The
Judgment
of
Richard
Richter

The
Judgment
of
Richard
Richter

IGOR ŠTIKS

Translated by Ellen Elias-Bursac

amazoncrossing

Text copyright © 2006 Igor Štiks
Translation copyright © 2017 Ellen Elias-Bursac
All rights reserved.

Previously published as Elijahova stolica by Fraktura in Croatia in 2006. Translated from Croatian by Ellen Elias-Bursac. First published in English by AmazonCrossing in 2017.

Published by AmazonCrossing, Seattle

www.apub.com

Amazon, the Amazon logo, and AmazonCrossing are trademarks of Amazon.com, Inc., or its affiliates.

Excerpts from Lawrence Durell's poem "Sarajevo" and his translation of "The City" are reproduced with permission of Curtis Brown Group Ltd, London on behalf of The Beneficiaries of the Estate of Lawrence Durrell Copyright © Lawrence Durrell 1951

ISBN 13: 9781503946668
ISBN 10: 1503946665

Cover design by David Drummond

Printed in the United States of America

To my parents

Elijah's Chair: Richard Richter's Manuscript

PROLOGUE

I mean to record here everything that has happened to me during the last few months. Will I succeed, and survive? Perhaps this writing I'm undertaking, the setting forth of facts that now begins, is merely a way of staving off the inevitable. I'm beginning to believe that one cannot move forward after learning that all of life's foundations are deceit, fantasies, even outright lies, behind which crouches a truth recognized far too late, like a snake one steps on at a precise, predestined moment. A viper striking at one's most vulnerable anatomy, delivering poison that assures a long, agonizing death. When a person feels life slip out from beneath him, he grabs for any hand that's offered and, often, drags down the very person who extended the hand.

In my case it wasn't a viper. Rather it was a sort of species that generously allows the victim to choose, himself, his own death. No serum can be had, nor will there be one. That moment of choosing comes at the end of this story, the story of my rebirth. Recently I've come to believe I was born twice, first in Vienna in 1942, and then in Sarajevo, a half century later.

This is about that second long and harrowing birth.

I

THE BLUE NOTEBOOK

1

My hand moves in fits and starts over the page; I'm balking, not sure how to tell what there is to tell without skipping the particulars, the moments, the events, even the most trivial, as I try to offer all the proof for how, out of matters that seemed at first so trifling, so negligible, the weights were placed on the scales of my fate, and her fate. Until now I've been a nimble scribe of the fates of others, a keen compiler, the "quick-witted storyteller" as some insist on calling me. Yet here, today, I stand powerless before the material of my own life as it interlaces with the lives of those whose dramas birthed me, and with the lives I've turned into drama. At times, they are one and the same. The truth hasn't struck me alone; that snake lurks and will lurk still, so long as there are those to stumble across it on their path. Perhaps it would be best for all this to end with me, for me to carry my venomous knowledge to the grave, slink off without a word, as I did, after all, not so very long ago.

I thought to capitulate. I tried pulling the trigger. I couldn't. I still cannot. I sit at the desk and can no longer hold back this story, which is on the verge of spilling out of me like lava from a late-stage volcano. The last it will ever spew forth. Once it's over, the flow will be simple to quell, to extinguish.

I feel all the helplessness of a writer faced with facts whose trajectory can no longer be edited to satisfy the narrator's whims. The bitter truth at hand resists my attempts to massage it into something like a novel, a trade I mastered long ago. Mastered it well enough that I was able to guide others, my grateful apprentices who don't know—and perhaps never will—that all this "knowledge" they drew from my books isn't worth a schilling. Exactly. Still, old habits die hard. That's probably why I can't step into the story of my own life and that which led to my demise without digression, without imposing on the material a sense of order and purpose. I'm organizing it as if I can still picture my future readers right here in front of me.

What I'm writing is perhaps no more than a feeble attempt to present the incredible discoveries that led me back into a world that had been lost with the death of my mother, Paula Müller, married name Richter, whom I never met—she having died shortly after I was born—and the suicide of my father, Heinrich Richter. The insights began emerging with a coincidental—that word now makes my skin crawl—discovery in Vienna in early May of this year, 1992; a discovery like the tip of an iceberg, whose invisible, vaster part lay in wait for me in Sarajevo, and into which I would crash full speed, at a velocity of fifty years of lies. This would drive anybody to procure a pistol with all due haste, just as I did upon my return to Vienna from Sarajevo in the second week of July. The pistol now lies on my desk beside the very hand with which I write these words, as laconic as an executioner who muses not on the person he puts to death or on the credibility of the sentence but only on doing his job well—with no superfluous questions. Perhaps what I'm writing is my way of justifying the way out to which my revolver points, and maybe I'm hoping this chronology will bring me forgiveness, at least from beyond the grave.

Yes, I know, all this should be buried with me in my dark tomb, but I don't believe there is a coffin spacious enough. Perhaps that's precisely the purpose of this writing exercise—ridding myself of the heavy ballast Charon won't allow on board his boat. And soon I'm due to cross the Styx.

How did it all begin to unravel? Who pulled the accursed threads? I gaze out the window of the hotel where I've been staying, incognito, since my return from Sarajevo. Below me stirs the Naschmarkt neighborhood of Vienna. Youthful, happy voices rise up to my room amid the serenity of the summer dusk, a stark contrast to the troubling story taking shape. I accept the calm with mild distress, because every thought returns me to that city that disappears even as I write and where, as I now know, I belong, though I've only spent a brief time there, a city where I've always belonged, despite all the years when its existence was no more than an ordinary geographic fact of general historic importance for me, no different from any other. Photographs are strewn about my desk. My favorites are up on the wall right above me and all I have to do is look up to see the city, a building near Titova Street, the banks of the half-dry bed of the river whose strange name I've come to love, the shattered roof tiles and glass shards scattered on the Baščaršija pavement, Ivor's grin, the balcony from which Alma's eyes watch me full of blame . . . Did she ever guess?

Alma . . . I seldom say her name, and then only softly so that God, resourceful old meddler that he is, doesn't strike me down . . . out of fear that I'll hurt her even more.

Who could have guessed what lay ahead when in early April I packed my bags and decided to return to Vienna after so many years in Paris? *You're fifty now, Richard,* I said to myself, *and Vienna is a city befitting your years. A city that will give you a spate of calm, quiet leisure for the "mature phase" you're embarking on with precious little baggage,* or so it seemed. *The serenity, steadiness, and predictability that Vienna has to offer are just what you need, you decrepit bachelor you, so buy your ticket and ride the train home to where your aunt Ingrid, the only mother you've ever known, still lives, though long ago she'd stopped hoping you'd come back.* To Vienna then! The city that will become my tomb. Not a city of taste, measure, calm, and spiritual contentment as they'd have us believe. Vienna prevaricates, with its appearance and its residents. It is inhabited by the past's demons who flock onto the Donaukanal quays, scramble out from sewer tunnels, crumble off dilapidated façades, clamber from cabinets discarded on sidewalks and out of the suits of dead aristocrats, stream out of old cafés as witnesses to the tragedies shared or plotted over the rickety tables—clutching plaques that testify to demolished buildings and lives erased; they switch road signs at crossroads, or simply sleep, lulled by the dark among the decaying walls, until they are stirred by an unwieldy hand, which will be, for the stirring, terribly punished.

This is *my* Vienna. The tomb of Richard Richter, into which he has voluntarily stepped. A trap. A blunder. Or, simply, the badly angled blow of a mallet.

No, I did not arrive in Vienna with a great deal of life baggage, nor was there anyone at the Gare de l'Est to see me off. Except the taxi driver, of course. There were no tears or fond farewells, and I did not stare, my face at the train window, until the contours of the city I'd so loved faded from view. None of that. I can only say that when I boarded the train that would take me to Vienna, I was not overly moved about leaving my Parisian life; I was too caught up with the notion of return, this new page of my life, to a place where I once knew every nook and cranny, yet now know nobody. Though they claim to know me from my books, and my picture is apparently often on display in the city bookstores. *Interesting,* I thought, *a new chapter is opening, buttressed by some old foundations, so let us stride into this life as if it were the dwelling of an old friend, gladly and freely.* This fresh start would, presumably, prove to be better than the end of the long period to which I was bidding farewell, as I shook hands with a person I was meeting for the first time and with whom I settled my last Paris bill.

I smile sourly now when I think of myself standing on the almost-empty platform, waving good-bye to the nameless taxi driver and stepping onto the fated train, ignorant of how the *show* had already begun, not knowing that I'm its star. Everything that had come before seemed, at this moment, like an invitation to give in, an invitation I unconsciously rejected as I strode, head held high, straight to my downfall. Perhaps I exaggerate, perhaps all the signs seem obvious to me now, perhaps only now in hindsight all the particulars swim to the surface of my muddled brain and acquire some sort of *loftier* heft. Even my wife Marianne Berger's departure some months ago seems ominous, as if this had been a thoroughly planned move in a demonic plot in which I'd be the victim. Not the only victim, sad to say. No doubt I exaggerate. Kitty, as I called her, was right when she finally ditched our long-since failed marriage, our extinguished love, our finished partnering. Today I don't blame her for anything, and yet I haven't the strength to pick up the phone, though I'm sure she watches the news each day and imagines me lying dead on a Sarajevo sidewalk, one more victim of a savage sniper in a city whose name she pronounces wrong. Still, I am not capable of contacting her after the vortex that began sucking me in after her departure, and which swept me up with all its force one day, in Vienna, in May.

I absolve her of all guilt. With her departure Kitty merely hastened the day when everything began to unravel. The day is precise, April 6, 1992. The day I left Paris. The day when, far to the southeast, the calamity of the city began—Sarajevo, a place I'd never been, where I'd be born again to learn of the stark truth of my life, which had been lying in wait for me patiently all these years. Sarajevo, which would give me, for the last time, the lips of a woman and would lay bare all the despair and mortal danger of that love, and which would, in the end, have only one direction in which to send me, only one exit. But I am pleased by the thought that the city, unlike me, will survive, even if barbarians occupy it for hundreds of years and even if no single stone is left standing. My only hope is that with it will survive those who are dearest to me today, whom I forsook with no warning, no word of farewell, like a coward or, more aptly, a traitor. In my defense I need to say that I had no choice.

Yes, I had no choice.

2

Signs, warnings . . . were there any? The train was late leaving the station, and there was even a rumor that the trip might be canceled altogether because of mechanical failure. Still, at the last moment the crew fixed the engine and the train pulled out, a lumbering armored device holding a motionless passenger hurtling to his own particular hell, *nel mezzo del cammin di nostra vita* . . . , a fresh copy of *Le Monde* in his pocket. The passenger in the seat next to me opened the same paper, leafing through it so that I could easily see the articles he had read or passed over with disinterest. He held it open wide and once he'd scanned both pages he'd close the paper to turn the page and spread it open wide again, leaving both himself and me with two pages to read. I amused myself by reading the paper under his guidance and selection, too lazy to retrieve my own copy from my pocket. After a while, my fellow passenger lingered on an article, engrossed, apparently, by the information he found there. While I was left in this odd readerly symbiosis on the previous page, which he had skipped, I could barely make out the words in the headline because of the jostling of the train: ". . . truth . . . trapped!" Only when the train steadied could I read the whole headline—"Seeking the Truth I Found Myself Trapped"—running above a story about a French priest who'd discovered he was actually the son of Jewish parents, not the French country folk to whom his parents had entrusted his care during the war. His parents never returned from the camp, and the caregivers never found themselves inclined to explain to him how he'd come to be in their home. They raised him as their own child, never concealing their delight that *their* boy had become a preeminent priest. This discovery about his background, as *Le Monde* quoted him as saying, rocked all that he'd believed in until then and reduced him to such a state that he concluded there were truths one shouldn't seek—and besides, he said, whose right is it to say that those to whom he owed his filial love had, in fact, wronged him by concealing his true origin? Had they not saved his life? The past was a trap, opined this unusual priest who continued, sermon-like, about how we mustn't allow it, our fated past, to govern our lives. Not only at an individual level—said this earnest member of an organization for promoting religious dialogue—but also collectively. I was on the verge of sardonic applause when I reached the end. Yet another one of those classic stories that the newspapers were so full of daily and which were all the rage over the last few years. Origin, iden-tity . . . identity, origin—the two-beat rhythm of our time, I sneered. My fellow passenger didn't budge from his clearly more compelling article on the other side of the page. I began to fidget. I was curious about what my neighbor was examining with such care, so I waited on edge for him to move on. Instead of opening my own copy, I passed the time observing the man's somber visage. He was at least sixty. As he shook his head in dismay, a gray lock of hair bobbed atop his head like a helmet plume. Then he finally turned the page with a loud sigh.

The first thing I saw was an eye-catching photograph of a crowd of people in a panicked fracas in a town square. The people were clearly fleeing something terrible, and there were bodies on the ground. Something dramatic was going on, demonstrations or riots, but I couldn't quite read what it was about and where it was happening. The answer to that question was hardly foremost on my mind. I was drawn to a woman's image that occupied a full quarter of the photograph, pivoting, aghast, toward the source of what was obviously horrific. My fellow passenger suddenly turned the page, catching my disappointed look as he did so. This made him register, with a discreet cough, my strange behavior. Hastily I pulled my own copy of the paper out of my pocket, which probably seemed odder still, and found the photograph and above it, typical for *Le Monde*, the headline: "*Once Again, Deadly Shots Fired in Sarajevo.*"

It was happening in the square in front of the parliament building, with demonstrations of some kind and shots fired from a nearby hotel. The face of the woman compelled me to read the article, from which I gathered that the war had spilled over from one republic of the ex-Yugoslavia to another, a theme about which I knew precious little, and, exactly like my fellow passenger a moment before, I sighed deeply. I thought about the woman, asking myself pointless questions about the tragedy she was facing. It had nothing whatsoever to do with me, but I wasn't any less upset by such scenes. The thoughts of an average, casual European traveler dismayed by bad news from the other end of the continent while beginning a journey of his own are so completely ordinary. Once more I peered into the paper, avoiding thoughts about the troubles of the world. A beautiful woman, yes, I noticed, and this was all that occurred to me as I looked at her staring somewhere skyward, her lips slightly parted, as if determined to gaze as long as possible into the very face of evil.

"*Quel beau pays, la Yougoslavie!*" exclaimed my fellow passenger. "Look what it has become! Terrible, too, too terrible. Why this war? Where is such hatred coming from? *La folie des hommes, mon cher monsieur!*"

Yes, no doubt, I responded to his multiple questions, *la folie des hommes* who shoot at beautiful women in a faraway place. My answer didn't leave enough room for the conversation to proceed, so he merely shrugged helplessly: "And what can we do here, my good man?!"

Not a thing, my good man.

I folded the paper and was suddenly overcome by anxiety, or maybe I was evading further conversation with the elderly gentleman who, having finished his paper, already appeared bored. I flew out into the corridor and headed for the bar. There I found a free seat and in peace and quiet opened the paper again to the same page. I tore out the article with the photograph of the woman—and on the other side the priest's photograph and life story—tucked them into my breast pocket, and tossed the rest of the paper into the trash. It's still with me, that scrap of newspaper, among the things I brought back from Sarajevo.

Maybe I should have disembarked at the first stop, or at least in Nancy, and returned to Paris by the next train, but after Kitty left I no longer knew whom I'd be going back to. I was not, therefore, altogether sincere in saying I'd left Paris on a whim, borne by pangs of nostalgia and fuzzy plans for a future in Vienna. The taxi that dropped me off was merely an apt illustration of the reckoning in my life after the long and painful demise of my marriage, which made me believe I had touched the very nadir of loneliness and I'd never again rise from it, that I was too old to be able to pull that off. Oh, how wrong I was! What I had touched was a false bottom; there was so much more room, as I now know, to plummet deeper. Kitty had left me in a life that still held hope, at least. Here, where I write these lines, that hope is gone.

I needed a fresh start. Both of us did. When I closed the door to the apartment we'd shared—which I'd generously chosen to leave to her—and stepped out onto the boulevard and hailed a cab, everything had already, as I see it now, been determined. As if an invisible hand were propelling me, as if I were unable to alter a thing.

My mother's elder sister, Aunt Ingrid, the hovering moon of my youth, was an old woman now, nearly eighty. I called her from the station as soon as I arrived, giving her such a surprise that she nearly fainted. She embraced me at the door to our old home, not releasing me from her bony arms for a long time. She was still in fine mettle. I stopped at the threshold and, before crossing it, took in that special aroma of my childhood and youth residing among these walls. *I've come home,* I thought brightly. I couldn't know that this apartment had been guarding a dangerous secret during all those youthful years. As if I'd been waltzing on thin ice the whole time, only finally to tumble through it into the chill water of all the things left unsaid. The snake was stirring. I'd stumbled into its lair.

I surprised my aunt again by wishing to return to my boyhood quarters, and my uncomfortable old bed on which I slept for the first few weeks. She wasn't pleased that my marriage had ended, and she was generally concerned about my frame of mind, but she was far too glad about my return to venture into these painful topics. She could see I needed peace and she offered it to me in abundance. We were together again after so many years, and those first Viennese days passed exactly as I hoped they might, in serenity and calm. I had disordered her life with my return, but this, it seemed, didn't bother her. As if she'd been waiting for decades for the return of the only son she'd ever had! She was afraid, of course, that I might leave again, and with guarded hope she listened to me talk of return for good, of a fresh start in life, of a new stage in my writing career.

In spite of our wishes, however, things soon began to elude her control and mine, and now I'll do what I have to do—I'll leave again and this time I'll be going for good. I hope she'll understand in the end. I hope she won't blame herself for speaking out after all these years. She couldn't have imagined what was in store for me. She still doesn't know that I managed to reconstruct the story, the whole troubled story to which I owe my existence. She doesn't know, nor will she ever, that this truth—no matter how devastating it might be!—would not have pushed me, in and of itself, to the edge from which I'll soon throw myself. She doesn't know what happened in Sarajevo, she doesn't know how viciously fate has toyed with us all.

On these hot July days, Ingrid doesn't know I'm back in Vienna now, returned from my fateful journey. She'd seen me off, choking back tears and pangs of self-recrimination, and she still doesn't know that I succeeded in plumbing the depths of my story in the besieged city. Like a first-rate detective of the Oedipal variety, like certain characters, in fact, from my own novels—how ironic is that!—for whom their writer always prepared challenging tests, finding a special joy in the impossible predicaments he placed them in from which there were only two ways out: madness and, of course, death. Ingrid is probably sleeping now, while I write this in a Naschmarkt hotel room, a room that seems perfectly suited to writing the story of a ruined life and, after that, for the protagonist to shoot a hole through his head.

I will remember April of 1992 as one of the most beautiful months in the last few years of my life, but they say that after a disaster this is the impression one usually has of the days leading up to it. Perhaps, but I have to say that I truly found balance and a strange peace despite the frequent shifts of weather that gave us clear days and freezing rain, cold mornings that confirmed winter had not yet relinquished its grip, followed by early afternoons in which we rolled up our sleeves so that we could sun, for the first time, our pale flesh. The turbulent arrival of spring fused with my serenity, light reading in an overheated apartment, and reliving memories of the days when I was growing up with Aunt Ingrid. For Easter, on April 19, we celebrated once again the long-since abandoned tradition of a holiday dinner, the children's game of cracking dyed eggs, and a leisurely and ample meal, so typical for those days. I remember well that there were newspapers on the table and that before we began eating I glanced at the headlines. This is one more of the images that will be etched in my memory, though then, on Easter, I dwelled on it for no more than a second or two. The Austrian papers published photographs, with an article under the glaring headline "*War*

Ablaze in Bosnia," taken, apparently, at a checkpoint on the border between Bosnia and Croatia. The people were waiting in a line on a bridge, frightened and anxious, while several soldiers in camouflage uniforms inspected their papers. Much later I found out that Brčko is located in the north of Bosnia and that the bridge these people were crossing was shelled several days later and shut down for good. In the foreground of the photograph is a woman of perhaps forty warily eyeing the soldier examining her documents. He is scowling. She has wrapped her arms around a dark-haired teenage boy, who is staring just as intently at the soldier and awaiting the man's decision, and a young girl with curly blonde hair who has turned away from the camera to look at their destination, the other side of the river. She has spread her bare arms as if trying to protect them with the only weapon she has. "*Refugees from Sarajevo,*" says the caption. I flipped the paper closed and pushed it off the table. My aunt brought out bowls of steaming soup.

Easter passed and soon I realized that this return to my younger days, my old bed and room, had become a burden and that I needed to make a few changes in our apartment, in which I still intended to live. Compelled by an urge, I decided to connect two rooms by demolishing the wall that divided them to create a living space and, I hoped, space for my future work. Ingrid resisted the idea of remodeling, but in the end she gave in, prepared to accept even the most radical demands as long as she could keep me there. After more than twenty years away, I'd been home for slightly over three splendid and, for my nerves, exceptionally beneficial weeks. With joy I spent them with Ingrid, the only woman who loved me unconditionally, and who'd softly close the door as I went to sleep and serve me breakfast in the morning as if I hadn't turned fifty, as if I were about to dash off to school. I didn't protest much. I spent my days, as I said, doing some reading, jotting down sporadic ideas for my writing, and, of course, taking long walks. With no radio and no television, news from the outside world came to me here and there from my dear aunt and I made no effort to hear more. I was also enjoying the total anonymity I felt then, because the Viennese, despite my modest literary celebrity, didn't recognize me on the street. My business obligations were also blissfully left behind. I imagined the phone ringing off the hook in my former Parisian home, until the calls began to thin out, as the callers were discouraged by the words of my wife, who, making the effort to be dispassionate, would say I no longer lived there and that she didn't know where I was now. I even relished the notion of their surprise, as well as the concern that must have stabbed Kitty's heart as well, lacking any news of me for such a long time.

A fine state of affairs, I told myself then, *remarkably productive for work.* A new novel was an effective cure for a collapsing relationship, and that was something I knew all about and intended to employ the method again. I laugh now at my literary ambitions; they all seem so pointless to me, and my career a crushing failure . . . All the themes, stories, ideas, the hundreds and hundreds of pages I wrote, convinced of my firm grounding, and which now seem worthless, empty, unconvincing. Swept away chaotically by the wind that has driven me here. But at that time, early in the month of May 1992, there wasn't the slightest breeze to be felt. Nothing augured it.

The ball of yarn began unwinding one afternoon. To begin the remodeling project I bought myself a mallet on sale. It was, I might add, a sculptor's hammer for work with marble, specially suited for gravestones. That sunny afternoon I was ready for a job I was not particularly skilled at, but I was determined to do it myself. I had the time, after all, so I moved the furniture and emptied the room. The old bookshelves were a particular challenge, and I spent several hours inching them away from the wall, as well as looking after the venerable, nearly century-old books. The big mallet was magnificent, entirely suited for waking the dead or releasing demons from the walls so that they'd flit around us like bats before our startled gaze. But one thing at a time.

The work proceeded with no significant setbacks, and the wall on which the old bookshelves had always stood shrank slowly under my blows. I was not a little surprised when, near the last stage of the demolition, the mallet plunged through the wall without resistance and met not brick but something metal mid-wall. I moved closer to the unexpected hollow in the wall and began pulling away chunks of wallpaper and plaster. I came upon a small metal box covered in dust, hidden all these years by the bookshelves, the massive tomes of an outdated encyclopedia, and several layers of wallpaper. *"What is this, for God's sake?"* I wondered aloud. At first I was entranced, transformed into a child beguiled by a mysterious discovery right there in his own home: a little combination safe!

All too soon, to my dismay, I would uncover its contents, which, like a time bomb, would demolish the pillars of my own chronology, blow it to smithereens so thoroughly that after I'd been turned to stone and had my reason borne away by what I'd learn, I'd be scattered into thousands of little pieces.

Irretrievably.

3

I never knew Paula Richter, my mother. I knew nothing about her beyond what my aunt Ingrid, her sister, recalled. Soon after I was born she died, "of complications," as Ingrid put it, at the age of twenty-four. I had no reason to believe Ingrid was hiding anything. In fact it's not so much that she ever lied but—now I can see, fifty years hence!—she just omitted what she felt I didn't need to know. How wrong she had been! Because such secrets age well—like wine stowed away in dry, dark cellars, in dust-covered bottles draped with thick spiderwebs; such wine is worth more, its bouquet is richer, more robust, and, of course, deadlier for the uninitiated palate.

A photograph of my mother had always hung in my room, and at night I'd hug the image of the unfamiliar woman, sobbing the way children sob out of loneliness and their ache of feeling misunderstood. She always remained for me the person in that picture and scarcely more. A shadow that birthed me about whom I didn't know what to think, how to love her, or how to grieve for her. It was so strange, visiting her grave each month! Paula Richter née Müller died, as I've said, a few days after I was born, while my father, Heinrich, was off somewhere on the Eastern Front, where it must have been hellishly cold that January of 1942. And that's all I knew of my mother for all my fifty years of life. But it turns out she'd left something behind when she went. Paula's message, although it wasn't penned to me, was waiting for me alone, hidden for half a century, sandwiched between the walls in a small metal box, between the covers of a blue notebook, on pages I never should have read.

I met Heinrich Richter, my father, only when he returned from the war late in the summer of 1945. I was only three, so I can't rely much on my own memories of him, and by my fourth birthday Heinrich Richter was already laid in his grave, having died by his own hand. My memory of him mingles with Ingrid's stories and a surprising dearth of photographs. But one thing is certain: he appeared at the door to our apartment an emaciated phantom. He wasn't yet thirty, though he seemed far older, a somber figure whose hands trembled, who seldom left the house, who chain-smoked, and who was unable to restart his life. Yes, this was the man who, Ingrid told me, was my father. Was his end hastened by remorse? A sense of guilt for mother's death? Or was it things he'd done, as I sometimes wondered? Now that all the pieces of this troubled puzzle are here before me, I cannot avert my eyes. It's as if I'm staring into the very watery depths in which I'll drown myself.

In the autumn of 1945, Heinrich hanged himself. My aunt was the one who found him and had him buried as her sister's husband, the father of her nephew and adopted son, though not alongside Paula in the Müller family tomb. I didn't know what to feel when we stood by his graveside, though I wondered about it less and less because we so seldom visited the place.

So before I reached the age of four, I was bereft of parents, knowing only fragments of the stories of their deaths. As I write this tale of family tragedy, which, following the trajectory of my life, stretches onward fifty years and which, I hope, my death will bring finally to an end, I know far more about it than did those who lost their lives along the way. Now that I've amassed the documents and testimonies, I can reconstruct the course of the river and the meanders of our misfortune. Its streambed will run dry with the help of the pistol I stow at times in the drawer, at times on the desk, and at times on the pages of this manuscript so that a sudden gust won't blow them away. Patiently it waits, guided by the perfect certainty that the manuscript will soon reach its end and the pistol will provide the final punctuation mark.

I drew the box out of the wall. I tried opening it right away, but it didn't readily release; this only fired my imagination and resolve. The workmanship was quite old but remarkably sturdy, and the little dial had too many possible combinations. Where had this small safe come from? To whom had it belonged? Previous tenants? What was inside? Gold? Worthless currency from the age of the Habsburg monarchy? Childish thoughts possessed me. I'd begun ordinary renovations, and now I was embarking on a bona fide adventure here in my own home. Within minutes I was marching down the street to purchase a blowtorch. I was euphoric when I brought back the mask and the apparatus—the work could begin! Luckily, I'd sent Ingrid off for a whole day around town, so I was on my own and entirely free to immerse myself in the game. Thanks primarily to my resolve to discover the contents of the small box, the edges melted swiftly away. Once I'd pried off the back, I could see a bluish object through the haze and shoved my hand into the shambles of the box. What a shame that, as I melted the metal, I didn't scorch the blue notebook beyond repair.

I was cautious—it had lain there for over fifty years—and gingerly eased the notebook out into the light of day. I could see as soon as I'd read the first few lines that I was holding in my hands a missive written by Paula, an unsent letter of some sort from the time right before I was born. I was astonished by what seemed, at the very least, bizarre. The small box contained nothing else. I sat on the floor with the blue notebook in hand, incredulous. I jumped up, clutching the notebook, and strode out of the dust-filled room. I splashed my hands and face. I was delaying the moment when I'd start reading. Before I sat down at the dining room table, I locked the apartment door so that Ingrid wouldn't discover me while I was reading, though she probably had no idea the notebook even existed. I brought out the picture of my mother from my boyhood room. Those eyes, which had spoken nothing to me throughout my childhood years, now watched me tenderly and, mute, left me to discover everything on my own.

Before me lay the notebook, a precious treasure dredged from the past, something no other eyes had seen, a manuscript of inestimable value finally brought out into the light of day, like a text that awaits its first reader, its first addressee, for whom it bore a message that mattered much too much, though, I repeat, it was not meant, initially, for me. I studied the 1940s notebook carefully. It was an ordinary blue notebook purchased for some other purpose (perhaps for lectures my mother attended at the university while she was still young coed Müller?), and then, perhaps at a moment of crisis, the notebook became a sanctuary, perhaps the only shelter during the days she describes, with their burden that would ultimately crush her. I sensed its threatening content as I ran the tips of my fingers over the cover, and my eagerness gave way to an uncomfortable twinge of dread. With my fingertips I palpated its smooth surface warily, as if caressing a dagger held sheathed so as not to inflict injury. The first sentences proved the accuracy of my forebodings. And when I read the last words (*Your Paula*), I knew I'd have to embark on a reconstruction of the events, armed only with the limited insights of one side in the drama, insights that my mother conveyed in her letter to a man I knew nothing about. As I opened the cover, the stiff paper protested; the pages were stuck together, not having been turned for so long.

It took strength to start reading Mother's words. The fact that she'd written the letter in the notebook and never torn out and sent the pages was already enough to scare me. A letter is a form that doesn't offer the interloper much purchase. The author has no need of explaining things to the reader; it's enough to use the unique code they share. The writer codes the message even more if they fear the contents might fall into the hands of outsiders, relying on opaque allusions, comparisons, initials, and elusive references. And so the contents are governed by the position of the author, the intended reader, and, ultimately, the fear that somebody uninvited might broach their intimate space. For the outsider, such a document may easily mislead. What the sender cared most to convey to the recipient is often precisely that which is unstated, erased, or left out. Perhaps this applies to most letters, but it is certainly true for those exchanged between lovers. This letter from my mother written in late 1941 to an unknown man was no exception.

I leafed slowly through the notebook, carefully separating the pages before I undertook the reading. I shivered as if this were a sacred text, because I could see clearly by its date, by the exclamation points and question marks studding each page, and finally by the small box it had been locked in, that this was a letter pertaining to some sort of calamity that had predetermined my existence. Even before I began reading I felt the ground slipping out from under me. Because a person who, amid dramatic wartime and personal circumstances (a month before my birth!), begins to write to somebody who is, presumably, absent, and then locks the unsent letter up using a combination safe and stows it away in a secret niche behind a bookshelf must have been forced into isolation by an unforgiving sequence of events out of which they were trying, desperately, to send a message that mattered. To a person who mattered.

As soon as I read the first few sentences of Mother's letter, I snapped back as if scalded. I was momentarily overwhelmed by a terrible (dare I say existential?) fear of reading her words, still not entirely comprehensible, and my hands began to shake. Still, I went back to the text and the more I read, the more the dread was confirmed. To have this notebook in front of me, to be able to read her missive, was like peeking into God's archive where everything is written down in black and white, without the ability to shield myself, without any, even the slightest, chance of blessed lies that might offer respite. I read about the events to which I owe my birth, about the immutable facts that my mother chose to keep secret. Nevertheless, she hid this document away so that her death wouldn't take it from the face of the earth, so that one day somebody might bring it out into the light. Instead of burning it all, destroying it, ripping it to shreds—perhaps not this last, because who knows what sort of wind might reassemble the pages—thereby protecting us all, she locked her diary in the box like a small explosive projectile aimed at the future, destined to be opened, as every safe is, at some point. The letter would fall into the hands of an intruder and Mother's side of the story, whose reconstruction I'd begun, painfully, that afternoon, despite myself, would be explained in her own words.

Writing now about the very beginnings of a story in which I'd play the leading role, I wonder, nearly three months after that fateful day: Am I not now doing precisely what my mother did as she penned her futile last record? To whom am I sending mine? Why haven't I stopped myself, burned what I've written so far, fallen silent for all time and strangled the viper? What sort of future do I imagine for my missive? Why do this when pulling the trigger would do the trick? Sometimes I think I'm writing out of fear at the prospect of the end where my faithful friend the gun awaits, patient because it knows that what I have to say will sooner or later be said. Human misfortune is, as we'll agree, boundless, but a text that is written about it has only a finite number of pages.

After my initial reluctance, I read in a single go the rest of Mother's letter she'd written to somebody named Jakob Schneider. I rose from the table where her notebook lay. The surprisingly warm spring day was nearing its end. The sun set, drawing down with it orange, red, and violet streaks.

An early-evening stillness settled over the streets of Vienna. Perhaps that was just as it had been that distant June day in 1941 when Mother learned she was pregnant. On the decisive day she wrote about in the letter, that day in Prater, it would have been warmer. I imagined their faces, the sunlit avenues, an indescribable peace within which two people hold an important, intimate conversation interlaced with reverberations of the current events: German troops in the Soviet Union!

I read the letter that was not intended for me, and the edifice of my biography began to sway as if it had never had any foundation, as if by some weird magic (which had finally run its course) it was resting on nothing at all—air, lies. I tried then to rebuild what I knew of myself as I sat there on the floor of the apartment in which I'd been born, to make an inventory of my own chronology, my own *self*, to rely only on the known facts, or rather on those I'd been led to believe were known, and then, so armed, to return to the letter. It was still waiting for me on the table, at the beginning of the old blue notebook, into which Mother, one night, a few weeks before my birth, wrote a letter to a man I never before had heard of; then she closed the notebook, perhaps in hopes that he'd come back to her, that she'd send the letter one day when she had an address to send it to, but she never had the chance because I was born and she died.

Still, I know there to be a story of my life, and it is not so bad nor is it completely lacking in coherence, and it goes like this: I was born in January 1942 to mother Paula and father Heinrich Richter. I was baptized as Richard Richter. Period. My parents married in July 1941. Shortly before they married, my father donned the Wehrmacht uniform, and like so many other men of his age, he soon found himself in the new waves of the campaign into Russia. My mother died a few days after my birth while Father was somewhere far to the east. Nothing unusual. It happens. After the war Father came for his son. He had no serious political problems to answer for regarding his service; the fact that together with Mother he'd been involved in some form of anti-Nazi activism in close-knit circles after the *Anschluss* and until 1941, a fact that my aunt proudly trotted out at times, could only serve to help him integrate into the new postwar society, being, indeed, one of "the first victims of Nazism." Still, he did not prevail. So at the age of four I was an orphan. Again, nothing unusual for my generation. Ingrid Müller raised me, giving me always these same stories, and they were my truth. Entirely adequate for anchoring my personal and suprapersonal self. And then all of a sudden, here I was, sitting on the floor, waiting for my aunt to come home, because now I knew that what she'd told me was not the truth, or at least not the whole truth, and because Mother's letter required explanations Ingrid had never intended to offer. But the day had come for a reckoning. There was *something* there on the table, pulled out of a rotten wall, its dusty pages bearing a toxic substance that placed a sinuous and malignant question mark over everything, and my life was slowly but surely crumbling into a dust that no force would be capable of putting together again.

I felt I could go no farther. *I should leave this all be,* I thought at one point. Shaken as I was, it occurred to me to burn the notebook and push what I'd read deep into myself so that it would dissolve there in all the pooled bitterness. Maybe that would have been better. It surely would have been better. I hoped to stop the questions that were mounting inside, driving me to look in the mirror and wonder whence came the man there before me whose face seemed so familiar, whose two-day stubble, eyes, mouth, and cheeks, his wrinkles and the patches of gray hair all told me this was, indeed, *my* own face. Better yet would have been to forget it had I been able, to turn back time, to destroy the paths leading to these just-learned facts in my overheated brain that, since discovering them, hasn't known how to think, giving in to panic and reducing to rubble a system that was no longer defensible.

If only I'd been able . . . Instead, I went back to the table and sank once more into the letter, glad to have this, at least, to grab hold of, letting my own mother and her words serve as my guide in a mission that could no longer be deferred.

4

Jakob Dearest,

or should I call you *Andreas*, as we've all been calling
you, as we still do? No, I'll use your real name, the
name you entrusted to me in the strictest of confidence, a name which, these days, is a danger for those
who bear it. Because these days, as you said yourself,
that combination of first and last name may be deadly,
and that is why I am writing this letter in the middle of
the night, in a locked room with the curtains drawn,
while all, I hope, are sleeping, and I don't know if
you'll ever read it . . . if you are even still alive. That's a
wretched thought, and to dispel it I keep writing with
no address. I write as if this were a diary. I've no one to
confide in. I want to say what was left unsaid between
us, though I have no hope of it ever reaching you.

I can confide in no one but you, my dearest, but
it's all too late. This conversation is only with the shadows. What is there for me to hope for? I must continue, I must write everything I had no chance to tell
you when I should have, what I had no opportunity
to tell you before what happened happened, before
they came between us, before they took you away. No

news of you for months, not a word, nothing, yet the child is growing inside me, Jakob dearest, and soon it will be born.

Christmas 1941 is nearly upon us. What a dreadful year this has been! The Third Reich has just declared war on America. Marvelous! This accursed year brought you and took you, but it did leave something behind for me going forward—a child whose heart I hear beating and whose kicks I feel with joy. Outside it's fiercely cold, the snow falls in a hush over blacked-out Vienna. I wonder: Where are you? Do you have a place to hide? What have they done to you? These are the questions I keep asking myself, but I do believe, despite everything, you're still breathing this same air, watching this same senseless world . . . you're alive. Perhaps it would be wiser to resign myself to what seems so easily predictable and accept your death as a given just as everybody else has.

Oh, I want to rip this letter up, what's the point! I picture myself struggling on, writing it for days, years to come, storing on these pages everything I'd so much rather be telling you myself. To write to a man who has disappeared, isn't that like beginning a task that can end only when I die? How much longer will I keep at it? It looks as if I'll never see you again, but my trembling hand goes right on writing in this war-ridden night. I am a desperate woman whose love—so brief!—was snuffed out by the war. I am carrying a child whose father must remain nameless, who doesn't even know he is to be a father, who might already be dead. Oh, this lie we live has been destroying me ever since you were arrested, but I know this way is best, I know you'd do the same, "reasonably," "as conditions dictate" . . . Yes, says Ingrid, you would surely do the same. Without her I don't know how I could go on living, for her sake I kept the child, but also for one more reason—the infinitesimal chance of your return. Perhaps this might all sound strange to you, but Ingrid saved the child with her pleas. You know it was not easy for her to embrace our love, just as she found it difficult to bear the fact that I'm pregnant—*why with you of all people?!*—but ever since she has been completely with me. I wonder how you'd handle it, this fact that you'll be a father, if only I'd had the courage to tell you then, our last time together. You were caught up in your analyses of the latest developments in the war. Then you stopped talking. The birds were too noisy that day in Prater. Hardly anyone nearby. I thought it was the perfect moment. I said nothing. Later you took my hand, you went on speaking of the "situation," a little kiss to the brow, as if encouraging me, and on we walked.

Ingrid awaits the birth with bated breath, almost as if she were the one expecting, and she's doing everything in her power to take care of us. After your arrest we thought we'd be next. But I knew you'd never betray us, no matter what they did to you. We ceased all our activities—no more meetings, withdrew into the apartment, and Heinrich enlisted (he'd been expecting to be drafted anyway!!). Now he's off somewhere on the Eastern Front in faraway Russia. His last words came to us from Kharkov!! He thought this was the best way to protect ourselves and the child, just as Ingrid and I felt it best for the child if we took his offer and I married him before he left for the Front. There, I said it. I hope you'll understand. I'm consoled by the thought that I would have given my blessing had our roles been reversed, after all you yourself know best what chances a half-Jewish child has for life in this world.

Heinrich has always been fond of me ever since we were young. Now his love has found the right expression, and he has acted like a true friend, exactly like somebody who embraces all conditions without complaint, even our love and *your* child—all of it. He wanted to help. I thanked him by accepting the marriage and his paternity for our child. I'm sorry I'll never be able to return the favor in equal measure. It was reasonable to take this step, to name Heinrich Richter, German soldier, the father of my child. You'll forgive me, I know, in this world or the next. I did everything I needed to do, love here took "second place under the circumstances," as you put it.

Yes, *love took second place,* exactly as you phrased it on that June day in Prater when I was certain of the pregnancy and had resolved to tell you. Yes, I realize German tanks were already deep into Russian territory and you had many reasons for concern. Forgive me for imagining aloud, with what you called "bourgeois sentimentality" and "immature daydreams," what it would have been like for us to have children, marry, live together, even in the city you're from if that were your preference; at that point none of it mattered to me. You had no idea why I was saying those things, while I stupidly believed myself to be laying the groundwork for breaking the big news. I guess I was testing your love. You shook me—remember?—and told me to stop the chitchat while the Nazis were marching on Moscow, to stop this claptrap about children when you had no idea whether you'd still be here tomorrow, because all that now took "second place . . . love, children, marriage . . . We are at war, woman, Yugoslavia has been occupied . . . Who knows what's become of my comrades, family, relatives, friends . . . What are you talking about, Paula . . . I am sitting here with you, useless, twiddling my thumbs, doing nothing, waiting for a signal . . ."

"And meanwhile you're busy fathering children with the naïve girls you beguile, just to pass the time while you wait . . . for a signal," I wanted to snap back. And so you sit, twiddling your thumbs with me, doing nothing . . . Do you even remember this? I so ached to ask you that, if only I'd seen you again. And I'd have told you I was sorry I hadn't divulged my secret, which you had the right to know, because I was so childishly hurt and I doubted your feelings. Ultimately your words were borne out. A few days later you were gone, "first-place" reasons interfered and took you off in a direction you hadn't meant to go, put an end to your struggle and to what was between us, the outcome of which you'll never know, because that afternoon in Prater I stubbornly refused to speak of what was already growing inside me perhaps since that night in early April when those same German tanks rumbled into your country. Tonight I deeply regret this. I regret that your words kept me from telling you of the child you'll never know.

It's already much too late and I'm so tired I can hardly hold my pencil. I am thinking of you, Jakob Schneider, of our child who will soon see this imperfect world. I am thinking of Heinrich freezing somewhere off in the east, in icebound Ukraine. I am thinking of Ingrid who fusses over my "mistake"—she no longer even speaks of you—yet who cannot conceal her delight at the prospect of the child, as if she's the one who will be giving birth, as if this were meant to be, as if you had chosen her instead of me, and as if this child, now that the "mistake" has happened, will compensate for all her betrayed hopes. I am thinking of you. I cannot forget you, though I, too, no longer speak of you; I, too, have relegated you to silence. There are things that must be done, as Ingrid would say, and we justify them to ourselves because there is no other way. No one dares say it's too late for you, Jakob. No one speaks of you, yet you're always with us. Who knows, perhaps the child will remind us of you more and more as it grows. What will we tell it? What will be the truth we tell? Will we keep up the lie we repeat now every day?

Will we ever learn your fate? Who betrayed you? And besides, who knew who Andreas Schubert really was? We thought Ingrid knew more. She was the one who brought you to us, into a world you changed forever. In a way, perhaps only I knew you. Or am I merely flattering myself? So many questions remain unanswered and their numbers mount as soon as I look down at my belly, big enough now to rest the notebook on.

The child is kicking, perhaps it can't sleep while listening to the pencil scratch the truth onto the paper, and it's asking in its own way for me to put out the candle, put down the pencil, shut the notebook, and wish for you the very best, Jakob Schneider, wherever you may be . . .

Your Paula

5

The sun has already set. It seems as if a silence blankets the city in the early evening: passing cars are rare and people speak in near-whispers. The streetlights will soon come on. This is the oft-evoked time of day—only a few minutes before another night begins in earnest—when there's a sense of inviting imbalance and mild tipsiness, when all the charm and triviality of surging emotions reach their apex, only to evaporate in the harsh imposition of the city lights. I was sure that Ingrid would hurry to get home before darkness fell. She had left me more time than I needed for the work she had so resisted. Had I respected her protests, I would not be waiting for her here at dusk. She must have been anxious to see what I'd accomplished, though she probably was afraid of the damage I might have done.

I didn't switch on the light. It suited me that the city was slowly sinking into gloom, and my gaze was drawn to the glowing ember on the tip of the cigarette that lit my dust-white fingers. I sipped whisky, and its harsh bite soothed me and kept me from dwelling too much on the substance of Mother's letter, from facing all the implications of what I'd just read. The blue notebook lay there, open to the first page. *Jakob Dearest* . . .

Everything seemed clear now, at least as far as paternity was concerned. Jakob Schneider was my father, there could be no doubt. Heinrich Richter was merely a good friend who made a sacrifice to protect her and her child, perhaps hopelessly in love. A man who had every reason to despise the foreigner. But the circumstances of the story from 1941 eluded me. I was not impatient, however, on that day of discovery because Ingrid was on her way home. Mother's letter had brought much to light, but there was more in those sentences I was unable to understand in full, to assemble the entire mosaic. I was an interloper, after all, eavesdropping on an unrealized act of correspondence between lovers, the difference being that I hadn't barged in as a total outsider, but, as I knew just in the past hour, as their very own son.

Who were the protagonists in this play? How to sum it up? Starting with myself. As the plot unfolds in the theater piece described in Paula's letter, I am still gestating inside her, starting somewhere in Act II. My arrival is intimated with *since that night, perhaps, in early April when those same German tanks rumbled into your country* . . . Gradually Paula herself notices the stirrings of the new character, and by the second half of the month of June she is absolutely certain of its existence and of the likelihood, obtained by a simple calculation, that I might make my entrance in late 1941 or early '42. Still, with her mixed feelings and a conversation with her lover held at, historically speaking, a bad moment, she decides against informing the biological father of my increasingly evident self. He never learns of me. My entrance coincides with Mother's exit, following the directions of some nameless director who, ruthlessly, prevents an increase in the number of characters onstage. I, the future Richard Richter, am apparently, judging by it all, a half-Jewish child who can only be saved by a protective Arian nod from Heinrich Richter, my father according to legal documents and my aunt. But who was this Jakob Schneider, my father according to Mother? A communist? Very likely. Jewish? Evidently. (He is, after all, the father of a *half-Jewish child*!). Country of origin: Yugoslavia (*We are at war, woman, Yugoslavia has been occupied* . . . *who knows what has become of my comrades, family, relatives, friends . . .*). Vocation, hair and eye color: unknown. She, my mother, has fallen in love with a man who presented himself as Andreas Schubert and who will be arrested by the secret police, which means his definitive stage exit and, most likely, his imminent demise. Ingrid, Paula's sister, seems to have had her own dubious bond with this Andreas, and there are hints of sibling rivalry. In short, Ingrid, who brings Jakob/Andreas onto the stage, loses him to her sister's embrace, until she, as consolation, is left with their child. Heinrich shows up at the end of the play, returning from the Front to familial desolation. The woman he loved has been dead for years, his competitor was pulled offstage by the dreaded hook, and the only one left is the child, a boy barely four, as a memento of unrequited love. And so Heinrich, his nerves shattered after the tragedy of war he's been through and the wounds he undoubtedly bears from it all, realizes he has no recourse but a noose with which to end his wretched existence. Ingrid and the child are left alone onstage. The end of this play and, for the attentive, the hint of a sequel can readily be discerned in the version of the story Ingrid passes on to the boy, hoping to secure him a better life than the lives seen so far onstage. The curtain falls.

The audience, deeply moved, leaps to its feet, clapping in erratic bursts of applause because it's tricky to brush away the tears and applaud at the same time. Dear sirs, because they, the audience, know the boy will grow to be a man, and he'll move to a different city, write books about the experience of the post-Nazism generation, about rebelling against one's parents, against the fathers and grandfathers who hid all the crimes and took part in the Holocaust (actively or passively, regardless) and all the other big questions of the age, and he will become famous and return at fifty to his hometown and find his mother's notebook (in one of the earlier scenes the audience saw the mother writing the letter and hiding the blue notebook behind the massive library tomes), which will wash ashore like a message in a bottle borne by waves of cruel fate onto the sandbar of life on which Richard had already run aground (the Kitty debacle—case in point). And now that he's read it—this terrible message that erases everything, which opens the original lie of his life—he stares at a seascape that offers no answer. Zilch.

I soon heard her footsteps on the stairs. I surveyed the room in disarray, the half-smashed wall. She didn't ring the doorbell, not wanting to bother me in case I was writing. I heard the rattle of keys and there she was, stepping breathless into the pitch-dark apartment. I used the opportunity to stub out my cigarette and toss back the last of my drink. She groped for the light switch, patting her hand along the wall, and finally flicked on the light, gasping at the same time.

"Richard?! What are you doing sitting in the dark for God's sake?!" she said, alarmed at seeing me seated at the table. Bewildered by my silence, she continued: "How you frightened me! What is it? . . . Did something happen?"

"Yes, something happened. Don't be frightened; sit here at the table," I calmed her. "There's something I have to show you."

"What is it?" she asked in a hushed voice, and quickly took a seat at the table without removing her jacket, placing her purse on her lap.

The play's sequel had begun. I regretted frightening Ingrid because of the impact my discovery would have on her. The demons of the past with whom she'd battled for so long had survived after all and they were all around us, more alive than ever. All she'd done was go for a walk, leaving me a few hours alone, and here they were, ready to finish their work, fulfill their mission of many years ago, the simple act of whispering the truth into the ear of the very person who mustn't hear it.

I pointed to the notebook on the table.

"What's that? An old notebook?" Ingrid looked at it, surprised, but with no particular interest.

"Look." I handed the notebook to her. She took it and turned it over in her hands, baffled. She didn't recognize it. She didn't understand what this object had to do with my sitting in the dark.

"I don't understand," she said sincerely. "Where is it from? And why the secretive behavior? Is this some kind of joke?"

"Read it, Auntie. I came across it today hidden in a niche in the wall behind the bookshelves. In a small locked metal box."

"What small box?!" She was shocked. "Locked? In my house?"

"Yes. You had no idea, but it was right here." I pointed to the smashed wall. "Where Mother left this blue notebook."

"Paula?! Whatever could Paula have to do with this?!" Now she was surprised and her tone grew more shrill. She protested. "Please explain what is going on here, Richard. What is this?" She stopped and then asked in amazement: "Wait, you mean Paula, my Paula?!"

"Yes, Ingrid, *your* Paula! This is her notebook. Don't you think you ought to read what she wrote?"

"Fine, fine." She nodded. "Yes, of course . . . it's just that I don't understand . . ."

"Read. Just read."

I stepped out onto the balcony to leave her to read through Mother's letter in peace, as many times as she wished, and to think about everything. After that she'd know herself what questions I'd be asking and what answers I'd be after. I watched her from the balcony. She sobbed but kept reading. Then she stopped, shook her head left to right, incredulous. She wiped away tears. She'd never wanted to tell me the secret. She planned to take the truth to her grave. I followed her reading and knew where she was because I'd already memorized the letter. From time to time she looked over at me. She took out a handkerchief. It's over, Ingrid, the boy has discovered the long-guarded secret. Some sort of creator decided, with a warped sense of humor, that for the development of his madcap story he needed to have me discover everything. He wasn't on your side, that's all.

After some ten minutes Ingrid finally mustered the strength to look straight at me. This is a tense moment in dramatic terms, after which the actors are obliged, as in a courtroom, to tell the truth, the whole truth, and nothing but the truth. She nodded to me. She was ready to talk. By then I no longer knew whether I was angry or just impatient to learn what I'd always had the right to know, or, more accurately, to receive the final confirmation of Mother's words. I couldn't tell where all this was going. As I came back to the table I was suddenly hit by a powerful swirl of dizziness, but that was, perhaps, the whisky.

Looking down, Ingrid stared into her lap, the notebook shut, and before I could say a word, she'd begun speaking in her defense: "I want you to know that I always did everything only for your sake, Richard, for your sake alone, believe me." Again she dissolved into tears, so I took her hand and rubbed her shoulder to comfort her.

"I know. I know you only meant the best for me, but I have the right to know who I am, and now I need to know everything." I tried encouraging her to speak. "All of it, right to the end?"

"What more do you want to know?! Paula said everything in the letter. What more could there be?!" She choked on her tears and my patience frayed.

"You know exactly what I want. I want you to tell me all about it. There is no more point in keeping secrets! For God's sake, they've all been dead for years!" I shouted. "And now I know Heinrich wasn't my father. The act you've been playing your whole life is over now!"

"I'm sorry, please, I'm sorry. It was all for you . . ."

"*For me?!* For me you hid the fact that my father was somebody else, this Jakob Schneider who was killed even before I was born? Why?!" By now I was shouting and pacing around the room. "Why didn't you say something? Why?" Ingrid pleaded with me to forgive her. "This is not about forgiveness, can't you see? Why can't you see what's happening? I don't know who I am anymore, nor who my mother was, or my father, or you. What happened? Tell me everything!" I pounded the table with my fist. "Now!"

She couldn't stay the tears, but at least she nodded. While she collected herself I poured another whisky and went over to the window. What a backdrop. An agreeable, warm Viennese evening outside, and in the apartment a family drama reaching its climax. Random passersby, couples, on a mild May evening, and at one window there's a man looking out at the street, whisky glass in hand—nothing strange, an ordinary sight—while behind him an old woman is crying. She has just learned not only that her secret has been exposed but also the bitter fact that her beloved sister in the days before her death had no one to confide in but the man who'd left her with child, that she hadn't stopped loving him, that she hoped for his return despite it all . . . And the tear-stained old woman must now come clean to the very person whose right to know who his father was had been brutally violated. And all this is not easy to endure, dear readers, because the boy you recall from the end of Act I, covering a half-century span, the boy who grew up to become a man and wrote "authentic novels about the state of mind of the postwar generation" and about "the evil of history," that very boy as a man of fifty will flesh out what he knows of his origins by questioning his aunt, and these facts are now seeking their rightful place, even if they elbow out both his work and his life in the process.

"What do you want to know, Richard? Say what you want."

"What happened? What happened with Mother, with all of you before I was born? Where did Jakob Schneider come from? What happened between him and Mother? Everything you know."

"There's a lot you could gather from your mother's notebook." Ingrid began talking and the words were hard in coming after all the years of silence. "Andreas—"

"Jakob," I interrupted.

"Jakob, if you prefer . . . is your real father. I never told you because he was gone before you were even born, and because I didn't know how it would help you in your life to know that aside from losing your father and your mother, your biological father was also no longer alive. After Jakob's arrest, we talked it all over and Heinrich decided to acknowledge you as his child and he proposed marriage to your mother. We accepted. We thought it best that way, especially what with all the circumstances of Jakob's arrest and his background. Can you imagine what would have happened to you if they'd learned he was your father? You know full well. I thought, afterward, that it would be better if you never learned the real truth. I simply thought this would be better for you, for your development, for everything. Yes, I thought it best to forget this and you have every right to be angry with me, but I'm still convinced that it would have been better if you hadn't demolished the wall. Unfortunately, Paula died immediately after you were born. Maybe your mother would have told you. I don't know. Maybe poor Heinrich would have told you. Forgive me, but I could not. I wanted to put an end to the horrific story that took from me everything I loved—everything but you."

"Well, you must know you wouldn't have lost me. You were my only mother, for God's sake!"

"I don't know. I didn't want to lose you and allow what destroyed our lives to destroy yours as well."

"I'm not blaming you. I just want you to tell me about everything. Who was this Jakob Schneider? How did he turn up in your lives?"

"My fault." Ingrid smiled grimly. "I introduced him to Paula and Heinrich. You read that in the letter. We were among the few who were opposed to Nazism and the *Anschluss* but hadn't left the country. At the university where I was working at the time, we formed a secret group. There were only a handful of us, maybe a dozen, and we were fully aware of what we were risking. Various ideological orientations merged here in our common hatred of Hitler. I included Paula, of course, as well as her friend Heinrich. Our activities were small gatherings in private apartments, discussions, several secret publications, and so forth. Nothing major, nothing earthshaking. At some point in early 1941, I met Andreas Schubert through a trusted contact. I say 'Andreas Schubert' because that is how he introduced himself to us, because those were the documents he carried and I had no reason to doubt him. He said he'd come from Yugoslavia, which explained his slightly odd accent, though his German was perfect. A Yugoslav German, there, that's all, with measured left-wing political views. This was the image he wanted us to have of him. He was never overly vocal, never impulsive; he never took initiative in the group, limited his role to that of an observer. But I sniffed out that he was a true communist, perhaps because I, myself, had leanings in that direction in my youth. With age and all that happened to us later, my confrontational attitude was largely softened. What I mean to say is that I recognized in him somebody who might be playing a more serious role than just keeping company with a few politically incompetent oppositionists, but I had no proof and, in general, Andreas had an air of secrecy. Perhaps that was what attracted Paula. I don't know. She was young."

"And you? What attracted you?" Ingrid now looked over at me with mistrust and for a moment didn't say anything. "What was Jakob Schneider to you?"

Ingrid was silent first and then she answered, deliberately sidestepping the question.

"Your mother wrote the letter at a moment that was trying for all of us. You mustn't take everything written there at face value. That was a very troubled time. Andreas was arrested . . ."

"Jakob, Jakob is his name."

"Jakob was arrested, Paula was pregnant, and Heinrich had gone off to the Front. We were left alone, and it wasn't easy. There were many quarrels and accusations."

"What happened after that?"

"Your mother fell in love with Andreas, that's what happened! I met him in early 1941. He earned my trust. We saw each other often at that point and I truly believed we'd become friends. Then I introduced him to Paula . . ."

"And he?" I interrupted. "Jakob?"

"I don't know. I realized something was up. I tried to warn her. He soon changed in relation to me. I think they'd already started seeing each other in secret by then. I learned about it all much later. I tried to dissuade her. And then one evening she announced she was pregnant. Something happened at that moment. I think things weren't going well between them. Jakob was later arrested and that ended it."

"What happened to him?"

"Heinrich was the first to learn of the arrest and brought us the news. Word spread quickly through our little circle. We could find out nothing more. It was obvious we had to stop meeting. Somebody had betrayed him. It was after the attack on the Soviet Union. Everybody was terribly frightened. We had to think about you. It was a trying time."

"How did they arrest him? How did they find out?"

"I don't know. After that he vanished and that's it."

"Where to?"

"How would I know? They killed him probably. I don't believe he could have survived."

"But still, you can't be sure. You never heard he was killed, did you?"

"No, but can't you see, it was obvious. I'm sure he was killed. How could he have slipped through?"

"But you can't be a hundred percent certain!" I persisted as if the door had opened a crack with her earlier *probably*.

"Richard, this is the truth. You cannot imagine he could have survived. This was 1941! Maybe they killed him later, maybe he died in a camp. And besides, you know how things went for Jews."

"But wait. According to Paula's letter he was arrested as a communist, wasn't he? Maybe they never realized he was Jewish. He had falsified papers, and I am certain he never would have let on about his background himself. Maybe he did survive after all," I mused while Ingrid shook her head helplessly. "I heard many stories of German communists who had better conditions in the camps than the Jews, and some of them spent as many as ten years there. It's possible. It happened."

"You can't start thinking like that," she said sternly, as if frightened by what she'd just heard. "Yes, he was arrested as a communist, but they must have realized who he was and then that was it. And besides, even if things went as you suggest, even if he did survive the war, the camps, and who knows what all else, which I doubt, he could have died since then a million times over!"

"He could have, of course. How old was he?"

"I don't know. Like me. A little older."

"See? Today he might be how old? Eighty? Not more. You're seventy-seven and you're still going strong, right?"

Ingrid said not another word. I had the impression she couldn't speak anymore, that she was petrified. Then I began to understand why she hadn't told me who my father really was. The possibility I'd voiced was at the root of her fear. I stood. I could no longer sit at the table, could no longer remain in the apartment; I needed fresh air. The dizziness was back. I turned to the door. Ingrid went on sitting, motionless, staring at something, lost in thought, back in a past that had finally reached her, a history she'd tailored to suit her and whose seams were now ripping apart.

I was already at the door when a question popped into my head that hadn't been answered precisely in Mother's letter or in this conversation.

"One more thing." I turned. "Please, just one more question tonight." She looked over at me, resigned, as if ready to take one more blow, and nodded. "You said that Andreas claimed to have been from Yugoslavia. A Yugoslav German. But what about Jakob? Was he, too, from Yugoslavia?"

She was startled by the simplicity of the question. As if she'd expected I'd want to know something bigger.

"Yes," she said after a few moments. "He was from Yugoslavia as well."

"From what part?"

She hesitated for a moment, plumbing her memory. "Paula spoke of it once . . ." And then from this she extracted the fact that seemed to pull together all the recent events into some sort of inscrutable and inimical order, and that pulled the already-shaking ground out from under my feet. "Yes! From the city where they assassinated the archduke. It is constantly in the news these days."

6

When the United Nations transport aircraft took off from Sarajevo on the morning of July 7, I was convinced that shame would strike me dead right there if I looked back once more at the city. I stayed in the seat I'd been assigned and fended off the desire to gaze one last time through the window at Sarajevo as I fled. I held my face in my hands, dropped my head to my knees, and didn't even rise to lift a hand and wave to the besieged city I'd arrived in as a journalist in mid-May— only to desert it that day like a coward running from my own personal catastrophe, which had intertwined so strangely with the city's calamity. Coward-like, I repeat, with no word of farewell. Or better, like a beggar in disguise, because there was nothing left of the old Richard Richter but, perhaps, the name on the accreditation ID that allowed him to board the aircraft as simply and painlessly as if hailing a cab to whisk him away from a war he had no tie to whatsoever.

And the tears that dripped onto the grimy iron deck of the aircraft, finding their way through his tightly squeezed fingers, might be perceived as nothing more than a perfectly reasonable human response to what he'd been through, a reaction to the stress that is invariably a part of the work of a journalist, a release of emotions now that the danger had finally passed, after our famous writer, valiant correspondent, and shrewd analyst of this tragic European war at the century's end had chosen to withdraw. Perhaps to write a fat new book about his experiences and the bravery it took to be there, on the spot, before anybody else could, to open the eyes of Europe—as long as the honorarium was generous enough. No one knew that the man they took pains to extract from the plane that hot day in Split when the plane had landed was no longer the man listed on the ID attached to his shirt. No longer did he answer to that name.

When I arrived in Sarajevo in mid-May as an analyst for the German papers, a field reporter, a European writer acting in solidarity with the cataclysm ongoing at the center of the continent, my eyes were wide open. Behind the official function that gave me access to Sarajevo, already under siege for several days—a siege that is unlikely to end anytime soon judging by the most recent news coming in as I toil over my final manuscript—hidden from view was the personal piece of my mission: to deliver my mother's unsent letter to the person she'd intended it for. The resolve with which I set out on this task was shaken from time to time, either by Ingrid's insistent pleas or my own doubts that this search for a father—undertaken by a man of fifty pursuing only sketchy clues dating back to a long-ago war—was tantamount to madness, an irrational whim on the threshold of old age. But I wasn't feeling the slightest bit elderly then, as if all the remaining strength I had left was surging inside me, regardless of the cost of seeing this absurd mission through.

I knew there'd be no return to the pre-blue-notebook life that night when, after my words with Ingrid, I dashed like a madman out of the house to wander the streets of Vienna, to cross the square where the central Gestapo headquarters had been and where today there stands an unassuming monument with a yellow star to remind us of all who disappeared into those cellars. There, not for his *race*, I thought at the time, but for his convictions, might have ended the days of the man who made me. Somehow I found myself by an open newspaper stand

and requested the most recent edition of the evening news. The papers, it seemed, were not covering the war in Bosnia much. Only a brief article about a clash between the former federal army and forces of the army of the young state suggested that the situation was worsening in Sarajevo, with alarming news about hostilities and massacres elsewhere in Bosnia.

Sarajevo?

The fate of that city had had an entirely different import for me earlier. Yet now it was . . . what? My own place of origin? The very thought of such a thing was weird. A place where I, in some sense, belonged? Or, perhaps, where I ought to be right now?

To do what?

Find my father.

Who had probably died before I even came into the world. And even if he'd survived and was still alive, to go there, knock on the old man's door, and declare, "Hello, I'm your son"? What was the point, after all this time, of complicating things, as if it wasn't enough that a fifty-year-old man had discovered the truth of his background. Wasn't it his problem, at first, to wrestle with? My father was somebody else, okay, but did that mean that now I needed to go charging into the fray? Ultimately what did I, Richard Richter, being who I am, have to do with all this?

These questions had been spinning in my head since I read Mother's letter, and they heightened in intensity just at the moment when Ingrid mentioned the news which, at regular intervals, broadcast images of Jakob Schneider's city. For God's sake, these weren't news stories about Wiener Neustadt or Eisentstadt, but about a city that was besieged, a city I knew nothing about! *What can I do?* I wondered, holding the newspaper with its bits of news about the mounting casualties in Bosnia, completely immersed in my intimate cross-examination, when the news vendor startled me out of my reverie with a wagging finger, pointing to the prominently displayed sign that the newspapers at his stand were to be "paid for, not read." That legendary Viennese sense of nuance! I smiled with understanding at the vendor and reached for my wallet. Then I remembered I'd left it at home and started riffling through my pockets in hopes of turning up a schilling, but to my surprise instead I pulled out a folded newspaper clipping. Like the vendor, I was startled. But as soon as I saw the text in French, I realized I was holding the *Le Monde* article I'd read on the train for Vienna, and which I'd forgotten all about the instant I stuffed it into my pocket. I unfolded it nervously and saw again the image of the woman—Sarajevo again, it was cropping up everywhere!—her head pivoting toward something horrific that seemed to be coming from the very heavens, which, as I later learned, was a rain of bullets fired from the Holiday Inn. I flipped over the clipping and there he was again, the unhappy priest whose fate I'd mocked on the train, not for its drama but for the media industry that had made the story their special purview. Why, I'd sneered at the time, is it today a bigger deal to discover your father is Jewish instead of the local postman? It was not easy for me that evening, coming across this Catholic priest who confessed to being part of the same people as our savior Jesus Christ and who, as printed in this little scrap of newspaper on the back of the picture of Sarajevo, understood that nothing would ever be the same again and that life could not go on as it had before. *Il faut aller jusqu'au bout!* thundered the priest from the crumpled page, and by now I had far more sympathy for his predicament than I'd had on the Vienna train.

I cannot say it was this example that tipped the scales in my predicament, or that I'd decided to take his advice, but when I scanned the story on the back, when I'd once more seen the eyes of the Sarajevo woman, I was astonished by the coincidence, the fact that an unconscious hand had linked in one place these two stories, stories which for the rest of mankind were entirely separate, yet at an exactly chosen moment were conjoined into a precise message, even an imperative for only one person on earth, now standing there by the newspaper stand.

My limbs frozen, as if a spider had wrapped me in a web, not a single strand of it spun in vain, I was snared in a mechanism of accursed threads whose purpose would be clear only to the corrupt gods of antiquity. Like a rabbit motionless on a road, its eyes glued to the glare of headlights it sees for the first and last time. To take this to the end, no matter what that means.

And, indeed, the feeling that the die had already been cast took concrete shape over the next few days through several contacts with acquaintances from the news world, who did not want the conflict in Bosnia to go unreported, as it was increasingly compelling in terms of victims, blood, and complexity. I organized a contract to report from Sarajevo and provide commentaries along the way for events as they occurred in the ex-Yugoslavia. An article every few days would suffice. Word soon spread and several German papers asked if I'd write the occasional piece for them as well, something with a "literary flavor that would describe your experience of this incomprehensible war." I worked out an arrangement with an Austrian television station that I'd be an official part of their team in exchange for the occasional on-screen appearance. My decision was seen, of course, as just another step taken by a once-passionate intellectual who'd embraced similar tasks and taken outspoken stances in the past about, in ossified journalese, the all-too-complex political circumstances of the day. But there were colleagues who were quick to spread rumors that this was all really about reinvigorating his career, which had recently been limping, and that the writer was, in fact, in it to attract readers and the media spotlight. If only that had been the case, that would have been an easy task, safe—more or less, a little buzz to jazz up my profile along with a collection of essays about the war to spark interest in my next novel, a tried-and-true routine that would indeed have been a much happier outcome for everybody.

◆ ◆ ◆

Over several days in May I scrambled to prepare for my departure for Sarajevo. At the National Library I read everything I could get my hands on about Yugoslavia and the seething conflict (a relatively brief bibliography at this point, mainly newspaper articles, written at the dictate of events and media demand), histories of Bosnia, Sarajevo, the assassination . . . Once I'd made the acquaintance of the librarian in the Balkan section, who clearly admired my novels, everything went smoothly and the books arrived quickly; I asked, timidly, about sources on the history of Bosnian, or actually Sarajevo, Jews, "about whom—*if I can trust you, ma'am, with a secret*—I'm writing a new novel." The able librarian invested considerable effort to dig up a study by Moritz Levy—written, thank heavens, in German!—about the Sephardic community of Bosnia (*Druck und Verlag von Daniel A. Kajon*), published in Sarajevo in 1911. A very rare edition, as she remarked. What about the Ashkenazis? Was there anything about those Ashkenazis from Austria who went there after the occupation? I sought additional material because in the index of Levy's short, wonderful book, there was no mention of the name Schneider, nor was it in any of the name indices of the many books that I leafed through, fueled not only by my desire to find my way through the Yugoslav drama but also by the peculiar hope that I might simply stumble onto a clue in my game of detection. I soon realized that this roundabout search was not going to produce any results, but I persisted, nevertheless, in preparing intellectually for the conflict ahead of me and whose actors, development, logic, and consequences I gradually came to know.

Ingrid had already given up on her pleas and dissuasion. I tried to learn more from her about Jakob, Mother, and what really happened in the spring of 1941, but we kept circling through the same things. There was a point beyond which I could not go with her, and for this I might have blamed her obstinacy or her faulty memory, or I could simply admit that she had no more answers to offer to some of my questions.

Finally, early on the morning of May 10, I left for Sarajevo, driving an official Austrian television–station vehicle, the team of reporters with me. We traveled through Zagreb, where we sent off our first report, then down to Split, and then it was our plan to enter Herzegovina and make our way through to Sarajevo, which was closed off. Fierce fighting continued in Sarajevo between Bosnian Serb rebels, backed by the Yugoslav federal forces, and the defenders. After violent clashes in early May and the arrest of the president, the situation had reached a fever pitch. There were television teams already in the field, and we hoped we'd soon catch sight of the city with the passes we'd received from both the warring sides. By then I'd committed to memory the names of all the main streets, the unpronounceable name of the little river, as well as a few basic words in Serbo-Croatian, if that language is still today called by its hyphenated name. In Zagreb I met with Mr. P., a publisher who had once evinced an interest in my novels. To his question of why a writer at fifty would give up his comfortable Paris life to come to the Balkans, I answered with the first words that came to mind, hoping to duck behind their trite ring: "*I'm searching for inspiration for a new novel, just as my colleagues have been saying. Joking, joking, of course.*" I received in response a sour smile and the comment that I must send along the novel once I'd written it. Many of the friends I was soon to make in Sarajevo asked me the same question, including *her*, and to all of them I offered insufficient answers, and their faces, much like the face of the publisher Mr. P., expressed doubts about my good intentions and the certainty that any foreigner coming into their war was pursuing a personal agenda. They were not wrong, though in my case it would cost me dearly. They couldn't know that the essential difference was that in Sarajevo, like Oedipus in Thebes, I was no *foreigner*.

II

Richard in Sarajevo

1

I left the hotel today for the first time. It was around eight in the morning, but I wasn't able to sleep last night, anyway. Writing kept me up, and then I listened for hours to the voices of the Viennese summer night, wrestling with my drinking, my scattered photographs, my rowdy monologues . . . I left the room this morning and must have alarmed the desk clerk for whom I'd been nothing more than a voice at the other end of the phone line until now, ordering food and drink with reckless abandon. He almost jumped off the chair behind the counter. I'm certain my reclusion has had a less than salutary effect on my appearance, already marked by a shaggy beard when I arrived, but that matters little to me now. There's no turning back the clock (and besides, I'd have to turn it all the way back to 1941!), and there's no way back to Sarajevo, though my whole being is pulling me there, as if battling opiate addiction to the point of physical pain. But then there we are again with a new bottle and back to the manuscript we go. Like every true addict, I know I cannot survive either the source of my addiction or the withdrawal from it which healing requires. For it isn't the war, or the ever-tightening siege around the city, that keeps me from returning.

"Mr. Schneider, Mr. Schneider!" the young man called after me. "Should I leave your lunch at the door as usual, or . . . ?"

"Yes. And don't go in, please. I'll be back soon."

He nodded. And I meant it. I didn't intend to venture beyond the open market. While I was leaving the building and blinking into the morning sun, I thought, *This is all wrong.* I've cut myself off from the world since returning from Sarajevo. My previous daily ritual of sipping something on a café terrace makes no sense. I'd be stepping away from this self-imposed penance, a cowardly attempt at mitigating my guilt, a heretic wish to reestablish contact with a semblance of normal life, no matter how small. Besides, I fear somebody might spot me; I might even run into Ingrid. After all, she frequents this part of town on her shopping excursions. And things might escape the control I've imposed on my fate, or what is left of it. But when the young man at the front desk used that last name to call to me, a name they could easily have found is an alias had anyone checked my papers, I felt the name was actually sheltering me. I am nothing more than an anonymous, bearded stranger. Who knows, the young man at the front desk might even have called the police had he caught on, and the phone would've rung in an office much like the one where somebody, a half century before, had betrayed the original Mr. Schneider, though he, too, had used another moniker for introductions. If somebody were to give me up, their call would usher in—to the world of spies, betrayal, and anonymous tippers—a weird diabolical equilibrium, in which all names are stripped of their meaning. The whole great secret would be laid bare: the father would be a father to his son, and the son a son to his father . . . and though the path to this blood-based tautology was strewn with thorns, it would finally be successfully outed. A father to his son and a son to his father . . . Besides, the last name has always been *mine*; I have the right to it according to some sources, according to the apocryphal truth I uncovered and based on which I've been drawing up my foundational document, the essential piece of my reformed personal canon.

This encouraged me to act on my intention and venture out again among people, while never emerging from the cave of my intimate catastrophe and knowledge, nameless under this new/old name, a prophet only freshly in from the desert, and as such I'd observe that life goes on: but as something to which I no longer have any right. And besides, the young man's reaction to my appearance confirmed that I have nothing to fear. *No one will recognize you, son of Jakob, in the city where you were born.*

I sat on a terrace in the Naschmarkt and sipped the first espresso I'd had in days. I listened to snippets of conversation in foreign languages and watched women order fruit and vegetables in halting German while calling to their children. A woman near me shouted, *"Emina!!!"* tangled in language and currency, in a panic because her child had run off somewhere. *"Emina!!!"* The little girl came back; she seemed to be about ten, and annoyed, she mocked her mother: *"Eminaaa! Eminaaa! What you do want now?!"* Then she translated for her mother from Bosnian, and while her mother packed up her purchases, the child looked around impatiently. A child like any other. She noticed me, nudged her mother, and pointed my way. She asked something, then pulled free, came over, and said in passably good German, "Mister, why are you crying?"

"Because I thought you were lost," I told the child without trying to hide my tears. I was shaken. "Joking, joking. I like your name."

"Why?" Her mother called to her again and nodded, cautioning her not to bother the gentleman.

"I knew a little girl who had the same name as you."

"So I remind you of her?" she asked, curious, her eyes wide.

"In a way, yes."

"And where does that girl live?"

"In Sarajevo. In Bosnia."

"I'm from Bosnia, too!" she crowed proudly.

"I know."

"So, why were you crying?" Finally, she asked what was really worrying her. "Was it her? Was it about the girl?"

"A little bit of everything."

"Somebody else?"

"Maybe."

"Somebody hurt you?"

"I hurt somebody."

Emina didn't know what to think about people hurting each other and then crying over it, and so she turned to her mother who was listening and trying to follow what we were saying. She hurried the girl along while repeating, *"Entschuldigung, Herr, Entschuldigung."* Before she obeyed, the little girl sighed as if she understood everything perfectly, as ten-year-old girls are wont to do. She skipped over to her mother. After a few steps, as much as was needed for Emina to communicate the gist of our conversation, both of them turned to face me and waved with pity and compassion. It was the nicest thing that had happened to me since I came back from Sarajevo. A sure sign that I must not go out again.

Will Alma understand? Understand and forgive? Or at least one if not both? And will Ivor, for that matter, forgive me? It's different with him. Who could have imagined that day when I arrived in Sarajevo that I'd find them, that I'd find love and friendship were still possible for a man of fifty who'd arrived like a wrung-out sponge—ready to absorb but not to give in return. Perhaps I'm writing this text for them and will offer these pages instead of an apology or an excuse. I could not reveal to them then—when I arrived in the city during those relatively calm days after such savage fighting, through the morass of checkpoints of well-armed Bosnian Serb rebels, discordant men from the Yugoslav army, and poorly armed but fervent defenders—that I knew full well, unlike the tragic king of Thebes, that I was coming to this city determined to learn something about my father.

Even as I was traversing Croatia and a stretch of Bosnia, I grasped the gravity of the war I was plunging into, but when I saw the first signs of the shelling and fighting in the Sarajevo neighborhoods, the burned-out frames of tram cars and vehicles on Skenderija, and the rubble of glass, brick, and mortar on the streets of the Old Town, I realized I'd reached a moment when my clandestine, poorly designed plan would have to adjust to the all-too-real siege into which I'd ventured. My eyes were opened wide when—after five days on the road—we reached Sarajevo and I recognized, with the thrill of a child, the buildings and monuments I'd been reading about. I was able to regale my fellow travelers with stories of the city, show them the place where young terrorist Gavrilo Princip started the First World War and the bridge that bears his name, recite the names of the mosques and churches, and teach them a crucial name from the city's history: Gazi Husrevbeg. They repeated it after me. I pointed to the pink-hued synagogue, admired the vibrant colors of the newer building near it, and described the architecture and style of the City Hall. Along the way I explained to my collaborators the task awaiting us now that we'd arrived in the capital. As we stepped out of the car by the hotel and found a bullet hole in the chassis, we realized that our naïve display of the "PRESS" sign provided us with no safety whatsoever. We looked at one another and, wordless, entered the hotel we'd been told would be safe for foreigners.

We were greeted by several local journalists who, like the hotel staff and so many others we'd meet those first days of the war, wanted to tell us all about what they were going through, in the hope that their truth would burst out onto the world stage and put a stop to their tragic destiny. Unlikely. Teams of reporters were out patrolling the city, and all the people of Sarajevo could hear was how their words were being pieced together on the channels of world television stations into a war mosaic that made things sound increasingly *ethnic*, *religious*, veering toward the *primeval* and, ultimately, *inevitable*—a conflict there was no point to getting embroiled in, a predetermined catastrophe rooted in the history of the region—these sentiments interspersed with carefully chosen quotes from their very own writers . . . But one of my organizational flaws became immediately apparent as I talked with these good people who, doing their best to communicate to us the state of affairs and explain what was really happening, kept referring to the tangle of political or historical relations—without always being able to find the most fitting English expressions, thereby only deepening our misunderstandings. Due to my own poor grasp of their situation, I was unable to divine their meaning, while at the same time I found myself sidestepping any questions I thought might dishearten them. At that point I still had no translator, or, I should say, interpreter, working with me who could guide me through the city and, ultimately, the war.

This overdue realization was what led me to Ivor, who would become my last friend, last, indeed, though not least. The need for an interpreter that I'd already sensed the first day quickly proved a vital necessity. While the television journalists could tailor their information to the mind-set of their media, I soon saw that for the commentaries I'd begun writing, the news gathered at the press centers or from other colleagues and agencies would not suffice. I contacted Vienna to say I'd need an interpreter and the funds were approved, while the hiring was left to me. Musing about where I might find a translator, I remembered a letter I'd received a year or two before from a young Yugoslav student of German studies who was interested in my writing and had taken up translating my novel *Closing Time*. I couldn't recall receiving a copy of the published translation, and in fact the whole thing had slipped my mind. I chided myself for having forgotten that the letter had come to me, straight from Sarajevo. I remember noticing when I first saw the envelope that the young man's last name had a German ring to it, but I couldn't dredge it up. Luckily, my shaky memory had retained his first name: Ivor.

Ah-ha, I thought with excitement, *I have at least one contact here, though via a letter I never answered.* I set about searching for Ivor. I gave my Bosnian colleagues his name and no more than half a day passed before somebody had figured out who that might be. Sarajevo is a small town, so Ivor got in touch quite soon, but the fighting during those days prevented us from arranging a meeting. This was when telephone connections were gradually vanishing. Ivor finally simply came to our hotel and decided he'd wait until I showed up so that we could meet. That day we were out filming a hall used some years before by the Olympic Games as it burned; I remember how the copper-colored roof buckled with shrill creaks from the heat. The whole team was uneasy, a premonition of the likelihood that we could be killed, a fate that was by no means reserved for the beleaguered residents of this city and country, and my jitters were heightened by the alarming flow of events that was pulling me farther from my personal goal. I could not find moment or method to move forward with my personal story, which was what had, initially, brought me to this hornet's nest.

When Ivor showed up, it was the first good thing to happen to me in Sarajevo. He was twenty-five and looked younger still. Maybe that's why he shaved only infrequently, his face streaked with scraggly black stubble. He wore small round glasses behind which one could see his large dark-brown eyes. He looked as if he'd only recently sheared his hair short in response to the wartime conditions, and he appeared that day in a plain red T-shirt with a faded inscription, beneath one of those US Army field jackets from the 1970s. He was, as I told him later once we'd become friends, the spitting image of a Brooklyn intellectual, anguished by his stabs at grasping the essence of life, replete with indeterminate heritage and fuzzy leftist leanings. In our later banter, I asked him how he'd found himself there in Sarajevo. He shot back that the description I'd offered of him was not very original. He was born here, but luckily he still looked nothing like a *Mitteleuropa* salon intellectual who'd never set foot in the Paris metro, who had played, at the dictates of his political engagement, with all the wrong regimes of this world until he'd finally discovered the Balkan crisis, which explained at least partially how *he*, the *salonista* such as he was, had found his way to Sarajevo. These labels that we so often, and so liberally, affixed to one another are only evidence of how quickly we'd become friends.

That first evening, after he aired his considerable surprise at my arrival in Sarajevo "in the middle of *all this*," describing it silently with a sweeping gesture, we spoke of work. He said he was interested in my writing, and I asked about the translation of the novel, the manuscript of which, Ivor informed me, was stowed away somewhere in a drawer at the leading publishing house. It didn't take long for us to dispense with formalities and embark on a more personal conversation, beginning a lengthy, ongoing dialogue that by necessity careered through literary and cinematic passions to some of the weightier political themes. This first episode of our friendship, lubricated by home-brewed brandy from the hotel's own reserves, ended in the wee hours of the morning.

"I'd pictured our encounter differently," said Ivor then. "The translation was done. The book would be published sooner or later, and you'd come to celebrate its launch. As it is, instead of coming to a book event, you've come to a war, so we do have a common denominator for all this, and this—no matter which way you look at it—is that fate decided you were meant to come to Sarajevo. And we, of course, were meant to meet. But, while a tourist visit to an exotic small city in the Balkans to celebrate the launch of your novel would have meant a moderately interesting yet incidental life step for the famous writer, I must ask you what drove you to turn up here precisely at one of the worst moments in this city's history?"

"What can I say? I guess I've been searching for inspiration for my next novel," I said with a deep sigh. "You know how it is with us politically engaged writers . . . The worse it is, the better."

"Reason enough," said Ivor with understanding. "When you finish it, send it to me for translation. And besides, I assume the theme will be local, will it not?"

"You have my word."

He rose to walk home with caution. *"Ivor!"* I called after him when he'd only taken a few steps. He turned and looked back, eyebrows raised. "Do you have a Sarajevo telephone directory?"

"I believe I do . . . ," he said, startled. "I think I have one somewhere. But . . . why? What's it about?"

"Nothing much. Please, bring it with you this afternoon. I'd rather not explain just now. Let's say I need it for the novel I'm writing."

2

By late May I'd slowly but surely relinquished my role as television reporter and with growing clarity had embraced the fact that the search for my father was doomed from the start to fail. It seemed absurd in a place where people were murdering each other with abandon (let the massacre on Vase Miskina Street on Wednesday, May 27, serve as illustration; we filmed the horrific carnage and dispatched it to Vienna— what a coup for my journalism career . . .). By then we'd already begun to realize that either this city would greet the winter still under siege or the defenders would succumb, which—we all believed—would lead to an immense catastrophe. How I admired Sarajevans for their bright spirits during those days, their conviction that they'd soon be freed either by their own efforts or by international intervention after the discerning Europeans had reached their limit. The magic word became *deblockade*, and it spread through the streets like good news. People began believing that simply by repeating it over and over and over, they could change the unacceptable situation.

By early June my fears were confirmed. Confirmed with each new journalistic report from a battlefield of the daily bloodshed, with each new sniper victim, with our trips to the Serb side where the attackers openly jeered at world opinion and conscience—if there even is such a thing!—shamelessly flaunting their deadly arsenal not merely to badger their opponents (who already knew it quite well), but to provoke the international military and political institutions who, after the two months of fighting, had dared to raise their voices in alarm about where the situation was heading. That no response was forthcoming to the brazen challenge—to the humiliation of those who'd been challenged and the glee of the challengers—was ultimately confirmed by Mitterrand's visit to Sarajevo. And we, the *foreign journalists* here on the ground, became both witnesses to and perpetrators of the tragedy playing out not only in Sarajevo where the cameras were rolling, but, as we know today, in other parts of Bosnia as well. I found the futility of my work ever more glaring: my political engagement useless; my remonstrations inaudible; the value of my role and my writing pure fiction.

In such a context there seemed to be no point at all in pursuing what might have been a simple enough search for Jakob Schneider, if, indeed, the man named in my mother's letter was still alive, and if this man had chosen to reside in his place of birth, of all places in the world where his life might have taken him, and (yet another if) if under the circumstances such as they were, he no longer had any way of leaving so was now managing as best as he could to live from day to day somewhere in the city of Sarajevo. Had I located him despite all these ifs, I'd have to figure out what to do then, what to say. What is there to say to one's own father who never even knew you existed? "Hey, Dad, let's hang out when all this simmers down; we should go for a picnic and get to know each other—after all, we're father and son, flesh and blood!" or some such drivel. I am not writing this to evade responsibility for the subsequent turn of events that whisked me along as if I were a foolish tourist straying from the beaten path, only to be swept away by a wild river. I might—and I say *might* again in my defense—still have been able to influence the course of events had I dared to ask the occasional question, had I done what I ought to have done and packed my suitcases and simply headed home. With my pocket full of pay, which skyrocketed as the subject matter became ever more urgent, I could have traveled off to French Guiana—why not—and swum there with the tapirs in the gold-bearing streams, far, as far away as I could go, from Sarajevo, a city that was rapidly fettering my hands and feet and thoughts with the agreeable ties that bind until one can no longer shrug them off.

In the fifteen days or so that followed the evening when I first met Ivor, my urge to shake off the role I'd saddled myself with, and my desire to abandon exploration of my genealogical vagaries, swelled in me hand in hand with the wholly irrational and mildly romantic compulsion, albeit fueled by a different impulse, to stay on in the city, to identify with its residents, to live from one day to the next as the people around me were living, despite the price so many of them had already paid. I knew the idea bordered on lunacy—for others certainly, for me somewhat less—and that it said more, perhaps, about my mental state, so I was reluctant to show the thoughts that were prodding me, and I did what I could to fend them off with the everyday routines of a war correspondent. The idea, however, gradually shifted into my resolve to remain in Sarajevo. This decision would ultimately bring me more joy than I could believe was still possible and more misery than I could fathom, after which no classical blinding or death could offer relief. But this wretched report will find its way there if I do not rein myself in, if the story doesn't come bubbling up out of me too soon.

With Ivor during those days I made the rounds of the battlefields, the military press centers, and the Pale rebel stronghold. I met with local intellectuals, activists, politicians, and musicians. I interviewed people on the street, came to know the streets, and adapted to the impossible, dilapidated turn-of-the-century passageways, wartime drinking holes, marketplaces, the parks through which one no longer strolled but ran, following now—instead of tourist maps—the marks that were being drawn on the fabric of the city by the snipers and Serb artillery. Meanwhile, the authorities in the free areas limited movements in their own way, attempting to protect the civilians, introducing more controls on an already constrained situation in which the military and political hierarchies were evident.

Ivor's arrival heralded a major change in our team. Indeed, the support I'd hoped for, that my interpreter would at least be able to explain the situation we were faced with, Ivor supplied far beyond the call of duty. He explained fully to me, the foreigner, the phenomena we were encountering—sometimes getting swept up in the process, never satisfied with easy explanations—which required encyclopedic knowledge, especially when he had such a blatant ignoramus as his student, and from Day One I felt I was absorbing a vast amount from his tutelage. He could have been my son in age, but I was glad to cede to him the lead as instructor. I have to admit I listened to Ivor's explanations, arguments, counterarguments, and erudite monologues with genuine relish. I grew fonder of Sarajevo with each passing day as our journalists' byways led us farther from the official press releases to the real life of the city that pulsed, strangely, ever stronger the more fiercely the siege tightened around it. Soon the Yugoslav People's Army abandoned the Marshal Tito barracks, an event Ivor and I celebrated in the company of his friends with my bosses footing the bill, and the government declared a state of war at last and announced a draft. My joking enthusiasm at the idea of reporting for military duty was rightly understood as hypocrisy, plain and simple, and earned me a chilly response from Ivor, who feared the very real danger of finding himself in the trenches tomorrow. He'd been told by his father—an officer who'd retired from the very same army that was now attacking us—ever since he'd been a little boy to stay far away from uniforms and weapons, passing on to his son all his contempt. I apologized to Ivor for the fact that, as he put it, I wasn't born long enough ago to fight in the Spanish Civil War.

It was obvious that I was beginning to incline more to the Bosnian side in my writing and in daily life, which brought me grumbles from my employers in their capacious, air-conditioned Frankfurt, Berlin, and

Viennese offices, who, in the name of their celebrated "objectivity," were demanding that I bring more balance to my tone. Thus began the first hiccups in our collaboration, though offers of new contacts also materialized, as did my disdain for myself, for the role I was playing in this theater while the directors were maneuvering me into the position they'd reserved for me in the media machine that we all served and which, after all, paid our bills. "Where would we be without Sarajevo, my dear Richard?" quipped my editor, a cynical old friend who at least made no effort to mask the true state of affairs. But it was becoming harder for me to act the celebrated *war-zone* writer while being critical of my government; angry at Europe, at America, at Kohl and Mitterrand both, including Mock; and angry at being merely a cog in a mechanism that was at work, democratically, to prevent things from moving out of deadlock. I say all this only to make it clear that my decision to stay on in Sarajevo, despite the meager results of my personal search, which I was doing my best not to think about, had already taken shape by then inside me.

The moment that definitely pushed me over the edge was something that happened in the second week of June. The city was being shelled at that point almost without reprieve. During one of the brief respites, Ivor, the team, and I crawled out around the neighborhood near the Markale marketplace. We found a nearby café open where the proprietor treated us to a round of brandies, whereupon we realized we had before us somebody we could interview, and he agreed to say a few words for our camera. His serenity and dismissive shrug surprised me, as did his recognition of his own powerlessness to which he added a blunt and clear, even quick-witted, judgment about the things going on around us. This was an affluent man with many acquaintances who, as we could tell from the first words he exchanged with us, had, with his skill in communicating, earned the esteem of his community, a wide circle of friends, and a respectable income. I listened to Ivor's translation and explanations with impatience, observing this man who wore the symbols of his social status with discretion. He'd spent his life negotiating the fringes of the demimonde and was proud of his experience, which anchored his thinking and his appraisal of the war, human nature, friendship, betrayal (this, apparently, hurt him the most deeply; he could not get over it), and the future. We thanked him for the conversation and decided to head back to the hotel to have a look at what we'd recorded with the aim of sending off a short piece characteristically framed with the comment: *life under siege*. I could already imagine notes from the conversation in my writing project, and I was pleased with the footage we'd taken. We said our good-byes to the proprietor. We'd walked hardly a block from the corner of the building when several blasts threw us to the ground. We knew at once that the shells had hit near the café where we'd just been sitting. We ran back to the scene, quickly enough that we could see what a shell could do to human flesh, quickly enough for us to add that footage to what we had, quickly enough for me to join in the rescue, to the surprise of my team and the medics and helpers who came to retrieve the human remains and carry out the wounded. Maybe because I saw Ivor doing this and because I felt ashamed at being so shielded, in some way, from their fate, not being a resident of this city. This was not slated to be my fate even if it should befall me, because Paula, after all, had chosen not to tell Jakob back on that day long ago in June 1941 that a child was growing inside her, and therefore, as a result of how things unfolded, the tragedy of these people was not, at least officially, my personal concern.

The shelling in its wake left three dead and ten wounded. Among these last was the café proprietor, the person who had told us several times just moments before that "this evil, too, will pass" with an optimistic wink. We carried people out for I don't know how long, running wildly, howling like everybody else out of fear, misery, horror. The smell of blood pushed all of us onto the other side of life, and we stopped, fearing a new shell might fall and hit us. In the end, once the dead and wounded were transported by cars to the hospital, Ivor and I sat down on the curb, smeared with the blood of strangers. Ivor took my hand, clasped it, and I could feel how my sense of touch was unpleasantly met by the bond of blood, sweat, and dust. The blood of strangers, the blood of our fellow citizens, made us brothers in blood. I threw my other arm over his shoulder as if to console him, but inside I knew, though it hadn't reached my brain yet from my heart, that there was now no turning back. I would no longer reply to the letters and messages Ingrid was sending me brimming with concern and, most recently, others sent by Kitty in panicked shock at my new place of residence of which she'd learned via the newspapers. They would not hear my voice again, and neither would my publishers, who were fretting over the bottom line, nor the handful of well-intended friends I could count on the fingers of one hand, the writers union, television producers, universities reaching me from a world that was distant and—from that day forward—foreign, to which I no longer intended to return and from whom I was reneging on my membership. Flight. Retreat. Displacement. Sanctuary found in a besieged city in the year of our devil ninety-two.

I carried inside me the weight of that event over the next few days while we did what we could to go on living and continue normally, if that's the word, doing our job. Although I felt revulsion at what I was doing, I kept at it, as if we were all part of a choreography of horror, with the executioners, victims, and observers all assigned their roles in advance. Here they all were: the UN Blue Helmets, Europe, NATO, the journalists, the commentators and interpreters, the fighters for human rights, the spokespeople for one or another of the "warring sides," those who recognized in this war the campaigns they'd already been waging every day in their boring countries and which they decided to wage somewhere new, on the backs of the Bosnians, the enthusiasts for the patriotic causes of small nations, the multiculturalists, the pitiers and the sympathizers, those who sent packages of medicine designed to treat diseases that were ravaging some other continent, pop stars whose careers were on the rocks, humanitarians, dealers, adventurists, racketeers, perverts, fools, and bystanders. All of them now showed up in Sarajevo and ran their part of the circus with its twisted entertainment and sense of humor warped by disease, yet nobody was willing to remove it from the European repertoires after such a wildly disproportionate audience response.

One evening in a similar mood, I was going back to the hotel. The city had already sunk into dusk, lit only now and then by the flash of a tracer bullet. The driver cruised through the Sarajevo streets where the streetlamps were off, and only occasionally did the hand of a policeman or soldier wave to guide us through the straits of the besieged city. Our hotel had already been turned into a bunker packed with sandbags, the remaining windowpanes naïvely crisscrossed with duct tape. Among the many incoming media mercenaries were those who boasted of still carrying, in their backpacks, grains of Mesopotamian sand, while there were others whose self-promotion and clamor found justification in the fact that for over half a year they'd been making the rounds to one place after another; they'd seen the devastation of Vukovar, filmed the shelling of Dubrovnik, or witnessed the occupation of Bijeljina and the murders that happened there. There was no shortage, in this cozy crowd, of thick-skinned photojournalists who were already seasoned in the logic of war; it mattered not at all to them whether they were working in the neighborhoods of Beirut, Belfast, or Jerusalem, or under the terror of Latin American dictatorships. They listened calmly, nosing around to find a good spot for taking pictures, and they refrained from commenting on or assessing the situation itself.

Of course we also came to know people who earned our respect and who knew what they were doing in this hell, with a well-grounded stance on the events they were tracking. They dispatched disturbing facts to their faraway home countries and had the power to convince their readers that they, too, were a part of this war that must, as they said over and over, be stopped. These rare examples weren't what bothered me; it was the clamor of the languages I heard spoken at the hotel—at least the languages I knew—with the torrent of stupidity about the current situation: people placing bets on how events might evolve, professional clichés spun out about how crucial our work was. In short, the talk was all ignorance, hypocrisy, scorn . . . And the very thought that these people were lying in wait for me was enough to make me nauseated. I'd had enough. I asked myself what I had in common with these folks flocking around the carcass whose decay had begun to distress me intimately. I felt my own decay merging with the city that will be both my tomb and my birthplace when the time for that comes. I hated myself, probably just as all the rest of the people in this city hated themselves: such easy prey, defying everybody's expectations, unyielding to attacks, refusing to die as the cameras roll; instead, they went right on trumpeting about their moral advantage over their vicious attackers. And besides, what else could they claim when they were so thin in the weapons department. There was a surfeit of vultures, I have to say: not just the big-name media players in the field but also their editorial boards, the channels, viewers, readers and listeners, the shortwave and longwave, the satellite television, the wide-circulation pabulum and illegible academic publications, and the newspaper vendors whose pages carried a daily report on the state of death. All together now they circled the corpse like those bare-necked scavengers—concentric, serene, with no doubt of their success.

I had trouble reining in my rancor, and finally it spilled over. Unfortunately, or—now that I think about it—fortunately, I chose to sit in the hotel foyer right next to a table occupied by several of my international colleagues. I was working on the piece about the café proprietor who was now lying in a ward at the Koševo hospital, but I couldn't move beyond the first several sentences because my thoughts kept being interrupted by the direction of the discussion at the adjacent table. Sitting there with two Americans was an Italian, a subject of

Her Majesty the Queen, and two Gallic characters, all of them newly arrived and rife with superficial impressions of a country about which they clearly knew little. I didn't want to listen to them carry on about the bad roads, Bosnian backwardness, greedy Croats, magnanimous yet barbaric Serbs, the provinciality of the Muslims whose devious nature should not be underestimated, the widespread crudity of the "parties to the conflict," the fine food at the cafeteria for the international forces, the lavish reception up on Pale, the halting English of the Bosnian president, the good-looking women of Sarajevo who might be had for cheap ("Give nylon stockings a try," advised one), the old ladies harvesting blades of grass in the city parks, the hatred radiating from everybody, the outlooks they'd visited above Sarajevo where they enjoyed sweeping views—and from where one could hit any window in town, the pitiful naïveté of the stories about coexistence. The pedestrian who insisted on waiting for a traffic light to change though none of the lights were working, though snipers' bullets whistled all around him, and though they were all calling to him to take cover. The man crossed the street, unharmed, once he'd decided the light had changed, and he asked one of them in flawless English, *"Have you nothing better to do than film people crossing a street?"* *"What a fool!"* one concluded. *"What a damned fool!"*

Of all that happened next, the only part I regretted was the fear on the face of a woman who worked at the hotel and happened to be standing nearby when my fist smashed the table so hard that the wood cracked and the taped windowpanes rattled. I even thought I might have fractured a bone. My act produced both a biblical silence and the frightened glances of the people who'd been caught up in the cozy chat that fueled my mute rage, my glare of primordial hatred, and my readiness to throttle them all, and this with the woman's penetrating cry of true panic made my gesture all the more dramatic and telling. The group looked at me, amazed, with no idea where I'd come from.

"You bloody cretins!" I said as calmly as I could and spun around to go to my room. Behind me a few seconds later I heard a murmur and then one of the Americans daring to ask, *"Who is that guy?!"*

"A fuckin' German, man."

"A Nazi!" his French colleague concluded softly, but not softly enough that I couldn't hear it.

That is why I went back to their table, to their shock, and explained in a quiet and steady voice that I'd be off to my room now and back down in fifteen minutes, at which point I did not want to see any of them around this table. *"D'accord?!"* Their silence confirmed they understood I'd be forced to employ rougher methods if I caught sight of them while I was walking away, forever, from that hotel.

Ivor had good reason to be surprised when I knocked at the door of his apartment that same evening, a half hour or so later. He spread his arms in amazement when he saw me with my luggage at my feet. And before he could say a word, I lobbied my request: "Could you rent me a room for a time? I'll pay you well."

"Excuse me?" he said, at first astonished.

"Yes or no?" I asked.

Ivor paused, mulling over it, and finally said, "Okay. In principle, why not, it might even be fun." He laughed and shook his head in surprise. "Come in!"

I knew Ivor wouldn't turn me away. Not only had we grown close over the last twenty days or so that we'd been working together, giving me reason to believe he wouldn't turn his back on me when there was no going back to the hotel, but I happened to know Ivor was living alone at his parents' place. They'd been at their house somewhere on the Dalmatian seacoast when the war began. Ivor sent them a simple message saying they mustn't try to return to Sarajevo, and so he lived alone in the spacious apartment. He could certainly let me have a room, and

I was counting on it. We quickly overcame the oddity of the situation and began sharing the apartment with real success. We laughed late into the night about the scene at the hotel and my theatrical exit.

"And no one was there when you came downstairs?" asked Ivor, incredulous.

"Like I said. Not a soul. They fled to their rooms and were probably peeking through the keyholes until the old Nazi crank evaporated. I understand them, they'd rather die on a battlefield than so unspectacularly at the hands of a colleague. And besides, I can't guarantee how I'd have reacted if I'd seen one of them there. I figure they realized this was no joking matter."

"Whatever the case, I'm glad you're here. However, there is one little thing . . ."

"What?"

"I'm troubled, you see"—said Ivor, looking at me in all seriousness—"about the fate of my telephone directory."

"I'm not going back there, absolutely not!" I shouted, clutching my head. "You can't make me. No way."

Ivor laughed. I promised I'd obtain a new directory for him when the war ended and the phones began to work again.

I'd forgotten Ivor's telephone directory for the city of Sarajevo in my room in the scramble of my exit. And while we're on the subject, I should say that this apparently paltry item played a small, but not insignificant, role in some of my decisions. Ivor had, indeed, brought me the directory as I'd asked, accepting this absurd first request as part of the job with his mildly eccentric employer. After I returned to my hotel room that day, I'd taken up the directory and begun looking through it, focusing my search on the surname I hoped to find. And though I knew the directory was not a complete list of the residents of Sarajevo, I somehow imagined flipping through the directory like they do in American movies, ripping out the pages so as not to waste valuable cinematic time, then dialing my father's number or finding his street address. This, despite what my rational mind had been whispering to me from the very outset, and what I soon discovered: the name *Schneider, Jakob* was not listed in the Sarajevo telephone directory. This little discovery, and the picture I suddenly had of myself—in a Sarajevo hotel after having left behind my life in Paris only two months before, with a detour by way of Vienna, and now here in the middle of this cursed war, flipping through a telephone directory in a city completely foreign to me until only the day before, searching in it for the name of my real father—all this revealed to me the true nature of my undertaking: lunatic, witless, moronic in the extreme. I stowed the telephone book away, took from my breast pocket that carefully folded clipping, and looked once more at the picture of my brother-in-genealogical-endeavor and told him aloud that he was wrong. Unlike the face of the woman on the other side of the page who—in that fraction of a second when she looked up and her face was captured by the lens of the camera—saw everything that would happen, what was happening, and what would go on happening.

It was too late for me. And after the evening I moved into Ivor's apartment, I could no longer separate myself from the city.

3

August afternoons in Vienna persist in an almost country quiet, and I feel at times that if I were to howl from the hotel window, no one would hear. My voice would be swallowed by the shimmering swelter. I gaze out at the empty marketplace, the shuttered shops and cafés, the drawn curtains. Everybody flees the merciless sun, traveling as far away as possible from the scorching city; everyone except those who have nowhere else to go, the isolated elderly, the impoverished, the bad students, the refugees newly arrived, the suicides biding their time. I don't know exactly what day it is today, or the date; I'm not interested. I no longer leave my room. I feel just like August: tired, heavy, and listless as I inch autumn-ward. When I'm not writing I lie naked on the bed, surrounded by photographs of my Sarajevo friends. Slowly and bleakly the hours tick by. I try to speed their movement by writing, but then night comes and only rarely now do I turn on the light at dusk; into the darkness I slump together with the city that crackles as it cools in the evening breeze. My manuscript guides my jumbled recollections and pushes me to strive further to recall my, our, story—every detail, every word that might explain, to me as much as anybody, how it all played out, how it could have happened. I give in enough to the internal mechanism of this manuscript, battling despair, madness, nostalgia, fear, and my own intentions, to ease the imperative of remembering.

The text seeks forward momentum, so I shuffle through the photographs until I find a picture in which Alma is gazing out the window of Ivor's apartment, her back turned to the camera, her hair down, her bare white arm resting on the window frame. And then I see her again on the street and she is smiling at me and even now I feel my desire to touch her as I felt it then. Here are the three of us—Ivor, she, and I—our cheeks pressed together to fit us all into the frame. Her porcelain complexion. Behind his glasses Ivor has squeezed his eyes shut like a purring cat. My face looks so youthful here that I can barely link that man to the bearded ascetic I am today, who writes while shut up in this room as if in his own desert and who cannot make his body die, once and for all, by so wishing. Ivor's balcony, the friendship, the war, desire, the city, betrayal, longing . . . And again, looking at us, I cannot help but think of that long-ago summer of 1941, of Paula and Jakob, of Ingrid and Heinrich, because we are all part of this same story, which is slowly devouring its characters. Will the story outlive their demise?

I return again to the thin line of my memory, to our city under siege on the verge of summer, when I began my stay at Ivor's, when I met Alma Filipović.

Sharing the apartment with Ivor proved to be an excellent decision. I stopped my work as a reporter, retaining only the option of the occasional longer piece when I was so inclined, and limited the rest of my journalism to those newspapers where I planned to go on publishing critical commentaries, and perhaps excerpts from my diary, which I'd already provisionally titled *Diary of a European War*.

Ivor went to the hotel to explain the new work situation to the team and returned with a camera so that we could continue our wanderings, filming only that which we really wanted to record. I had no lack of funds, there was plenty even for wartime Sarajevo. The payments arrived regularly so that Ivor and I could live, even with the steep rent

I'd insisted on paying for the room, without the fear of hunger or thirst that was beginning to be felt in a city that was rapidly using up its supplies, and as supplies dwindled, so, accordingly, soared the prices.

I was revived by my move to Ivor's apartment. He gave me his parents' capacious bedroom, with his father's desk, their library, many photographs, documents, and artifacts from his family's history on both sides, and a roomy double bed. The bedroom faced the inner courtyard that, according to Ivor, was the safest side because the shells from the hills couldn't reach it. This claim would have sounded encouraging, except we were all fully aware that there was no target in the city the Serb artillery couldn't hit; the skill of the enemy after two and a half months of war was no longer in doubt.

So I made myself comfortable in a room that, in a sense, held the history of Ivor's family. In a war of clashing ethnicities, in which religion, background, first and last name played a key role and could determine life or death, or which camp or refugee destination to head for, or whether one was qualified to receive humanitarian aid from this or that charitable organization, Ivor preferred to define himself as a citizen of his besieged city and of the dismembered Bosnia. With disdain he dismissed ethnic pigeonholing, considering it the ultimate stupidity that so many people willingly gave up their earlier role of citizen to become mere Serbs, Muslims, or Croats. He was irritated by queries about his own background and refused to tell anyone anything about what he referred to as his "blood group." His first and last name offered nothing but a challenging riddle within the claustrophobic terms imposed by the war, and Ivor was eager to complicate things with data from his family tree, claiming himself descended from Herzegovinian tobacco traders, Dalmatian peasants, Austrian merchants, Hungarian craftsmen, Dubrovnik diplomats, fallen Bosnian nobility, Danube dames and gardeners, Pannonian Talmudists, prewar communists, nineteenth-century religious converts, and Yugoslav army officers. I dubbed him a mythographer, though I assumed there to be at least a kernel of truth in what he said, as confirmed, in part, by the family inventory in my room. With pleasure I listened to him belittle ethnic backgrounds and spin colorful tales about his ancestors, and I forgave him the occasional exaggeration, biting my lip, envious. What could I say to him on the subject, I who never knew my mother or my father, who came to this city precisely to explore this very mystery that Ivor so frankly, backed by convincing arguments, deplored? The famous mystery of one's origins! As if this would change anything, as if life could be any different?! Or could it?

As we no longer had to hustle around town every day, labor over reports under the pressure of broadcast deadlines, or cover the details of the war, Ivor and I were almost on vacation, if such a thing is even possible during a war. Ivor often went off, pursuing his own interests and habits, while I, when circumstances allowed, poked around this city I was coming to know. I'd encounter the occasional colleague, and often I'd run into a Sarajevo acquaintance, mainly from the circles of culture and journalism, acquaintances whose number kept growing and who always invited me to spend the day with them consuming an assortment of beverages and improvised food obtained in all sorts of ways. Thanks to the respected accreditation documents I carried, we did not always have to obey the curfew, and we never ventured beyond the town center. On the days when it was impossible to stick even a nose out the door, we'd spend our time writing and reading, adamantly refusing to take shelter in the cellar. Ivor was writing for a new journal, so he'd dash off his article and go to the editorial offices; now, that publishing endeavor was a bold adventure. Ivor also had literary ambitions, and I had the impression he was laying the groundwork for his first fiction project. I was meanwhile expanding my notes on the war, developing an outline for a future book. There aren't many of those notes left. No matter. What happened later rendered them moot.

As night came on we'd light candles in the kitchen and open a bottle of brandy, and we wouldn't put it away until we'd reached the bottom, while warming up for our ongoing discourses and debates. It was a genuine pleasure to converse with this brilliant young man, who would sometimes, because of his inescapable youth, react to the outpourings of my middle-aged crabbiness with childlike fuming and huffiness. Ivor was one of those people who had learned most of what he knew so far through intermediaries, whether via books, art, or other sources, rather than the experience of his own skin, so my irony and bitter relativizing of things sometimes hurt him. But with awe I watched as the scales of his reason found their own equilibrium. I loved hearing his disquisitions into which he wove literature, film, and philosophy (yet another follower of Derrida! Foucault!), meanwhile working to situate all this in the war of which we were a part. Yes, I could easily have sneered at his illusions as do so many crotchety old men, but I would have missed drawing nourishment from them. Ivor breathed new air into my failing lungs.

From one day to the next, our friendship grew more sure-footed, aided by our sharing of the same roof. As the imperatives of professional collaboration became less pressing, we began moving through the daily reality of war, guided by our own thinking, and Ivor took me, with joy, through his own private Sarajevo, which seemed more natural with no camera on my shoulder, and also through the city's recent history, which everyone discussed as if it had been a golden age (the 1984 Olympics, literature, the rock 'n' roll scene, the new primitives . . .) before the pending calamity. He spoke to me of typical Sarajevo life, the mind-set, the way local people drew on a particular brand of humor, a worldview, and the place within it that was cultivated here in this valley. He also spoke of provinciality and flashes of cosmopolitanism, of the importance of the minor distinctions, and the general tendency to assign equal blame to all sides for what was happening. With his guidance I came to know the popular gathering places during the war, even during the siege. Along the way I met a host of interesting people, with whom we sometimes partied at drunken bashes washed by benign marijuana smoke and the seductive perfume on the throats of Sarajevo women, the quantities of which were steadily ebbing in the little bottles in their boudoirs. I was feeling much better and, I have to say, younger after having come to stay at Ivor's and after I'd begun believing that I, too, was part of this city, while I cut my links to the outside world back to sporadic signs of life: the occasional published article as a signal to my nearest and dearest that I was still alive.

Maybe it was, ultimately, all Ivor's fault. He set things in motion, albeit unknowingly, over the last fifteen days of my stay in Sarajevo that would change forever the trajectory of my life, and not just mine. There's no point now in seeking a culprit, and it would be too easy to attribute everything simply to fate. Whatever the case, it was Ivor's idea for us to wrench free of our lassitude and do something, make a contribution of our own, within limits, of course—film something, take an active role—because something had to be done. The situation was only getting worse: we were shelled daily, the hospital was overfull with the wounded and the dead, and there was no point in sitting at home in terror of ever stepping out into the street. I agreed. And besides, we had the camera, the passes, an array of options allowed by my privileged status, a team ready to do our bidding, and all we still needed was a fresh idea for a short documentary that we could later send to Austria or Germany. I proposed we film the people living in and around the stairwell in our apartment building—the men, women, and children who did not leave the building, our neighbors, who had become our friends and fellow sufferers, the families and their lives during the war . . . Ivor didn't find the idea unacceptable, but he felt, and, again, I had to agree, that we should go beyond simply sending out Sarajevo images of suffering; rather, we should give examples of people who were continuing to work at an enviable level at their ordinary peacetime jobs under these disastrous conditions. We quickly narrowed the professions down to artists and others involved in cultural activities, because cultural life truly was intense during those days, as much as was humanly possible, with daily improvisations and despite all the obstacles thrown up by the wartime conditions. Exhibits, concerts, plays . . . Here is where we sought our subject matter.

The next day Ivor came home thrilled by an idea—yes, it came from Ivor again—which sounded by far the best. He wanted us to make a short documentary about Sarajevo actors, or more precisely about a wartime acting troupe that was organizing performances on an almost daily basis to packed audiences, though the audience members, and the actors themselves, were risking their lives to go to the theater. He wanted us to interview the actors, directors, and audience and film the conditions under which they were working, the play itself, the vitality of the theater, and the passion of the audience. The idea sounded similar to some of the others we'd entertained, which had, I suggested, been even more attractive—the idea, for instance, of making a documentary about the journal he was writing for—but ultimately I relented after Ivor insisted. And besides, being as he was fiercely determined, he'd already set things up with his friends at the theater, and the next day we'd have our first meeting. We could begin filming soon thereafter, crowed Ivor, and now all he needed was my approval.

"But I know nothing about this!" I shouted. "And besides, I've always found theater tedious. I don't know what to ask these people, or what I want from them."

"We'll manage," said Ivor. "It's a fine topic. Everything we record will be first-rate. A little editing, improvisation, and we'll have a fifteen- to twenty-minute movie we can send right off. We really must do something. We're not going to just sit at home, twiddling our thumbs. That couldn't be why you're still in Sarajevo. Work on your memoir somewhere in the French Riviera, Richard! After the war."

"Okay, okay. Let's spend a little time with the actors, and we'll see what comes of it."

So I agreed. And the idea began to grow on me. That night I thought long and hard about the movie and worked out a structure for it, which I meant to present the next day to the theater crew. It would come in handy, I thought, to stretch my legs a little and really do something in a city where all our efforts thus far had seemed so pointless.

We went off the next day to what was, Ivor said, one of the finest of the city theaters, where we made the acquaintance of the portly theater director who presented his acting troupe of mainly younger actors. They were inspired and talkative. The theater manager appeared in a rather serious-looking suit, but we soon realized that behind his gesture of formality this was a true man of the stage who laid out for us the ambitious repertoire they were taking and which, despite my doubts to the contrary, they were slowly but surely staging thanks to actors like these who worked tirelessly, feeling that in this way they were at least doing something in the midst of this unjust war. The manager took us through the house, introducing us to stagehands who complained of the working conditions and a few of the director's impossible demands. Then, along with the smiling director who was already sweating heavily—this was, after all, the second day of summer, 1992!—he took us to his office. To welcome us he took a bottle of brandy from a drawer in his desk—the "war reserve," he noted with a smile—and offered us each a glass. These people behaved as if they'd heard of me, knew why I was in Sarajevo, and appreciated the fact that I'd chosen to share their troubles with them, though they found it surprising. Ivor explained to me that Sarajevo was a small town and the story of the famous writer had already spread, so I could be sure that though the city was under siege, people were reading the articles I sent out into the faraway world, meaning they knew full well what I was saying about them.

We soon began discussing the idea for the movie and the actors joined us. Ivor set out our plan. In short, we wanted to show what it was like to put on plays in Sarajevo in this war year of 1992. He explained how we envisioned the film, with interviews and portraits of the actors, culminating with the play they were rehearsing. Soon we'd realized that the movie, if it should ever see the light of day, would be significantly longer than the running time we'd originally planned. Our hosts also offered us interesting ideas. They talked about the repertoire for the summer and fall. Planning any farther ahead would be folly, as they said. They were considering, for instance, staging *Mother Courage*, but the director was rooting for *Ubu Roi*. Sartre was a possibility, and there was talk of Camus's *The Plague*. A dramatic staging of Max Frisch's novel *Homo Faber* struck me as the oddest choice of all.

They were eager to hear what I'd have to say. I warned them I'd be frank and wanted their responses to be so, too. I felt the mere fact that somebody risks their life to perform Sartre in Sarajevo wasn't enough to raise an eyebrow among the European audiences to whom we'd show our movie. What I wanted to know was: Why? Why theater when there are bombs dropping from the sky? What was theater for, anyway; why was this a weapon against the siege? During my feverish monologue I said I'd recently come to believe more in bombers and cruise missiles than in the power of the word. What we wanted to know—and I made no secret of the frustration that they, too, knew so well, nor did I hide my own bitterness at the state of affairs, and I had the impression that I might have even alarmed or demoralized them—is the relationship that your work has to your everyday life, before and during the war. What does the theater mean to you really, and what do the people who watch you mean? How do you choose the plays you do? Brecht, Sartre, even Frisch (for this last one I asked for further explanations)? Why perform while people are dying and fighting only blocks from the theater building? Why do you think it's worth anything? Why not, instead, make Molotov cocktails and improvise bombs? I paced around the manager's office, circling nervously and addressing their serious, silent faces, noticing here and there somebody's impulse to answer, say something, protest, or agree with what I was saying. But they heard me out patiently. (By the way, I couldn't fathom the patience the people of Sarajevo showed in hearing out and reassuring all the foreigners.) I could give hundreds of reasons, I claimed, even outside the context of our preparations for the movie, with which I'd ridicule the Sisyphean task you have undertaken, to say nothing about how important it is to conserve energy for the difficult days ahead, for the winter that will come instead of the deblockade, for anything other than risking one's life to do something that will change nothing and which will never convince those who are shooting at you, and at me along with you, from the hills to relinquish their mission, nor will it flush them out. For if they, one day, come down from the hills to town, they will be the victors, and don't go thinking that the international community, Europe, the UN, and others like them will withhold recognition. I'd like to hear from you: What good is there in this theater of yours and this prancing about on the stage?

After my final question there was silence. Ivor stared out the window with an expression that told me he thought I'd gone too far, but that it might not turn out so badly after all. The manager tossed back his shot of brandy and then stared down into the shot glass as if looking for the last drop, while the director fanned himself with a document of some sort. And then I heard a voice from behind me, the voice of somebody who must have come in while I was talking so heatedly, because until then I hadn't registered the speaker.

"I'd say . . . that the point isn't to make the person who's shelling you more humane, but to help those of us who are being shelled to maintain our humanity."

"Yes, but . . ." I turned, surprised, and saw the woman. "What can I say—isn't it just a little naïve to believe that theater is what makes us humane? Sustains people or keeps them human beings? Do you not have a Shakespeare scholar among the rebel leaders, dear lady?!"

She stood there, leaning on the doorframe, glaring at me angrily, preparing to answer me with ferocity. She finally, clearly, gave up; all she said was: "You're a cynic."

"So maybe I am." Stung by the tone of her answer, I did not want to retreat. "Maybe I am, dear lady, but this is not about me. In the movie I want you to show me why you are right, and not, God forbid, them. And why your work is not ultimately . . ."

"Sisyphean?"

"Yes, probably, yes . . . In fact, I'm glad you responded to my provocation precisely as I'd expected." I was aiming to strike a conciliatory note.

"You know everything, is that it? You understand everything?"

"As I said, dear lady, this is not about me."

Again, silence. I looked at her. I met her eyes, which she then shifted to the window. Silence. Ivor stared at the floor (a bad sign), the actors at one another, the director sought something in his fan of texts, and the project seemed not off to the best start. Then the cheery manager clapped his hands, in an attempt to shift the mood.

"Mr. Richter, may I introduce you . . . This is our main actress, Alma Filipović. Alma, this is . . ."

"I know who you are," Alma said coldly, without proffering her hand. "I'm glad that we'll work together, even if you aren't convinced there's any point."

"Far from it, but . . ."

"The adaptation of the Frisch novel was Alma's idea, Mr. Richter," interrupted the manager, intending to smooth things over and retain the cooperation of his main actress in a project that was obviously important to him.

"Ah, indeed. Very interesting. I am wondering why you don't put on the Beckett. Wouldn't it be more apt? Aren't we all waiting . . . ?"

"I'm delighted to surprise you, Mr. Richter," concluded the bold young woman with poise. "You're clearly expecting someone in this city to prove something to you, but I'm not sure the answers to these questions should be sought here, in this theater, or even in Sarajevo, and I don't believe our efforts are likely to convince you. Still, perhaps your movie will convince somebody somewhere in the world, so it's worth a try. We have no choice, anyway, but to work with you and the likes of you," she said, placing emphasis on the last words so that her disdain for people the likes of me would be crystal clear. "So see you tomorrow, Mr. Richter, when you are filming."

"And, please, don't be late as you were today, Miss Filipović, to our conversation."

"*Mrs.* Filipović, Mr. Richter. Mrs. Filipović."

She walked out of the office, leaving us in silence. This is how she and I met. I felt nothing special during our first encounter except the usual sense of challenge stirred in me by a feisty woman. I felt myself looking forward to continuing the dialogue we'd started. And yes, she was beautiful, which was not insignificant, though in admitting it I felt I shouldn't allow myself at this age to be impressed so deeply by looks. This, and nothing else, was what was running through my mind, while the manager reassured me of Alma's qualities in dramaturgy and acting, assuming that I must have been offended by her behavior. And truly nothing more, even when the director elaborated on her plan to adapt Frisch's *Homo Faber* for the stage, asserting that hers was a truly splendid project. How did that text ever become so entangled in this whole story?! How did she ever come up with it?!

4

We began our work on the movie the next day. We filmed actors rehearsing a scene, the hovering director, the building—the ordinary routines of work in the theater, the sorts of scenes you could film anytime and anywhere. The difference in Sarajevo was hidden in the context of working with people who, if they were even to show up at work, had to get there on foot, sometimes from neighborhoods far away, negotiating their way into the center of the city, dashing across intersections where a sniper lurked, fearful of shelling, in order to take part that day in rehearsals or to perform for free before full houses of people who also had to dodge these obstacles in order to attend the performance. Not to mention that they were then faced with the return home, which made all the art in this city, here and now, an undertaking entailing quite a remarkable degree of risk.

This was what we'd hoped to film, but we got so much more because the story of each of our actors is unique. Bojan joins us at the theater only when he isn't out on the defense lines. Aida has a three-month-old baby and lives in a part of town near the Grbavica front line. Mirza cares for his ailing parents, and his girlfriend recently left for Belgrade; he hopes they'll find each other somewhere when all this is over. Vanja lives near the television station, and the routes she takes into the center of town each day are arduous—recently her father was killed. Lejla dreams about going out to the coast; she met a local boy there, apparently, last year and wonders what happened to him, there's a war going

on there, too . . . The rest of them hadn't yet managed to get to the theater that day. I felt I could have filmed them just like that—while they
were talking about the everyday realities of their wartime lives—and
we could have made a movie about these young people, but we didn't
have that much screen time. We decided instead to apportion more
minutes for interviews with the manager, the director, and, of course,
Alma Filipović. After that we'd film the performance and the audience,
take a few statements, and proceed with the editing, which we'd already
made arrangements for at the television station.

We decided Ivor should speak with Alma about filming at her
apartment in a day or two. Later I realized he'd been admiring her long
before they met. He considered her a superb actress and remarkable
person, head and shoulders above those around her. It crossed my mind
that he'd organized the making of the movie just to work with her.
Then he confessed he was interested to find out what sort of impression
she'd make on me. That was why he hadn't mentioned her before then,
although he'd already assigned her a central role. In his eyes, she was
carrying the theater and its wartime repertoire.

I received a rather cold greeting from Alma the next day, which didn't
surprise me. She went straight to work, paying no attention to the camera
Ivor held, while capably juggling any number of other details, and ignoring my directorial prompts in English. (An odd situation, but since Ivor
and I were new at this, I'd say things went reasonably well.) Ivor explained
that we wanted to film a longer conversation with her, at her apartment,
to give the movie a certain depth. We wanted her to tell us about herself
and her ideas, the life of an actress during the war, et cetera. Alma nodded,
glancing my way a few times. They talked a while longer, clearly more
relaxed, judging by their smiles. Ivor, it seemed, was softening her cold-
ness. Finally, she tossed out, *"Bis bald, Herr Richter!"* and before I had the
chance to respond, she'd slipped out through the foyer.

◆ ◆ ◆

Our plan, that first day, was to interview the theater manager. Over the next few days we'd be filming the play's director while he worked with the actors, starting with him explaining his concept on the empty stage, shedding pages from the bundle of papers he always had tucked under his arm, sweating like a steam engine while apologizing for it and raising his hands to the sky that, along with everything else, was bearing down on us with heat. The manager received us, of course, in his office in a freshly pressed suit, ready for his great speech before the camera. It was actually quite engaging, what he had to say, the gist of which could be summarized as "the role of our theater in the war of defense." And though he drew his inspiration from the Partisans of the Second World War, whom he evoked, he said that under the current circumstances, in the contemporary world, such as it was, there was no place for traditional patriotic theater. In fact, the most patriotic theater in the Bosnian situation could only and exclusively be to work on first-rate European theater, a modern staging of classics or recent texts, because, as he said, this is the only way we can fight the barbarians, clearly showing on whose side we truly stand, with a "united Europe and the civilized world," which, both Europe and that world, sooner or later, would come to understand and put a stop to the bloodshed by justly punishing the aggressor, the manager concluded optimistically. I let him speak his piece, not to muddy his trust in imminent salvation, and, besides, the speech was calibrated for foreign audiences and had its place in the movie, so I saluted him with a revolutionary clenched fist. I was thinking that such slogans would please only aging leftists, of whom I was one. Some of them had not yet grasped that the Berlin Wall was down for good. A few hangers-on were still stubbornly voicing their support for Milošević's side in the Yugoslav wars, admiring him for his open scorn of the capitalist West, his voluntary isolation, and his resolve to continue on his path, taking others down along the way, and, ultimately, his own people. But I thought it better not to talk to the manager about that; I let him think things would eventually fall into place.

I was surprised by the altogether different ideas about the war we heard from Alma Filipović, ideas I did not, at first, fully understand, though they did make an impression on me. As time passes I see with greater clarity that, unfortunately, Alma was right.

Alma Filipović. I'm skipping over a host of details about the days we spent filming in the theater building. I'm skipping ahead because I want to write about Alma and I can no longer rein in the story and slow down the gallop of events, as if there were some way to change things by so doing, as if I could believe that this is a novel and I possess the power to steer the plot. Unfortunately, it is rather the opposite: the plot is sweeping along the protagonist who is, in fact, the author himself. In the moment he describes, he was walking through it all blindly, unable to foresee what the plot held in store for him. Even when the Sarajevo episode ends, the story goes on. It seems that he's recording all this at the will of the plot that took hold of him that April day and will eventually punctuate its own end with a period when the time for that comes.

Perhaps, after I left Sarajevo, Ivor finished the movie. Our little contribution might even be aired one day so what we, my fellow filmmaker and I, did during those days will be seen. I don't know. I fled too soon to find out what Ivor did during the days reserved for editing at the television studio. For me the movie will remain nothing more than how I found my way to her, the open door through which I stepped, and which then, unnoticed, shut behind me. Maybe nothing would have happened if we'd done something differently—any little thing—than what we, Alma and I, did. Just one decision, even the smallest, might have changed everything; and today I wouldn't be sitting here in the middle of the Viennese summer in 1992, and my sweat wouldn't be dripping onto the typewriter, my sole witness to the painful (shameful?) things I mean to describe. Something different, I say: a chain of circumstances, a different time of day, a chance encounter, the explosion of a shell in another place and another time, a belated arrival to an appointment, less hurry, a question asked of the right person, perhaps a slightly lessened intensity of attraction, another hair color, other arms, glances evaded, poorly chosen words, anything . . .

There's no point in guessing. We visited Alma at the appointed time, the day before the opening night. Luckily, she lived not far from our place. We had to climb uphill with the equipment, avoiding spots that were more exposed. We felt that, camera in hand, we were a choice target for an ambitious sniper. Ivor warned me several times that I should watch what I was saying, that I shouldn't behave, as he put it, like a "gnarly old goat," that I mustn't be as rude as I was that first day, which I duly promised. He was quite excited; he wanted everything to turn out exactly as he'd planned: he'd ask a number of prepared questions and then we'd let Alma talk, because without her, judging by Ivor, there was no way we could have made the movie. Fine, I nodded, fine, but I wasn't sure who was doing the directing here and who was assisting, which hadn't mattered much to us, anyway, since we'd begun.

The moment before we rang at Alma's door, Ivor told me, "Oh, and yesterday she asked about you."

"Really?" I was startled. "What?"

"Why you've come to Sarajevo, where I met you, how, that sort of thing . . ."

"And? What did you say?"

"That you had nothing better to do than to come poking around Sarajevo . . ."

"How dare you . . . !"

"And that you were doing it so you could write about everything that's happening here, raise the alarm out in the world and so forth . . . that even if you're occasionally a little heavy-handed, you believe in what you're doing, you're a famous writer . . ."

"Fine, fine . . ."

"That she already knew."

"Really?"

"Her parents, believe it or not, have several of your books in German . . ."

"So my books have been read here."

"But she admitted she hasn't read them . . ."

"There is, my dear Ivor, always time for the classics . . ."

I hadn't yet finished the sentence when Ivor rang the bell. Alma opened it almost immediately, as if she'd been waiting right behind the door, and I was even worried she might have overheard our conversation. She greeted me in German, which she spoke with some difficulty, then exchanged a few words in Bosnian with Ivor that sounded warm to me.

She brought us into the living room. She was living alone in an apartment where books elbowed videocassettes. Ivor had already told me her husband, Faris Filipović, was a prominent film director, and soon Alma would confirm that the war had separated them; he'd gone to Berlin on a fellowship at the beginning of the year.

"*Good timing!*" I exclaimed.

"*That depends*," she answered coldly. Since the war broke out her husband had been asking her to join him, but she'd refused. Why? Because at moments like this, one doesn't leave, was her feeling. I couldn't stop myself and said that sometimes the larger social and political situation gives people a handy alibi, but it is likely to be linked in some way to interests of a purely personal nature. Ivor shot me a sharp glance.

"Referring to yourself, Mr. Richter?" she asked.

"Not necessarily."

"Following one's personal interests, as you put it, needn't mean that one remains in a city where the shells are falling, does it?"

"Not necessarily," I answered, and we smiled at each other for the first time with greater warmth. Ivor breathed a sigh of relief.

There was a stunning view from Alma's apartment over the old part of town and the tall mountain behind it, but she immediately cautioned us not to stand near the windows for safety's sake. She led us through the spacious apartment with its modern furnishings. We were holding drinks as Ivor joked with her and I followed them, taking in the surroundings. Her laughter, dark hair—now clasped in a ponytail, her slender body in jeans, her summer blouse, her at-home manner, her shapely breasts, the makeup she'd probably applied hastily, her expensive perfume, the bare feet on the dark-brown parquet floor . . . How old could this woman be, I wondered; I was probably old enough to be her father . . . I felt over-the-hill with the two of them . . .

"Where would you like to begin, Mr. Richter?" I heard her question as if from afar, as if I were recovering from temporary deafness. "Mr. Richter? Are you with us? Mr. Richter?"

For a moment I felt I was getting dizzy; I also mused, sheepishly, that I was studying her a little too closely, that this was the wrong move and she felt it, and, besides, I was having increasing difficulty controlling the effect young women's beauty was having on me (how old could she be, I mused again, concluding she couldn't be over thirty). This loss of concentration, that annoying symptom of aging, was certain proof of the last atoms of youth evaporating in me and, with them, the painful loss of the illusion that a dalliance was even possible.

"Richard?" came Ivor's voice.

"Sorry, friend?" I started. "Apologies. I'm right here with you. I was just thinking of how best to start, and my thoughts wandered. Mrs. Filipović . . ."

"Please call me Alma, Mr. Richter."

"Please call me Richard, Alma. The *Mr.* makes me, I don't know, feel strangely antiquated, like a friend of your father's that he plays chess with on Saturdays."

"Never. My father's much, much older than you, so in the worst case I might treat you like a somewhat older gentleman. And besides, he plays chess on Sundays."

"You've consoled me, Alma, indeed. Thank you for that. And what do you say we leave my years be, which may, sad to say, add up to more than yours and Ivor's combined."

"Don't go pitying yourself like you're an old fogey," called Ivor, who then turned to Alma. "He affects innocence. Don't believe him." Alma laughed.

"But to get to the point, what do you say to us sitting here in the living room while you tell us about yourself?" asked Richard.

"Should I lie down, perhaps, on the couch?" asked Alma.

"Only if you tell us something about your relationship with your father. All for the movie, of course. After all, you like such topics, *Homo faber* and the like; that seems apt under the circumstances. Only, of course, for the sake of the movie."

"Anything you say, doctor." She embraced my jest. This emboldened me. "And that role suits you better than the role of *judge* you so often play, what with your last name being *Richter*. But a name is something that can't be escaped, can it?"

Judge? Alma was the first person in Sarajevo who'd mentioned the meaning of my last name, the name I was given by Heinrich. Alma reminded me for the first time in days—I'd been refusing to dwell on the big discovery of my mother's letter, of Jakob, of why I was here, of the unpredictable path on which my Viennese decision had led me. And suddenly the fact that I was in her apartment, with Ivor, that I was even in Sarajevo, in the midst of a war, besieged, seemed so remarkably bizarre. I was marveling at this, and I must have sunk back into my thoughts, because the next thing I saw was Alma's anxious face. She apologized, "*Sorry, are you all right? Did I say something wrong? So sorry . . .*"

She appeared to be genuinely concerned that she might have upset me with her innocent jest. Suddenly she lost all her hauteur. She seemed especially charming and also more sensitive, personal . . . I became aware of this, for the first time since meeting her, precisely at the moment she laid her silken hand on my shoulder and I shivered like a teenager.

"Is everything all right? How are you feeling, Richard?"

"I think I'm just tired, Alma," I replied and decided to check the flow of my turbulent thoughts and collect myself, so I clapped my hands. "To work! Quick!"

Alma took a seat in front of the camera and spoke in Bosnian. This was our plan. Ivor interpreted for me. She understood enough German that he didn't have to interpret back to her. I watched her openly as I adjusted the lens and Ivor's words reached me. She spoke about how she's living alone in the besieged city, how she readies herself each day for work, how she rehearses her roles, sometimes at night in a cellar packed with neighbors by candlelight; she spoke about the streets she travels every day, what she sees happening, about an everyday life lived within constraints, about how some things are becoming habit. Alma spoke and her chest, like a child's, rose each time she started a sentence; soon she was flushed. Her hands danced along with every word she spoke, and I could guess at what she was saying by their movements alone. One of her wartime duties was to look after her elderly father, and clearly she was deeply attached to him. This was no surprise: her mother had died a few years earlier and now they had only each other. She was born when her father was already well along in years. He was in excellent shape, though nearly eighty, and he read a lot in several languages, including, for example, German. He'd been a student in Graz before the Second World War. She was sorry he'd had to suffer through this war as well, after he'd only barely survived the last one; he'd even been interned in a camp.

Alma had a black cat named Kali—but it was not a harbinger of bad luck for its black fur or its name, as some of her neighbors who had a passing familiarity with Indian mythology feared. We let the cat curl up in her lap and loll about in front of the camera. Kali is the first to flee to the cellar during each bombing raid, and she waits there for her mistress and the other tenants. We all chuckled at the cat staring at the camera lens, then turning to the window as if portending what the enemy artillery had in store. We bantered while the camera rolled.

Then she spoke about her theater projects. About her acting, the roles she's preparing, the books she's reading. I'd saved for the end of the filming the question that had piqued my curiosity from the start, and I hadn't been able to imagine her answer.

"What made you want to adapt Frisch's novel *Homo Faber* for the stage and put it on in Sarajevo while the city is under siege? Why this particular text? Its connection to what's going on here is not an obvious one."

Alma took another deep breath before she launched into her monologue, and her words still ring in my ears, with far more clarity than they had then.

"Mr. Faber is an engineer who believes in technology and science, he believes in the *ratio* on which the modern West rests. He believes in mathematical calculations, uncontestable laws. He does not believe in human constructs like the soul or fate. As he says of himself: 'I don't believe in providence or in fate. As a scientist I am used to reckoning with the formulas of probability. What does providence have to do with it? I don't deny that it was more than a coincidence that made things turn out as they did; it was a whole train of coincidences. But what does providence have to do with it? I don't need any mystical explanation for the occurrence of the improbable; mathematics explains it adequately, as far as I'm concerned.' His name is Faber, which is itself not a coincidence. Names are never coincidental, are they? He is the *Homo faber*, as Hanna dubs him. Giordano Bruno defines him as a person who fashions his own fate. And, finally, Mr. Faber does just that; he falls in love with and sleeps with his own daughter, fashioning his own fate, a bitter fate indeed, despite all the warning signs. This engineer, scientist, mathematician, a true product of Western civilization, is incapable of the most rudimentary calculation, incapable of drawing conclusions from what so blatantly asserts itself, that the girl he has fallen in love with is his own daughter."

"The connection to Sarajevo, to this war, still eludes me," I interrupted her. "What's the point of staging Frisch's novel in Sarajevo today? Whatever for?"

"I was just getting to that. On the one hand, our company agreed that just because we're at war doesn't mean we should choose plays with an obvious message for the audience. I feel that we need to go on working as we would otherwise, in peace, as much as we possibly can, while trying at the same time to sustain a certain standard. Because, after it's all over, the story isn't what will be remembered, but the standard to which we performed it. The war will pass and we'll be left with top-notch theater, as good as any we'd have in peacetime. And that is what these theatergoers, who are suffering through the war, care about. Because of this I wanted to stage something I've been interested in for some time. Even before I saw Schlöndorff's recent movie adaptation. It was, if I can put it this way, a peacetime idea. However, the more I work on it, the more I see that Frisch's text brings us a message at an entirely different level, a message that's not easy to decipher, but may be of critical importance to us. Schlöndorff's movie couldn't have this message because it was pared down to the story of Faber the engineer's fate, and the chain of coincidences that brought him to his inadvertent incest. Unfortunately, this is bad news for the people of Sarajevo and Bosnia. Frisch's text helped me understand our plight, to begin thinking with a profound pessimism about our future, the days ahead, the siege which will go on and on, even if right now we can't even imagine such a thing."

"I don't see how this text, in particular, helped you understand the war," I blurted. "I'm really trying to grasp what that could be . . ."

"The message can't be found at the level of the novel's story line, nor in what the viewers tomorrow will see onstage, but if we have a discussion that starts with the text, we can ask ourselves whether *Mr. Faber* is, in fact, right. Isn't what happens to him about something rational and, ultimately, quantifiable? You don't need fate to run an ordinary calculation and understand the relationship of cause and effect that, no matter how unusual it might be, is, in fact, based on a series of plausible causes and effects. It's just that Mr. Faber didn't succeed in doing this, the basic mathematical operation, though it was right there in front of him.

"I see something of this in the situation facing Sarajevo, this country. Are we not naïve with all our surprise at what is happening, all our: How is it possible that the war happened, how is it possible that somebody is holding you in this citywide concentration camp, shelling you day after day, how is it possible that the world isn't lifting a finger to help when the injustice is so glaring, how is it possible that we who are defending the values of coexistence, multiculturality, tolerance, and the other grand ideas in circulation at the moment in Europe have received no aid from that same Europe, no aid from contemporary Western civilization which has built these values into its very democratic foundations, and how could it be that, ultimately, those who are acting in the name of ethnic purity, division, conflict, and war still go unpunished?! And along with all this, while we're trying to prove what's truly happening here, how could this same Europe be referring to the war as something 'preordained,' an 'avalanche of ancient hatreds,' 'madness,' 'misadventure,' a 'prophecy come to pass,' trying to explain this clear cause-effect sequence of the war by relying on irrational arguments? The fact that Mr. Faber—or our naïve Europe—miscalculates doesn't mean the formula isn't correct and that it wouldn't be simple to solve if only they'd open their eyes wide enough. And in the same way, Faber doesn't want to do that, because he's in love with the girl, so he ignores all the signs in order to get what he truly wants: her body and her love. Because as I see it, Europe and the West are actually standing on the opposite side of where the people of Sarajevo think they should be standing, on the opposite side of what Sarajevans are defending today, what they are invoking. Everything they're doing, despite the rhetoric, is confirming that they, whether they're fully aware of it, partially aware of it, or altogether oblivious to it, are on the side of those who dream of states that are ethnically and religiously pure, and they are prepared to send millions to their death or into exile to make this happen. Today's Europe may, in fact, have its true representatives in Karadžić's army, not in us. Karadžić's men are the heralds of the continent's future, of ethnicization, religious hatred, division, of racial purity and resistance to the demographic threats of the racial, national, and religious *others*, champions of the new European xenophobia; they are the truly European players on the Balkan playing fields, not us. Nothing here is 'predestined' or 'rampant,' yet the European *Homo faber* continues invoking destiny so rationally, while sitting there twiddling his thumbs. For now he's confused and apparently he'd rather not do the math: two plus two. He summons *fate* to his aid, and once it arrives in the Balkans and comes into its own, there is nothing to be done. So he sits, flaming the rampant forces of ethnic conflict to assuage his uneasy conscience. Yes, the European *Homo faber* is fashioning his own destiny today in Sarajevo precisely as he deeply desires—even if that means sleeping with his own daughter, and even if he has to do what he claims is impermissible to his rational order, and even if he has to trample daily on what he claims are *his* values, or simply allows others to trample on them, unpunished, right before his very eyes. Yes, the European *Homo faber* is constructing his fate in Sarajevo because what he sees here today is nothing more than a mirror showing him his own future. When all is said and done, he'll undoubtedly wonder how it could have happened that he was unable to do the simplest calculation, how he didn't open his eyes and look out through the window of the Balkans war into the front yard of his own tomorrow, how he didn't realize what was obvious, common sense, and how all that could happen to him, to Faber, to a modern and enlightened European?"

Alma was done. Ivor turned off the camera. I watched her breathlessly, trying to take in her words. This was more than enough for the movie and certainly provocative, though I wasn't sure that it all made sense. We got up in the strange silence that came over us following her weighty words. And even if I still couldn't easily come to agree with her arguments, I admitted her sharp mind, the lure of her thinking, and the impact of her conclusion. We thanked Alma and promised to leave her alone until the opening night of *Homo Faber*, which would also be the last scene we'd film. The manager had already invited us to stay on in the theater after the performance for the "reception," as he announced officially, for the actors and crew so that we'd have a chance to see each other then. Alma saw us to the door. The cat hid under the bed, scared by distant blasts.

I was troubled and disturbed by her interpretation of events. I could never have read Frisch that way, though I might have agreed with most of Alma's political conclusions. But I would have drawn them more likely from the everyday experience of the war, not from literature. Perhaps this was a question of vanity, I don't know, but I couldn't help but say, "I'm impressed with your interpretation, though I must admit I didn't fully grasp the link between the novel and all we see around us. And besides, you said this was a project you'd already had in mind before the war. You were reading it in a totally different light then, yet chose to stage the text now?"

"Yes, I understood it differently then. I was interested in the story, in human fate, in the unpredictability of life, the likelihood that something like what the novel speaks of can even happen, and that historical circumstances, human personalities, and beliefs can play their part. Fate, whatever that means. What I said, actually, was that this text helped me understand our situation better, not that I read it all from the story in the novel. My father has a similar way of looking at it. It was actually through our conversations about the adaptation that I came to these devastating conclusions. These are, to a large degree, his ideas as well. I want to say that, if the link isn't entirely clear, I am unable to explain it with crystal clarity—who would be, after all?—but it seems to me that at the political and practical level, things are looking more and more like what I described to you. Regrettably."

"The UN has issued Karadžić an ultimatum," said Ivor.

"We'll see. I hope I'm wrong. But the development of events won't change the essence of the thing. It seems to me that the logic of this conflict has already been endorsed by those who have issued the ultimatum."

"We'll see," I said. "It would be hard for me to accept your pessimism in its entirety, although I admit that you have laid good foundations for it. And besides, who would think to connect Frisch and Bosnia! But Frisch is not letting me go. How did you even come up with the idea of adapting it?"

"I love the text. I love the story," she said. "Simple."

"Oh, everybody loves it." My sarcasm was growing and I felt like needling her. Maybe her intelligence was starting to wear on me, her youth, her brash ideas, beauty, confidence . . . I hated myself for what I was saying, but a demon inside me drove me on. "Incest always has appeal, doesn't it? The war is one thing, but what drew you to this novel? Fear that something like that could actually happen? Fine, but you at least know your father. You have that advantage, but at another level, to use that word you like so much, a daughter can recognize within herself the fear that something like this really could happen to her, to sleep with her own father, as a source of fascination rife with sexual tension. If I understood correctly what the director said, you'll be playing Sabeth, the daughter. This is very interesting. Did it catch your fancy? Or was the idea of adapting the novel your father's suggestion? Which would be interesting, of course, from another point of view . . ."

"Clearly, it's time for us to move to the couch, but time is up on today's session. I'll have to disappoint you, or perhaps offer you more material for your unrealized psychoanalytical potential," she said, responding in kind to the barbs of my commentary. "You see, my father did tell me about this novel. I think he was reading it on an entirely different *level* from that of the story, and here, again, I disappoint you. Far from the shocking tale of incest, I think in his case this text was related, in a way, to his loss of faith in progress, in human advancement, in a better society, in change, if you like, on the one hand, and, on the other, certain important moments from his own life. But that, of course, is none of your business. Now I have to prepare for opening night. I hope I have helped you, gentlemen."

Alma opened the door. She exchanged a few words with Ivor, avoiding my eyes. I had made her uncomfortable and the tip of her nose jumped angrily as it had on that first day, perhaps precisely because everything had gone so well all afternoon, and I'd flattered myself that she liked me. Ivor was in a hurry to leave, before this swelled into a new clash, which was the last thing we needed at the end of our filming. He was already striding out through the dark of the hallway as Alma Filipović tried saying good-bye to me.

"Don't be so sure," I interrupted her, surprising myself with my words, clearly thoughts I hadn't been able to hold back in my own destabilized mind, "that your father didn't, like every man, have in mind the idea that perhaps there is a daughter of his wandering out there in the world, a daughter he knows nothing about, yet whom the theory of probability allows. Without underestimating Frisch, this is the secret of the success of this text for most readers."

"Mr. Richter," said Alma, shifting emphatically to her more formal tone, "you truly judge everything as if life is a courtroom and you are presiding over it, and you proclaim your judgment about all those who find themselves on your path, about whom you know nothing, and you are perfectly convinced that you are right and that God gave you the talent to judge people. And since you are a seasoned judge, you're unable to serve as judge for yourself, because it just so happens that within the jurisdiction you've built for yourself, you can't imagine that somebody could take your place and place you, for instance, in the chair of the accused. You ought to try that for once. It cannot be easy for you to judge justly day after day, to understand everything and everybody, and always be right. You do your difficult job with enviable ability, Mr. Richter, especially as it does not bring you, or any judge, for that matter, much love from those who are judged."

"Nicely put." I took a combative position. "Do you remember the story about the scorpion and the frog? The frog, surprised, asks 'why' after being stung in the middle of the river by the scorpion, which had asked the frog to do it the favor of ferrying it across the river on its back. Do you know what the scorpion answered before both of them sank?"

"I can hardly wait to hear."

"*It's in my nature!*' Miss Filipović."

"*Mrs.* Filipović!" she shouted. We must have been sparring loudly, because I heard Ivor hasten back. "Your story is instructive, but you still need to find that frog, Herr Richter, to confirm your own character. This will undoubtedly bring you happiness."

"Sooner or later I'll find it, don't you worry," I said nastily. "I always do."

"Best of luck!"

She slammed the door. I froze for a few moments, staring at it as if enchanted. I suddenly felt an inexplicable emptiness. I didn't know what I felt exactly, aside from a tinge of remorse at the words I'd said. I was surprised by the feeling that had been sparked by this conversation and which seemed unusually complicated despite the fact that I'd only known *Mrs.* Filipović for a short time. I couldn't understand how it had happened. It was one more in a series of strange feelings that day. I moved slowly toward Ivor, who was watching me with reproach from the stairwell. After two or three steps I turned suddenly, without any clear reason, back to Alma's door. It seemed only then that the cover clicked over the peephole from inside the door.

III

In the Same Cage

1

Among the things I brought back with me from Sarajevo, there is not a single item to remind me of Simon and our brief, strange friendship. Simon—unpredictable yet wise; the time has come for me to write about him, too. He and his story were linked in some fashion to my own, playing no small role in my detour, as I started picking up speed without even realizing it. I hadn't so completely lost my bearings yet that I was willing to believe how every single step I took from April 6, 1992, to my present roost in this kitschy hotel room at the Naschmarkt fell along a predetermined route, leading me to this vestibule to death. Not yet.

It is impossible to forget the day he and I met. For me, it was a few hours before the opening night of Alma's *Homo Faber*, for the newspapers and television news, it was the day when French president François Mitterrand visited the besieged Bosnian capital. An interesting array of circumstances, a string of coincidences, its upshot appearing to bear out Alma's dire predictions. The day marked the opening of an airlift for just barely enough humanitarian aid to reach Sarajevo so that the city wouldn't expire altogether. But the foreign arbiters didn't arrive to put an end to the blows that had already knocked Sarajevo down. This was a measured gesture by a worried world, again: enough so that nothing would change, yet thanks to that gesture I was able to leave Sarajevo when I chose to flee at dawn one day in July.

The conversation with Alma had a powerful impact on my mood. Her words thrust me straight back into my personal distress. Her jab about the meaning of my surname brought to the surface all I'd been suppressing over the last few weeks. Richard *the Judge!* She had sent me back to myself, in a way, to the question of paternity we'd batted about so crudely, at least for my part, and for which I owed her an apology, back to the question of the truth about myself, the puzzle of my birth, which I was trying, unsuccessfully, to push away, only for it to resurface now, requiring urgent attention, like a piece of driftwood that won't fully submerge in the waters of everyday life, that damned piece of wood that keeps bobbing up even during a siege at the end of the world. Ah, is there any such thing as success at repression? Has anyone ever succeeded at that?

What was I doing, still here at the end of the world? My "secret" mission had been abandoned, and I didn't know how to get back to it; the job, unfinished. The old Viennese riddle from which I was born remained an enigma, unresolved, perhaps forever . . . All I knew was that my name was not *Richter*; Alma, I have never, unlike you, met my *father*; indeed, *ma chère*, last names are coincidence . . .

That night I couldn't sleep, though unlike the residents of this city kept up by shelling blasts, gunfire, and frontline skirmishes, I couldn't shut my eyes because of something that happened more than fifty years ago. Am I capable of forgetting it and picking up where I left off with my life? I can't believe this, because my former life seems now like the dream of a sleepwalker who has been shaken awake, and I'm still drowsy and confused about my sleepwalking existence. All the lies, even my writing, which often revolved around the history that defined us as a generation, around us repenting the sins of our fathers, around our attempt to name a new trajectory, fully cognizant of what they, who made us, had perpetrated, around the inescapable *Judenfrage*, the ultimate drama of the German century, the famous German *Sonderweg*, and similar such nonsense; and then, on the heels of this: political engagement, communism, the pledge of an entire generation that nothing like this must ever happen again . . . So much was tied to essential questions of paternity, to our loathing for our fathers, and the fact that we were the progeny of the persecutors, not the persecuted . . . Amid the roiling thoughts that kept my eyes open through that Sarajevo night, Alma's words stung like wasps. She'd hit truly sensitive points without even knowing, and this was the reason why I'd struck back with low blows, of which, I confess, I was not proud. I couldn't stop thinking about that afternoon in her apartment, the slammed door, her eye hastily withdrawn from the spyhole . . .

In the moments when I got up from bed to get a glass of water, I'd wonder whether I was even sane, if I should start a raging fight with somebody I hardly knew, a mere passing acquaintance. I dismissed the possibility that I was attracted to her with a barking laugh, followed by an apology to Ivor's ancestors whose solemn *Austro-Hungarian* faces— among them a 1914 portrait of Ivor's youthful grandfather on his way, as a Hungarian soldier, to the Eastern Front—were watching me from the wall. I owed them an apology, too, for the troubles their guest was putting them through as he came unhinged.

I could find no peace nor sleep, so before morning I switched on the light and reread Paula's letter to Jakob Schneider. I reflected on my cruelty to Ingrid. I hadn't written her for weeks. I hadn't forgiven her for keeping silent all those years. She was guided by selfishness. Without a second thought, ummoved, she watched me build my life and work, all of it based on a lie. I thought of the promise I'd made to myself, of the role of postman I'd embraced when I set out for Sarajevo; of this whole circus I'd created of my life; of Kitty, of all the years we'd shared, of the rift we hadn't noticed growing between us, into us, under our skin; of Ivor, of the friendship we were still building, of the joy of companionship; of this city, which I'd picked as my dungeon; of Alma Filipović; of the accursed, blinkered Mr. Walter Faber . . .

◆ ◆ ◆

I couldn't recall what time it was when I finally fell asleep, but I'm quite sure I slept no longer than three or four hours. As soon as I was up, I went to visit the Jewish Community Office on the left bank of the Miljacka River, an Ashkenazi temple from the period of Austrian rule. Several of the leading community members received me. I introduced myself in my official capacity as a television and news reporter. I said I was interested in writing something about the Sarajevo Jews, their role in the history of the city and their position today. The community leaders were not surprised; every humdrum foreign journalist must have had this thematic card up his or her sleeve for the days when there wasn't much bad news to write about and yet the generous salary had to be justified. I had one request, an idea that might serve as a short-term focus until I'd decided what to do with myself: I wished to visit the old Sephardic synagogue at Baščaršija. I'd come up with the idea earlier, in fact Ivor and I had gone to have a look but found it locked; we were told to request access at the Jewish Community Office. At that point we were too busy to do so. This time, I didn't want to involve Ivor in what was too personal an affair. Luckily, everything was quickly arranged. A guide came to pick me up in the early afternoon and took me to the old part of town. He unlocked the old iron gateway to the yard, then the door to the synagogue, which had been turned into a Jewish museum long before the war, if I understood his gist. He told me he'd leave me on my own, he had things to see to, but he'd lock the outside gate after him to be safe. He left me the spare keys, showed me how to lock it all up afterward, and said he'd be waiting for me back at the Jewish Community Office in a few hours.

So that's how I ended up alone at the synagogue, a venerable sixteenth-century stone building. It was an unusual temple: the ritual objects now served only as museum exhibits, mementos of the days when the Torah was read here and there were whispers in Spanish in the galleries. A golden Star of David gleamed in the afternoon sunlight in a window that was almost entirely blocked by sandbags. Next door to the synagogue stood a madrasa with the spikes on its roof arrayed like upright bullets; a little farther off was the Gazi Husrev-beg mosque. All that was missing was the chiming of the Sarajevo church bells for one to experience with eyes and ears what the people of Sarajevo touted with such pride about the city's past—it's a miniature Balkan Jerusalem!—as if this were a source of consolation, while the city was being battered with each passing day. The blows striking Sarajevo were designed to leave scars, to change the nature of the city forever. "What will become of the city," I asked aloud. *What will become of me, for God's sake?*

The empty synagogue offered no answers.

After I'd had a look at the first floor, I went up to the balcony, drawn by an unusual exhibit on display. As I'd stood below, looking up at it, I'd realized there was something large and book-shaped up there, suspended from the ceiling, swaying ever so slightly in a barely noticeable gust breezing through the building. As soon as I went up the stairs, I saw what it was. It was in fact a book, its large pages covered with first and last names. It was a book of the murdered Sarajevo Jews! The surnames of the Second World War victims were listed in alphabetical order, the Spanish names intermingling with the German and, in a few cases, Slavic names. I was taken aback at how unusual the memorial tome was, but then I started, hands trembling, to read through the list of Sarajevans who were lost in the war. I saw immediately what great value this book might have for me, for my search, so fumbling hurriedly I leafed on:

Alkalaj,
Altarac,
Bararon,
Berg,
Finci,
Gaon,
Goldberg,

Goldstein,
Isaković,
Kamhi,
Kojen,
Levi,
Najman,
Papo,
Pardo,
Pinto . . .

Then even a *Richter*, though that was not the surname I needed today . . .

Rihtman,
Rot,
Salomon,
Samokovlija,
Silberstein . . .

And—at last . . . !

Schneider:
    Abraham,
    Amnon,
    Aron,
    Baruh . . .

In the fractions of a second needed for my eye to scan these names and send them to my brain, I felt as if I could hear my heart pound faster with each syllable of each new name, as if trying to leap out, almost to the bursting point . . .

Benjamin,
Daniel,
David,
Ester,
Isak,
Judita,
Josef,
Lea,
Max,
Moritz,
Natan,
Rifka,
Sara,
Zakarija . . .

And then came the next surname—

Schönberg . . .

And that was that. Once more I scanned the list of deceased Schneiders. I shut the book. There wasn't a single Jakob on the list of the dead! My father was not among them!

I slumped onto a dusty bench that was probably put there to serve weary readers of this sad volume, still suspended midair by my head. And then relief—even a surge of an odd joy—replaced the despair. I wondered if one of them might have been my grandfather, uncle, some relative . . . And then, after everything else, came the fear. As if I could suddenly see myself from the outside, I plunged my head into my hands and felt a stab of real anguish and fear for myself. I felt I'd go mad if I kept at this and I'd go mad if I didn't, if I failed to find out what happened to Jakob, if I never found him, even among the dead. The relief that I hadn't found him in the book was displaced by regret.

At least the quandary would have been settled. I'd have been free. I'd have found my *truth*; his death would have been confirmed with as much certainty as my mother's grave, and I could have walked away from this hell! To mull somewhere else over my sorrowful fate, or, like that accursed priest, plunge into the niceties of late-onset Judaism! I could leave here, damn it!

When I finally looked up, the synagogue had already eased into the afternoon stillness. The panic had waned, and the book was hanging there, quiet, as if no one had touched it, as if no one had disturbed the dead. The air that had been moving through the walls of the old building seemed to fall still for a moment. I hoped damned Mitterrand had already left Sarajevo, having done at least something worthwhile. I'd celebrated when he was elected president of France in 1981, but the gentleman had since lost my support. Time had passed him by. I hoped, nevertheless, that he might be able to dislodge this stalemate in Sarajevo. Soon enough we'd see the real meaning of his visit; the gunfire that evening would jolt us back to reality—it would show us who'd come out of this as victor, and disappointment would elbow out our hope. But while I was at the synagogue, I admit, I was submerged in the world of Paula Müller and Jakob Schneider, in the subterranean realms of our lives, clutching at my one link to reality, to the surface, just a tenuous thread: there was Alma's opening night to attend.

I came back down to the synagogue's first floor. A glance at my watch told me I had half an hour before I had to return the keys to the Jewish Community Office and then hurry off to the theater. The slant of afternoon sunlight transformed the synagogue. The part that was sunlit glowed, and standing in the shaft of light, I could barely discern what was in deep shadow. Determined to take in the scene, I perched on an uncomfortable wooden chair with a carved inscription. Outside, there was a war going on; inside dwelled the ancient past. And silence. Divine silence.

I must have sat there for ten minutes, sunken into the chair and thinking of nothing in particular for the first time, perhaps, in these exhausting nights and days, merely watching as the afternoon sun danced through the venerable Jewish temple. Then the silence was interrupted by nothing less than my own terrified shriek. A rumbling, garbled, diabolic voice had intruded into the divine silence, coming from somewhere in the shadowy reaches of the synagogue—from very near me in fact. The voice so startled me that I bounded off the seat as if catapulted from it and ended up crouching behind the staircase. My shriek still echoed through the space as I sputtered in German, French, and English all at once, shocked, frightened, and berating the motionless hulk I could just make out in the gloom. It took me a good ten seconds to collect myself and comprehend that the intruder's words had been spoken in Bosnian, and that this unexpected visitor had asked me something while standing right behind me, and that his tone was not, in fact, threatening at all, even if it had chilled the blood in my veins when he spoke at just that moment. I stopped shouting and the figure began to laugh aloud. I must have presented a comical sight for the surprise guest, but I was hardly reassured. Through the play of light and shadow that had taken over the synagogue, I could already tell that he was an older man with a long beard who was now trying to say something in a jumble of languages, clearly hoping we'd find a way to communicate through his hodgepodge: *"Don't be afraid, mon ami . . . pas de panique, ha-ha . . . It's okay, ha-ha"*—he couldn't stop laughing—*"moi, je ne te ferai aucun mal, ha-ha . . . dobro, dobro, alles gut, heh-heh, nema problema . . ."*

He stepped into the light, his hand extended in a gesture of reconciliation and hospitality. I walked warily over to him. If it hadn't been for his bright, disarming smile, I might have been afraid of him even in the sunlight. He was a very old man, over eighty or so he seemed, his face creased with unusually deep wrinkles, with a long white beard and a high brow. He was dressed, prophet-like, in clothes reminiscent of a well-worn monk's habit. Only his eyes, which shone like a twelve-year-old's, belied his Methuselah-like mien. I no longer feared him. Now I was merely cross and I spoke to him in English, which he readily embraced, leapfrogging over the gaps in his knowledge by interjecting French or the occasional German and Spanish word.

"Good God, man, what are you doing here?! You gave me such a fright."

"Heh-heh, shouldn't I be asking you that, *n'est-ce pas*?!" he answered, dropping his hand.

"The Jewish Community Office permitted me to be here. I mean, I have the key. I'm a journalist."

"*Bueno, bueno*. A journalist? Okay . . . But how could I know who you are and what you're doing here, sitting in the circumcision chair! And when you're asked, you hop around like a madman, as if the Devil himself were speaking to you in this place of God, heh-heh . . . ?"

"Sorry? What chair?"

"Circumcision." He made a scissor-like gesture with his fingers several times. "Snip, snip, heh-heh . . . That's what the inscription says here, take a look. They circumcised me on this very Elijah's chair. That's what we call it, Elijah's chair."

I looked again at the uncomfortable wooden chair and the inscription carved into it. Chances were it was exactly what he said it was.

"There, look." He pointed at the inscription, as if I could have understood anything, and then enunciating, he translated, "*Cir-cum-ci-sion*. See?"

This, too, was an exhibit. I stared at it, bewildered, unable to imagine that where I'd been sitting so cheerfully, people had sat to be circumcised. The old man came closer and then, again, extended his hand.

"Hey," he said, "I don't have all day. Now that we've had the good fortune to meet, we should introduce ourselves."

"Richter. Richard Richter," I said and shook his hand.

"*Enchanté*. My name is . . . Simon, Mr. *Judge*."

And so it was that I made a new Sarajevo friend in the old Sephardic synagogue on June 28, shortly before Alma's opening night, while the airplane carrying President Mitterrand was winging its way, carefree, to Paris, under the late-afternoon sun.

After the unusual introduction, the two of us were at a loss for words. I was reluctant to ask what he was doing there. As far as I knew, all the doors had been locked when the man from the Community Office and I entered. I wondered if my guide might have forgotten to lock the outside gate, allowing the old man to slip in. But I said nothing. Instead, I looked up at the synagogue's two tiers of balconies, admiring the simplicity and charm of the building.

"I heard that this synagogue is a replica of the former synagogue in Toledo." I tried to break the silence with this reference my guide had passed on.

"There are many such replicas wherever Sephardic Jews have set foot," Simon continued, in English. "I cannot be sure, but who knows, it's possible maybe that after decades of persecution, a Toledo resident might arrive in Sarajevo and build this synagogue moved by pangs of nostalgia for the image he'd carried with him along the pathways of his refuge flight, which had blurred over time in the lands of new. Who knows, heh-heh . . ."

Simon's English had a particular, elusive ring to it. He was clearly an educated man who spoke with ease in several languages, while knowing none of them perfectly. By combining them, he pulled off amazing linguistic feats so that he could be sure he'd be understood, in a flood of words, inundating the listener with what he had to say.

"Yes," said Simon, "perhaps just as the memory of Toledo he's known blended with the El Greco painting, so the image of the temple in Toledo for the Sephardim who came into the world with an inborn nostalgia for distant, exotic places gradually merged with their new Sarajevo temple. I can be wrong, but the imagination of refugees rises to strange things."

"You, too, are Jewish, I gather?"

"Heh-heh, a curious *čifut* am I, *cher camarade*." This was when I first heard the Turkish word, *čifut*, for *Jew*. Later, I found out it had a pejorative hue.

"Among the very last to remain, or so they're saying in Sarajevo."

"They say many things in Sarajevo." Simon paced around the synagogue, peering at its interior with which he was evidently familiar, yet his expression showed rapt attention as if he were spotting a new detail as we spoke. "*Der letzte Jude? Non, il y a toujours des juifs dans cette ville.* Of all that, truth is, when I was born, which was, frankly, a very long time ago, *mon vieux*, this city was bustling with Sephardim, and there were Ashkenazim, too, but the number has fallen today to a handful of us and death will soon fell us. As our number dwindles, so Sarajevo becomes less the microcosm that reflects the old Ottoman condition and the Austrian and Yugoslav monarchies. What can you do, Sarajevo is merely the last to fall to the curse . . ."

"The curse?" I asked, startled by the direction of Simon's reasoning. "You think this siege is a curse? A curse, maybe, of history?"

"Listen, friend, I think nothing. I sense, the older I get, a hellish logic, an ancient curse—we cannot remember how it came about—that is slowly but surely wiping from the earth all cities where faiths, peoples, languages, hues, complexions mix together like a pack of cards."

"You said 'last' . . ."

"Yes, the last, or maybe one of the last cities which are now giving their final gasp." Simon now looked up and pointed to the Star of David in the big window. "This is what I mean, if you make the effort and look through the star from all quarters of the synagogue, from upstairs and down here, inside its points you can see the rooftop of the madrasa, or a minaret, or the Orthodox church, or the Catholic church, all only an arm's reach away. This is not only a passive *coexistence*; this is a joining of all together in new forms, in the Sarajevans. It disappears. People disappear, only empty buildings are left, this synagogue, the museums . . ."

"But still, it isn't yet over and done with . . . All my friends . . ."

"Not yet," he interrupted, "of course it isn't, but the end nears. So I tell you Sarajevo is the last or one of the last; there's no stopping the dominoes. For years Sarajevo withstood. Its nature has been to welcome, since the Turks, since the city's beginnings; we've all shared it, the Muslim, Catholic, Orthodox, and Jewish. Here together lived Slavs, Turks, Armenians, Arabs, Arnauts, and *tutti quanti*. The *König und Kaiser* days ushered in with them the Austrians, Hungarians, Czechs, Ashkenazim, Poles . . . During the time of the Kingdom of Yugoslavia, all these people were moving around inside its borders, but then with the Second World War began the decimation, the curse. Still, the city came back, living on without its Jews, or with far fewer of us, only enough to keep alive the memory. Once again Sarajevo welcomed, mingled, made the Sarajevans, from those who are born here to those who pour in from elsewhere. During this war, this siege, the city is trapped and we all want to get away no matter who or what we are. It is not the Serbs, Jews, Muslims, Croats, the ex-Yugoslavs—don't forget them—who are fleeing, it is the Sarajevans who run, and each takes something of the city with him. Those people in the hills who bombard us are simply doing the work of the curse; I don't know when it started, but I think it has been alive and ripping at the fabric of these cities a very long time, a modern-age disease, if you will."

"What do you mean by that?" Simon intrigued me with his theories. "A disease? Or is this merely the doings of history?"

"Ecoutez," he went on, smoothing his long beard, "I'll start with the history of our day, which has been erasing slowly but surely the city-worlds, our latter-day Babylons, the sanctuaries in which even the simplest were born speaking several languages, but the soul—my

apologies for that tired word, but I have no substitute—is gone, carried off with people to graves, to exile. Let us start with an Alexandria with no Greeks, Jews, or Europeans, to a divided, troubled Jerusalem, to a Nicosia, sliced in two, to Damascus and Aleppo, to Beirut, warring within, to an Istanbul with no Greeks and Armenians, to a Salonika without its Turks and Sephardim, to give only the examples we know best . . . But the disease didn't limit itself to the Ottoman Empire. Tell me what is left today of cities such as Trieste, Vilnius, Königsberg, Warsaw, Lviv, Odessa, and Chernivitsi . . . ? Sarajevo, I fear, stands at the end of this list. Cities disappear; what remains are memories, empty houses, and the occasional witness like me."

"But the city has survived so far, it is raising a united defense . . ." I tried countering Simon's dark predictions. "Forgive me, I am a foreigner, but it seems to me that, regardless of what the masters of war—the politicians and leaders of the various groups here—have claimed, the war is not being waged 'between the Serbs and the Muslims,' at least not in Sarajevo. This is not an 'ethnic' clash, but a clash between those who are defending Sarajevo together and those who wish for the destiny you've predicted. The tactics do seem to be effective: a siege, crime, and a dirty war are the most effective ways to destroy, as you put it, the fabric of a city, its spirit, its soul or something else, which has held and still holds all the people together, or at least those who've stayed. I don't know, maybe I'm naïve. Maybe I'm wrong. I'm just a foreigner here, *un étranger parmi vous . . .*"

Simon listened closely, nodding and glancing up toward the hills held by Karadžić's militia every time he heard a strange sound.

"And I believe the aggressor will win the day," I went on, "if and when only one ethnic or religious group is left defending the city and the multicultural spirit is gone. Then the fight for the city will be lost, regardless of what happens on the fields of battle."

"Donc vous êtes d'accord avec moi!" exclaimed Simon. "This has to be about a curse and the troops in the hills, 'them up there' are merely

doing its bidding, while 'them down here' who believe they are defending the city as it truly is, belonging to everyone, intermingled, in the Sarajevan spirit, after all, are gullible—fighting against what destiny intended all along. For how can one defend against a curse, when one is up against an attacker who intends to change the city, even to the point of destroying it, and when the curse, the fratricidal epidemic, is laying a trap for you behind your back by eating away at the city from within. The success of the attack lies in how they are already spreading the disease through the defense lines, a disease that will devour the city. Then Sarajevo as we know it will join the ranks of the other dead cities I numbered, regardless of the occasional memento of the old days."

"I must confess to believing naïvely in this city, because if it fails, what does the future hold for the others? Forgive me my gullibility, but this curse, this disease you speak of, will not be spent and stop here . . . Instead, it will gain momentum, and then . . ."

"And then may God help those who sleep peacefully today . . ."

After his bleak forecast, Simon fell silent and bowed his head, pacing around me, stroking his beard, scowling. I glanced quickly at my watch. I had to leave that minute if I was going to reach the theater in time for the opening night. The occasional burst of gunfire was hardly promising. But just as I thought I'd say good-bye to my new acquaintance, Simon spun around and asked, "So, what are you actually doing here, Mr. Richter?"

"That's what I wanted to ask you."

"Really? Well, you see, I come and meditate here on the past. This is one of the few places where a person can truly be alone in the city, heh-heh . . . Of course, until an inquisitive guest shows up. You?"

"I am a journalist. I was given permission to visit the synagogue. A man from the Community Office unlocked the door for me and left me to have a look around, and so—"

"That's not my question," interrupted Simon curtly. "I asked you what you are really doing here. In the synagogue."

"And I said. I'm a journalist. *Un journaliste étranger, c'est tout.*"

"No, you're not entirely an *étranger*, *Herr* Richter, because in the middle of a war, amid the dying and suffering going on around us, a person who visits a synagogue, that person may perhaps be *un journaliste quelconque*, or whatever it is that you are, Mr. Richter, but you did not come here by chance."

"What do you mean? What is so special here?" I felt discomfort, even anxiety, as if Simon were reading my mind.

"This man . . ." Simon turned to me and, in a sententious tone, declared, "This man is seeking something."

"I'm seeking nothing. What do you . . ."

"This man did not come here just to have a look around." Simon stepped toward me, looking me straight in the eyes. "This man came to find something or, maybe, somebody . . ."

"No! Not true. I . . ." Why was I backing away and defending myself from this stranger's accusations like a child before his all-seeing father?

"So why were you leafing through the memorial book, then?! Ha?!" he shouted so loudly that I cringed. His deep voice rang throughout the synagogue. His eyes sank into the deep crevices crisscrossing his face. I felt my back against the cold balcony pillar. *"Pourquoi?"*

Today, I know that destiny was smiling on me then, that the flutter of its wings moved across my face and brushed me, that I was being honored by a quirk of fate, given a chance. Today, I know that Simon would have been able to help had I been honest in my answer to his question. I wouldn't be sitting here today, the revolver would not be rattling in the drawer as I pound on the typewriter, as if the more force I used to press the keys, the more bearable the story would be. Alma would never have happened. Things would have been easier.

But the wings merely brushed me and instead of telling the old man everything, I took a different approach and the moment passed.

There was no longer anything except the strange man there before me who kept trying to divine my thoughts; his eyes barely visible, a curious figure who had crept in here, he watched me, guessing at and slowly penetrating the sealed chambers of my most intimate thoughts, and he now stood there and waited for an answer that I did not owe him.

"You have guessed well, *cher monsieur*," I told him, head bowed as if conceding. "Indeed, I am not here merely to write an article."

Simon was surprised by my confession and, as if disarmed by the confirmation of his intuition, he peered at me with interest. His eyes surfaced, broke through the creases deep as scars.

"The story may sound strange to you, but that is because it is strange. I didn't lie when I said I'm a journalist. I am. I write for some newspapers and serve as a commentator for television news. But this doesn't explain why I came here—to this synagogue. You see, a few days ago a friend from Vienna reached me with a most unusual story and an even stranger request. It may sound incredible, but he is a dear friend, you understand. After more than twenty years he recently moved back to Vienna from Paris, and imagine! While renovating his apartment, he found a niche of sorts, a hole, I mean, in a wall behind a bookshelf where there was a little box, and in it he found a blue notebook. Now listen to this, in the notebook . . . Do you know what he found in the notebook? In the notebook he found a letter his mother had written to a stranger, a man my friend had never heard of, and who, it would appear, judging by the substance of the letter, was his true father. You can imagine what an effect this discovery had on him. Not only did he learn that his father was not his father, which, as I'm sure you'll agree, would shake the most robust among us, but he learned that his father, I mean his real father, had disappeared even before my friend was born. He was arrested by the Gestapo as a communist in 1941 under an alias. From his mother's letter, however, my friend learned his father's real name and something else, which is what brought me straight to this synagogue. You see, his real father was Jewish, from Sarajevo; can you imagine?! My poor friend now wants to learn something about the man. It's easy to assume that his *real* father died long ago, but that doesn't matter to my friend; he still wants to know what happened to him. He himself wanted to come immediately to Sarajevo, but then he heard about the war, so his search stopped there. Desperate, he was at a loss for what to do. But when he learned that I—his old friend—am here, right in Sarajevo, he turned to me for help. I decided I'd help him. So I did come here today for an official reason, as a journalist of course, but I saw the visit as overlapping with my detective work, with my resolve to help my poor friend. I've been trying for some time to find something out about this man and I haven't succeeded, so you can imagine my excitement, my relief I mean, when I caught sight of that *book* up on the balcony. There. A strange story, wouldn't you say?"

A half-truth is better than a lie. Simon studied me closely, showing genuine interest, and the earlier sternness with which he'd alarmed me vanished completely. He seemed to be still under the sway of the story he'd just heard.

"*Tiens, tiens* . . . This case of your friend's. Interesting, indeed. Hmm . . ."

"So perhaps you might be able to help me. Of course, only if you'd like." I couldn't believe my ears that I got those words out.

"Oh, yes, *volontiers*, absolutely, if I can help this friend of yours in any way. Forgive me for my behavior earlier; I had no idea. You surprised me: the way you were studying the book up there surprised me. I said to myself, this man is seeking something . . ."

"And you were right," I interrupted. "I know my actions might give an altogether wrong impression."

Still, I was tense and suddenly I wanted to end this encounter without saying the name *Jakob Schneider* out loud. As if I wasn't ready, after the previous night and this whole day, far too stressful a day for my nerves, to hear a stranger tell me anything decisive about him.

"Listen," I said, "I really have to get going. I think it would be best for me to write down the name of the person I'm looking for, and you think about whether you are able to help. My friend would be grateful."

The game was draining me. I scribbled the name on a scrap of paper and pushed it into Simon's hand before he had the chance to ask anything. He tucked the slip of paper into an invisible pocket in his robe without even a glance.

"It's dark in here. There's no longer enough light, and my eyes, you know . . . What an interesting story . . . But . . ."

"I'll give you my address." Again I interrupted him, hurrying to get out of there as fast as I could. "Or you give me yours and we can meet somewhere more suitable. I would like to continue our engaging conversation."

"No need for addresses, believe me, we will meet again . . ."

"How . . . ? You have no address, no nothing . . ."

"Don't you fret about that," said Simon and patted me on the shoulder.

"I assume I lock the door behind me," I said as I walked toward the exit, "and you'll find your own way out."

"You have understood everything, foreigner."

I shut the synagogue door and ran out into the yard. The outside gate was locked as the guide had said it would be. How had Simon entered? *Strange indeed,* I thought. I bolted the gate behind me, hoping Simon really knew what he was talking about. Then I set off for the Jewish Community Office. The sun was setting over the besieged city, with shells blasting in the distance as they had for many nights now.

Quel beau dimanche!

Adieu, Monsieur le Président.

But I didn't want to think, just then, about that. The opening night was ahead.

2

"Destiny is the most powerful coincidence of all," she said at the end of that day when I asked her whether she thought people find each other by destiny or by coincidence. She laughed; we were giddy, tired, tipsy as the lovely evening at the theater, the after-party for the opening night, drew to a close. Perhaps it was the drinks and the mood, but I asked her for a dance, squelching the fear a fifty-year-old must feel when facing a young woman. Still, I was sure by then that we'd reconciled. And more. I began to wish the dance would last longer than such songs usually do, aware only of the scent of her neck, of Alma's hand on my shoulder, of her fingertips in my hair, of my arms around her supple body, succumbing to the heat of her warm cheek while we danced slowly to music Ivor had chosen. He, too, was dancing with one of the actresses, and winked at me discreetly when our eyes met. I couldn't tell whether this was to encourage or mock me.

She whispered her answer, grinning. "*Destiny is the most powerful coincidence of all.*" Here in Vienna I say Alma's words out loud. The words gave me goose bumps when she uttered the sentence, more than a month before now as I'm struggling to describe the hours that would define my life, or, should I say, the little that is left of it. Her breath brushed my ear. At first I didn't catch the allusion. She explained, laughing at my startled expression, that this was the promotional phrase used to advertise Schlöndorff's movie. Ah-ha! Though I hadn't seen it, I said

I was convinced, complimenting her as an older man would, that her adaptation for the stage was far superior. I also said that under the circumstances her answer was apt, even if borrowed. (We said all sorts of things to each other, borrowing the words of others!) I drew her closer. She didn't pull away. *Destiny, nevertheless, is the most powerful coincidence of all.* We said nothing more until the song ended, and then we stepped apart, each to a different end of the room. Talking with others, a laugh and the occasional glance, a glass tipped in her direction.

A few days ago I saw the movie adaptation of *Homo Faber* here in Vienna. It was showing at a small cinema not far from my hotel. I came across a mention in the newspapers that the young man from the front desk has taken to leaving with my breakfast, probably intended to keep me at least a little connected to the outside world. I left the hotel at dusk and walked to the cinema. On the way I saw only a few others—Vienna is a lonely city in August. Ladies short of breath, slow red trams, half-deserted terraces . . . My hometown. When I reached the cinema there was only one other person who had a ticket, a woman in her late thirties, waiting for the movie to start. I thought perhaps this might be precisely the sort of soul the movie had been made for. Who knows, maybe she wasn't able to use her vacation time just then, she'd finished her workday, there was nobody waiting for her at home, her friends were out of town, and she had nowhere else to go but a cinema to catch a tearjerker. (In the end I was the one who cried, and she asked, kindly, "Is everything all right, sir?" "Yes, thank you, ma'am." "If something's the matter . . ." "Thank you, no need . . .") I was certain she'd read Frisch's novel. It is, after all, required reading. Waiting for the movie to start, she stole glances in my direction. I was only hoping she wasn't one of those bookworms who might recognize me—her glasses and the loose, messy ponytail suggested she was a high school teacher, perhaps one with a powerful appetite for reading, perhaps the very sort of teacher who awarded my high school literary efforts with low grades, along with comments like *Unclear, Psychologizing!, Main point missing* . . . (On the other hand, they may have been partially right, those teachers of mine. After all, didn't some of the more rigorous critics say those same things years later?) I hoped she didn't recognize me, but her eyes seemed more drawn to my prophet-like beard—even Simon would have been proud of it—and my sorry state. *Un homme déboussolé.*

A young couple joined us. Their impatience while kissing suggested a relationship of the briefer variety. We arranged ourselves in the cinema at a distance from one another. The woman rustled with her newspaper (the Viennese, so predictable), the young couple whispered and giggled; otherwise, the silence was strained as we waited for the movie to begin. How different this all was from the opening night in Sarajevo! The contrast was almost painful! I thought I'd burst into tears just recalling the moment when I arrived, out of breath, at the theater to see the play, so I was relieved when the lights dimmed finally in the cinema. At least I no longer saw the wasteland around me, the empty rows of seats.

When I reached the theater building after that remarkable encounter at the synagogue, I found a crowd gathered by the entrance. It had been a long time since I'd seen people so determined to get in and so patient. Evidently in this besieged city that had no working phone lines or any of the other habitual ways of spreading information, different but no less effective strategies for spreading the word had evolved. Inside, the theater was packed to overflowing, and this was not just because the show was free of charge. The audience sat elbow to elbow to free up as many seats as possible for those waiting outside. This was a collective act, so different from the numbered seats, reserved loges, privileged seating, and everything else that was so typical and customary elsewhere in theaters.

Luckily, the director spotted me in the crowd and shepherded me in as an important guest. I apologized. "Just as long as the shells don't start whistling," he said with trepidation.

Ivor shook his head, appalled, gesturing at his watch. The camera was set up and ready to roll. "Where were you, man?" he hissed when I reached him.

The audience let me pass without protest. "Out and about."

"Out and about?! It was all I could do to push the raising of the curtain a few minutes!" Ivor was nearly shouting, and I was saved from his lecture by the lights suddenly dimming, leaving the stage lit only with slightly flickering lights. The play began: *Homo Faber* on the Sarajevo stage!

Oh, how odd it was to revisit that same troubled story! It served as both the before and the after for *everything*! *Before*, in Sarajevo on the day that defined everything: the siege, myself, and, ultimately, *us*—and then *after*, after I'd left for Vienna. The same story had such different tales to tell! *Before*—on the Sarajevo stage, Alma as Sabeth, Alma as Hanna, the grateful audience packed like sardines into the theater in the shelled city, people watching a staging of one of the classics of German literature, drinking in the actors' every movement, word, gesture; theater that has meaning because it itself was the message, simply being there was the message, nearly an act of defiance or at least so it seemed to me . . . And then *after*—the movie in Vienna, so removed, the story about Walter Faber, with Sam Shepard and young Julie Delpy in the leading roles, the interesting destiny of a man, of course, our contemporary, roughly speaking, a product of our times, of the twentieth century; it was mainly about *his* destiny. The young couple who lost the thread of the movie after the first twenty minutes; the solitary woman, her head tilted slightly to the left; and the former Richard Richter, a man who had been in a small Sarajevo theater only over a month before, and in a synagogue before that. And a man who knows what happened after the opening night, who knows how Alma Filipović whispered that destiny is *the most powerful coincidence of all*, smiling, understanding his flirting, his clumsiness, his insecurity (his infatuation?); and now that same man in a Viennese cinema who no longer sees the movie before him but is back again breathing with those people who felt the noose of destiny tightening around the main characters while the thunder of war inched closer, and he, among them, thrilled by what he was seeing on the stage, even though he understood nothing of their language, yet knowing the story down to its finest details as it ground up its characters like a water mill, moved by his experiences that day, saying to himself that despite all that had happened over the last months, despite all the coincidences that had conspired to sweep him along and bring him to the dark of that Sarajevo theater, he still had the strength to tug the threads he was meant to tug, to take the thing to the end, to forge his destiny, even if his undoing was what he'd soon fashion for himself.

The Sarajevo Walter Faber character was believable. Perhaps a shade too handsome for Faber. He was played by an actor in his forties who could have stood in for good old Sam. Alma didn't wait long to enter as Sabeth. Her adaptation of the play actually started on board the ship when Faber and his daughter first meet. Alma as Sabeth, Alma as a twenty-year-old girl. I didn't take my eyes off her. Ivor relied on his judgment for the filming. My mind was not on the movie. Ivor was perfectly capable of taking command, and he already knew me far too well. There in the dark, surrounded by the warm bodies, I thought about the despair that had swamped me at the synagogue as I read the names of the dead Jews, the excitement pulsing through my confession to Simon—albeit in the third person—and the unexpected delight coming from the fact that I was here, that I was watching Alma from the dark without a thought to the meaning of what she was saying, that I was observing her lissome figure, her charming girlish face, the ponytail that bounced while she played the oh-so-symbolic game of ping-pong with Faber on board the ship, Alma as Sabeth, Alma as her own father's lover . . .

I thought just then of Max Frisch. I remembered meeting him in 1976 when he was awarded the Peace Prize of the German Book Trade. They summoned us young writers to keep the great Swiss writer company. I'd already published two books and was flattered that old Max knew a little something about them. We dined with him. Frisch joked and gave advice to the angry young men, avoiding a conversation about literature as a mystery, something akin to philosophy, the sort of thing we leaned toward. And of course we touched on *Homo Faber*, too. A colleague asked an artless question, the question we all were probably longing to ask, but because we saw ourselves as serious writers, we couldn't allow ourselves to ask it: Is the novel based on something the author or a person close to him experienced? Had he heard such a story; is there any *truth* to it? Frisch smiled while the rest of us sneered, making our colleague uncomfortable. The classic cruelty and hypocrisy of literary gatherings, which I would soon come to deplore. We didn't see that Frisch himself wasn't bothered by the question; his smile was in no way a sneer. He said that sometimes he thinks literature is based on the possibilities emerging from what happens to us or from the experiences of others. With an ambiguous smile he hinted that some of the events in his life or the lives of other people he knew had the potential to develop into the story that *Homo Faber* brings us and that he'd tapped into this potential when writing the novel. "I assume this is what you had in mind, young man, when you asked the question," he addressed our colleague, who, having not much of a choice, nodded. "Is there truth in what you write, gentlemen?" the author asked the rest of us, continuing quietly to putter with his fish. We bowed our heads like embarrassed schoolboys and focused on our dinner.

There must have been a smile playing on my lips as I recalled the episode. Then I focused all my attention on what was happening onstage, where the drama had reached its climax. And then, a surprise: Alma made her entrance as Hanna, Sabeth's mother! The romantic fling of Walter Faber's youth, which produced the child whose existence Faber discovers only too late, when a different sort of love—nothing remotely like paternal affection—had already blossomed, when Hanna appeared only after the accident put Sabeth to sleep forever so she'd never learn the horrifying truth about the man she loved. The trick took all of us by surprise, and there were audible gasps from the audience when Alma stood before Faber as Hanna, a woman of almost fifty, before Faber, who finally understands everything, who has woken from his delirium and opened his eyes; Hanna, who realizes what transpired between father and daughter . . . Alma as Hanna, a serious, seasoned, resilient woman. Alma in both roles: Faber's former lover and their daughter, who becomes her own father's lover. The similarities and differences between the mother and daughter played spectacularly. I could not shake free of the impression. Sabeth's innocent embrace with Faber; Hanna's fury, punching Faber in the face when the tragedy erupts and the truth is finally exposed, when destiny is the most powerful coincidence.

I sat there for a long time after the lights came up and after the solitary woman left the cinema, after she checked to see that everything was all right with me—that slightly odd fellow with the beard. The couple had vanished. The sufferings of others had little to do with them and rightly they rejected them. The movie's sad ending could serve as the perfect excuse for the tracks of my tears, streaking into my beard, and I wouldn't have attempted to claim otherwise. I preferred for that to be the reason why I kept right on sitting in the cinema for a few more moments of stillness. In my mind I was already far away, after all, in a place that nobody here knew anything about, in the place I come from, where, I believe, I belong, with the people I was with that day in the little theater. Here I can expect no understanding for the applause resounding inside me that erupted and lasted long after Walter Faber, the European *Homo faber*, died in Sarajevo from a tumor that was eating at his gut from the very start (a scene that was left out of the movie).

How the people applauded. I am not sure they all understood the message as Alma intended it, but they clearly knew they'd seen a superb performance and genuinely enjoyed it. This was what they'd needed, to attend an excellent play the way they used to in peacetime. To come nicely dressed to a theater helped them feel a part of something larger than the life they were being forced to live. It gives you the chance to feel human again in the midst of a war—the therapeutic value of theater at such moments is something that warrants research—to feel as you remembered yourself. The play was a success if it gave them back that feeling, and our movie would be a success if that is what came across, I thought as I stood there, clapping and cheering—"Bravo! Bravo!"—perhaps louder than all the rest. Ivor panned with the camera, Alma looked over at us for a moment, probably drawn by my cheers, first cautiously and then, when she saw my grin and clapping and Ivor's high thumbs-up gesture above the camera, she smiled with warmth. The director and manager came out. Everyone went right on applauding without moving from their places. When they finally did begin to disperse, the director signaled for us to stay. There'd be a little after-party right there on the theater stage.

Perhaps I should have left just as the members of the company were bringing tables and chairs into the empty theater. I could have hurried out with all the people who were now undertaking the precarious journey home, because despite Monsieur Mitterrand's visit, yet another cease-fire had floundered. "Now we have everything we need. I think that should do it," concluded Ivor, switching off the camera. Yes, the filming was done. Ivor did this with a flourish of unconcealed glee. My intimate concerns had pulled me away from our project, and Ivor was no longer angry with me for my lack of attention. We had hours and hours of footage for a movie that would last, at most, twenty minutes, and as we'd soon see, Ivor was the one who mainly worked on it over the next few days until my departure. From this perspective I can see that we no longer had any reason to linger at the theater, and had we left then, everything would have been different, without the coincidences that become destinies. Alma had vanished into the dressing room and hadn't yet come back out to the stage. Yes, today I know that we should have left at that moment. But, unfortunately, I was far from such a decision then. We were already helping to organize the celebration, food and drink were brought in from somewhere, and an agreeable mood was already in the making for the fifteen or so people who had put the production together and the two of us special guests. We should have expressed our gratitude to everybody, had a drink, and left. Asked the director to convey our congratulations to Alma. Slammed the door on our desires.

Say no.

Go home.

Find father.

There I was out on the street. It was night already. The sweet taste of summer air, infrequent passersby, and, from afar, the screech of a tram on a curve. Good old familiar Vienna. One of my cities. In the other cities I went from being a foreigner to being a domesticated foreigner, and finally to the right of citizenship. With Vienna it was the other way around, from full citizenship, through an estranged occasional host who only passed through, to what I am today: a man returned from a private odyssey who slipped in under an alias and isn't certain he landed on the right Ithaca, even though everything seems to shout that this is, indeed, the place of his life's origin. I stood on the road for a few minutes and had a look at the buildings I had seen so many times, the sidewalk, so familiar, the contours of the city, so much itself. With a slow step I returned to the hotel. Because I hadn't been able to tear my thoughts away from that Sarajevo evening, I'd been nearly locked in at the cinema. There evidently hadn't been an audience for another showing of *Homo Faber*. I could hear them locking the entrance as they shut the lights off again inside. I hadn't been bothered by the dark at that moment; indeed, the voices, laughter, clinking of glasses at our Sarajevo party, the songs, faces, even the ordinary background sounds of the siege . . . felt closer, more accessible.

The director was overjoyed with the opening night and he'd breathed a sigh of relief, or so he said, when he heard how pleased we were with the footage we'd shot. After a glass of wine he had to unbutton his shirt and then loosen his tie. We, too, were warming up from the excitement and the drinks. We talked about the play with the director and praised his work, and Mr. Big Belly made no secret of the fact that Alma deserved most of the credit, for, as he said, what was one, though only one, of the "high points of my career." The exaggerations were of the usual variety.

People took seats at the tables, sat on chairs they'd pulled out, or perched on the first rows of theater seats. Holding a glass they kept filling, I moved from cluster to cluster and all in all I felt terrific, even a little surprised by all the changes in mood and condition I had been through that day. All of us were waiting for Alma. I'd already wondered where she was hiding, thinking this late arrival to her own party was perhaps the behavior of a diva. The usual pretension of actors, which I have always despised, didn't bother me with Alma. And then somebody reported that she wasn't in the dressing room. A search began. Nobody could imagine she'd left to go home without a word. The mood deflated. Everybody had been looking forward to seeing the star, and her absence put a damper on the party that was only just starting. My souring mood, I admit, was of a different sort. This became clear to me when I set down my glass and began thinking it was time for me, too, to go home. I'd stayed in hopes that I'd be able to smooth things over with Alma. Suddenly I realized my aging heart was having trouble admitting it had been beaten. *Suck it up,* I thought as I headed for the door, laughing at myself—the fifty-year-old madman. I didn't even say good-bye to Ivor. I didn't want to taint his evening. But as I was reaching for the door handle, the door flung open toward me. There stood Alma, breathless.

"Mr. Richter?!"

"I thought you'd gone?" I stuttered, still reaching for the vanished handle.

"Uh, sorry, but . . . ," she said speaking quickly, "I couldn't resist it and ran over to Father's place. He was so thrilled about the opening night . . . Luckily, his place is nearby. I told him all about the show and tried to persuade him to come back with me."

"It wasn't prudent to go rushing off like that . . . without a word. We were alarmed."

"Nothing is prudent these days, is it? But he wouldn't. He's feeling too frail; that's why he couldn't attend our opening night, the excitement was too much for him."

"What a shame, I mean, that he missed seeing the play, but . . ."

"He even asked me to stay, but I couldn't. I simply couldn't."

"You should have. Something might have happened to you. Listen to the gunfire. I mean, you need to be careful . . ." I was sounding like an old codger. "I mean, this isn't New York, if you know what I mean . . ."

"Since when do you have such concern for me, Mr. Richter?" interrupted Alma, looking at me with curiosity. "I thought you were not so fond of me."

"Well, our interactions haven't exactly filled me with a special glow of joy," I started in the old vein, "but I'd still be sorry if something were to happen to you, especially after such a fine performance."

"Did you like it? Really?"

"I haven't enjoyed myself so much in ages. Congratulations!"

"Even though you didn't understand a word?"

"Plenty. It was enough to see you onstage. Superb."

"Thank you." The compliments pleased her. "Thank you. I might even forgive you your cynicism. Maybe . . . But where were you headed just now? We're standing by the door."

"I don't know. I guess I needed a breath of fresh air," I lied, and meanwhile the remaining shred of healthy reason in my brain was commanding me to go home immediately.

"A breath of fresh air?! You thought you'd take a little stroll, did you . . . ?! Well, this isn't Paris, Mr. Richter . . . You're in Sarajevo. Be a little more careful why don't you."

"Since when do you have such concern for me, Mrs. Filipović? I thought you were not so fond of me."

"Well, our interactions haven't exactly filled me, as you said, with a special glow of joy . . ."

We burst out laughing and then said, in unison, "*Let's go in!*" She took me by the arm and in we went to our friends.

We applauded Alma and didn't forget the effusive director or the agile manager; Mr. Faber acknowledged our appreciation while guzzling his many drinks; the young men and women from the company received their much-deserved share of the praise; and then all of them, at the manager's prompting, clapped for Ivor and me, and even Alma raised a glass to us, wishing us a good documentary. The antagonism was clearly behind us, and I had begun to see our quarrels as a sign of attraction. And then the power suddenly went out. We lit candles, sat around the table, and one of the young men picked up a guitar. I sang along when I recognized a song from the international repertoire, noting with some regret that I didn't know the newest tunes. It was touching to see people's faces in the glow of the candles. Ivor sat across the table. I raised my glass to him with gratitude.

At one point the playing and singing stopped and back we came to reality. It was difficult to ignore. There had been hopes the day would bring resolution in a different arena. Everybody knew Mitterrand had left having completed a mission that was of no help to us; the hopes of this morning were dashed. We exchanged several bitter comments, suddenly without a shred of optimism. Then we stopped talking; somebody nervously tapped their lighter on the table; the young man with the guitar leaned his head helplessly on the instrument, strumming the notes of a soulful *sevdalinka*; and others smoked and looked around like people trapped in forebodings of the dark days before us. I kept my eyes on Alma. She met my gaze. Then an actor began reciting a poem. Ivor came over and whispered to me that the poem was one by Zbigniew Herbert, a poet I admired, and that it was "Report from the Besieged City," a poem I, regrettably, did not recall. Ivor conveyed the gist of Herbert's lines, which the poet had written for a different context, a different siege, but the poem and our friend's voice compelled us to hear that today it was saying something vital to us alone of all people on earth. I felt a shiver as Ivor translated the lines about the chronicler of the siege, the enemies taking turns, the siege going on since time immemorial, the defense of the city and its ruins, the one who will be the last to carry the city within himself on the roads of exile and who will be the city, about looking in the face of hunger, fire, and death—but not *betrayal!*—dreams, which are all that has not been humiliated . . .

Our faces flickered in the rhythm of the burning candle. The voice dropped. Herbert's report was cruelly precise. It reminded me of verses by Lawrence Durrell from a poem that bore the name "Sarajevo" and which I'd come across in Vienna while preparing for this trip. I copied it into my notebook and later read it several times to myself, trying to imagine the city Durrell visited during his stay as a diplomat in Yugoslavia.

> And down at last into this lap of stone
> Between four cataracts of rock: a town
> Peopled by sleepy eagles . . .

Everyone turned to me. My memory had retained the disorderly assortment of lines, which I went on reciting:

> Where minarets have twisted up like sugar
> And a river, curdled with blond ice, drives on
> Tinkling among the mule-teams and the
>   mountaineers,
> Under the bridges and the wooden trellises
> Which tame the air and promise us a peace
> Harmless with nightingales. None are singing now.

> No history much? Perhaps. Only this ominous
> Dark beauty flowering under veils,
> Trapped in the spectrum of a dying style . . .

I stopped and looked at the faces around me before I gave the last two lines:

> A village like an instinct left to rust,
> Composed around the echo of a pistol-shot.

I stopped. The solemn faces regarded me without a word. "Lawrence Durrell, his poem 'Sarajevo,'" I said, a little sheepish, and they clapped, though just as solemn. I must have blushed. I looked at Alma. She hadn't clapped. I thought her eyes were shining—Durrell's *ominous dark beauty?*—or was that me hoping? My verses had touched her. When the clapping died down she began reciting in a voice that still rings in my ears, something which, I admit, I felt was meant for me alone, though she recited it for everyone. How fitting were the lines she addressed me with, how true they were, so true that they could stand at the beginning of this chronicle I'm writing, being a very different *report from a besieged city*:

> There's no new land, my friend, no
> New sea; for the city will follow you,
> In the same streets you'll wander endlessly,
> The same mental suburbs slip from youth to age,
> In the same house go white at last—
> The city is a cage.
> No other places, always this
> Your earthly landfall, and no ship exists
> To take you from yourself. Ah! don't you see
> Just as you've ruined your life in this
> One plot of ground you've ruined its worth
> Everywhere now—over the whole earth?

I had started when the young man shook my shoulder. He'd looked alarmed. He clearly hadn't expected to find anyone in the dark, empty cinema. He apologized that there would be no more showings this evening and asked me to leave. He probably thought I'd dozed off. I mumbled an apology and left. *For the city will follow you . . .* I repeated these lines to myself while walking through the streets of Vienna on my way back to the hotel, just as I'd repeated them—perhaps even with my lips moving—that evening as I followed Alma's every word. We spoke the poem together, our epitaph ominously carved in stone from the outset. Long ago I'd committed Durrell's English rendering of Cavafy's poem "The City" to memory. "The City" at that time might have been the Vienna I'm walking through tonight, but today I know Alma was right, though she couldn't have known it. There is truly no other land, no other sea; wherever I go the city will follow me after I leave it (that must be Herbert's *worst of all—the face of betrayal*). I left the city of Durrell's poem, Herbert's besieged city. Cavafy's *city* that is a *cage*. And just as I ruined it there, as the poem says, I ruined my life the whole earth over.

And, sad to say, not just mine . . .

The lightbulb flickered on after the poems' last line. The generators had been repaired at last, and the applause that was heard again was for both Alma and the anonymous repairman. As if we were fortunate that things turned out that way, the music began to play again, Alma smiled at me, and I raised my glass and drank to her. Dancing started, the lyrical moment had passed, and the party could resume. I waited to summon the courage to ask her for a dance. I explained my lack of self-confidence with the fact that she was a married woman, these were her friends, I was a recipient of their hospitality, and flirting in such a situation was not the wisest idea. I drank and watched her dance. I envied the director and Mr. Faber, whose real name I've forgotten. I tried looking to the side, I tried talking with others, I told myself it's not prudent to deepen the friendship, it's inadvisable . . . And a minute later we were dancing and I was asking her whether people find each other by destiny or coincidence.

I reached the door to my haven. I don't believe I'll ever leave it again. When we left the theater together that evening—quite drunk, giddy, and tired—we ran immediately into patrolmen who were satisfied with our passes and the manager's words, and they immediately said we should proceed straight to our homes. People arranged to stay in nearby apartments, and two or three of them even set out with us. But though Alma's place was near Ivor's, I didn't suggest I'd see her home. As I said, she was a married woman. The director assigned that role to himself. Then, though we hadn't exchanged any words since dancing together, she seized a moment just before we went our separate ways, when we suddenly found ourselves a little farther off from the others.

"Who are you, Richard?" she asked.

"What do you mean?"

"Exactly that—who are you? Simple."

"Listen, I am trying to understand that myself," I said sincerely. "And I'm having a rough go of it."

"And you came to Sarajevo to figure this out?"

"Yes, in a way. Not perhaps at the most auspicious moment, I know."

"Okay. If I can be of any help to you, I'd be most happy . . ."

"I'll hold you to that, Alma."

"Good night, Mr. Richter."

I was glad to reach the room. I threw myself on the bed and plunged my head into the pillow. The young man at the front desk had spotted me as I entered the hotel, and called, "Good night, Mr. Schneider!" I waved to him. I knew the night would not be a good one for Mr. Schneider, for entirely different reasons from the ones that kept Mr. Richter awake in Sarajevo as that Sunday, June 28, drew to a close. Mr. Richter was taken by delightful anticipatory shivers and so, not knowing what else to do, he plunged his head into his pillow in much the same way. Mr. Richter shivered because he couldn't stop thinking about Alma Filipović, and Mr. Schneider was shivering because he'd destroyed her life. The two of them should never have met in the same cage.

3

When Ivor woke me the next morning, I couldn't have known that the countdown to my last days in Sarajevo had begun the night before. I couldn't have known that at dawn on July 7 I'd go briefly to the apartment, and within a few hours I'd be gone forever from the city. Even a few days earlier I couldn't have imagined myself leaving. It was, I might say, the furthest thing possible from my mind. When Ivor woke me, I couldn't have known that just before me were the days that would seal my fate, the days that would crown with insufferable knowledge the rarest moment of joy, which at long last I'd come to know. Leaving was the only way I had of containing the tragedy, preventing it from reaching, at least in its sickening fullness, its last victims.

No, I couldn't have known that morning that the end of my stay in Sarajevo was so close. I woke up, in fact, absurdly happy. I listened to the reports from the Front and from the city, the international reactions, all with equanimity, and even decided, with a dose of cheer, to embark with Ivor on the adventure of visiting the television studio.

We jumped into a BBC vehicle—one of the upsides of some of my remaining international contacts—and began careering through the newer parts of town. I noted an exceptionally high degree of destruction—the gutted high-rise buildings along the avenue—after the barely three months of war since the first shots rang out before the now shell-pitted Assembly. One could almost feel the nearness of the Bosnian Serb positions; the sniper nests were quiet by the Jewish cemetery, or was that merely how it seemed as we hurtled down the street, as concerned about a car crash as about sniper bullets?

We were given space at the television studio building where we could work on our movie. It was with a remarkable burst of joy that we went to work that day. We explored our ideas. Ivor was gratified to see me so interested, though he was still chafing over my earlier neglect. This serious young man left nothing to chance: he cared deeply about the project, and I must have hurt him deeply with my behavior. But what could I say? Whenever I left my personal quest, my pilgrimage, behind completely, we functioned like a perfect orchestra. I liked to discuss things with Ivor, to rein in his creative overreach, to hold fatherly sermons and to accept his stings, the sort only a rebellious son or younger brother might come up with.

But, unfortunately, he couldn't keep me with him for long. The events of the previous day had turned me decisively toward the city, where I believed the answer to the questions of my origin was waiting, or so it felt, staring me in the face. I had no inkling that everything was going to play out with dizzying speed, despite my best intentions, just when I was most reluctant to pull back the veil from the events of 1941. We shield ourselves from certain desires; this is all I can still say. But these desires do not easily tolerate being ignored. Just when we think we're rid of them, they come surging in as a nightmare.

Eventually, I left the work on the movie to Ivor. He grumbled, but there was nothing he could do. I persuaded him he could do this part on his own, and justified this by saying I needed to write. That was, after all, why I was here! I decided to go back to the center of town. Ivor, my good friend, stayed on at the television studio. He could even spend the night there if he needed to, and behind those thick gray walls he was reasonably safe. He had everything he needed, the equipment and the people, to help him finish the project. And, as he said, he didn't care to test his luck every day on Sniper Alley. I promised I'd stop in from time to time and take part in the final editing once he'd sorted through the footage. He, in turn, promised he'd return home whenever he had the chance. The events to come would reunite us, sad to say, for only a few more happy moments, and all that remains of them are this handful of photographs. I'd drive right by the television studio on the morning of July 7, the gray building flashing by the window of the UN transporter. I thought of Ivor then, curled up on a studio floor or, bleary with lack of sleep, staring at a screen on which my face, too, appeared.

I may have woken up that day in high spirits, without dwelling much on what was happening in the city, but I certainly did get a sense later of what being out on the streets was like. I am not saying enough here about what was going on with the war. As if I've surrendered to the dictates of my manuscript, letting it lead me, letting me draw the city into the story in the ways best suited to it. (And besides, to write about the Sarajevo siege as would a journalist, a newspaper reporter, even as I might write an essay, would be to write something very different from what I have here. If I could be the author of that piece, I'd be one happy man.) The city is an essential part of this story. Only later did I realize the degree to which my story had melded with the city, or the city with my story, and that it governed the progress of my private chronicle of the Sarajevo siege, which is woven—one of the thousands of threads— into its tragic tapestry. This is why I can't possibly avoid writing about the city. So I must say that Dobrinja was shelled for hours that day, and other parts of the city were targeted as well (five killed, forty wounded); the images of the wounded and dead were broadcast on state television news, and the heedless behavior of the enemy continued—they shot again at ambulances, killing another six people. Five foreign journalists were wounded near the airport, and a reporter from *Libération* was seriously wounded in the leg. The UN was finally supervising the airport, and humanitarian aid was starting to arrive . . . An attentive chronicler of the siege, and there certainly are those in this city, will enter this news into their chronology of dishonor under the date June 29, 1992.

In my memory, particularly in contrast to what was to come, that day will remain one of the more peaceful ones. Or perhaps that was just me. The excitement I felt certainly owed something to the events of the night before, though I did fend off thoughts of *her*. My condition of mild giddiness quelled the agitation stoked by the visit to the synagogue. The lovely day was a personal cease-fire. Sad to say, it didn't last. But the sudden calm of that day helped me finally to drop off to sleep with ease, sleep soundly, and wake up the next morning rested. As if my body were bracing for what was coming.

I rose, shaved, ate breakfast, and didn't succeed in dodging the question buzzing around my head and loudly demanding an answer: *What now?* I wouldn't even have the time to mull it over when the answer came straight to my door. Meanwhile, as I'd later realize, there were two people looking for me in Sarajevo. It was only due to their keen detecting skills and to chance that they stumbled, sooner or later, on a person who could direct them to where I was staying, and this determined the sequence of their visits. Today, it seems that had the first visitor lingered just a little longer, all of this might—I can't bear that hollow phrase yet again—yes, everything might have played out differently . . . Nonetheless, when he appeared that day at my door, Simon had the honor of being the one to inaugurate the last stage of my stay in Sarajevo and accelerate the countdown.

But first, the knock. I was startled when I saw a little girl at the door. She told me in surprisingly capable English that somebody was looking for me and was already on his way up to the apartment. I have to admit I was alarmed that perhaps the person on his way up might be from one of the armies, or the police, or a search, that maybe they were looking for Ivor; and the loud steps I could hear sounded like a stalwart person in uniform, with important medals spread across his chest. I felt a huge wave of relief, but still confusion, when the guest hollered, *"Buenos días!"* and roared with laughter . . .

It was Simon. I let him in. By daylight I could observe him more closely. He had the bushy gray beard of a hermit and the tousled white hair that flew in every direction around the cap he had tossed on his brow, and was wearing a mantle of some kind. In short he looked like some sort of unofficial emissary from God, a defrocked priest. He said with his characteristic English that he wished to see me, that we had had a nice conversation the other day at the synagogue, and as we hadn't, he said, exchanged phone numbers . . . Besides, he was forced to express his doubt as to the smooth functioning of the public services of late, so he had the lack of *courtoisie* to visit me directly in my place of dwelling so that I, he said, would not have to trouble myself finding him.

"So kind of you, Simon! I am glad you managed to leave the synagogue, though I can't imagine how you did it. I thought I'd leave events to bring us together as fate would have it."

I was reluctant to admit that I'd been expecting him somehow or hoping I'd run into him again. At my words, Simon just waved dismissively, surprised at my naïveté.

"Mistake, *compañero*. Events generally, after all, take you in a direction you do not wish to go. Did you just leap into the river of events and swim out on the Sarajevo shore? Eh? Just like that? Not knowing where you were going or why?"

"How did you find me, Simon?" This interested me more.

"My dear *haver*, you'd never have found me even if you'd gone looking for me." He laughed, biting at the same time into an apple he'd found on the kitchen table. "So I made this little effort."

"Still, I don't get it. You didn't want my address or anything . . . I am staying here in somebody else's apartment."

"What good will the address do for me in Sarajevo? It would only have confused me. The addresses keep changing here, anyway. Like, the other day a shell ripped up a façade on Titova Street, and underneath appeared a plaque with the name of the old Nazi Ante Pavelić. *Brrrr* . . . Believe you me that gave me the shivers, it did, that moment. I'm an old man; I am beginning to believe that everything is possible. That is how I rely only on my nose. I smelled it . . . yes, that's how I found you, heh-heh . . ."

"And how do I smell?"

"Like a baffled cat," he answered, confident in his diagnosis.

"Like a baffled cat?! Now I really am baffled."

"Yes. A lost cat that can no longer find its way home following the regular system of smells, smells differently. While still seeking a thread that will guide it to its haven, it tries to master the new and unfamiliar territory, leaves a new smell, creates a new system for a new life, just in case the return home becomes impossible. That is how I found you. Regrettably, I cannot help you return home, as I do not know where your home is."

"Interesting."

There was something unsettling in Simon's words. I wondered who this peculiar man here before me was. Maybe he'd followed me. His secrecy was hitting its mark, and at the same time it sounded like pure rubbish. I attributed this weakness to myself, an oversensitivity leading me to see everywhere my own circumstances. What cats were these now, these smells, new life, home, nonsense . . . Simon clearly saw on my face that I was uncomfortable and he slapped me on the shoulders with glee, guffawing.

"Hey, don't be so serious, as if you're the judge, not me, heh-heh . . . That was a joke, the sense-of-smell thing. As far as cats are concerned, I have a few . . . but, fine, they are a topic for another day."

At those last words he sat down in an armchair in the living room and began studying the paintings on the walls. Then he looked out the window, taking in the scene, concluded that the position wasn't bad, in the military sense, of course—that is what matters most these days—and ate another apple. I watched him. Simon had to know what I was thinking; he had to know I was dying to ask whether he had anything for me. Then he spoke.

"You see, Richter," he said, "the days are numbered. The noose tightens."

"I don't understand; what do you mean?" I thought about how everything this man said sounded ominous. And ominously truthful.

"The truth will out. It always does. Awareness. And then will come the misery." He was at the window again, watching the children playing in the yard.

"What misery? What are you talking about?"

"Well, what we conversed about at the synagogue. What else?"

"Ah yes . . ." I tried to remain calm. I thought perhaps through Simon I'd found a shortcut to the solution of my riddle. "Is there something here? Do you know something, Simon?"

"Of course there is; of course I know." Simon looked at me, surprised as if this was something that was patently obvious. "Don't get too excited. This is destiny. The curse."

"The curse?"

"Yes, like I said, the curse. The knowledge will come slowly, then the misery."

"You're scaring me."

"I don't know what you have to be afraid of. Sure, it's one thing to be concerned for the sake of a friend, but it's not you who will suffer. You, Richter, can walk away freely. This is, essentially, none of your business."

"What have you learned, Simon?" Now I was impatient. Simon turned again. When he was perplexed, he'd press his lips together and tilt his head first to one side, then to the other, theatrically, as if he could not understand what sort of people these were, what these questions were, what nonsense . . .

"Learned? There is nothing here to learn. Everything is clear. I knew from the first day."

"You knew the person's identity?! Why didn't you tell me, Simon?"

"What do you mean, the person's identity? I'm not talking of a person, man! I'm speaking of the curse."

"The curse?!" I was losing my composure. "What are you talking about?! What do you mean!"

I believe I was shouting. I'd had enough of this conversation, the torment he was putting me through; I wanted to know everything right away, and right when I'd resolved to chase this thing out into the open, Simon spoke softly, "Why, the curse that is destroying cities, *Mensch*! Sarajevo is done for. Nothing will pull us out of this. Our last hope faded yesterday, or rather all hope of hoping faded. Who knows how long the siege will last. Winter is coming, freezing-cold temperatures, misery . . . I can't imagine what could be unclear here? Why so agitated?"

"Oh, that!" I shouted and began to laugh. "That's what you're talking about? Yes, now I understand, ha-ha, oh forgive me, ha-ha . . ."

This only astonished Simon all the more. He was bewildered, tapped his finger to his head a few times and asked, *"Ferikt?"* The way he mispronounced the German word only made me laugh all the harder. I apologized, but I was gasping for breath. Simon shrugged and again he flung himself into the armchair, waiting angrily for me to stop laughing over something that was so inappropriate for the guffaws that were erupting from me. As if a huge boulder had been rolled off my back, I couldn't stop.

And then again a knock.

It was the same little girl. And before I had the chance to get a word in edgewise, she launched in with: *"Somebody asks for you again. I ask why and she tells me it's important. I told her wait outside. What should I do? Let her in?"* She was so fetching that I was almost overcome by a new fit of laughter, but realizing that in fact I had somebody who was looking after me in the building, who was watching out for me and who alone had the power to issue passes to my guests, I quickly regained my composure and in a serious, conspiratorial tone asked her whether she'd checked on who this was, had she undertaken all the necessary precautions when keeping an eye on our entranceway. My assistant confirmed indeed she had, and she whispered to me that she thought the person in question was "okay."

"Then, do you think it would be all right for you to let her in?" I asked, and the little girl nodded, saluted, and off she went toward the stairwell.

"Hey, wait! What's your name, lieutenant?"

"Emina."

"From this day forward you're my right-hand girl, Emina." I grabbed a can of French beef, which I'd recently brought home to Ivor's delight. "I have something here for you."

"Wow! Super!" She quickly snatched the can. "Thanks. Mama will be so happy."

"How old are you?" I called after her.

"Eleven," she said, excited, and added, growing serious, "but I feel much older."

"You look older, too."

"Thank you, captain." Her eyes shone, then she saluted me again and off she went to bring the guest.

Emina ran along in front of Alma, shouting, *"Here she is, captain!"* while I tried to muster a proper welcome. As if I were in some sort of trap—Simon's baffled cat?—I started smoothing my hair, straightening my shirt, pants . . . Only later did I notice Simon behind my back pitying me with gestures and saying, in French no less, *"Dignité, Richter! Dignité! Ce n'est qu'une femme! À votre âge?!"* I didn't have the time to debate him. Alma was already here in front of me.

"Good day, captain," she said. Her hair swinging, dressed as if for a summer stroll through a chic vacation resort, she was wearing ballet flats, a knee-length skirt showing off her shapely legs, just as her shirt, clinging to her slender frame, drew one's eye to her throat at which flashed a silver necklace. Emina, Simon, and I must have been staring at her as if entranced. For several moments nobody knew what to say. Emina glanced back and forth from one of us to another with a question in her eyes ("I'm the lieutenant," she told Alma); Simon grew solemn and kept his eyes on Alma; she was slightly startled by this odd assemblage; and, stuttering, I finally introduced everyone.

I invited her in. One glance sufficed to explain to Emina that she should return to her sentry post, and Simon suddenly glanced out the hallway window, as if checking where the sun stood, and concluded, "Hmm, it's getting late. I'm oh so sorry, but I must hasten. I must feed my cats."

"What cats are these again? Wait, Simon. We didn't have a chance to talk."

"Next time." He took a pencil and scrap of paper from his pocket and wrote down an address. Once more he shot a glance, suspiciously, at Alma and then said, "Look for me. I'm not sure I understand what is happening, but I believe this could be a very urgent matter. I might be able to help you, I mean, with that friend of yours, you know . . ."

"Yes, yes, of course. I'll find you. Now that I have the address."

"Bye."

And like that he was gone. Nutty old man.

"You have not only right-hand girls but very interesting friends," said Alma.

"If you only knew where I find them . . . but let's leave that for now."

Alma apologized. She felt uncomfortable to be disturbing me, but there was no guarantee we'd see each other again, so she'd decided to look for me. She hoped she wasn't a bother. She said she'd enjoyed the evening and the time we'd spent together had somewhat changed the impression she'd first formed of me. How had she found me? Ivor had once told her where he lived, so she'd decided to see what she could do. If it hadn't worked, she'd have left us meeting again to the fortunes of war. After two or three people helped her locate the building, she came across the little girl who led her to me, for a few bills, it's true.

"Yes, that is my lieutenant," I confirmed.

"A slightly corrupt lieutenant," Alma concluded.

"What can you do, this is a war . . ."

Actually, she didn't want to stay long. If I wasn't opposed, she'd take me around town, though taking a walk sounded absurd in this situation, she said. That is, she hoped I'd be willing to escort her around while she took care of some errands she had to see to today. Yes, indeed, why not, now that I'd finished my work, I might as well stretch my legs . . .

The day was a little quieter, at least in this part of town. A warm summer day full of people who'd come out onto the streets as soon as they'd felt there was no immediate danger. No one can live in cellars all the time, but then how many lives does the first shell take when it ends the temporary lull? I, too, had picked up this bad habit in the besieged city. Perhaps this time I was even less wary. In a way I was relieved when I saw Alma. Simon had managed again to disrupt my equilibrium. Perhaps I should avoid the oddball. Maybe he was pulling me out onto thin ice; perhaps he was toying with me and my nerves. I tucked the scrap of paper into my pocket. Alma's presence was helping me forget my unhappy search. In a way she had also saved my honor—my "dignity," as Simon said—because I had a compelling urge to look for her myself. It would have been preposterous for me at this age, like a university professor bored with his career and marriage, to chase a young woman, who was married to boot, to ask after her around Sarajevo with pathetic excuses . . . This way I simply went along as her escort, worry-free. And after all, I consoled my pride, she had sought me out.

She takes me to the Markale open market. Alma says one can come to know the inner spirit of Sarajevo here. She isn't referring to the black-market sale of everyday food items that are ever scarcer for ordinary folks, but to the things that filled the apartments and homes of local people just the day before. And it's true: we find people here who are setting out their valuables for sale, or at least the things with which they're willing to part. Today they're selling books—I muse as I follow Alma through the crowd, listening to her chat with people, greet, inquire, move on—along with the less valuable paintings, porcelain, useless decorative things, dominoes, tobacco pipes, antiques . . . And tomorrow they'll bring out the silver, gold, diamonds, precious items; they'll sell their collections, amassed for years, all kinds of things, the costliest dinnerware, the most intricate Persian rugs, the family heirlooms that will be valued in handfuls of rice, kilos of flour, two or three eggs, spoonfuls of oil . . . Simon is right, the noose is tightening. First will come knowledge, then despair. Perhaps the looters who profit from the anarchy and cart things out of abandoned apartments sense this or already know. How surprised their owners—now perhaps off somewhere in a refugee camp or over on the Bosnian Serb side—would be to see how little their belongings are selling for that day at the Sarajevo wartime market!

Alma tells me that at first she'd buy rare books or the occasional small household item, even some antique jewelry, but now she realizes it was lunacy to think the war would be over quickly, so sometimes she stops by this place just to see what the city has been hiding. Now she's no longer surprised, she says, to find the most improbable things here. The sealed cellars have been opening, as have old safes and drawers and the partitioned sewage tunnels (some may even run under the encirclement, far from the siege, who knows?), and works of art, stolen or stowed away, may see the light of day; somebody one day might wrap up a kilo of precious meat in a worthless Rembrandt self-portrait.

"Why not," I say. Cities scrawl their history onto walls, in fact, and not into treacherous and corruptible human memory. This is the only way. Do we not register our lives in all those objects, in diaries, in jewelry, in carefully dried roses that illustrate in the best possible way the fragility of our memories and emotions, and so our lives mingle with the life of the city, with other similar attempts at marking our passage across the earth. And so both people and the city inscribe themselves where they can, what they want us to know and think about them, as well as their secrets. Perhaps we wouldn't like everything that these opened cellars, rusty safes, or the inside pockets of our grandfather's suits might disclose. Perhaps in those hidden sewage tunnels there are thousands of fat rats that will gladly, if disturbed, launch an attack, obstruct the passage, and in doing so contribute in their way to the siege of the city.

We examine the books on offer. People are selling their home libraries, mainly older people who no longer receive their regular pension. Most of the books are in Cyrillic, or they are works of Marxist literature. For books in this last category, nobody thinks they can be of help to anybody. Among them there are a few that still command a price. People find it hard to part with their favorite books, and there is no guarantee that they'll sell you the book in the end. People like that are extremely rare, and besides, the market is unforgiving here at Markale. There are even people who sell books they have found in other people's apartments. One among them set a price—each book costs one deutsche mark. I'm not sure how far he'll get with that. To buy books instead of pasta, for example, is pure lunacy. Yet many people gather around him, looking, leafing, handing back, reaching for their wallet and then changing their minds . . . A pile of books, tossed one on top of another, rises there beside him, clearly brought in from all over. Here and there I recognize the name of an author, a title. Spinoza, Hegel, Plato, Hobbes, Homer, Dostoyevsky, Cervantes, Stendhal, Nietzsche, Babel, Musil, Joyce . . . Old friends, they're all here. Now they're only paper, things which should be gotten rid of for at least some sort of price, because soon they'll be superfluous, maybe only worth a little as kindling. One deutsche mark! "I have the feeling," I say to Alma, "that the deutsche mark has never been more precious."

I find some teenagers selling only very old books. They must have robbed an antique bookstore or picked up the books that a shell blast had scattered from somebody's valuable library. They have no idea what it is they're offering. I begin to believe Alma when she says we will come to be surprised by all the things the city has been hiding. I quickly pull out a dusty and tattered volume of Diderot and d'Alambert's *Encyclopédie* . . . I see a shabby school anthology of classics from the late monarchy in the first years of the last century; I find and leaf through the technical statistical study *Das Bauwesen in Bosnien und der Hercegovina vom Beginn der Occupation durch die Österr.-ung. Monarchie bis in das Jahr 1887*, edited by a Mr. Edmund Stix, then a first Gallimard edition of Malraux's *La condition humaine* from April 1933; I skip over a number of titles in the local language; I see Enzo Strecci's *Canzoniere*, the first issue of Karl Kraus's journal *Das Fackel*, a velvet-bound edition of de Sade's *Justine*, and finally I pull up a German translation of Shakespeare's *Merchant of Venice* from 1935, printed in Gothic, missing, of course, Shylock's famous monologue from the third act. I recite it to myself from memory: *Hath not a Jew eyes? Hath not a Jew hands . . . If you prick us, do we not bleed? If you tickle us, do we not laugh? If you poison us, do we not die? And if you wrong us, shall we not revenge?*

I ask one of them where he'd found the books, but he just shrugs. He asks whether they are worth much. "For somebody maybe," I tell him.

Alma calls to me. She has found something intriguing at an antique dealer's table. She shows me a pocket watch, the image of a girl etched on the lid who, muse-like in a glade of trees, is reclining her head on her arm. She is clothed in nothing but a diaphanous shawl, and her eyes are fixed with an intent gaze on the distant horizon. On the opposite side is etched a soldier, his gun laid across his knees, on guard and gazing with melancholy eyes over the fields into the distance, to wherever his beloved is. Alma opens the watch. We are surprised to see it still works. On the inside of the lid is an inscription in German: *Dearest Rudi, with every second the war comes near to its end, and we—to one another. Your Teresa, Prague, 1914.*

We wonder what happened to the star-crossed Prague lovers and how this watch found its way to Sarajevo. The seller has no idea. The lovers' estimate of when the First World War would end was overly optimistic. I wonder whether Teresa went on waiting for him through all the years of the war. The cold Prague nights require a warm embrace, is my opinion, and a soldier's grief requires respite, so I wouldn't have been surprised if Rudi found consolation in the traveling Galician brothels. Alma doesn't much like that epilogue. But she isn't so sentimental as to think that the lovers were reunited after the war, married, and lived happily ever after until, say, 1939. Had that happened, how did the watch come to be in Sarajevo? Alma thinks that in that unlikely case, ham-fisted Rudi got his watch stolen by a Bosnian buddy from his regiment. No. Alma is certain that Rudi, having undergone ghastly wartime traumas, as his Bosnian buddy knew so well, chose to spend his leave, at the urging of his trench mate, in Sarajevo in the summer of 1918, where he met the buddy's sister. Love had its way, and despite his Bosnian buddy's initial protests—our buddy, after all, wasn't keen on having his sister marry his best trench mate with whom he'd frequented those brothels, and he knew the degree of distress somebody felt who'd fought in the Austro-Hungarian army for nearly four long years and was, to say the least, a touch *überspannt!*—it culminated in a wedding. On the second day after he was married, Rudi sold Teresa's pocket watch, deserted the Austrian army, and as the Serbian royal army marched into Sarajevo, he hid in the attic of the family home of his charming spouse.

To parry her at least a little, I claim that things went a little differently. Oh yes, Rudi, remembering the pleasures Teresa often gave him in the cellar of her father's tavern, and remaining at least a little sentimentally attached to his former life in Prague, hid the gift. Now it is brought out into the open, like all the things for sale at the Markale market in the summer of 1992. "And Teresa?" asks Alma. "What happened to her?" Teresa gave up her work at the tavern and left it all behind in 1915, running off with the first officer who held a rank higher than lieutenant to appear in her life, thereafter living the nomadic life of the regiment whose wanderings were guided by the fickle fortunes of war. The grief of her father was boundless, which goes without saying.

We chuckle at these fates we shaped to the caprice of our fancy. In any case we kept the lovers alive: this calls for a celebration. We are in fine spirits, and I ask her if she wants the pocket watch.

"Then the message would have to be changed," she says. "If you were to give me this watch, what would you inscribe on the inside of the lid?"

"Dear Alma, I am not certain I can wait for the war to end. Your R. Sarajevo, summer 1992," I say quickly, pouncing on the chance.

I watch her, breathless, awaiting her answer. Surprised, she tries to divine the weight of the words I just said by studying my face. Then she spins around and goes on walking as if she didn't hear me, as if the last few minutes of the conversation didn't happen. She looks left and right, exhibiting genuine interest in the items on display, sparking brief conversations with the vendors; she asks for the price and moves slowly away. I will never forget her walk through the crowd of the wartime market. Not a sign that what I said was heard. I stand there, motionless, watch in hand. She finally turns around and beckons me to join her. Nothing has happened. The stroll can proceed. I embrace the game. During all this, the price of the watch has mysteriously risen from ten to twenty deutsche marks. The vendor clearly has been following our conversation. To my surprise, he just shrugs: this is a war market, no point in attributing emotions to things. I don't buy it. Ultimately, only Teresa and Rudi could have understood it—this story about nearing and distancing—in short, what wartime love is supposed to be like.

On we went in silence. I didn't have the courage to look at her. I told myself that an intelligent person should draw a conclusion from this. Hadn't Alma allowed me to extricate myself in the most painless manner possible from the mess I'd made with my lack of forethought? An advantage of being this old, I realized with bitterness, lay precisely in this, in the respect that others show you, their desire to preserve your dignity when you slip. Still, her indifference stung me. We climbed uphill in silence. I didn't ask where we were going. We walked side by side in silence.

"You aren't asking where we're going?" she said finally.

"You took me for a walk, Alma. I trust you completely."

"As I asked you to come along with me today, I'm obliged to tell you where we're going."

"I wait to hear with bated breath."

"I want to introduce you to my father. I told you so already. He and I are very close as you've seen. I visit him every day. I've already told him a lot about you. We have one of your books on the shelf that he remembers reading years ago. He is an avid reader and reads a great deal in German. I think he's eager to meet you."

"You mean right now? I don't know, can I go like this?" I protested.

"Come on, Richard."

"Fine, fine, whatever . . ." I agreed, though the truth was I'd have agreed to almost anything to stay with her for as long as I could. Even more than a single visit to an elderly gentleman, who promised to be only a mild bother. I asked where her father lived.

"Thank you," she said. "On Bjelave. Not far from here."

I didn't know where Bjelave was so I continued, "Anyway, it's always a pleasure to meet my readers. I never pass up the opportunity. Especially here in Sarajevo, where except for Ivor my only other reader may well be your father."

"Don't be so sure. Somewhere in that pile of books for sale for a deutsche mark, we might have found one of yours."

"That would finish me off. Though perhaps the market down there is the most objective way of evaluating literature. Perhaps all my novels together would bring enough for a decent Sarajevo omelet!"

We climbed up to the top of the hill. I tried to read the street names. I hadn't been good at remembering names for the neighborhoods, particularly those that were tricky to pronounce, let alone the street names. But there were a few that I'd memorized far too well. I felt sweat trickle down my back, and several droplets pooled in the lovely dip at the base of Alma's throat. I looked over at her now and then, my pride still a little stung. I kept up with her pace, trying to give the impression that the twenty-year difference between us was not glaring in terms of my physical condition. We soon reached the building where her father lived. We hadn't entered yet when an elderly neighbor explained to Alma that her father had just stepped out. Alma was surprised and concerned. Although he was quite old, her father hadn't given up his habits when he felt up to it. He'd go off for a walk, a visit to friends, a round of chess, the market. Alma had been urging him to stay in the apartment the last few days, "until things quiet down," but this clearly was not working. Had we left the market sooner, we'd have found him at home. "He doesn't usually venture out. I don't know what got into him today. He knew I'd be coming over." For a while she hesitated, musing whether we should wait for him up in the apartment. I convinced her there was no point in waiting. I wasn't burning with the desire to meet her father, especially not today. After what I said at the Markale market, it would feel odd to chat with the man, or flirt with his daughter in his home while we waited for him to return. But I promised I'd come to visit another day.

"I'm still here. There will be other opportunities."

"All right. Then at least see me home. I'll come back later."

"If we'd only gotten here a few minutes earlier . . . ," said Alma. *If I hadn't said what I said . . . ,* I thought, not knowing exactly what would have happened. On we walked. Perhaps the silence, which had grown between us back at the Markale, saved our lives. We walked beside each other, our shoulders brushing now and then, and we didn't pull back, we didn't pull away. And then we heard the whistle of the shell breaking the tenuous cease-fire in this neighborhood of Sarajevo. We had maybe a second or two to fling ourselves down behind a wall, and for me to draw Alma to me at the moment the blast reverberated.

The shell hit the roof of the building under which we crouched. The façade spewed bricks, plaster, wallpaper, and pieces of furniture from the top-floor apartment, all strewn around us on the road. We were coated in dust and plaster; nothing could be seen through the smoke, and we waited for our hearing to return, not knowing if we ourselves were groaning in pain or if we might hear others who'd been hit. I scrambled up and helped Alma to her feet. If somebody had passed us at that moment, they'd have seen two people touching each other, inspecting the other's limbs with both hands to make sure they were still alive. Not a drop of blood, only the grit of dust on pale skin, dust that had blanketed our hands, clothing, shoes, neck, and hair. If somebody had happened by, if somebody had looked out their window while the dust was settling around us, they'd see a man white with dust taking in his hands the face of a woman white with dust and kissing her. And they'd see the woman accept the kiss and then turn and continue walking down the street . . .

If only . . . then it might have . . . or wouldn't have . . . Again I am trapped in the painful game I've been playing over and over as I type this text. If I hadn't said what I said at the open market, if we hadn't been playing with the story of somebody else's love in a long-ago war, wasting valuable time, then we'd have reached Alma's father's apartment before he went out. If that had happened, we wouldn't have been strolling in silence, the shell wouldn't have exploded above our heads, it wouldn't have blanketed us in plaster spray, we wouldn't have kissed, we wouldn't have tasted the dust grit in each other's mouths. The ending to my cruel game is always the same: everything would have turned out differently. I could write thousands and thousands of pages of this manuscript, but I can't stop the events that are pounding at the door to my story, demanding to be let in and telling me clearly that I cannot escape myself, or that day, or what was to come.

This must be shock, I thought on my way back to Ivor's apartment. I'm still in shock. In the mirror I saw a dust-white man. I was surprised that despite my hair being thick, I didn't look as old as usual. More like a vaudeville entertainer, as if I'd slathered on cake makeup, the wrinkles had disappeared—all traces of aging were gone. Only my lips against my pale face looked oddly red. I touched them and told myself all of this was shock, just as the kiss had been. And in my state of shock, I could still see Alma walking away, and, finally, as if on a stage where the smoke has cleared, I saw myself standing there alone on the empty street.

I stripped off my clothes. The faucets produced no running water. I picked up the bottle in which we stored water and started slowly pouring from it, gradually rinsing away the filth, sweat, and dust all over me. It had been a long time since I'd felt my body so taut, firm, powerful, pulsing so positively, desirous of life. The shock, the anxiety, the dread, the doubt, the pain, the despair—all washed away, swirled down the drain, leaving calm and resolve. When I looked again in the mirror I could feel a change. As if I'd passed through a deranged rite of passage, now I'd rid myself of all traces of the ritual, all the grime of the obstacles I'd overcome, all the low blows of fate, all the intrigue and cunning of the enemy, and I'd earned the right to step into a new phase: I'd earned the right to have more. I decided to find Alma.

I sprinted to her apartment like a man possessed, ignoring the people shouting from their windows, the warnings from the few pedestrians I passed. I couldn't care less that distant detonations and bursts of gunfire echoed across the summer evening. I had already learned enough about the different calibers of the mortar and gun shells and all the different antiaircraft weapons whose munitions were raining down upon us. None of that interested me then; I ran through the streets while here and there deadly fireflies sliced across the Sarajevo sky above me. I followed only what I remembered of the route I'd taken once to Alma's apartment, and in my mad dash managed to lose my way, turn into streets I didn't know, backtrack hopelessly, and finally, breathless, arrive at her door. I knocked. Nobody opened. I knocked again. I feared she was refusing to open the door for me. I rang the neighbor's bell. I asked if they knew where she might be. I probably didn't look too trustworthy, asking in English, out of breath and impatient. To reassure them I explained this was urgent: we worked together; I had to find her. They said she had only barely survived the shelling that day; she'd come home and left an hour later. Perhaps she was at her father's. I said I'd wait. I was determined. I sat down on the step by her door. The neighbors slowly withdrew into their apartments, with suspicious sideways glances at the foreigner who was asking for Mrs. Filipović.

I don't know how long I sat there on the steps. It was completely dark. I thought of nothing but waiting. Perhaps somebody might have called this shock, but I knew I had never been thinking more clearly. How long did I sit there, waiting? A little less than an hour, perhaps? At one point I started shivering in the cool air in the stairwell. Alma hadn't come home, and my resolve had begun to flag. I knocked for the last time at the door. And then yet again for the last time.

I ventured out onto the dark street. I felt broken. I nearly sobbed. But tears were powerless over the hopelessness that had engulfed me. I imagined that someone who might have seen this man earlier as he ran, brimming with resolve, clearly on his way to meet his destiny, might now be watching him drag himself slowly along the same route in the opposite direction. All his strength sapped—perhaps the shock was only now abating?—and his age and anxiety surging back with more dread than ever. I was pained by the illusion, only moments before, that things, life, could be changed; the feeling that love—an old man's pitiful infatuation!—could correct the wrong course I'd pursued so long ago. I trudged toward home, longing to die, and loathing myself for lacking the strength to do it myself; I hoped something more precise would do it for me, a shell, a stray bullet, a sniper. I waded through a war that was not mine, and the war treated me like a foreigner that night. It had nothing to do with me; even as a victim I was of no interest. I encountered no patrols or soldiers; no one demanded my ID. They may have seen me moving phantom-like down the street. The war had already sent some into madness, and people were used to seeing them out and about, and perhaps wondered who was, in fact, the worse off. I probably looked exactly like one of the mad, lost in thought, deaf to reality, beyond a fear of war and death.

I reached Ivor's building and trudged slowly up the stairs to the apartment. I thought I'd never get there, that I'd be better off sitting down at the bottom of the stairs, resting my head on the cold iron banister, and falling asleep forever. I heard quick footsteps pattering down the stairs and then suddenly there was Emina in front of me in the dark. I had no resilience left so I passed right by the child, wordless, barely dragging my feet. *"Shhh!"* she whispered. I told her I wasn't feeling up for banter tonight. *"Shhh!"* she insisted. *"You'll wake her . . ."* Who?

Maybe the only thing faster and louder than my feet as I bounded up toward the apartment was the pounding of my heart. Alma was sitting on the landing by the door. There was no time to think. There was nothing I cared to think about. I felt as if everything between us—the years, languages, history, misunderstandings, fear, background—had all melted away . . . She was sleeping. Like a little girl who'd forgotten her keys to the house, curled up there by the door. When I lifted her, she began to stir. She wrapped her arms around my neck. Wordless. I carried her into the apartment and shut the door. I carried her to the bed.

I felt tears drip from my eyes, and then there was no holding them back as they spilled over her body like the first heavy drops of rain. I collected them as I kissed her hair, throat, ears, feet . . . wordless . . . following their tracks over her belly, nipples, her thighs . . . The sound of bodies twining and untwining, shivering skin pulling away and then surrendering again, the sheets rumpled under our backs, the pillows hiding our faces, our fingers clasping in a fast, convulsive knot.

IV

THE HOURGLASS

1

The sand begins piling in the lower chamber of my Sarajevo hourglass. One week. Even less. The unstoppable enumeration of minutes, hours, and days by grains of sand in the hourglass doing, inescapably, what it does. That night an unseen hand had turned it over behind our backs, with no chance for reversal. Nothing would remain of those moments, not the tiniest shred of the pleasure we enjoyed so briefly, oblivious to the sand grains careering madly through the neck of the hourglass, accumulating onto the dead mound at the bottom of the cruel device. Everything is forever smothered in that sand.

Today, I find myself wondering why that unknown being who measures time for all things chose, in this case, in my case, to use my hand for the doing? Was it not my own hand that flipped the hourglass over that last week, the hourglass whose ratio of sand in its upper and lower chambers showed, like the most precise machine, the reach of my, of our, calamity? It was the hand with which I caressed her body that summer night and on whose palm her face so often rested over the next five days—before time accelerated the rhythm of the last grains of sand sliding away swiftly before our eyes, exposing the utter irreversible emptiness of the upper chamber—the time fate had given us, the time we'd spent. The tender lover's hand, the gentle hand that brought bliss, calm, solace, and promise became the selfsame hand—we'd soon find to our wonder—to wreak irreparable harm. The hand of a criminal, whose fingers will stop typing these very pages, will pull the trigger on the pistol in the drawer, and that will be the last thing he does in this world, knowing that this will not, even in death, be forgiven.

I summon the courage for a way to write about the last days and their painful end, which will stand in sharp, unbearable contrast to what happened between us from the moment when I thought, too lightly—while I carried Alma in my arms over the threshold and into Ivor's apartment—that thanks to the whims of a God who was on my side, I'd been undergoing all this travail as a test, from the Gare de l'Est in Paris, through Vienna, to Sarajevo under siege, so that I could begin a new life that very night. It didn't last long, only slightly over 120 hours, and then to dissolve, disappear, be gone—irretrievably, irreparably—as if dropped into the powerful acid of events: love, happiness, discovery, knowledge, death, flight, and despair . . . everything whose sequence was dictated by a joyless God as if in a bad joke. And again—I cannot stifle the question—was it not I, myself, who chose my fate and the fate of those who stood in my path? Did I not write out my own story, did I not guide every part of it, was it not my hand that found Mother's notebook, and did that same hand not reach for Alma's body? Did I not shift this story into gear every single time it slowed to a halt?

I watched, motionless, spellbound, as her body surfaced from the summer night, lit at dawn by the first rays of sunlight. I couldn't take my eyes off her supple form; her sleeping face in my lap; her full lips, a little dried from the kisses, sleep, thirst; her consonant breasts; and the dark place between her pale thighs where the traces of that first uncertain, clumsy, unexpected lovemaking were still hidden. I covered her then with the sheet and fell asleep. We must have woken at the same time, or waited until the other's eyes were open so that we could deal with that first flush of self-consciousness about waking up together, facing a morning that should be wiser than what the night brought with it.

About morning-after wisdom, so often mingled with remorse, I can only say that as soon as we caught sight of each other naked in the morning light, we burst out laughing as if we weren't a day over seventeen and went right on making love as if we'd only just discovered all its delights. Everything else between us had disappeared the night before, there, in that bed. Nothing more, just two people making love one morning in the bedroom of an apartment in a building in a besieged city from which there was no way out.

So began the first of five happy days. And just as all happy days are alike, to reach for that nugget of Tolstoyesque wisdom in this impertinent manner, so every unhappy day is unhappy in its own cursed, unhappy way. I'll write about those later when the hourglass, with its measure—precise down to the grain of sand—tells me the time has come. The sand, for now, is trickling only imperceptibly into the lower chamber, and the stores of time remaining are sufficient for the lovers' secret life in their friend's Sarajevo apartment, in early July of the first year of the siege, to proceed without hindrance. I say "secret life," because ours, when everything else is stripped away, was also a case of adultery and I had to consent to the secrecy. Besides, it was easier for me because I was never in Alma's position of having spent the night at Ivor's apartment and watching out to be sure not to encounter anyone I knew, taking care that nobody suspected, that my behavior didn't expose me, that my friends, colleagues, neighbors, or father didn't find out. The very fact that I waited for her in such a frenzy on the stairs by her apartment did require an explanation. I don't know what Alma told her neighbors about that bizarre episode. I suggested she could say I was one of those foreign nutcases—the journalists, humanitarians—with whom she was forced to work in order to earn a little as a translator, people who didn't understand that there was nothing so urgent at the Sarajevo UN headquarters that it warranted intrusion into her private life. The issue was, after all, a serious one. Her husband was a famous man, and this was a small city, even smaller given that several neighborhoods were being held by the Serb forces; the news would have spread very quickly, indeed.

Her marriage was something we seldom talked about. It had nothing to do with us—it didn't touch these two people who'd found a sanctuary at an address where nobody would come looking for them (except, perhaps, Simon, if he decided to drop in again, or Ivor, if he came home)—perhaps because her marriage had nothing to do with the war. As if the marriage had been left behind once the war began (I wondered what her husband thought, up there in Berlin, about that), a peacetime relationship with no connection to this new reality that brought everything, as Alma said, into question, which changed our habits, lives, our feelings . . . "*Love, too? Maybe,*" she couldn't say. She felt no twinge of guilt and this didn't surprise her. She didn't deny still loving her husband but felt no remorse. The three months of war had ushered in new rules of play. You cannot feel remorse for something that has been left behind; you cannot betray somebody who is not a part of your present, who is not *midwar*. This new reality had imposed two temporal categories on the city's classic time flow: *prewar* and *midwar*. We still didn't know when this duality would collapse with the arrival of the third category, being the dreamed-of time of *postwar*.

We did know how we couldn't display openly what was happening between us. And besides, we said, taunting each other, who knows, maybe this is just a momentary trance, a passing crisis, a brief infatuation, lust, sex, taking care to avoid the word *love*. It is too early, we said, feeling, in fact, afraid, feeling that this word was already pressing on us with its obligations, responsibility, its untamable will to upend the lives it overwhelms, stripping them, if possible, of all regret. Except, of course, for those who fall out of play.

Something of this change had already happened in our lives. Wasn't a page turned with finality the moment the whistle of the *Société nationale des chemins de fer français* blew and the train pulled out of the Paris station, just as the war in this city was beginning, changing the lives of its inhabitants with the first bullets fired? While the war was blazing here, and the siege was building, I was finding a letter half a century old. Didn't Mother's words shake my life to its very core just as the war was changing Alma's? Weren't our lives unmoored at the same moment, only to be brought together in this city, each along its own independent, jagged path?

When she said that the war—largely a negative phenomenon—had brought with it at least for now two good things: her independence ("a newfound maturity in life and art") and me, Alma was wrong. "If it hadn't been for the war," she said, teasing, "you never would have come here to supplement your income with our distress, would you? I'd never have met you. Nor would I have found myself in such an unseemly situation, cheating on my husband in your friend's parents' bed." She didn't know that something entirely different had brought me here, that this war of theirs started as a secondary concern for me, that though it sharply and irreparably divided her life, I turned up in it led by a personal mission, and in fact I was suspended in a vacuum between the life from which that train had borne me away, rendered worthless by my Viennese discovery, and a brand-new life that was ahead of me now, whose contours I couldn't quite discern, which would only crystallize—yes, at the time I did believe this—once I'd learned the truth of my parentage. I felt as though I couldn't say a word of this to her. To be honest, I shrank from even thinking of it during those days, which seemed like a respite, a fresh start, a promise that somebody, something, was coming to my aid or even was at hand to pull me from the ruins of my former life, which had come tumbling down when I learned that its foundations were rotten, so to speak, from their very beginnings.

The rhythm of those five happy days didn't allow me to turn to the personal reasons that had brought me to Alma. And even if I had, I'm sure I'd have sworn that any reason was worthwhile if it brought such a woman to my door. Paraphrasing Alma, I might say that the discovery of the family secret that led me into the war—of course, largely a negative phenomenon—brought with it two things: a crisis in life and art, and her. To define the negative and the positive in this from where I'm sitting now is a complex challenge. These days of happiness, the hours spent with Alma, stopped me from thinking about the address Simon had left with me and which rustled now and then in my pocket, about his message of urgency, the conspiratorial summons to visit him as soon as possible. Besides, I was already highly suspicious of the weird old codger, and I was concerned about the impression that his charm and very appearance had made upon me (I couldn't forget the way the deep creases on his face converged and dispersed in the gloom of the synagogue).

Is it not madness to expect salvation from such a man?! And yet, all my searching came down to that, to waiting for glimmers from a dubious informant. I didn't have the strength for anything else, admitting that perhaps somewhere deep inside I was afraid of a successful completion of my investigation. Whatever the case, I was more and more certain that Simon would never bring me to Jakob Schneider, perhaps for the simple reason that reason itself tells us the man is probably no longer among the living. I was also beginning to worry that I might discover Simon to be an unhinged old man who, with malice, was manipulating my lack of compass. Whatever the case, I fled from the pain that the question of paternity brought with it, savoring the days with Alma as a gift that satisfied the most surreptitious and the boldest desires of a fifty-year-old man.

When these days were over, there would no longer be any time to raise the question, the answer would already be there, and its substance would guarantee that I drop from suspension in the vacuum between my two lives, certain in the knowledge that one life had, indeed, ended but the brand-new life would never begin, a fresh start would, simply, never be in the offing. *Ah, can you not see, just as you ruined your life here, you've ruined its worth everywhere now—the whole world over . . .*

Irreparably.

Alma was in and out. She strove to maintain the customary rhythm of her life, go regularly to her job at the theater, keep up with her colleagues, visit her father, show up often enough in her building, both for her reputation as a married woman and because of the rumors about people fleeing the city. There was somebody leaving with each day via various channels and with the help of connections and money, to Serbia, to Croatia, and farther; families split, friendships ruptured, the departures hurting those who stayed behind and blame scarring those who left—contempt, of course, additionally dogging those who crossed over to the other side. People moved from one neighborhood to another; they broke into empty apartments to loot or seek food and a roof over their heads. Alma spent the night in my bed while telling the neighbors she was at her father's, meanwhile telling her father she was at home. The torched post office on the Miljacka riverbank was inadvertently complicit in our arrangements. The difficulties with reaching most people by phone helped us from being exposed in such a flimsy lie.

During those days we were away from each other for no more than a few hours at a time. I never left the apartment, always waiting for her to return. Maybe I jotted down a few words now and then, building mainly on my old idea about a journalistic diary-essay sort of book on the encircled city, a thought I found increasingly compelling; I was feeling a new surge of energy. The happy days went on between the kitchen, where we tried wartime recipes with the little food and reserves left; the bathroom, into which we'd scramble every time we heard water gurgle in the ever-emptier Sarajevo pipes; and the bed—or more precisely, lovemaking on the bed and in every other corner of the apartment with a stamina that sometimes surprised me. But that must be how tenderness is exchanged in times of plague and siege, with ferocity, as if for the very last time. We took one another boldly, never depriving ourselves of even the slightest pleasure, as if our bodies anticipated the brevity of the joy, harkening to the sound of the slow, unstoppable seeping of the sand through our hourglass. Perhaps Alma drew from me something of my experience. I most certainly drew my strength from the body, will, and imagination of a woman who was still poised at the threshold to maturity. Every separation, no matter how short, crazed us with new hunger and desire. And while I quaked with fear that something might happen to her, trembled like a twig while listening to the shelling blasts, I'd be there to welcome her, waylaying her as soon as she stepped into the apartment, demanding love right there on the floor of the front hall. It was only five days.

Irretrievably.

We did not, however, remain altogether secluded. The secret of our tryst was shared with two more people: Ivor and Emina—my youngest Sarajevo friend. Ivor showed up at the apartment on our second day. I was already wondering what had happened to him, and had the feeling he'd stay on at the television studio, though I was afraid he might turn up at an awkward moment or find Alma scantily clad. When Ivor walked into the apartment, we were, it so happened, fully clothed, but the situation he found left him no room for doubt. I didn't insult his intelligence by trying to hide anything. The expression of astonishment on Ivor's face was something to see, his gasp of surprise as he sorted it all out, surely wondering whether I'd come back to the apartment that day because of this, and whether there had been this other plan in action ever since the night at the theater.

He frowned at the two of us with suspicion, searching for proof on our faces of the thoughts that were racing through his mind, and then he took off his glasses and, scowling, tried to clean the lenses on his T-shirt sleeve; then he gave up, put them back on his nose, and said, first in his own language, *"Dobro, dobro . . . nema problema,"* only to translate this into German for me, unnecessarily, choosing a slightly different nuance for his commentary: *"Alles in Ordnung."* We laughed with him. And that was that. We knew we had a devoted friend in Ivor.

Unfortunately, he and I would not get the opportunity to speak just the two of us. Perhaps, if given the chance, he might have said a word of warning about how unseemly the situation was, might have urged caution, mentioned my age; he might have held it against me, perhaps jealous that of all women it was Alma Filipović who ended up with me in his parents' bed, but again, I may be flattering myself, he might not have been more than merely taken aback by the turn of events.

Ivor stopped by that day to get some rest, pick up a few things, and return to the studio. The movie was coming along well, he told me, pleased. He was sorry I was unable to take part in it myself, but promised me good material for the final phase of the job. I told him he needn't go off to the studio, he could stay here; the "circumstances"— yes, that was my word choice, not finding one more apt—did not require it, but Ivor insisted, not only because of the new "situation," but because he felt compelled to work, to be useful, to finish the movie that was now his central focus in the war. He said this must be a new brand of wartime psychosis, compulsive activity that helps one sustain a more or less normal frame of mind. He was not concerned about where to sleep. All he cared about was working, selecting the material, editing with the help of his studio colleagues. I asked him about his fiction writing, his journalism. Wouldn't that be a safer avenue? "You could call what I'm doing journalism," he said, "and as for the former I have no will or desire; I see no point to fiction. All my literary ideas are passé, they date from *prewar* times; today they are worthless. New ones have not been forthcoming. And besides, young people are often tricked into thinking that the occasional well-written passage means literary talent." He made me promise I'd stop by soon. He said he needed my help, admonishing that I wasn't going to be able to wriggle out of this. I asked him when. "In five or six days," he said. I promised I'd come.

Ivor appeared once more at the apartment on the fifth day, just as I was on my way out to look for Simon. I don't know how long he stayed; he wasn't there when I returned from the visit with a new slip of paper in my pocket, this time with an address that was supposed to be the very door I'd been hoping to knock on since I'd arrived in Sarajevo. During our overlapping minutes together I promised once more that we'd get together by the day after tomorrow at the latest at the studio. He winked to me as I left the apartment, as if giving his blessing, as if he understood being in love, as if he were my older brother. He couldn't know that I wasn't off to see Alma this time. He even went out to the stairwell and watched me descend to the ground floor, waving good-bye to me finally from above, calling, "*See ya!*" I imagine how he waited for me in vain these days. I waved in reply. I didn't know I would no longer, by then, be in Sarajevo.

The photograph with Alma, Ivor, and me posing, our arms around each other, on the balcony—which I keep on my desk while I write these lines, as if seeking their encouragement and support—was taken by Emina during that first visit of Ivor's. We sometimes let the girl join us in the apartment when she'd knock at the door and declare all sorts of important reasons why she'd come, and we often invited her in ourselves to join us for a meal. Ivor told me her father had been killed in the first days of the war and her mother was looking after her two-year-old brother. Emina sometimes stopped by when she saw Alma going out. Then the wild red-haired creature would pester me delightfully with endless conversations and amuse me with her ideas, nudging me to think that my paternal instinct might not be gone for good after all. And ultimately Emina, too, in her own way, enhanced the happiness of those days. I wonder what happened to my youngest Sarajevo friend, who was, along with Simon, the only witness to my disgraceful escape. Did she pass on the message I entrusted to her that morning?

It took us a while to get to know each other. Though the past was behind us, left in *prewar* times, it still couldn't be swept away altogether. The occasional anecdote, the references that tended to crop up in our long conversations, passing jokes, the confessions and clashes of thinking, the discovery of affinities, allusions—even the ones we suppressed—helped us slowly build an image of the other. Was five days enough to build the image we meant to offer of ourselves? I don't know. I'm only sure that I wanted to know so much about her, and there was so much to tell her about myself that in the end I fled so that I wouldn't have to share the whole truth with her. I also know, and I write this with heart bared, that I love her no less, that I desire her no less because of the truth that came between us. Each of us was left with only scattered islands of knowledge about one another, forever dappled in shadow. I pore over what I came to know about her, over this archipelago, as if poring over a map that ties all those reefs and atolls to her name. I repeat the stories about Alma to myself, using the words she used to tell them to me, doing what I can to link them into some sort of whole, like a puzzle for which I'm missing the big picture.

I imagine her as a child on the Adriatic, splashing with joy in the green-blue estuary of the Krka River. I imagine her struggling while she practiced the piano and giving it up. I imagine the rock thrown in a child's game that gashed her head and left a scar that I kissed twenty years later. I imagine her waving a youth-brigade flag, or lighting her first cigarette, or how she showed her breasts to a school friend, or how surprised she was when Tito's death didn't leave her feeling quite sad enough, how she passed her entrance exam for the drama academy, how she fell hopelessly in love with a professor, how she traveled around Europe with the first big love of her student days, how her head reeled from smoking weed in Amsterdam, how she discovered Paris on one July evening at the top of Montmartre and was amazed by the hues in the sky, how she promised herself she'd live there one day, how she was given her first leading role, how roses showered down onto the stage of the National Theatre, how her mother died—Aida was her name—how she got to know her future husband in a smoky counterculture café, how she fell in love with him for the resolve with which he went about seducing her and because of his beautiful eyes and, of course, the unusual ways that he saw things and people, which she took for originality, a word with real weight in those days, how they were married at the Old Town City Hall and went off on a trip to Italy—their tour of Rimini, San Marino, Castello Mardi, Cesena, Forlì, Ravenna, Bologna, and then south to Florence, and later, of course, to Rome in April . . . then came their apartment, the first marital discord, his fellowship, the war, her maturation in life and art, and . . . me, Richard Richter. But the last part of the puzzle doesn't fit; it spoils the picture, skews all the puzzle maker's hard work.

Her curiosity outstripped mine. And besides, agewise I had more to tell and, of course, not to tell. She often came back to Kitty. She was surprised that Kitty had left me, then later decided she could understand. She urged me to talk about '68, Paris, the first mansard apartment in the tenth arrondissement, then the larger apartment on the Canal Saint-Martin as my readership grew and the advances on my book contracts climbed, as the literary prizes began coming in, the fierce debates of those years, the revolution, socialism, the constant Sartre-izing, then *The Gulag Archipelago* . . . I told her I'd been raised by my aunt, about how I was orphaned, about my Viennese childhood, the bleak postwar years, the fact that I first slept with a woman at the age of twenty due to extreme shyness. "I'd say, and reading too much," Alma teased me. I shrugged. She was proud she beat me at this; she, apparently, did it at fifteen. I shook my head. *Kids these days.* I told her about the relationships that failed, the wrenching breakups, my long crush on the wife of a close friend only to have all those feelings evaporate one day as if they'd never been there and with them the friendship, about Kitty, who found me when I was nearly forty and hadn't published a sentence in years, while trying to fuel my imagination with ever greater quantities of alcohol . . . My dear Kitty, I wonder what she thinks when she watches scenes of Sarajevo always in flames—because there is always something burning in the city these days, in several places at once—what she feels while she imagines me killed, wounded, hit by one of the hundreds of shells that fall on the city today, as reported by France 2 or 3, whatever . . . and finally, what she would say if she were to see me alive and well in Alma's arms. I know she'd breathe a sigh of relief, that this image would please her far more than the one in which I'm writhing on the pavement, while the cameras of the world's news agencies are rolling, and I know she'd go right ahead and chide me that the girl would break my heart as had happened several times before while we were still living under the same roof . . . Warm-hearted Kitty. I hope she has replaced me with a decent lover.

Who knows what more we'd have learned about each other had we had more time. There might have been a lot we wouldn't have liked. Who knows whether we'd have come to hate each other in time; who knows where this would have taken us. Guessing now is pointless. I know it hurt her when she woke alone that day, just as I know she cannot comprehend why I left her, no matter how many times she tries to assemble this puzzle of mine, she'll always be short a key piece she doesn't know, the pattern, the basic information that's missing that determines the big picture, without which none of it makes sense. Any despair is futile; I wish I could say to her, "Live on. Survive." I keep hoping she'll sidestep the shrapnel, the bullets, that she'll never walk into the sights of a sniper, that she'll evade hunger and thirst and cold, and that she'll hate me as the most reprehensible foe, as the foulest of villains, as a serpent, a thief, and that from her hatred she'll draw the strength she needs to go on.

The sands in the hourglass counted the fifth day. A little more than 120 hours was the time accorded to our love. Alma wanted to bring me, at last, to her father that day, to introduce me as a friend. She knew the old man would enjoy talking with me. He was isolated after all. He was awaiting my visit with impatience in the late afternoon for an early supper. Reluctantly I agreed. Alma was pleased. A little after noon she went to her father's place to prepare the food. She'd come back later to get me, and this time her father would be at home; I needn't worry. I decided to look for Simon, hoping the old man might indeed know something that would help me bring my search to an end without embroiling Alma. This was something for me alone. The street name and house number were barely legible in Simon's handwriting, but nevertheless I managed to locate it on a city map. As I dressed, Ivor showed up; I left and walked hurriedly to Simon's address. I found it behind the synagogue, near the Old Orthodox Church; then I went up a steep street above Baščaršija. The grains of sand followed the rhythm of my footsteps, swiftly sliding through the narrow neck of the hourglass.

2

I was perplexed when I found a dilapidated wooden fence at the address Simon had given me. I could barely make out the house number on the rusty old plaque. Through cracks in the fence I could see a yard overgrown in weeds and a run-down two-story house. And two cats who peered out from behind the bushes, watching me, curious. I pressed the old metal doorbell several times, but the wires seemed to go no farther than the gate. I knocked, even called Simon's name. After a few minutes I began to feel ridiculous. It occurred to me that I'd fallen into the old crackpot's trap, that I'd gullibly come looking for him at an address where nobody had been living for at least a decade. I turned to go back to the apartment. I crumpled the note up into a ball and angrily flicked it over the gate. I hadn't stepped back more than two paces when my ball came zinging back and bounced at my feet on the sidewalk. The gate opened with a creak. The first cat's head poked out, and then I heard Simon's voice: "Throw trash into your own yard, foreigner!" He quickly gestured to me to step into a yard that was a jumble of grass, weeds, and volunteer plants leaving only a narrow paved path leading to the front door of the house.

"You wouldn't believe me," said Simon, pointing to the jungle around us, "if I were to tell you that in the old days, soirées were held here, right here in the garden, during the time we were under Austria. A colonial scene it was: Viennese engineers, Czech schoolteachers, the occasional clergyman, maybe a deputy to the regional parliament, Hungarian businessmen, little children chattering in four languages at once, and their genteel mothers who could barely teeter on the cobblestones of the courtyard. It wouldn't have been viable without local color, so there'd always be a few of the prominent Sarajevans; you could tell them from the others by the occasional oriental detail in their impeccable modern attire, *à la viennoise*, as befitting loyal subjects of our good emperor and king. My young father buzzed around, the host of the soirée; he'd climbed the social ladder of the day as a physician, a pharmacist to be exact, the successor in a long line of Sephardic medics in Bosnia, running here and there, muttering nervously in Ladino along the way to the servants. This was on the eve of the war so that's mainly what they talked about: Will they, won't they, yes-they-will, oh-no-they-won't . . ."

"I assume that you, too, were there among the children."

"Wrong, Richard. Wrong. I wasn't yet born, but I came not long after. As soon as the war ended, as soon as the peace treaties were signed, as soon as the chaos was at least somewhat reined in, I appeared on the scene. The only plus in my father's books, if one could put it that way, from the utter catastrophe of the war that buried his ambitious dreams under unpayable debts. If you also know that your child will only add to the debts, then you haven't much cause for celebration. Bankruptcy, my friend, bankruptcy. This serves as an answer to your surprised bourgeois look at the condition of the façade. No, we haven't redone it since, if you must know. Do come in."

The house was in almost-total darkness, which I gradually acclimated to, knocking into indiscernible shapes, while following Simon, who could have cruised through the phantasmal labyrinth blindfolded, I'm sure. He clearly lived alone, not counting the cats; I'd seen five and assumed there were more. Thick drapes covered the windows, candles were lit here and there or a wick burned in oil, and from time to time I heard the meow of a domesticated inhabitant of the ramshackle structure. The occasional shaft of light from outside found its way in and lit furniture from various eras that crowded the interior as much as the weeds crowded the yard. Simon led me into the "salon," as he called it, the large central room of the house, just as overfull as everywhere else, with a dusty piano, bookshelves on two walls, paintings hanging every which way, and heaps of wax drippings in the corners where candles flickered. Simon settled into an armchair. A cat immediately hopped into his lap, another nestled at his feet. He sat there amid all these things probably preserved since the floods of history, while the flames and shadows danced phantom-like across the creases lining his face. I shuddered, feeling the three pairs of eyes on me, staring, curious at the intruder. Stroking the cat, he finally spoke: "I was expecting you sooner, Richard. What kept you?"

"You know how it is, something interesting is always going on in this town. I've been busy. Reporting is exhausting, and you must believe it isn't easy counting the dead and rushing to the sites of tragedies all the time."

"No doubt. But that is not your reason for forgetting your friend."

"Listen, I can't always be thinking about that friend and his problem. And yet I know I'm his only hope. I imagine him biting his nails in Vienna, waiting for news from me."

"That's the reason you're here?" asked Simon, and only then did I understand the double entendre of his question.

"In part, yes. On the other hand, I've been looking forward to seeing you. Conversations with you have an unusual dimension, and I have to say I have been looking forward to more."

"I hope I'll be able to help your friend. Though you're fully aware of how thankless a task this is. The man may regret his search. Because of what he'll find."

"That's his problem. My job is to lend a hand. If you, too, can help him, I would be most grateful, in his name of course."

"Of course, of course."

Simon rose and paced around the salon, sighing several times, linking his hands behind his back as if wrestling with weighty thoughts. Then he came over to a kind of pedestal on which there was an open book, and he glanced at a page. I didn't want to lose my patience. I knew he'd tell me, sooner or later, what he knew, if indeed he knew anything. He was pleased I'd come to visit—the condition of the house left no doubt that a very solitary man lived here—and it was clear that he didn't want the visit to end too soon. I, myself, was less nervous this time, pretending that the help for the imaginary friend was only one of the reasons for my visit. I took in the books on the shelves, the motifs on the paintings, the Ottoman-period sabers, the platters and cups in which they'd served tea, perhaps at the soirées that Simon had described . . .

"And the girl?" he asked casually, while flipping through the pages.

"The girl?" I blurted at first, continuing as calmly as I could. "What girl?"

At that Simon gave a dismissive wave of his hand as if he couldn't believe that somebody could dissemble so poorly.

"*What girl?* You ask me, 'What girl?' Ridiculous!"

"You mean the woman you met at my place? Alma?" Simon now watched me impatiently without a word, waiting for me to finally answer his question. "Well, nothing. Nothing. We worked together on a movie. My friend Ivor and I made a documentary about Sarajevo actors. She's an actress. She'd come to talk to me about it that day. That's all."

"That's all?"

"Yes! That's all. What else would there be?!" I shouted.

"Nothing, nothing," said Simon as if defending himself. "I said nothing. Just asking. So interesting."

"What is so interesting?"

"I don't know. You, her."

"There's nothing. She's married." I began defending myself and then rose to my feet, hoping to be taken more seriously. "I am fifty years old.

Do you think such a young woman would even consider me? Or that she even needs a lover?"

"I don't know, these days . . ."

"Come on, Simon. She's just a good friend."

"You didn't ask for her help with the search for that friend of yours?"

"No. Why?" I asked, and Simon only shrugged. "Simon, I'm not asking everyone I meet on the street about the father of some friend. I have better things to do, I told you. This is not a question of life or death. And besides, I don't know her well enough to involve her in this. Do you understand?"

"Yes, of course. Forgive my curiosity. Don't be angry. What does it matter to me, anyway? No need to get upset. I was just interested . . ."

"About whether I have something going on with her? No. I do not."

After he'd responded with a long, drawn-out "*Okay*," Simon went into the hallway, leaving me alone in the salon. I went over to the pedestal with the book. I tried to figure out what it was about. There was a picture that looked to be of wartime Leningrad, something about the siege of Leningrad in any case. Next to it was a book on whose title page was the famous photograph of the Madrid street during the Spanish Civil War with the banner declaring *"No pasarán!"* hung between buildings. And next to that, a novel by Albert Camus. I checked the title. *La Peste*. Simon came back to the salon, carrying a large and obviously very old brass key. He handed it to me and said, "With this key, you could open the door of a house in Córdoba, Richard, if the house still stands. Or so the legend says. You are holding five hundred years of exile in your hands, my dear friend. This key was brought by my ancestors to Sarajevo. Or so they said. They carried it from the day they last locked their house in Córdoba, so "far away and alone" as good old tragic García Lorca would say. Forced by those fighters for a pure Christian land, they boarded ships to take them through Constantinople to Salonika, bringing their children to this mountain valley, where the fogs linger long, a place so different from Córdoba. Or so says the legend that obliges you to drag seemingly worthless things wherever you go, that obliges you to have children and live alongside this key that declares your exile, reminding you that your home is elsewhere, in a distant land whose language you still speak among yourselves, even if it has become contaminated in the time you've been far from the homeland, which, of course, isn't your real homeland, as the book you revere tells you. This is how you are born and die, stricken by the illness of a nostalgia for which there is no cure. And now, looking at this key, which will remain in the ruins of this house because I have nobody to pass the burden to, as you can see, I am imagining what would happen if by some mercy of God it had been possible to return to that house in Córdoba, being still in the identical condition it was in when we were ousted, with a lock that could finally receive this key and a door that would open with one happy *click*? What would it be like to put the key in the lock of your house and step back into it again—the wild dream of the displaced!—to return again to Córdoba? Would we be happier? I wonder whether our Sarajevo key would chafe us in our pocket, less vintage yet still the key to our house, and wouldn't Córdoba seem foreign and wouldn't a new nostalgia eat at us while we had children and grew up with a new key as a reminder, hung on the wall? The house in Córdoba is longed for until the moment when you step into it; this key is most valuable while it's useless, while it cannot open any door."

Simon fell silent and gave himself over to his thoughts. I turned the ancient key over in my hands, ran the tips of my fingers over its texture just as many had done for centuries before me. Under the sway of Simon's words and the mystical silence that ruled these rooms lit by the flames of many candles, I wondered whether I was not also seeking the lock of the house whose key I'd found hidden behind the bookshelf of our apartment in Vienna, a key which I was trying in every door. Shouldn't that house, that father's house whose existence I discovered, remain locked and its owner, if he were still alive, be left undisturbed?

His head bowed over his chest, as if he were sleeping, Simon appeared to be completely lost in thought. I stood and, still holding the key, closely perused the titles in his library. I noticed a great deal of legal literature in various languages, and it became clear to me that the big volumes on the shelves were old legal codices. I remembered Simon's pun with my surname. Hadn't he said something similar at our last meeting? It seemed to me that I might finally learn something about this mysterious man.

"Forgive me, but . . ." My voice rang out loudly in the silence. Simon started. "Although we've met twice and we're in your house, I still know nothing about you, and I find it difficult to decipher some of your allusions. However, if I were to gauge you by your library, I'd say you're a lawyer . . . or a judge. *Richter*, am I right?"

"Judge ye well. Felicitations. Do not betray your surname, though that's the thing with surnames, they're given to us by fathers, and the thing about paternity, well . . . it never is entirely clear."

"The example of my friend confirms that, does it not?" I said swiftly. "But let's leave him be. So I guessed correctly. A judge."

"A former judge, retired, to be precise."

"A glance at the collection you have here suggests that you have been doing that your whole life!"

"In a way, yes, though I stopped many years ago. Many years. You know, the law is an inexhaustible source of insufficient answers, and when skepticism takes root judging becomes a tricky profession. It's a little like with the clergy. Once they start doubting, the work becomes challenging, awkward, when problems begin to trouble them for which they won't find a sufficient answer in the books in which they believed until yesterday. So it is with people of the law, there is always a moment when sufficient and just answers to the complex predicaments of life cannot be found in the available legal codices. Situations never before described—a web of circumstances that revisits the concept of justice, righteousness, good and evil, and forces you to ask whether, now that you are aware of this, you can continue judging."

"So you gave up?"

"Perhaps it could be said that my profession gave up on me. I no longer fit in its framework."

"How so?"

"You see, Richard, you're old enough to know that there are border-line cases which bring everything into question. Afterward one merely draws one's conclusion. It's as simple as that."

"Maybe it's not quite as simple as you say. What was it, if I may, that drew you to conclude you should quit?"

"You see, I've been speaking about all this in general terms. I drew my conclusion from my own experience and the experience of others. We don't have to go through things ourselves to understand them, do we?"

"I agree. Yet something must have pushed you to such a decision."

Simon again dropped his head to his chest and sighed several times. "Yes, there must have been something . . . ," he said. The cat moved back to his lap. I sat again on the sofa, watching him like a pupil who waits with shining eyes to learn yet another lesson. I finally set the key down on a tin table, and after the metal *zing* rang out, Simon looked up, as if pulled back from the distant past, and began his story.

"Yes, something truly did move me to decide to quit the judiciary. It needn't, as I said, have been something that happened to me; it needn't be from personal experience. Profound doubt in the profession of administering justice, a calling which, as I said, *deserted* me precisely because I no longer believed in it. Just as sometimes a lover leaves their partner not out of their own lack of love but out of fear that the partner has stopped loving them. Just as God abandons his preachers as soon as they doubt his existence, and decides to seek simpler souls to spread his glory o'er the land.

"I will tell you a story of a colleague, also a judge, a story about a friend, a peer, a Sarajevo Jew, the story from which I finally drew that conclusion.

"This fellow judge, you see, let's say his name was Daniel, was born to an impoverished family of former doctors and small businessmen. His father succumbed to drink after a series of business and personal missteps caused by the war, poor investments, and nervous breakdowns, so he took his own life, leaving behind seven-year-old Daniel and his mother, Rifka, in a home much like this one to manage as best as they might. His remains lie at the Jewish cemetery from where, perhaps even now, a sniper is picking off new victims. A widow in debt, Rifka had to overcome her genteel pride that dated from the higher moments of her husband's career and social standing and accept work less respected in this society of ours, cleaning the homes of the wealthy, becoming a washerwoman and a seamstress, finding consolation in the fact that the good Lord would compensate her for all the troubles of her people by giving her a son who would be a good Jew, one day a rabbi, a doctor, or, at least, a lawyer. Rifka was a young and handsome woman, and only three years had gone by after his father's death when our Daniel saw in their home for the first time a Mr. Kraus, a prominent businessman who commanded respect. It should be said, perhaps, that Mr. Kraus had a nose for the zeitgeist, and in the nick of time, just after the First World War but before the Second, he'd jettisoned the unpopular faith of his Middle-European ancestors by marrying a Catholic woman in Sarajevo and blending in with the local Catholic community. Uncle Franjo (formerly Franz) Kraus would visit Daniel and Rifka's home for a few hours, mostly on weekdays, bringing Daniel gifts, usually books, and closeting himself with the boy's mother in her private rooms. Sometimes Daniel would find them together when he came home from school; sometimes they'd dine together; sometimes Franjo would set aside his workplace finery and kick a soccer ball around the yard with the boy. The poor child grew fond of the gentleman, who from time to time in a, shall we call it, occasional way, stepped quite smoothly into the place of the boy's late father. There was no need, of course, to explain to Daniel that the presence of kindly Uncle Franjo in their house was something he shouldn't share with others, even if everybody already knew—in our little city such things seldom passed unremarked—and that the continuation of his visits, and with them this essential surrogate for paternal affections, depended precisely on preserving the secret nature of the thing. Because Daniel knew Mr. Kraus had a family with whom he lived in a nice house on the other side of the river, and more than once Daniel had seen him on a Sunday in town with his wife and little daughter—about Daniel's age—hurrying to mass at the cathedral. These close acquaintances would never greet each other then. A quick exchange of glances would suffice to reinforce their tacit agreement.

"And Daniel respected the agreement, no matter how hard this was for him, no matter how envy stung his child's heart. Still, he couldn't complain. Wasn't it Franjo who had given him his finest set of clothes for his bar mitzvah and a gift certificate with the admonition that he must use it for books and dictionaries—because the shrewd business-man was convinced that knowledge of foreign languages never hurt, and his celebrated instinct told him that among them, English was preordained to take the lead? Hadn't this man helped Daniel solve challenging homework problems, hadn't he congratulated Daniel with a pleased pat on the shoulder for his successes and criticized him kindly when the need for that arose? Daniel even wondered whether it might have been Franjo who, with his characteristic discretion, settled the family's debts, and hadn't Franjo—more than once—bailed Daniel out of trouble with the police during his rebellious teen stage for fervent communist agitating, which was when Rifka relinquished her first dream of her son the rabbi and began to dream of her son the doctor, and hadn't he been the one who had seen to it that Daniel was able to enroll at the university? Here Rifka, with Franjo's help of course, won at least one victory, persuading her son to study law if he wouldn't be a doctor, to the great regret of our Daniel, who was wild about novels and philosophical claptrap.

"His youthful envy, however, never left Daniel's heart. How many times had he slipped into the Kraus's yard and, from the dark, watched the idyll of Franjo's real family life, the harmonious marriage between Mrs. and Mr. Kraus, the Christmas parties, his own mother scrubbing the floors in their home, and above all, their beautiful daughter, let's say her name was Jelena, as she grew up in a happiness that was beyond his reach, as she became a beguiling young woman. And, of course, not much time would pass before our Daniel, by now in his last years of secondary school, would realize that all his envy—fed by those occasional spy missions, which he couldn't bear to give up—had transformed into an obsession for Franjo's daughter. All his interest shifted from their familial bliss, which was not perhaps quite as idyllic as it had seemed (over his years of spying Daniel had witnessed many bitter quarrels and the lady of the house, let's say her name was Ana, often sobbing behind locked doors), shifted from that bourgeois illusion, as he surely would have put it at the time, to the girl's thrilling intimate life, which, while he sat on a branch of the walnut tree so close to her window, unfolded as if on a movie screen, except that unlike in the movies of the day, there was no censorship.

"Yes, this lasted for a while. Our Daniel tried several times to approach the beautiful Jelena for whom he longed, but, what with his shy nature and his lack of experience, he never managed to even start. Until, as is often the case, the girl took things into her own hands; opening the window on a chilly night between awful 1940 and even worse 1941, she beckoned to her admirer, the maid's son, to come in finally off the creaking branch—which his frequent climbing could soon force into a snapping capitulation—and come inside into the warmth. Need I add that Mr. Franjo Kraus knew nothing of what was going on in his only daughter's bedroom. Daniel began visiting her after that night the same way Mr. Kraus had visited Daniel's home for years, secretly and to the delight of the woman receiving him. And it bears saying that there were times when Franjo would be at Daniel's house precisely when Daniel was at Franjo's, yet Franjo knew nothing of it, which was a terrible source of glee for our Daniel. Jelena, of course, had no illusions about what her father might think of these trysts or what he would have said had he found the boy in her room or, heaven forbid, in her bed. But what she didn't know was that Daniel and Franjo already shared a special bond; they were, so to speak, stepfather and stepson—and here Mr. Kraus had to be credited with leading a successful double life, though there were signs that Mrs. Kraus's bitter tears were shed for this very reason—so what Jelena couldn't know perhaps made her father's reaction to come even more heartless.

"Yes, one night Franjo heard a vase fall to the floor in Jelena's room, and in a panic he rushed to her locked door. Daniel scrambled to pull on his clothes, Jelena was already opening the window, and Franjo, with all the noise but no word from Jelena, was overwhelmed by paternal panic and decided to break down the door. When he did so, well, there was Daniel, half-dressed and ready to leap out the window. Franjo blanched and briefly froze, collected himself, and without a word—and most fathers would at least have spat out a curse or two—grabbed the intruder and, hitting him, dragged him outside, threatening to 'flatten him,' in those words, if Daniel ever came near their home or Jelena again. Daniel responded brashly with the very same threat, adding that for every time Franjo hit him, Daniel would pay him back with double. Surprised, Franjo released him. So it was that they parted, blistering with recriminations.

"Daniel respected only the first of Franjo's two warnings. From that evening on, Jelena came to him. Sometimes Daniel would see Franjo nosing around the house, trying to figure out whether Daniel was there before he dared knock. Daniel exulted at the bone-deep fear Kraus felt, but he didn't want to interfere with Kraus and his mother. In short, the two men avoided each other. They'd pass one another on the street without a word, though Daniel had the satisfaction of Jelena's visits, until one day chance brought father and daughter to the door of the two-story house at the same moment, after which Franjo locked his daughter up at home. Whether Mr. Kraus intended to continue visiting Rifka we'll never know. German troops marched into the city that very day, ushering in the Ustaša regime, and Mr. Kraus could no longer be seen in the vicinity of a Jewish household. Rifka sewed a yellow star and a big letter Ž onto her clothes, as required by the new regulations, and Daniel then found himself escaping through the city's underground with his comrades, and later, of course, the partisans. The war took him through Bosnia and Croatia until finally in late 1945 he came back to Sarajevo, where he continued his studies with the rank of demobilized captain. Rifka was sent to a camp in 1942. The last news of her came in 1943, before she was sent to a place from which neither she nor anybody else who knew of her fate ever returned.

"The house was in shambles. The people who'd been squatting there didn't manage to cart off all the furnishings when they vacated the premises in the spring of 1945. Daniel learned how during the war Franjo Kraus had served the regime faithfully with his business acumen, and paid priests and Ustaša officials to confirm his religious and national purity, protecting his family. Daniel was surprised that the new government hadn't already arrested him, only to learn that Kraus had donated a generous portion of his gold to the national liberation struggle, insuring himself from that angle as well while the war was still going on, in the years when it wasn't easy to predict who would come out victorious. His instinct, yet again, served him well.

"Daniel decided, finally, to pay a visit to the Krauses, encouraged by his age and experience and still full of youthful hope that the war hadn't erased Jelena's memories of those prewar months. Of course Daniel was sorely disappointed when he found at the Kraus's house a high-ranking officer of the victorious army—let's say his name was . . . let's say his name doesn't matter—who held a key political position in liberated

Sarajevo. Daniel was surprised to hear that their wedding date had been set, and he was thrown out of the house for a second time when he furiously reminded Jelena of her oath of love to him; she averted her eyes as her fiancé demanded—invoking his rank—that Daniel leave at once, and then he asked Franjo Kraus why he hadn't helped Rifka, who hadn't had the gold with which to buy her life and who had been his loyal mistress all those years. This was the final straw: Mistress Ana burst into sobs, Jelena shot him a glare of either surprise or contempt—he couldn't tell which—and a paunchy officer from the People's Army threw him out, shouting that if he valued his life, he would never set foot in that house again.

"And he never set foot in old Kraus's family home again, even when he was later begged to come back. Jelena married that man who'd climbed the ladder of the new social order, and his positions in the Party and executive bodies of the Bosnian and Herzegovinian government brought him power and stature. Emboldened by a few shots of grappa during a reception, Daniel once more approached Jelena and asked her whether she still remembered his room, because he vividly remembered hers, or something along those brash lines. Jelena, again, averted her eyes and the next thing he knew, somebody had grabbed his arm, smashed his nose, battered his ribs, and tossed him out onto the sidewalk; the officer informed him that the next time he saw Daniel anywhere near his wife, he'd cut Daniel's handsome face. After that evening Daniel gave up on Jelena; he threw himself into his studies, along with the occasional romantic fling, determined to begin a new postwar life, avoiding the officer and his wife when he saw them on the street, following her husband's political career only through the newspapers, and pretending not to see the already bent-over Mr. Kraus whenever he walked by. And though Kraus always stopped as if he had something to say to Daniel, the young man wouldn't give Kraus the satisfaction of listening to his excuses. Daniel mastered his studies and was hired to work on the Sarajevo bench, where he soon became one of the youngest and most promising judges.

"Daniel thought the whole thing was behind him, he thought he'd overcome the humiliation and hatred and love, as well as the allure of revenge. He had ceased caring. And then on June 28, 1948, Stalin announced the Cominform, severing relations with Tito and isolating Yugoslavia. Immediately afterward in Sarajevo many Cominformists—whose sympathies were alleged to remain with Stalin—were arrested and many a career on the bench was snuffed as well, so Daniel, as a resilient young judge, rose quickly up the vacated steps of the internal hierarchy of the courts, loyally determining the cases he'd been assigned at a time when judges were expected to be settling accounts vehemently with Moscow-inspired conspirators. Swept up by the backlog of cases, and prepared to issue evenhanded judgments based on the evidence or free the accused of the accusations (whether fraudulent or genuine) put before him—here he cannot be faulted for his objectivity and loyalty to the letter of the law of the day—he ceased to dwell on his earlier humiliation. As I said, he was convinced he'd mastered the hatred, that he'd matured, ignoring thoughts of the rejection that sometimes surfaced. That was behind him . . .

"And so it would have remained, far behind him, if one day he hadn't been entrusted with deciding the fate of a high-ranking Party chief, one of the first to join the cause at the start of the war, and until days ago a prominent politician, the very man who'd promised to cut Daniel's face if he ever came near his wife, the same man now in a cell at the Sarajevo jail, accused of endorsing the Cominform Resolution and taking part in a Stalinist conspiracy against the federal authorities.

"As soon as he was handed the fate of this person he so despised, Daniel knew that the revenge he'd forgotten had not forgotten him, keeping to the age-old adage that no injury suffered goes unpunished, that the pain of an eye lost can be assuaged only by the eye of one's enemy, as with a tooth knocked loose. And so he was patient, even calm. He visited the defendant in jail. Jelena's husband had been quite badly beaten, and the last ray of hope vanished from his face when he realized that Daniel would be his judge. Daniel questioned him by the book. The man swore to his innocence, his loyalty to Tito; he spoke of bureaucratic errors, treason, conspiracy, a tale so familiar to investigators that it did nothing to deter further beatings. In many other cases, the investigating judge would already have received a signed confession and the prisoner, after being tortured, would readily confess to acting as an accomplice to crimes they'd never even heard of. Daniel, after examining all such evidence, if it can be called evidence, was expected to send him off, in the name of the people, to hard labor on Goli Otok or one of the other prison camps set up by the fledgling government. In this case, to everybody's surprise, he demanded privileged treatment for the prisoner, halting the torture and personally assuming the role of eliciting the truth. He requested that they accommodate the fallen comrade in a cell of his own, and sought to prolong the investigation because of the so-called vital information he intended to draw out of him.

"Daniel had studied the case thoroughly and he realized that the man was telling the truth: he'd genuinely had nothing to do with Cominform, and his loyalty to the regime was beyond reproach. It was clear to Daniel that the charges were trumped up, as was the role he was expected to play in all this. It came down to issuing a summary conviction and putting an end to the man's political career, possibly even his life. Daniel was expected to visit the cell of his victim when he chose to, demand new information—other names, threaten him with torture and camp, whisper the name of his wife, describe the horrors which awaited him, and patiently transform the initial defiance into despair, the pride of the formerly powerful man to abjection. On the one hand, he knew he'd be sending an innocent man to a camp or even to death, and he found it troubling, despite the allure of revenge, to acclimate himself to this thought, wondering at the same time about how many people he'd already dispatched to this fate without corroborating the information he'd received, without allowing the prisoner a chance to prove his innocence, acting only as a cog in the roaring machine of revolutionary justice. Daniel balked at taking the next step and letting the man out of his hands, because at least under his purview the man had a modicum of security, and this was how he placated his troubled conscience. On the other hand, he awaited impatiently the inevitable moment when Jelena came to his door to plead for clemency.

"And so she did. She heard who'd be in charge of her husband's case and she came to Daniel's office, distraught and abject. Gone was her pride, the contempt with which she'd averted her eyes, and the social status and power she'd briefly enjoyed. These were now irretrievably behind her, and she was merely a wife pleading for clemency. She must have swallowed a great deal in going to him, but she was equally certain that he could help her, hoping his hatred hadn't overcome all his memories of her. It is a strange thing to decide somebody's life as if the life is one's property. With her arrival, Jelena offered him her life and her honor in return for mercy. At first Daniel set out for her the gravity of the situation, the fact that his hands were tied, the predicament she was in as the wife of a traitor, leaving only a small window of hope that the investigative process, who knows, might possibly vindicate him. There was no need to add that a positive outcome depended on her. Jelena had been prepared for something like this. When she began taking off her clothes, Daniel felt all the joy, and the heartache, too, of revenge. Again after all those years he reveled in her body on the floor of the office; she gave him full freedom to do whatever he wanted. But her silence pained him. She never, that time, so much as sighed.

"The investigation continued; Jelena visited him regularly, and he often went to her home, demanding and getting whatever he desired. But Daniel's revenge couldn't be gratified in the way revenge itself demands. It tormented him that exacting his revenge wasn't satisfying. Daniel realized that the hatred and scorn fueling his revenge—and at times he felt he was avenging the very first day he saw Franjo Kraus in his home, all of Rifka's scrubbed floors, the fact that Franjo was alive and she was not—were retreating in the face of the love he felt again for this woman. And yes, he made one more mistake; he desired his feelings to be returned in the same measure.

"Not a day passed without him seeing Jelena, without him desiring her. He brought news about her husband, sustained her hope, and the hours they spent together truly did, finally, build a certain intimacy. Her resistance seemed to be waning, the disgust melting away, her body responding more and more, her sighs or laughter unforced, the old passion stirring again despite the humiliating relationship he subjected her to. Or not? Meanwhile Daniel visited the prisoner regularly and their relationship, too, began to modulate. The humiliations of the investigative process turned into long conversations. Daniel's interest in the prisoner's story grew. Her husband divulged to him the mechanisms of government and the injustice that had been visited upon him. Daniel began to sympathize with the man and a vast, forbidden doubt began nesting in Daniel. He'd secured the best possible conditions for the man; there was no more he could do. And besides, the prolonged imprisonment of the man afforded him access to the body and promise of love of the man's wife. But, as I said, doubt began to swell within him, skepticism about ideology, the system, justice, personal integrity, about everything. Revenge had begun to eat at him from within, and he was finding this more and more difficult to bear. He'd turned the woman he loved into a whore who was pandering herself for the life of her husband. He was holding an innocent man in prison, thereby implementing the will of a system in which he no longer believed.

"Daniel would never forget Jelena's radiant face the day she opened the door, expecting him at the hour they'd agreed upon, anticipating the continuation of her servitude, dressed as one dresses when expecting a lover, excited by what his visit would bring. And he would never forget her surprise when instead she saw her husband, gaunt, hollow-cheeked, much drained by his lengthy imprisonment, 'cleared of all accusations,' as Daniel announced in the company of two other officials. Jelena embraced her husband, sending Daniel a last glance over his shoulder, a message whose meaning he could not divine. Daniel wished them all the best and said, through clenched teeth, 'So you see, justice may be slow but is attainable.' He turned and went straight back to the court, where he requested a long sick leave.

"Over the next weeks Daniel sequestered himself in his house with the intention of smothering the love inside him, firm in his resolve never to come near her again, to face the injustice he'd visited upon them and which he had only partially remedied by freeing the man, saving his life. Daniel found the burden difficult to stomach, and illness finally joined the mix. He lay, thinking he was dying in the old house, without anybody to help him, the sole consolation being that it was all finally coming to an end. Just as he was beginning to convalesce her telegram arrived: *I am pregnant. I'll tell him everything*. No signature. Daniel did not respond. Was she thinking he would? That he'd act? He'd never know. Instead he opened the gate, unlocked the front door, and waited. He was expecting the man. Expecting his punishment.

"At dusk on the third day he heard pounding at the gate. Then he heard the gate open, steps in the yard, and the man coming warily up the stairs and inside to where Daniel was waiting for him. The anticipated, though uninvited, guest, deliberate, with clear intention, jumped on him immediately and began thrashing him with whatever he could grab. Daniel managed to pull away, but he chased him into a corner. Then he pulled out a knife, and the only thing Daniel remembers hearing from him that evening was the sentence whose truth was proved to Daniel over the rest of his life. The man said, 'Nobody loves a monster,' and then slashed Daniel's face. Another three or four times he slashed, and then Daniel shoved him back and they fought, clutching for whatever they could reach: there was smashed glass and furniture mixing with the blood that dripped from the gashes on Daniel's face but also from his assailant's wounds; Daniel had managed to stab him with a broken glass and nearly strangled him. The two twisted in a writhing mass, and whoever had the upper hand quickly lost the advantage; who knows how it would have ended, who would have killed whom, had a shot not rung out.

"Daniel felt his opponent's grip release; after the dead man slumped to the floor, he saw Jelena in the doorway, pistol in hand. He would never forget her stare, aghast, at the dead body of her husband and at Daniel's bloody, forever disfigured visage, just as he would never forget those moments of silence when he couldn't help wondering—as he did for the rest of his life—which of them she'd truly meant to shoot."

Simon fell silent, as if conjuring for me those moments of horror. The story seemed to have undone him: he was no longer present; he said nothing more. No commentary was needed. The cat hopped down from his lap and looked at me as if it wanted to announce that visiting hours were over. I stayed sitting there, still, letting each of his words sink in, under the sway of the story I'd just heard. There was nothing to add; any question about what happened later was superfluous. Simon's silence was unassailable. I didn't dare disturb him. I thought of Alma, waiting for me at the apartment. It must already be late. Gauging the hour was tricky with all the curtains drawn. I got up. Simon's face was hidden deep in shadow, and I couldn't discern any movement, as if my presence was no longer his concern. I decided I'd leave him in peace. I was certain we'd meet again. I turned to the door, a cat ran out in front of me, and then I heard him say my name.

"Richard," he said, as if returning from a deep sleep into which he'd sink again as soon as I left. "For you."

He extended his hand with a slip of folded paper.

"The address," he said. "The address which ends your search. The man you are looking for lives there."

I took the slip of paper and unfolded it: *33 N. Street.* Into my pocket it went. I sighed, thinking of the task that awaited me, tomorrow perhaps, and at that moment I was almost sorry Simon had fulfilled the wish I'd come to him with.

"Where is the street?"

"On Bjelave."

By now I knew where Bjelave was. I nodded and thanked him. Simon merely shrugged. I turned to the door and then heard him speak softly as if talking to himself.

"*You will die that day and be born.*"

"Excuse me?" I turned, surprised. "Simon, you speak only in riddles."

"Ha, Oedipus thought the same." He laughed softly. "But we all know there is nothing mysterious here, is there? Those are the words, more or less, with which Oedipus answers Tiresias when he asks the eternal question: *Whose son am I?* When he learns he'll die and be born again, and that day will be both his tomb and his birthplace. Tell that to your friend, the bit about the day on which one dies and is born again. Maybe he'll understand."

The cat scampered about in front of me as I went down the stairs. When we came out into the yard, it slipped into bushes. With some effort I shut the warped gate behind me and peered in, as I had a few hours earlier when I'd stood before it. The same scene of disarray. I felt as if I'd spent these hours with ghosts and was now on my way back to the world of the living, which began here, on this side of the gate. Maybe so, but from that world I'd brought something, the story about Daniel and Jelena, and an address. I looked once more at the house. A soft glow of light appeared briefly at a window and then was gone as if somebody had passed by holding a candle.

3

The fifth day is nearing its end. The sand is trickling. There is only a little of it left in the upper chamber of the hourglass. Now begins the last slide, and everything feels as if it's accelerating out of control. The last hours. As if I myself am disappearing with the remaining grains from that happy upper chamber, I clutch, cling, but in the end I fall and down I tumble—not even too roughly—to the tip of the sand heap in the lower chamber of the hourglass. The final grains of sand that are spilling onto my face tell me it's over. Time has run out. *You will die that day and be born.* Then silence. The silence of an hourglass that has done its job, the silence of the inside of the glass chamber. When the sand stills.

I'm amazed at the way my memory has preserved even the most minute particular of the rest of that day, as if I'm seeing it all again. I find it odd that I remember none of the sound attached to these memories. Actually, at the beginning it's as if I hear more, our voices, the voices of the passersby, the street, perhaps even the blast of a shell echoing in my memory, though I'm not sure of that because they rumble through all my memories of Sarajevo. Then the sound slowly fades as I stride toward my goal, my downfall, the end of my search, as I fall through the sand into a nightmare.

As I walked away from Simon's courtyard gate, I thought only of how I wanted to get back to the apartment as soon as possible and get through the visit that awaited us as quickly as possible so that we could return to the apartment, to one another. Simon's slip of paper, and the address at which he claimed my search would end (as far as this was concerned I held on to a skeptical reserve), I'd leave resting tranquilly in my pocket until tomorrow or the next day, although the street (*N.*) and its number (*33*) kept spinning around my mind, mingling with Simon's story, with his voice. I thought about how I'd already been to that neighborhood, how I might have even walked along that very street, how, if Jakob Schneider were indeed still alive, perhaps I'd walked right under my own father's window. The mysterious threads of fate. Today, I'd keep an eye on the layout of the streets, I told myself, to see if I could spot N. Street, so that I might orient myself more easily on the day when I used one of Alma's times away to set out on my new, perhaps final, search.

I ran. Although it was less than ten minutes from Simon's house to Ivor's apartment, I was still late. Alma was waiting for me, on edge. She couldn't understand how I could have forgotten that we were already supposed to be at her father's, evening was coming, there was a curfew on, and so forth. Who was this Simon now?! What did I have to do with the weird old man?! Although I'd bounded up to the door barely breathing, she didn't let me in even to change. We left immediately for Bjelave. Her father would be worried if we didn't arrive at the time we'd agreed on, she said sharply. I followed her, head bowed, even lagging a little. There was no dread. An agreeable stroll over the sand that was trickling away underfoot.

I wondered who I was supposed to be that evening, what role I should play. I asked her whether she'd told her father about us. "No," she said. She couldn't tell him such a thing just like that. Why did she ask me to come, then? It was what she wanted. Besides, she thought that one day it would be easier this way if . . .

"If what?" I asked.

"I don't know . . . If this is *it*."

"If it's what?"

"What do you mean 'what,' Richard?"

"I don't know what." I was stubborn. "You tell me."

I stopped her midroad. Alma glanced over at the other side. "What?" I asked. She didn't answer. The creases puckered around her eyes, as if angry she pressed her lips together, her small nose twitched as if she were about to punch me, punish my stupidity.

"Between the two of us," she said. "Between the two of us, *it*, you see?"

I turned her head tenderly toward me. "This is *it*," I said. "This is it," I repeated.

She smiled. Her anger ebbed. She seemed happy. And a little worried. Wary. Then we kissed for the first time outside our sanctuary, midday, among people. *This is it.* There was a strange glee in the way all the people walked right by us and paid no attention. Even she didn't swivel around. She accepted the kiss there, in the middle of the road. It was a nice gift. I felt grateful. This was what the last days had portended. Five days and counting.

On we went. We were truly happy, climbing up that hill. We were happy as we walked toward Bjelave. I was happy that I'd acted the role she'd set for me. In yet another of Alma's theatrical adaptations that was, I thought, playing to my advantage. We walked side by side without touching. Alma explained that I shouldn't be any different from who I am, or who I was before whatever happened between us happened. She'd already told her father I was there as a visitor. A writer, journalist, a new interesting friend, simple. All right, I consented like an actor who trusted his director. Everything would be fine.

While we were walking, I did what I could to decipher the illegible street names, just in case I might catch sight of N. Street. I twisted my tongue trying to pronounce them and ultimately simply focused on the first letter. That street had to be here somewhere. I thought how much easier it would be for me to find it now that Alma had shown me the way.

"You seem distracted. Is there anything wrong?"

"Everything's fine. Sorry."

"You weren't talking. That's why I ask."

"I was thinking about a story Simon told me," I lied. It was the first thing that occurred to me.

"What story?"

"About Daniel and Jelena, about Rifka and Franjo. About matters which are challenging to judge."

"Sounds interesting. You'll have to tell me the story," said Alma.

"I could tell you now, if you like. I haven't heard a story like that for quite some time."

"Gladly, but we haven't the time right now," she said. "We're almost there. We're already on his street."

I turned and saw a familiar building. I'd already been here. I asked what the street was called. I felt a small, muffled blow in my gut when she said the name, though still no dread. We were only at no. 3 on N. Street.

What a remarkable coincidence. I walked along slowly, gazing down the street. I recognized Alma's father's building on the odd-numbered side, and I tried gauging where no. 33 might be. The building we were walking toward would be, by my reckoning, somewhere around no. 21, so I projected no. 33 to be a red five-story building. My calculations kept adjusting, and I couldn't determine the sequencing of numbering precisely. New buildings became visible along the way. Glancing at the numbers I saw my estimate was off.

"Richard?" she called to me just as I'd recalculated her father's building to be no. 29, and was figuring my destination for tomorrow or the day after would be a gray three-story building that I was studying just at that moment. "Hey?! You wandered off again."

"I'm here, right here." I felt my throat go dry. Still no dread.

"I'm interested in the story. Tell me about it on the way home. Okay? Who is this Simon fellow, anyway?"

"Believe me, I don't really know myself."

In my memory from that moment forward, silence reigns. Only Alma's lips move. From them I read, "Here we are! You remember the building, don't you?" She smiles. The dread is suddenly here. My feet are leaden, but I still manage to resist the absurdity of a thought that has just occurred to me and which I cannot shake loose. Again it comes from afar, muffled, but then I take a blow to the gut that I can't ignore. The building, which I was sure is no. 27, turns out to be no. 31, and the one I thought surely is no. 29 is, in fact, no. 33. Alma pulls out her key for the front door. I remain out on the street. Motionless. Silent. Not a single thought. Only the mute incomprehension of coincidence. And only one or two words racing around my brain. *Coincidence. Remarkable coincidence.* Alma frowns. She doesn't understand why I froze. She beckons. *Coincidence.* I stare as if hypnotized at the blue plaque on Alma's father's building with the name of N. Street and, under it, no. 33. I have the same address written in Simon's handwriting in my pocket. I am musing on the coincidence. The place where my search ends is, according to Simon, this white building. A thought surges through my mind and raises foul, unimaginable dread. Is it possible that our fathers live under the same roof? Did some weird fateful mechanism line things up? All I can do is shrug if that is the case and try to locate Jakob Schneider's apartment on our way up to her father's place, where in the next few days I'll be ringing the doorbell, because today, regrettably, I cannot. The schedule for this afternoon at this address is already full.

Emboldened by the thought that I might learn where my father's apartment is in the building (perhaps right above her father's, maybe the two of them get along well, neighbors, of a similar age?), I think about how fate—I can't come up with a better word at the moment—is easing my job with its bizarre twists. The dread is gone, the muffled blows to the gut ease up, and I even hear Alma's voice again. She urges me to come in. She's frowning and smiling at the same time. My feet move of their own accord.

We're in the building. The ascent up the stairs to the apartment takes forever. Her father lives on the top sixth floor, she tells me, and goes skipping up the steps in front of me like a little girl. I slog along behind her. On the first floor I quickly scan the surnames on the mailboxes. I look for Schneider, I scan for Sch . . . , Schn . . . , Schnei . . . but I don't see it. It must be on a mailbox I miss because I'm following Alma, who summons me again, by now alarmed at my peculiar behavior. She is a floor ahead of me. We climb. Alma keeps going a floor ahead. I lag. She calls after me as if I'm a child who is trudging up step by step, resisting going home. She gestures. Faster. Faster. I climb up at a snail's pace. I hesitate. I peer at each surname on each door. The building is six stories tall and there are two apartments on each floor. The calculation is simple. I have already passed the Hodžićes, the Markovićes, the Kebos, the Alijagićes, the Ilićes, the Marjanovićes . . . and we are already on the fifth floor. Still no Schneiders or any sign that would help me know that I'm truly at the end of my search, as Simon predicted. Absolute silence reigns. On the fifth floor the dread is back like a boomerang, like the fresh assault of an illness on a wasting body, from the gut, the muscles, the temples; my pulse quickens, I feel myself perspire, but I still cannot accept its terrible whispers.

I want to say her name: *Alma*. To say *Alma* as if I'm calling for help. Better to say something than listen to what my brain is telling me. I call her. She turns. She looks at me, questioning. She's almost all the way to the sixth floor. It occurs to me that I never asked for her maiden name. Curious that she never offered it. *What a coincidence!* I reject the thought as the product of the dread that has so paralyzed me that I can no longer feel my arms or legs, and I've lost my hearing. Alma now looks at me a little worried. The Begovićes and Detonis live on the fifth floor, I've just learned, and it must be because of this information that I am looking poorly. *Curious, so curious,* I say to myself, *that I never asked her what her father's name is, that she never told me, after all the time we've spent together. The time since we met is not so short that this question wouldn't come up.* I call her once more. She comes back down a few steps, a bit worried. Clearly she's asking me what's going on. I can't utter a word. She gives me her hand. She forces us to keep going. On we go together. I have no strength to lift my eyes to the doors of the remaining two apartments. *The chances are now fifty-fifty, Alma,* I think. *It might be better for us to leave, go somewhere the two of us can be alone, like that first night, without age, without language, without background.* I think of Ingrid. I think of the picture of my mother. Nothing makes sense anymore. I'm deadened by the thought that is banging at the door of my consciousness, that has just smashed its way in. I close my eyes. We're on the sixth floor. We've obviously stopped at the door to the apartment we're going to. I can't tell because I've closed my eyes. I feel her hand on my neck. Then I stand in front of her with my back to the door, and I don't dare look at it. I stop her hand that moves toward the doorbell. I ask for her maiden name. Her lips ask me if I'm okay, is everything okay. I'm ashen, she says. She runs her hand through my sweat-drenched hair.

"Is everything okay, Richard?"

"No, it's not," I say. "Your maiden name? Tell me."

Alma looks at me in surprise, even a little frightened. Now she doesn't understand a thing. Her lips don't move. In despair she drops her gaze. She asks, "Is everything really all right?" She says we don't have to do this if I don't want to. She's alarmed by my appearance. Once more she asks me to explain what's going on. She says we needn't do anything I don't want, I am not obliged to her, I can live my life.

I ask her again, "Tell me your maiden name, Alma."

"What does that have to do with anything?" she asks. "Where is that coming from now?" She frowns. I'm tormenting her.

"Tell me your maiden name."

She shakes her head, miserable. She doesn't understand. In the end she gives up all resistance and points at the plaque on the door behind me. "See for yourself," she says. Instead of turning and doing what she suggests, I muster my courage and decide to read what is written on the door across the hall, behind Alma's back. My last chance. Failure. The Delić family lives there. I tell her I love her and that I'm sorry: this is all a crazy misunderstanding. Then I spill in silence through the neck of the hourglass. When I hit the floor I feel nothing, as if I dropped into the sand of our spent happiness. I don't hear a sound, but my eyes are still open. Before I completely lose consciousness, I see the plaque by the door. I already know what it will say. But there is still something that surprises me and if I weren't unconscious, perhaps I'd have a good chuckle over my dismal fate, my stupidity. "ŠNAJDER." On the door it says "ŠNAJDER"! What a joke! My eyes shut. So here the surname is spelled *Šnajder*, not *Schneider*! What a bad joke! I had to come all this way to find this out. What a stupendous mistake! I think back to the telephone directory. What idiocy! I think of leafing through the book of the dead at the synagogue. At that other side of my consciousness, I laugh myself silly to the point of tears that later will not stop flowing. I see the door open. I see an old man in the doorway looking at my body lying prostrate on his doorstep. Here ends the search. *You will die that day and be born.* He leans over me. He hoists me up under the arms. Alma lifts my feet. They carry me, dead, into their home, into the home of my father

and my sister.

4

We were back at Ivor's apartment just before curfew. I feigned exhaustion. Alma brought me headache pills. I asked her for a pill to calm me down. She made me damp compresses that were supposed to help me wrest myself free of the sudden lassitude that had come over me; Alma blamed it on the sweltering heat. This understanding of my spectacular fainting spell gave me the opportunity to act the listless patient, not in the mood for conversation, even though for a time now, since waking in Jakob's apartment, I'd had both feet firmly on the ground; I was completely self-possessed, meaning I was fully aware of what had just happened to us. Better said, the outcome was crystal clear even if I'd still not succeeded in figuring out how we got here, how could such a thing possibly have happened, what bitter destiny was toying with us.

I went to bed. With the compress draped over my forehead, I pretended to be dozing off, feverish—sleep being the best cure for sunstroke—and what I needed was quiet. Alma came in, brought me a glass of water, and ran her hand through my hair, sending me off to sleep with kisses as if I were a sick child who'd woken in the middle of the night in the glow of a yellow light from the hallway, with somebody close at hand to soothe him, a mother, grandmother, or . . . a sister. I dove into the pillow, pulled free of her hands, pulled the sheet over my face, hoping this was just a nightmare from which I couldn't seem to wake, but which would soon come to an end, as does every dream, and

I'd wake up next to the Alma I knew this morning, an Alma whispering in my ear while her body told me that all this, despite the place where it was happening—despite the war surrounding it—had a future (how fatuous that word now sounds), next to an Alma with whom I don't share a father. She left the room, not yet ready for bed. She closed the door, the yellow light was gone, and I was covered in sweat under the sheet, my eyes opened wide. They'd close only once, briefly somewhat later that evening, to persuade Alma that I was fast asleep. There would be no more sleep for me in Sarajevo, not that night, nor the next long day, nor the last night after which I fled.

I lay on my back, eyes fixed on the ceiling. In her sleep Alma slid her arm over my chest. I listened to her breathe, the kind of breathing that showed she was in a deep, guileless slumber. Oh, how different that night was from our first night when I'd kept watch over her as she slept! Since then I'd gotten to know every part of the body that was now sleeping at my side, knowing nothing, oblivious of the tragedy that had begun that first night, tossing and turning fitfully and muttering, snuggling up to me and demanding sleepily that I welcome her embrace. I didn't dare offer her more than that. The love that, despite everything, was still there was forbidden to me. I was afraid, with every new kiss, of magnifying the trouble I'd brought upon her. On the other hand, I didn't know what I could do to ease it, diminish it, make it less wrenching. There could be no expiation here, nor forgiveness. The deed, though inadvert, as if that made any difference, was done. I hope she never learns what really happened. To violate the right to truth of a person whom this truth could destroy is not a sin but a duty. That is at least what my guilt whispered to me as it clutched me ever more tightly around the neck each time I looked at Alma, whenever I reached for her.

Good God, she must never find out. This was the first thought that came to me when I regained consciousness. I didn't open my eyes. I heard

Alma and her father talking softly, taking care not to wake me. I didn't want to open my eyes. I didn't know how much time had passed since I'd fainted by Jakob Šnajder's front door, by the door of the man I'd come to Sarajevo to see and to whom I'd finally found the way, but not thanks to Simon, as I'd hoped. I found my father, who was also father to a sister I never knew I had. I'd come to know her as a lover, and came with her to the apartment where I now lay as if dead and laid out on a bier, and I couldn't bear to open my eyes for the disgrace of it, for the fury, for the despair, for the helplessness. To die and be born again—Tiresias was right—and then to live as a blind man. Oedipus had the right idea, Simon. I thought about how it would be best for things to stay this way, with my eyes shut to the world forever. For the first time in my life I thought of suicide as I lay on that couch. Then I tried to figure out where I was by squinting through my lashes. Alma and her father were sitting at the table. After a few minutes Jakob looked over in my direction, and then he said something to Alma. Alma came over and kneeled so that she could whisper in my ear.

"Are you awake?"

I mumbled something inaudible, confirming that I'd heard her.

"Thank goodness everything's all right! Have a little water, Richard. Are you okay?"

"Think so," I answered.

The hiding was over. I opened my eyes. I was born again. Jakob handed me a glass of water, smiling and nodding warmly. He said *Willkommen* in German. My father was welcoming me at the moment of my new birth. All I could say to him was *Oprostite*. That's what I was thinking: *Forgive me*.

"What matters is that you're okay," said Jakob. "How are you feeling?"

"Sunstroke?" added Alma.

"Yes. I think it might be. The sun."

"It's so hot."

"Unbearably so."

"Forgive me," I said once more.

"What matters is that you're back with us. I'll put dinner on the table."

Alma got up and went off to bring out the food. I looked at Jakob Šnajder. The old man studied me with curiosity. We smiled at one another. His hair was a charming shade of gray. Still a full head of hair, a dark complexion, and strikingly brown eyes. He was clean-shaven as befits an elderly gentleman. Regardless of his age, he seemed robust, energetic. A handsome older man. He must have been dashing in the early 1940s. Hardly surprising that he'd seduced the Müller sisters. I wondered what I'd inherited from him. The build. The lips maybe. Not the eyes. Mine were blue like my mother's. The lines of his face perhaps; I wondered pointlessly whether I'd look just like this were I to reach his age. I smiled at him again. The old man watched me with lively eyes as if trying to read on my face all about the guest who'd come for a visit. I was almost ashamed. I felt as if he'd succeeded in his intention. That already he knew everything.

"Alma has spoken of you a great deal, Richard. She told me she hadn't met such an interesting man as you in a long while."

"I'd say she's exaggerating a little. I've also heard a lot about you. I am so glad to have had the opportunity to meet you, despite this little incident."

"Don't you worry about that. So nice to have you here. Alma's friends are my friends, too, you know, and I'm always glad to meet them."

He spoke German fluently. Masterfully. Then he went on looking at me. I looked around.

"You have a nice place" was all I could think of saying, hoping to delay the inevitable question that was part of all my Sarajevo introductions. I failed.

"Tell me," began the old man, and I already knew what he'd ask, "whatever brought you to Sarajevo at such a terrible moment?"

My reason for coming, he'd asked my reason for coming! I thought of Mother's letter. The blue notebook. Alma served the meal. I balked. It would be so easy to speak the truth and with one stroke to change their lives, everything they knew about themselves, see the horror register on their faces.

"Richard is a writer and journalist. He's reporting from Sarajevo. He is filming and writing. I told you about that."

"He writes, what's more, with great skill"—my father complimented me—"at least as far as what I have had the opportunity to read is concerned. I still have your novel here somewhere. I bought it when I was in Germany. I was intrigued by the title. *Die Loslösung*. What was that about?"

"Ah yes. *Secession*. About an angry young man who secedes from his country, a country whose recent disgraceful history belongs to his parents' generation. His is a demarcation from his parents, from history, from their crimes, from their worldview. It is a political secession which, in my character's mind, passes first through a final severing of bloodlines, a break with his parents, with everybody who is older, with the perpetrators, with the criminals. What can I say—that was one of my first novels and I was the *angry young man* who refuses to carry the guilt of others, who's out to judge others, those older than himself who brought him into the world, without mercy."

"I remember. You impressed me with your daring. How did your parents react to such a position?"

"I don't know. I never met my mother. She died when I was born, and my father killed himself after the war."

"So sorry," he said sincerely.

We ate in silence. Alma gave her father the latest news from town. They commented on the war and the political situation. I said nothing. I admired their closeness and love. I admired Alma. *This is it.* The love hadn't lessened, she wasn't frightened, and she hadn't gone anywhere now that I'd learned that she was my sister. I didn't know how I could possibly understand this. I didn't know anything just then. I simply watched these two clueless people. Maybe it's the bloodline, the intimacy, the love, the respect, a stronghold built from birth. But what about adoptees? What does the bond of blood mean in our case? Who were the parents against whom I'd risen up? The old people I saw as criminals because they'd stayed silent, they did not repent, they called for others to be asphyxiated in gas chambers? I hated them because I was one of them. That's why I wrote *Secession*, out of rage and disgust. What should I think now about this bond of blood that put me on the side of the asphyxiated, and at the same time was tearing her away?

Questions swarmed through my mind. I had no answers then, nor do I have any today. I watched them and envied them. I felt like an intruder holding their destinies in my hands. I thought of the damage I'd do to them. I thought for the first time that I must leave Sarajevo, must get out of there as soon as possible. That would be easier than for her to learn the truth. She'll get over me. She'll go back to her husband. I thought about how this old man didn't deserve to learn that my existence was bound to his, that he was somebody else's father, that my mother hadn't informed him of her pregnancy, that life later had its way. He admired the younger man for his bold reckoning with the past, a past in which the younger man was tied by the great burden of kinship to crimes committed, as well, in his name, in the name of a future for a pure race—but the younger man had made a crucial error right from the start and he, this gray-haired man with the lively eyes and the death-camp number tattooed on his lower arm, was the younger man's trueborn father. I thought about how it would surely shake him to the core to learn the real reason I'd come to this city, but I wasn't sure he'd then survive learning about the true nature of Alma's and my relationship. What he might have sensed, read in our gestures, on her face, in Alma's game of hide-and-seek. She must never know. Never. Leave Sarajevo. That seemed the only fair decision. The only way out. I needed, at least, to save their lives. Mine was over. I'd died and was born again to do penance for my sins, and I did not wish to do any more harm. I would take the secret of the incest to my grave in the hopes that my next death would be without a rebirth.

"Alma tells me you, too, lived in Austria," I said, although only a moment before I'd sworn I'd leave the old man alone. "That must be why your German is so fluent."

"My father taught me German. He was from southwestern Hungary, a little town on the Drava River; he spoke fluent German, Hungarian, and the Croatian spoken around there. Afterward I studied in Graz in the late 1930s. Then I lived in Vienna for a time, working for the Party under an assumed name until the summer of 1941, when they arrested and deported me." Jakob showed me his arm as proof.

"You were lucky to survive."

"Yes, clearly. But I'm not sure I'll survive this war as well. Who could've imagined something like this would happen?! In Sarajevo! Again we are being interned! They don't allow us water, electricity. They shell us."

"Now, now, Father, calm down," said Alma.

"All right, all right, Alma, dear. And anyway, to change the subject. I wanted to ask you where you live in Vienna? I knew that city quite well, long ago."

"In the ninth *Bezirk*, on Berggasse."

Jakob himself offered me the opportunity to begin the game. I could have simply lied. But I knew he'd react to the street name and I couldn't resist.

"Indeed?!" he asked first, incredulous. "What a coincidence! I had friends who lived on that very same street."

"At which number?" The game was rolling along of its own accord.

"I believe it was number 17."

"Why, that is the number of my building!" I exclaimed, feigning surprise.

"Is that possible?" the excited old man asked. "Their names were Paula and Ingrid Müller."

"I believe there is an elderly woman in the building by that name . . . Yes, Ingrid Müller."

"Really! Ingrid is still alive?!" exclaimed the man, only to blanch and with a hushed voice—or at least so it seemed to me—to ask about Paula. "And Paula? Do you know perhaps . . ."

"No, I don't know her," I answered him in a panic. "I'm only a neighbor."

"We were very close once long ago," Jakob went on. "Paula and I."

"Father's Viennese romance," Alma added, "until she turned him in to the Gestapo."

I started as if stung, as if I'd been hit in the face and it had woken me up and enraged me. As if I were protesting a glaring injustice, I shouted, *"Sorry? What?!"*

Seeing the surprise on their faces, I realized how inappropriate my reaction had been.

"You were betrayed by one of the Müller sisters," I said, calmer. "Why? I don't understand."

"Why, you ask? I don't know. I never will."

"What did she report you for?"

"My Jewish background, of course! Simple and sufficient, as you well know," said Jakob in a conciliatory tone, shrugging. "You look surprised, Richard, but that sort of thing happened. Did you yourself not write about such people?"

Yet another surprise. I was looking at him, amazed, not because I couldn't grasp his words, but because Ingrid and Mother's notebook suggested that Andreas Schubert had been apprehended for something altogether different, for spying.

"Didn't you say you were working for the Party at the time? Under an assumed name? Might they have arrested you as a spy?"

"That is what I myself assumed when the Gestapo picked me up. Then I soon realized they'd arrested me as a Jew hiding under falsified documents. They'd been sent a report that there was a Jew hiding illegally at that address. When they began questioning me I realized they knew nothing about my work as a communist. In a way I was relieved, because the whole network would've been threatened. That's why I confessed. I thought that under the circumstances it might even keep me alive, because as a spy they'd have tortured me and shot me quickly."

"How do you know it was she?" I stuttered.

"Simply. As I told you, I was in Vienna on assignment under an alias. Nobody knew of my background except for Paula. In moments of intimacy, when you think you're with a person in whom you can confide your deepest secret, the secret that your life depends on, as if confessing it will bring the two of you even closer, I made that mistake and put my life in her hands. And she betrayed me. It could only be her. That's how I know."

I wanted to tell him he was wrong, that there was a letter. I pulled myself together. Nothing could set it right without destroying something else.

Still, I asked him, "What happened to her? Did you ever . . ."

"No! What good would that have done?! I don't know what happened to her or even whether she is still alive."

"Didn't you want to know?"

"No. I survived the camps. For me the story was over. I didn't want revenge. I didn't want to know her or anybody like her. Why would I seek out my executioners, take an interest in their lives, ask why they'd done what they did? It didn't interest me."

"You never learned anything more? After the arrest, I mean."

"I wasn't interested, as I said. I made no effort." Jakob stopped talking. This bridled him. He'd revisited bitter memories while I wondered who else could have known he was Jewish besides Paula.

"Forgive me if I've upset you, reminded you of those things. It's just that I live in that building."

"No, Richard, it's nothing. Just life. And besides, I often think of those terrible times. Today, perhaps especially because I knew you were coming and you're Austrian, I thought back to those days several times. A curious coincidence, I must say, that you live at the exact same address."

"It happens. Not my fault."

Alma stroked her father's head. Tears welled in his eyes, which turned them from flashing to muddied. I thought he'd start to cry. But he collected himself. There was nothing more to add. I said I was still feeling a bit wobbly. Alma suggested we get going. The old man saw us to the door. He shook my hand firmly, amicably. He said I must promise to come again. I said I would while promising myself that this visit had been my first and last. He waved to us as we went down the stairs. My father. Jakob Šnajder.

As I lay there, sleepless, that night, my plan for a speedy exit from Sarajevo was already in place. Alma would leave the apartment in the morning, and as soon as she left I'd pack my things and go back to the safe zones where the great names of world journalism were gathered, from where they dispatched their reports on the besieged city. I'd make contact with anybody who could help me leave that very day on a transport aircraft, hoping circumstances would so permit. And so I would forever vanish from the lives of these people to whom I was a threat. I could hurt them. I hoped our pathways would never cross again. This is what I had to do; it was the only solution. The window was open and through it came the familiar voices of a Sarajevo wartime night. Somebody is dying. Somebody feels the pain of a wounded body. Somebody is mourning. Somebody is squeezing a trigger. Somebody is snuffing a candle. Somebody is making love. Somebody is living their last days. Somebody will soon leave the city.

I got up. I'd hidden the blue notebook in the wardrobe under my clothes. I went into the kitchen, checked that all the curtains were fully drawn, and lit a candle. Again I read Mother's letter to the man I'd now met. Her desperate letter to a lost lover whose child she'd soon bear. The letter that would remain forever trapped within these blue covers, that no post office anywhere in the world would be able to deliver, to a man who since the moment of his arrest to this very day tasted the pungent tinge of betrayal, unable to make sense of her reasons, hating the woman who gave birth to me and who wrote him a letter that left no room for doubt. But who did, in fact, turn him in? Had Ingrid known Jakob was Jewish? Even if her sister had divulged the secret, I was sure Ingrid would never have taken such a risk. She, too, was implicated in the whole story, in the secret circle, and it would have threatened her own life, her sister's life, and, ultimately, mine if Jakob were to confess under torture to what he'd been doing in Vienna. She couldn't take that chance. No, she didn't seem capable of such betrayal. And besides, didn't she care for Jakob herself? Was it Heinrich? Had he known? Maybe Paula told him at a moment of loss and fury. Maybe she hinted at the secret. Or he guessed. Maybe he tried his luck? He was close to her and he had certain motives for pushing Jakob aside. Perhaps that way he'd win Paula back; she was in no position to refuse marriage. Didn't he enlist right away? Didn't he propose to Paula immediately? Did he kill himself out of guilt? I had no proof. Somebody else altogether might have betrayed Jakob. Maybe information about him surfaced in Yugoslavia? Or in Russia? Then they would have arrested him as a communist as well as a Jew, and not just as a Jew, wouldn't they? I was maddened by my attempts at solving this mystery that was only a little older than I was, and which would determine my whole existence, my work, my views, my life's path, my literature. The riddle seemed insoluble. I wanted to smash the kitchen table with my fist, and I'd have done it if Alma hadn't been sleeping in the bedroom; I might have even broken something, because I realized I'd break the promise I'd made myself when I shook Jakob Šnajder's hand. I couldn't leave this city until I'd delivered the letter to him and removed the blemish of betrayal from my mother.

5

There are days like yesterday that seem to swallow the events of the surrounding days, weeks, months, and—like black holes hidden in the calendar—they steal all their vitality, promise, and substance. They suck up everything, squeeze the surrounding days dry like overripe oranges, and then out they spill in a rush, all within the bounds of a single day. These days mark our muddled lives with milestones, signs by the roadside that alter the complexion of the phases behind them, and open before us stretches of road on which we had not expected to tread. Yes, I knew this was one of those days. But I was wrong in thinking the day would end by the next morning, that the black hole would be satisfied. The day would spill over into the coming twenty-four hours, because a new milestone was being embedded in my life bearing the simple message that its end was nigh.

That day I would tell everything to my father. Simon hadn't instructed me on what happens with a father when he meets a son he'd known nothing about. There must be a prophecy on this theme. Didn't cruel Laius lose his life when he met his son? It needn't always be that way. Didn't old Laertes, in another story, grow more youthful after discovering his son Odysseus in the orchard? But the comparison is flawed, because the man who set out for Bjelave to go to his father's apartment that morning, blue notebook in hand, is a son whose father never lost him the way Laertes lost Odysseus; the father would only be meeting this son now for the first time. There'd be no place for celebration in this version, nor would Athena with a single blow end the pointless war so that father and son could live on in amity, allowing the epic poem to wrap up with the help of a little cunning on the part of the blind singer, already weary of the vast scope of his endeavor.

It must have been Simon's influence that had me remembering the last book of the *Odyssey*. I always loved that moment in the epic. The moment of recognition. Yet another instance of Odysseus's cunning, this time to the delight of the father he'd deceived.

I did what I'd set out to do that day. I stood before my father feeling no regret or pain or fear but the bluntness of the truth, the bald facts, the cold chiming of the historical clock, the vacuity of what—with a thrill—we call destiny . . . only to have the events that followed to the end of that overlong day stoke fear and pain and, finally, regret. I would carry all this with me the next morning as I fled.

I set out for Bjelave not long after Alma left the apartment. I had no idea at that point what I intended to do except to deliver Mother's letter to Jakob Šnajder. It said all that needed to be said about the betrayal and, of course, the child. I thought I wouldn't tell him I was the child in the letter, the one kicking his mother's belly with little feet as she penned it in late 1941. I knew if I did there was great danger that Alma would learn about it all very quickly. I wasn't able to think clearly about what I was doing. After the events of the day before and the sleepless night, I could only follow the thought that had led me to Bjelave and told me that Jakob Šnajder must not die before he saw the letter. My plan to leave Sarajevo that very afternoon seemed ironclad.

That morning Alma found me, awake and irritable. She thought I was ill; she said maybe I should go to the hospital, that she'd go with me. I refused. I had no idea we'd meet again at the Koševo hospital that very afternoon. I also had no idea there'd be one more time, one more night. "I'll stay here in bed," I said.

"I'm already starting to miss you," she said and ran her fingers through my hair. "When I come home, greet me as only you can. I'm losing my patience." I could barely stop myself from asking her back to bed. Everything hurt, every word, every kiss, her scent, her preparations for going out, what she didn't know, my fear that I was holding her for the last time, that I was feeling her tongue in my mouth for the last time. I did not succumb to my body, and this was not just because we were bound by the same father but also because it seemed that making love with her that morning would be an even greater betrayal, once I'd gone. I decided to do what I felt must be done and leave her forever. For the good of all of us. Suffer the sacrifice for future happiness. Hers, foremost, because I no longer entertained illusions for my own.

We agreed we'd meet at the apartment as we'd been doing every afternoon. I thought about these everyday, ordinary words and the gestures we'd begun to use as our farewell, or at least what we called our good-byes—her parting smile, the kiss she blew as I lay in bed, her brace for the gentle ache of separation, consoled by the sure sense that we'd see each other again soon, a brief wait until I blew my kiss back, her wave, her lips mouthing *Love you* and then the *click!* as she shut the door. Her steps moving away down the stairs.

I no longer needed a guide. I remembered clearly the route we'd taken the day before, and so I was soon out in front of Jakob's building. From time to time I slipped my hand into the bag and touched the blue notebook as if afraid I might lose the central piece of evidence in this belated facing of the facts—my own sort of birth certificate. Along the way I met a small number of people hurrying, and a group which were doing what they could to barricade the cellar windows and entrances to their buildings with whatever they could get their hands on, whether boards, sheet metal, or sandbags. Yet another day of war. Shells had rained down overnight, and there might be wounded. A boy had written "CAUTION: SNIPER!" in big red letters. The message was for the pedestrians who were coming from my direction, and it took effect immediately. Nobody could complain they hadn't been warned. The boy looked at me with surprise as I walked by him slowly, and then he pointed with his brush to what he'd written and off somewhere in the distance to where the sniper was probably hiding. The logic was rock solid, but I didn't care. I simply felt apart from all that. As if I no longer shared their reality, as if it had been that way from the start, as if I were just passing through their troubles, immune to the bullets, though not to the lethal arrows that had reached me from faraway 1941. I was somebody for whom no well-intentioned instructions for surviving the siege were of any merit—a foreigner clutching a blue notebook in his hand as if clutching an ominous talisman! It had brought me to this tragic city, and it would take me away!

For the second time in as many days, Jakob Šnajder was surprised by the sight of me at his door. He barely summoned the words to greet me courteously, saying he'd hoped to see me again but hadn't expected me quite so soon. He didn't ask why I was there but threw open the door. He gestured to himself as if to apologize for his appearance, as if he weren't dressed properly for the occasion. In a worn bathrobe, old slippers, slightly ragged pants, and unshaven, his hair still uncombed, he seemed older than he had yesterday. *Laertes in tatters in the orchard,* I thought, looking at Jakob's figure. I felt sorry for him. I was sorry that I was about to burden him with new trouble, yet in I strode into his apartment as if I were there to read his judgment. I said coldly, "We have to talk, Jakob." We stood facing one another in the living room. "Last night I was not entirely frank with you."

Worried, the old man asked me what this was about and sat down in an armchair as if expecting a terrible blow, as if steeling himself. I didn't know where to begin. Only then did I realize I had no concept, no plan. The old man looked at me, afraid.

"Does this have anything to do with Alma?" he asked impatiently, watching me closely.

"Oh, no! No."

"Thank goodness!"

His greatest fears were assuaged, and he now seemed prepared to accept whatever it was I had to tell him.

"No, this has nothing to do with her. It has to do with our conversation yesterday. Something we discussed."

"Vienna, am I right?" he asked impatiently as if he'd been expecting exactly that, and then he rushed on without waiting for my answer. "But what about?! I had this feeling. You see, even before you came I was thinking about what happened then. Because of your visit, probably. And besides, I knew a man who had the same last name. Our conversation yesterday left me in quite a state. I hardly slept a wink all night, thinking back to the war. The war of the 1940s, not the one now. This is not your fault. How could it be?! I am an old and lonely man who gets easily sideswiped by memories . . . Am I right? Something about Vienna?"

"Yes, you're right."

"But what?" Jakob went on groping for answers, giving me no chance to speak, as if he feared what I had to say, though he could never have guessed, no matter how deeply he delved into the past.

"Whatever could you possibly have to do with it except for living at the same address? Or am I wrong? I don't understand. What's this about, Richard?"

The old man was struggling. Just as Laertes did in the orchard.

He doubted whether to embrace him, kiss him, and tell him all about his having come home, or whether he should first question him and see what he would say. In the end he deemed it best to be crafty with him . . .

"When I say I wasn't being entirely frank with you last night, it actually has to do with that address in Vienna. I live today in Ingrid Müller's apartment, Jakob. I was recently doing some remodeling there and found something which I believe belongs to you, something you should know about. I couldn't speak of it yesterday in front of Alma. When you see what I'm talking about, I believe you'll agree."

"What do you mean? I don't understand a thing you're saying." He rose abruptly from the chair and took several steps around the room. He was visibly agitated. "You came here yesterday to my house as Alma's friend, you lied to me, you spoke of Vienna, and today you tell me you live in Ingrid Müller's apartment and you found something that belongs to me which I should know about?! This is madness! What game are you playing?!" shouted Jakob. "What does Ingrid have to do with this?! Or Alma?! Who are you, Richard?! Who sent you?!"

Who and whence are you—tell me of your town and parents? Where is the ship lying that has brought you and your men to Ithaca? Or were you a passenger on some other man's ship, and those who brought you here have gone on their way and left you?

"Allow me to explain." I strove to calm him down. "Have a seat, Jakob, please."

"Don't torment me, Richard, please. Explain or leave at once!" He gestured at the door and then, out of breath, returned to his armchair, focusing somewhere up at the bookshelves.

After a few minutes, in a more conciliatory tone, he said, "Speak."

"Paula Müller is not the one who turned you in. I don't know who did but it wasn't she. I think that's important for you to know. At the moment when you were arrested, Paula was carrying your child. She did not betray you. That's all."

The old man struggled again out of his armchair. He opened the balcony door to take a deep breath. Then he went to the kitchen for a drink of water. He leaned with his hands on the stove and tried to calm himself with steady breathing. He was clearly thinking about what I'd told him, staring frozen at the floor with the glass trembling in his hand, thinking about my role in all this, yesterday's meeting, Alma . . . After a few minutes of silence it was as if his very sense of reason rebelled against my words, as if he'd come up with a saving grace, a way out of the tricky situation I'd imposed, and he asked, "How can I trust you?"

Poor Laertes . . . *you must give me such manifest proof of your identity, as shall convince me.*

Then back he came to his armchair. He stared at me fixedly. "How can I trust you?" again he asked. He waited. I knew the feeling. I knew his incredulity and his fading hope that this was all just some big misunderstanding. I knew all this because I already died and was born again.

The comparison is flawed. Odysseus showed the scar from a wound a boar had dealt him when he went to Parnassus to his mother's father. He pointed to ten apple trees, thirteen pear trees, and forty fig trees, which, along with fifty rows of grapevines, had been promised him by his father. It was easy for Laertes to recognize him. I died and was born again so that I'd take the blue notebook out of my bag that day and place it on the table that stood between us.

"I found this recently in Ingrid and Paula Müller's apartment, this notebook, hidden behind bookshelves in a niche in the wall." I opened it to the first page—*"Jakob Dearest . . ."*—and handed it to him. "Read."

I watched the old man's face as his expression changed. The twitching of his cheeks, the contracting and spreading of his wrinkles, the dilating of his pupils that drank in Paula's words . . . the grinding of his teeth, the occasional release of troubled sighs. I'd delivered to Jakob Šnajder what was his. I'd done my job. My mission was done and what had to unfold afterward I let happen, knowing I'd be leaving his and Alma's life in a few hours. *She'll understand why I left,* I thought, *when Jakob tells her the incredible story. Maybe it's better this way.*

Jakob took a long time with the letter as if measuring every word, as if every sentence required multiple readings so that the message wouldn't be wrongly understood, as if weighing the document, its authenticity and worth, as if he were giving himself a little more time before he raised his head and looked at the foreigner who this letter had turned into his son.

At one moment Jakob quickly stopped a tear, as if it would be unseemly to cry. Then he closed the blue notebook and tapped its old cover several times with his fingers while still not raising his eyes. As if he were garnering the strength to ask, finally, "You're the child, are you not?"

The last shred of doubt melted away with my silence. Jakob nodded, resigned. Then, as if splashing his face, he buried it briefly in his hands, then his face slowly emerged; yet the scene had not changed: I was still right there in front of him. His son. And the silence between us was an irrevocable answer.

With the tips of his fingers, Jakob caressed the cover of the blue notebook. It bonded us. The words of a mother who hoped, one winter night, that the father would know the child who was soon to be born.

And her wish was granted.

"Yesterday you said . . ." Jakob spoke again in a hoarse voice, losing the last word. He coughed. "You said your mother died after you were born and your father killed himself."

"Yes, I wasn't lying."

"So that means she . . ." Jakob fell silent and looked to me as if pleading for help.

"Yes, Paula, my mother, died soon after I was born."

Jakob's chin trembled as if beginning to grieve for a friend whose tragic fate he'd only now learned of, or maybe he was apologizing to Paula for the injustice with which he'd branded her memory, for the arrogance of the betrayed, for half a century of bitterness.

"So Heinrich recognized you as his son."

I didn't answer. I wasn't sure if that was a question.

"What happened to him?"

"I didn't lie. Heinrich, my father, I mean the person I thought was my father for fifty years, killed himself after the war. Ingrid is still alive, as I told you. She raised me."

I don't know how long we spent in silence, looking at one another, before Jakob coughed again, as if weighing the meaning of my gaze, the purpose of my visit, my patience in waiting. As if he were facing an unconditional reckoning, he took a deep breath and began to tell, with a telegraphic clarity and without a pause, the story of the year 1941—as if this were the only thing in the world he had to give me.

"I met your mother in early 1941. Ingrid introduced us. I'd come to Austria on assignment. The Party needed people inside the Third Reich, and I was the perfect candidate for the mission. My father had taught me German, I'd studied in Austria. I presented myself as a Yugoslav German. I had falsified documents and the alias Andreas Schubert. And another advantage (or perhaps drawback) I had over the other candidates for the task—as one of my comrades told me—was the imperative of celibacy. The comrade told me that women are the greatest danger for a spy and that at least I didn't have to worry about that, because under the Nazi regime the fact that I'd been circumcised was the perfect guarantee I wouldn't stray.

"I was sent as part of a campaign to observe the conditions and link the various little groups that had formed to defy the Nazis who might be of use to us. My reports were dispatched to Yugoslavia and then probably on to Moscow. My task was to live in Vienna, find a job, open my ears and eyes, or simply do nothing and wait for further instructions. With this in mind I found a job at a restaurant where certain highly positioned Viennese Nazis gathered. I had several reliable contacts through which I sent information. They pointed me to Ingrid.

"I quickly got to know her and earned her trust. I liked this forthright, learned woman who'd succeeded in attracting a certain number of her students and friends to the resistance circle—amateurs at least as far as I, as a communist operative, was concerned. If one could even call what they were doing resistance. They were mainly social democrats or simply democrats: in short, anti-Nazis. In an operative sense there wasn't much potential, but there weren't many people to be found in Vienna at that point who were prepared to offer any kind of resistance. I took care that my activities didn't make the others appear too suspicious, while at the same time I made as much use of them as I could.

"Your mother was also in the circle. And Heinrich. The first time Ingrid brought me to a secret meeting in their apartment at Berggasse 17, where they mainly discussed the war situation, newspaper reports, news from banned radio stations, I spotted Paula. And while your aunt, Ingrid, was a remarkably levelheaded woman, an organizer and a leader, Paula enjoyed a rich internal life in Ingrid's shadow, quietly waiting to come into her own. She loved her sister and appreciated her maternal shade in whose shelter she hid while waiting for somebody to come along and draw her out of there. Or at least that's how it looked to me. Ultimately, perhaps she is what drew me, the young woman—a sanctuary from the history that was tumbling down around our heads.

"Heinrich was endlessly devoted to her. A friend from childhood, an ever-besotted companion. In fact, I didn't know the true nature of their relationship. She loved him, that was certain, but it was also clear that she wanted something more.

"I still remember her chestnut hair and that slender little nose, and those curving dark lips. To stroll with her in the early spring of 1941 along the Ring meant not to belong to the reality surrounding us. Your mother simply shrugged it off, and she generously welcomed me into her hideout from the world to which we were born. It was easy to fall in love with Paula, Richard. She brought me something I hadn't known, caught up as I was as a youth in the undertow of our century. She spoke to me of things I didn't even know existed, little things I'd never even noticed or which did not exist in *my* world.

"I don't know what attracted her to me. But, whatever it was, it led her to my door one night. She'd had a fight with Ingrid. I asked why. She told me candidly that this was all my fault; she was in love with me. I will never forget that feeling. Never again have I known it. No matter how much I loved Alma's mother, through the shared decades of our life together, I never again felt what I felt as Paula and I stood in the doorway on the night she describes in her letter. The night she believes you were conceived, the night in which she made me forget so many things, including the advice from that comrade of mine.

"Perhaps for that reason the betrayal hurt me so deeply. And, indeed, just as the letter you brought me says, that night was the beginning of the assault on Yugoslavia. So it was that our relationship began. In the context of the larger events, it lasted between the two German invasions: the swift occupation of Yugoslavia and the invasion of the Soviet Union.

"When the Gestapo arrested me, my first thought was that the close-knit network had given way somewhere—information had been leaked and certain death awaited me. I was taken to the central headquarters in Vienna. As they were escorting me into the building, one of my guards shouted to a comrade of his, *We found a Jew!* as if he'd trapped a rare wild animal. Immediately I grasped what was going on. I confessed to my origins. My confession allowed me to cloak myself so I wouldn't betray things which mattered much more to me just then.

"From that day forward until now, I thought of your mother as somebody who'd allowed me to feel the sweet, sometimes even unbearable, joy coming from joining with a beloved being, but also something very different, the dull pain from the deep stab of the dagger of betrayal which, unlike the brevity of that first feeling stirs from time to time at its own murderous pace. Thanks to you and the letter you've brought, what's left of my life will at least be free of that burden."

The history of my parents. Because of this I'd come to Sarajevo. Jakob told their story and then dropped into silence, his eyes wandering over Paula's letter. I listened calmly, even surprised, with a tinge of regret at how the story of my arrival into the world was actually a matter of a few well-formulated sentences, taking up the space of no more than several handwritten pages. Still, the story I wanted to know was not complete.

"Doesn't this leave you wondering who did betray you?" I interrupted Jakob's stillness, and he looked up abruptly, chuckling softly at my naïveté.

"I'd be a happy man, Richard, if I didn't have to wonder that. Now, since I've read Paula's letter, I am wondering whom to install in her place. For a half century I thought I'd been the victim of someone I'd trusted, someone who'd seen the long-hidden sign on my body and hadn't even blinked when she realized what it meant. I wonder, but I cannot find the answer, and I may never know. Perhaps there's no point in seeking it. Unlike most of the members of my family who all met the same fate, I survived. I survived the fate that was meant for me. The fact that your mother, judging by this letter, preserved the secret is far more important for me at this moment . . . It's as if I've reconciled with my ghosts . . ."

Jakob rose to his feet. The time had come for this conversation to end.

"I hope you'll tell me, one day, about all you've been through," I said, knowing that day would never come.

"Just as I hope that you'll tell me more about yourself, Richard. When we get to know each other better, of course."

Perhaps he truly hoped for that. I nodded. He gave me his hand, and I pressed it firmly. The blue notebook remained there on the table between us.

I turned to leave and was at the door when I heard Jakob behind me in the hall.

"Richard!" he said as if recalling something important. "One thing you didn't explain. A thing I still don't understand. Please don't take it the wrong way, and answer me honestly."

"About what?"

"How did Alma get involved in this story?" he asked, his voice trembling. In the gloom of the hall, he seemed bent down under the weight of the question, as if preparing to deal a blow or fend one off. His face darkened and narrowed, wrinkling his skin.

I recoiled as if caught in a trap. I felt the fear take over my feet and climb upward, caressing my tense belly and squeezing my throat. My skin crept with sweat, droplets of cold water that slithered down my spine. I started. "Entirely by coincidence."

"Can I believe you?"

"Don't you worry. It's pure coincidence. Trust me. We're friends."

"I want to trust you. I also know my daughter. I saw you two yesterday, Richard," Jakob chided me.

"We're friends," I repeated. "Trust me. It was entirely by chance."

"Just tell me, did you know she was my daughter?" he asked me once more as if he hadn't heard what I'd said.

"No."

"Does she know you are . . . ?"

"No."

I cannot forget his eyes. The answers did not reassure him; they did not relieve his fear. He didn't change his posture; he went on standing there motionless in front of me, distrustful and befuddled, unsure of how to continue. It seemed both of us were thinking the same thing, the difference being that I knew the truth while he was still groping with shades of the unimaginable. His fear stole his breath and his words.

"You know that would be . . . ," he stammered.

"I do."

The old man pressed his lips together. Breathing deeply I withdrew and nodded as if he had no choice but to believe me, as if trust in this foreigner standing there before him, in the son he'd only just now learned of, was his only defense against the image that had already invaded his mind and with which he was wrestling. And it was as if only his firm human conviction in the impossibility of such a thing ever happening on earth prevented him from succumbing, from tearing out his scant gray hair, from mutilating himself.

I closed the door softly. I ran my fingers over the plaque with the name "ŠNAJDER." Laertes remained on the other side, in his orchard. *I'm leaving him forever, unhappier than when I found him, unhappier than he was before, without his son.*

For the second and last time in the home of my father, I concluded, erroneously, as I went down the stairs.

6

The comparison was flawed, but I still can't shake it off as I write about that day. It was flawed because the war raged on, because there was no goddess to come down among people as Minerva had done long ago on Ithaca, and, having had enough, said, *Men of Ithaca, cease this dreadful war, and settle the matter at once without further bloodshed.* Because more blood would be shed that day, but it wouldn't be the blood of warmongers as it had been in the *Odyssey*, when the gods meted their just punishments. Their absence in this war forced me to wonder whose side they'd chosen and to suspect finally that their role had been assumed by the European and international community. Oh, how bitterly disappointed Odysseus would have been! Nor would he have done so well had he wandered into Sarajevo these last days. Yes, the comparison was flawed from the start.

It took me longer to reach Ivor's apartment than I'd hoped. Every few minutes I had to stop and duck into the entrance of a building or behind a car, and once, when the shells began falling so close that I had the feeling they were exploding right over my head, I went into a bomb shelter for the first time, an ordinary cellar, not very well barricaded. Still, I left the cellar as soon as the intensity of the shelling let up, despite the building's residents' warnings in their rudimentary English. I couldn't stop; I couldn't wait. A burst of gunfire from the nearby hills rang out, and I could only imagine what was happening on the front lines, especially where they cut across city neighborhoods and houses. I couldn't stop. I needed to get to the apartment, throw my things together, and go to the hotel where my reporter colleagues were staying, find a connection to the UN or something similar, and get out of the city as soon as possible. I must reach the apartment before Alma did and vanish from there for good. Never ever see her again.

This internal command, this imperative bolstered by the last image of our father—as he stood in the hallway, facing the threat I represented with an unspoken warning on his lips—propelled me through the empty streets from Bjelave to Ivor's apartment, as if a higher power were pushing me along that I could not resist, as if the very tip of its sword were prodding me in the back and telling me that any further delay would only compound my misery, multiply the evil. My mission was over, and all that was left was for me to exit the shell-gutted stage.

The war raged on, even though the son found his father. The war raged on, and because of this it took me nearly an hour to reach the apartment instead of fifteen minutes. With relief I saw that Alma had not yet returned. "It's better this way, much better," I whispered to myself, stuffing clothing into my suitcase. I lurched around the apartment, searching for things I had to take with me, though it was less and less clear what my criteria were in doing so. Into the suitcase I stuffed papers, texts, several books. I took out a few things that were condemned to remain in Sarajevo. I felt like a thief who knows that the owners of the apartment might appear in the doorway at any moment. An encounter that I must avoid at the cost of my life.

I found our photographs—developed the day before—that Alma had brought to Ivor's apartment. Our pictures: the proof of our love, the proof of my friendship with Ivor. I didn't know what to do with them. Should I destroy them right there or take them with me? Leave her no trace of what she must forget, help her erase my face more readily as she rages at being abandoned? In the end I did neither, but divided them up, hastily sharing the photographs with Ivor and Alma. As if my very being rebelled against the attempt to expunge myself from others' memories, against my impulse to control them, against the injustice.

Mechanically I swept up the clothing left on the bed and chairs in that room where our five-day love, banned by God and the laws of man, had lived. But the suitcase refused to take in all the things. I pushed them in angrily and tried, using hands and feet, to close it, as if its disobedience were the only thing preventing me from leaving, walking away from this place, from a story I myself had created along with its characters, whom I'd turned into my victims. When, hopeless, I realized I wouldn't be able to overcome its defiance, I swung the suitcase high above me and hurled it with a roar at the facing wall.

The overturned, broken suitcase now lay on the floor amid my shaving kit, notebooks, odd socks, a jutting shoe, several photographs wedged between Alma's dark-red bra and a silk handkerchief with a serene Asian design of high mountain peaks and streams with red fish, among her hairpins, her cosmetics, her mirrors. From the bag, consorting with my trousers, peered her underpants with Snoopy standing guard over the crotch and a T-shirt, an ordinary white T-shirt, sporting the faded logo of the Winter Olympics on the left side of the chest—*Sarajevo '84*—in which she slept.

I sat down on the floor of the bedroom in Ivor's apartment with that ordinary T-shirt in my hands, under the disapproving looks of his ancestors, some of whose frames had been badly tilted by my altercation with the bag. I breathed deeply through the T-shirt that still held last night's smells, a hint of her scent, of her slumbering body, Alma's fragrance, from her breasts, her back, her belly.

The smell of my lover with whom I share the blood of our father.

The smell of my sister.

The smell of my half sister. As if this half that we didn't share somehow eased things, as if it could diminish the incest committed unknowingly. I buried my face in the T-shirt with this knowledge that hadn't yet been driven from me, a demon who had fettered itself to my feet like an iron ball to prevent me from leaving the apartment. Time stopped. I was like a burglar waiting for the owners to return so that he could show them what he'd meant to steal and accept his punishment with grace. I was in no hurry. Her T-shirt soaked up my tears, mingling them with the sediment of her nights.

I decided to wait for her, sitting there motionless on the floor, surrounded by our jumbled belongings, with the overturned suitcase, with Ivor's aggrieved ancestors, with her *Sarajevo '84* T-shirt clutched tightly in my hands. I decided to tell her the story that had tricked her, seduced her, and swallowed her, the story that used her to swell into its own horror, to mow us down, to create and demolish a love between two people who were supposed to be separated by the different languages, ages, origins they trusted and the life trajectories that emerged from them. The story about a blue notebook, its history, its surviving message, a story about the effectiveness of fate's postal services at bringing an undelivered letter across half a century from a distraught woman who'd bear a son to a father who was condemned to death, the gas chambers and the crematorium chimney, himself the future father of a daughter who would find herself in the embrace of her brother during yet another war. The daughter would fall in love with her brother who would fall in love with his sister. With no regard for the means, using their love, destiny would finally deliver the letter to the addressee, confirming once again the reliability of its channels, no matter how enigmatic, deranged, or terrifying they might be.

After I'd resolved to tell Alma the story as I knew it with all the traps into which we'd stumbled, I was mollified by the decision, this reconciliation, yet another task to do before I left. It would hurt her, there'd be fear, anxiety, tears, and there'd be blows. None of them as harmful as the cause itself. My responsibility in everything that had happened to us required, as I could finally see, that Alma should hear the truth from my lips. I mastered my cowardice. The story I planned to tell her opened only one door, the door through which I'd leave. My departure wouldn't be an escape, but a step that was understood, which shouldered responsibility, perhaps even a sort of mercy to allow the perpetrator to leave the place of his crime and carry out his own punishment so that nobody else's hands would be soiled by him.

Perhaps a little more than an hour passed while I waited, much reassured, for Alma to appear at the door, listening without a shudder to the distant shelling and gunfire. I'd say I spent a whole hour in that dazed state, waiting with Alma's T-shirt in my hands, as if sinking, carefree, ears full of water, deaf to the world, senseless to life . . . when a thought sparked panic that catapulted me from the depths to which I'd consigned myself and, like a drowning man, I clawed my way to the seemingly calm surface and gasped for air with my emptied lungs, screaming with horror, *"She already knows!!!"*

I recalled those last words I'd exchanged with Jakob and finally understood the true meaning of what he said. I could guess what he'd done as soon as I'd shut the door to his apartment.

She already knows.

I imagined Jakob dressing in a panic, stripping off his at-home attire, pulling on a shirt, clumsily tying his shoes, and hurrying off in search of Alma. The father who must prevent the horror or at least put a stop to it if, God forbid, it had already happened.

She could already know.

I ran into the street as if it were any street in any city. I ran along the empty thoroughfare full of sunlight, shards of smashed glass, dust, the stench of gunpowder and burning buildings; I ran as fast as I could toward the theater. Soldiers stepped out from behind a shelter, pulled out their guns, and forced me to stop, but I produced my press accreditation card, my magic pass, and waved it around before the anxious, startled young men. I shouted that this was urgent, that I had to reach the theater, that this was a question of *life or death*, at which they all began to guffaw with laughter. They let me through. Nobody had time to bother with me. On I pushed through the labyrinth of streets, not knowing where the bullets were coming from, and the whistle of shells forced me, several times, to throw myself down onto the ground. Finally, covered in dust and sweat, I reached the theater.

They were all in the cellar, and astonished to see me. My appearance probably alarmed them. I said nothing, nor did I acknowledge their questions. I walked among them, looking for Alma. She wasn't there. I found the manager at the back of the cellar. He was genuinely concerned. He stopped me and asked me to sit, to calm down. I couldn't. I peered feverishly around me and fidgeted around him. They brought me a little water. He asked what had happened. He wanted to help. "*Is Alma here?*" I asked. He said that she wasn't, but . . . "*Was her father here?*" I interrupted him edgily, halfway through his sentence. The expression on his face showed he hadn't been expecting that question, and his bewilderment was heightened by the fact that he still couldn't understand my presence in the cellar. I moved around him impatiently and, still breathless, waited for him to answer. I grabbed him by the shoulder and shook him. "*Yes or no?!*" I shouted in his face, which abruptly darkened. His brow furrowed and he looked at me askance with open enmity.

"*Mr. Šnajder, Mrs. Filipović's father,*" he said suddenly with an officious tone, loudly so that everybody could hear—that is just the way he said it, *Mr. Šnajder, Mrs. Filipović,* as if scolding me for my too-intimate *Alma,* for the *her father* with which I was asking about something that was none of my business whatsoever, to which I had no right—"*is seriously wounded, Mr. Richter, and he's been rushed to the Koševo hospital.*" He continued, "*Mrs. Filipović, Alma*"—stressing her name with a brief pause afterward, as if drawing a distinction between us regarding our right to use her name—"*is with her father. Is there anything else I might help you with, sir?*"

My head began to spin. I wanted to lean my brow on the cold bricks of the cellar, let my pulse slow, give myself time for this to sink in. I apologized for bursting in. I said this was important. "*I'd say it can wait, wouldn't you agree?*" he said with derision. As if seeking a justification, I answered that this was a question of life or death. I couldn't come up with anything better. "*More likely death than life,*" he said coldly. I turned to the exit followed quietly by the eyes of the men and women packed into the musty theater-building cellar. The dizziness returned on the stairs, but I managed to break through to the surface. I came out again onto the street. The afternoon sun blazed. I was surprised that cities can be so fervently demolished on such a beautiful summer day. Sounds began to come back. I didn't know where Koševo was. I didn't know which way to go.

Then the door behind me opened. It was the leading actor from Alma's show, Mr. Faber. He asked if I'd come back inside to wait with him in the cellar until things quieted down. "*Mr. Faber,*" I said, grabbing his hand desperately like a beggar, "*help me, Mr. Faber. You couldn't help yourself. Help me now. Don't start in with your theory of probability, of risk, of providence, when both of us know the truth, isn't that right, Mr. Faber?! Help me.*"

The man was bewildered, then perturbed. He smiled as if he understood what I was saying, as if it all made perfect sense. "*Let's go back into the cellar, out here is too dangerous,*" he said as he placed his hand on my shoulder and with gentle pressure tried to steer me back.

"*No,*" I said to him. "*You're wrong again, Mr. Faber. Now. Help me now.*"

Seeing that his solicitous tone was getting him nowhere, he seemed to resign the goal of returning me to the cellar, and asked, mystified, "*How?*"

"Where is Koševo?"

"Don't do it. Come back inside."

I calmly placed my dust-covered hand on his shoulder. *"Faber, you're the last who should be saying that."*

He relented and said, *"All right."* He told me I wouldn't make it to Koševo alive.

"Faber, enough predictions." He pointed me in the right direction, gave me instructions for the first few streets. I ran off before he could even finish.

After I'd made my way through those streets, I had to follow my instinct. I began despairing. I began believing I wouldn't make it alive to Koševo. To Jakob and Alma. I didn't know which direction to take next. I'd gotten turned around in the little streets. I finally recognized the street I'd been on a few minutes earlier. This was a labyrinth. A shell-riven labyrinth. Then I heard a car on a side street, the screech of brakes and the loud rumbling of the motor. I leapt out in front of the car. The driver and passenger looked as if they'd fly through the windshield, he slammed so hard on the brakes. The man howled something. I just kept repeating, *"Koševo, Koševo."* Then the back door swung open and I flew inside. A wounded woman was lying there, unconscious. The floor was soaked in blood, and my shoes sank partway into it. The car took off. A boy, about fifteen, was sitting on the front seat holding his bent arm. Only then did I see that the driver's face was covered in fresh wounds that didn't seem too serious. In the few words we exchanged, the boy explained to me that a shell had hit their apartment. The woman whose head I now held on my lap was not moving. The boy kept speaking to her. I held her so that she wouldn't tumble off the seat as we swerved into the turns. The ride took just a few minutes and then we were at the hospital, where they were taking in the wounded and the dead.

I eased the woman carefully off the backseat and put her in her husband's arms. Blood trailed after them like a red thread with me holding the end. The driver gestured to the boy with his head, then disappeared into the building with his wife. I helped the boy out of the front seat. Only then did I realize he'd been wounded in several places. I carried him into the hospital. Two men in white coats smeared with blood pointed me to a room where I laid the boy on a table. They pushed me aside. The boy moaned as they cut away his clothing. I turned to look around. There were at least twenty people receiving help or begging for it. Screams. Panic. Fear. And that smell, a mixture of blood, sweat, and rot. I peered around. The half-naked wounded. I didn't recognize Jakob among the bloody, bruised, disfigured faces, the bandaged heads, nor was he among the ashen, stiff faces of people nobody could help anymore, among the desecrated bodies. My feet kept wading through the blood clotting on the hospital floor tiles. My shirt and pants were soaked in the blood of the boy and his mother. The boy kept groaning while two medics did what they could for him with skilled movements. Somebody asked me something. Then they led me out of the room. Again I was at the entrance. Total chaos reigned there among the medics, the wounded, the dead, civilians, and soldiers. The cacophony was deafening; people bumped each other, swore, fumed. At one point a soldier shot off his gun, and after the silence that briefly followed the shot, he loudly ordered the medics to take in his wounded comrade. The man was long dead; everybody could see that. Perhaps he'd died on the front lines, but his frantic comrade would not desist. They brought in both of them. I followed them back in.

I wandered through the hallways, looking frantically for Jakob and Alma. Then a nurse stepped in front of me and tried to explain something. When she realized I was a foreigner, she asked if I was wounded. I told her I wasn't, but that I was looking for somebody who was. She took me to the main nurse, who asked for the name of the wounded person. *Jakob Šnajder.*

"How are you related to him?"

I didn't answer.

"Why are you looking for him?"

"I heard he was wounded today and was brought here. I want to know if he's all right. His daughter is here. I'm also looking for her."

"How are you related to them?" She was persistent.

"That doesn't matter. Can you please tell me if they're here?"

"You aren't wounded?" she said again, relenting a little, and began shuffling through the papers scattered around her as if she knew what to look for and where. I was surprised that in all this chaos there was still some kind of order, or that somebody was at least trying to create it.

"No."

"You look as if you are."

"This is not my blood."

"You're lucky."

I didn't understand what this last comment referred to, because immediately after she said, "*He was brought in today. Wait. I have to check where he is.*"

Then she shuffled again through the papers on her desk. She clearly knew what she was doing. She closed one book. She picked up another, this one dark blue. She closed it, too. Then she took up a third, a black register. She flipped through the pages, seeking a name with her finger. Then her finger stopped. Calmly she shut the register and put it back in its place.

"I'll show you," she said.

We passed through corridors crowded with wounded. As soon as they saw the nurse, they began to cry out, and hands reached out to us, blocking our way, beseeching the mercy of her care. She paid no attention. She passed through the multitude without halting. We went down a flight of stairs and several long corridors. There were fewer and fewer wounded. We passed two medics carrying a body. Then we went down another floor into the cellar, passing several dead bodies in uniforms laid out on the floor one next to the other. It was cooler down there.

This whole journey through the hospital was a kind of preparation, from people with minor wounds to those who were half-dead, and finally to the cold rooms intended for the bodies. I knew Jakob Šnajder was dead even before the nurse, at the door to the morgue, said that he'd died shortly after they'd brought him into the hospital. She looked in through the little window on the door and said I should wait. She went in. I looked through the little window and saw at least fifty dead bodies laid out on the floor, of whom some were in plastic bags while others were simply lying there, some with their jaws tied shut, one among them with his arm raised as if greeting us from the other side. The dead who had stiffened with their mouths agape and eyes open looked as if they'd been interrupted in the midst of an important sentence, almost affronted. Around them were members of their family, I assumed, or friends. I watched the nurse as she cruised around among the bodies without looking back, without surprise. Death had become something that did not merit attention. She knew it well. Death inhabited the black register on her desk. It was nothing more than that.

Alma was sitting by a bag from which protruded Jakob's head. Our father's head. The nurse laid her hand on Alma's shoulder. Alma looked up and the nurse leaned over and whispered something to her. Alma looked over toward the door. Then she got up from the body, wiped away her tears, ran a hand through her hair, said something to the nurse, looked once more toward the door as if thinking it over, as if she was uncomfortable that I'd found her here over her father's body, and finally she nodded several times.

I went in even before the nurse came back to summon me. Alma stood at the back of the room. I leaned on the door. We looked at each other for a few moments, frozen where we were, with the dead between us. I began moving toward her. "*She'll need you tonight,*" the nurse said to me in passing.

When I reached Alma she clapped her hand over her mouth. "*It's nothing. Just dust and blood,*" I said. "*Somebody else's.*" I took her in my arms. She sobbed softly, burying her head in my chest, as if taking care not to impinge on the dead and grieving. Over her shoulder I saw Jakob Šnajder's body lying there. The same face from this morning, eyes closed. No less alive. Maybe he'd only fallen asleep. I had the feeling that he might wake at any moment and curse me for what I'd done, for what I was doing. This man who lay lifeless at our feet, under our embrace, under Alma's body that was shaking with sobs, under my bloody shoes, I thought, *This man read the blue notebook a few hours ago and discovered that he had a son. And suspected that this son loved his daughter. And that's why he is here.*

That's why we're here.

We left the morgue. We sat on the floor in the hall. They were bringing the newly dead into the room. Alma said Jakob was struck near his liver by a tiny piece of shrapnel when he'd nearly reached the theater; he crawled there with his last strength. By the time she'd reached him he was already unconscious. While they were transporting him to the hospital, he'd come to and ranted, delirious. He held her hand tightly and spoke in a garble. He said something about Vienna, a notebook. (*Where was the blue notebook now?* I thought, alarmed, while she spoke.) He mentioned my name several times. "*Odd, isn't it?*" asked Alma, as if musing to herself, and then she went on. Jakob finally lost all consciousness. After they arrived at the hospital, he lived only another twenty minutes. I asked her whether he had anything with him. Alma found this surprising. I said he probably had set off somewhere, that he must have been carrying something, that he hadn't gone out for a stroll. Unable to understand why I was asking this, she answered that she didn't know, but if he'd had anything with him he'd probably lost it during the blast. I hoped so. She told me then he'd have to be buried this evening if it wasn't too dangerous. There was no room at the hospital, and the burial would have to be done in the dark, anyway, because of the snipers and the frequent shelling of funerals. There was no time to lose. There'd be no ceremony. The nurse who'd brought me to the morgue would send us a man who'd help us take the body to the cemetery, luckily only a few blocks from the hospital. We'd bury him by her mother, Aida, in their shared grave that same evening. I said nothing and nodded.

We sat on the floor, leaning against the wall. Her fingers, with traces of our father's blood, interlaced with mine. I wondered if the boy and mother had made it. Alma was crushed. The tears had already stopped streaming down her swollen face. "*Now I'm alone,*" she said. Again I said nothing. We sat there silently for a long time, propped against one another. Waiting for nightfall in the besieged city to bury our father. Then Alma suddenly sat up as if struck by an important thought. She asked me, slightly surprised, what was I doing here at the hospital, how had I found her. I told her I had been worried and went to look for her at the theater, where I learned what had happened and came here to find her. "*Thank you,*" she said after a few moments, "*it's comforting not to be completely alone in all this . . .*" I didn't answer. As if my silence confirmed her words, she kissed me. Or rather our dry lips gently brushed together. There were no witnesses except the dead soldiers on the hospital floor. Perhaps she was beyond caring. She clung to me. The moment had passed. I was taken by a powerful wish that she never know the truth.

We waited for nightfall to bury our father.

Dusk brought relief. The whole afternoon and into early evening, we stayed huddled together in the corner, in the waiting area of sorts that had meanwhile begun to fill. At one moment they began to deny entry even to those with ties to the dead behind those heavy doors with the little porthole window. Twilight passed with shell blasts that shot tremors through the building. Some people in the hall were waiting, like us, for circumstances to allow them to bury their dead at a cemetery, in a park, in their backyard. The sobs, sighs, inconsolable monologues of the living, the still-fresh wounds of the survivors, the whispering in the corners where their faces were beginning to melt into darkness.

From time to time Alma dozed off. She slept fitfully, and woke often, but was quickly overcome again by exhaustion. She could neither stand nor sit. She stretched out on the tiles with her head in my lap. At times she'd shake with shivers or sobs, her face plunged into my chest, and she'd only quiet down when she fell asleep, seldom longer than ten minutes. I could have stayed there for an eternity staring, eyes fixed, at the facing wall, keeping watch over Alma, running my fingers through her hair, and kissing her protectively on the brow while she shuddered, muttering.

Somebody spoke to me, then patted my shoulder. He realized I was a foreigner and merely nodded with compassion and condolence. I nodded back. Death had brought us here. We knew all there was to know about one another, at least, all that we needed to know here. We were here to bury our dead. A nod sufficed.

Several corpses were taken from the morgue. Medics came for the bodies and took them away. Then, once the darkness was total, that same nurse lit us with a flashlight. She said it was our turn and introduced us to a young man, one of the medics who would help us carry the body. He had a shovel in his hand.

We went into the morgue. We couldn't see anything beyond the circle cast by the nurse's light. She moved adeptly among the dead as if she knew exactly where each of them lay and which way to go. She lit Jakob Šnajder's body. Alma dropped to her knees and ran her hands over his face. I crouched by her and laid my hand on Jakob's brow. Alma looked at me with surprise but made no effort to understand my gesture. She was enveloped in her pain.

"Let's hurry," said the nurse.

The medic brought over a stretcher onto which we placed Jakob's corpse, just a length of canvas taut between two thick metal rods. He gave Alma the shovel and we set out for the cemetery.

From the hospital we walked along the road for a block or so. The medic pointed to the top of the white cemetery gate, the bottom of which was deep in tall grass. He told me we should hurry. I was drenched. My filthy shirt no longer absorbed the sweat, and I could feel it freely streaming down my back and legs. Alma ran her hand several times over my hair and neck as if to ease the strain, as if to thank me for everything I was doing for her. She didn't know I could have carried that body for hours without buckling. To her, the effort was a sign of my affection for her, while I was looking for some small penance to do. There was none. I felt almost sorry when we reached the cemetery gate. I wanted to carry him farther. I wanted to carry him until my body gave way, until my muscles stiffened, until my hands went numb, until I could go on no longer, to carry him on my shoulders like a dead king from some capricious Ithaca, with the woman who was a daughter, sister, and wife, walking alongside me who was a son, brother, and son-in-law, through a city that had been abandoned by the gods, in a war they did not care enough to end.

The medic hopped easily over the gate. While we were passing the body over, the stretcher caught on the gate spikes and the body almost slid off. Alma shrieked, but I managed to grab the upper part of Jakob's body. We lowered the body from the stretcher and passed them each separately over the gate. We laid Jakob in the grass.

"Where's the grave?" asked the medic and peered around in the dark. The evening was without moonlight, but we could still discern the irregular shapes of the tombs around us. I looked and saw a multitude of five-pointed stars gracing the graves. It seemed at that moment that I caught a glimpse of somebody slipping behind a grave some hundred feet away, as if he were hiding from us. I said I thought we weren't alone, but neither Alma nor the medic had seen anything. Alma led us to her mother's grave. We settled Jakob back on the stretcher and followed along the narrow avenues in the graveyard where partisans from the Second World War were buried, walking behind Alma. I started at a massive shape in front of us that looked in the dark like a great rock or some other looming object. The medic turned and, seeing my surprise, laughed. "*Lion, it's a lion,*" he repeated, giggling at my reaction. Then he caught himself, remembering the solemnity of the occasion. I stared at him with surprise. Maybe the young man had been crazed by the job he was doing. Everything seemed to have acquired unreal proportions, with the charred ruins of the sports hall only three hundred feet from us. The boulder began looking more and more like an oversized reclining lion. I, too, almost laughed when I realized it really was a large stone lion watching over the dreams of the dead partisans at the cemetery to whom we were bringing yet one more comrade. I turned and gazed around and again seemed to have caught sight of somebody hiding behind one of the tombstones at some distance from us. I thought perhaps my nerves were giving way with the exhaustion. Alma called to us from somewhere in the dark.

We carried Jakob gingerly as we walked across graves. We soon joined her before a tomb on which was written

AIDA ŠNAJDER   JAKOB ŠNAJDER

née Sarajlić

1929–1989   1914–

Alma was sitting on the concrete rim of the grave and fingering the gravel that was scattered over the ground. We held Jakob in the air, barely able to stay on our feet. The medic, breathless, said something to her and

Alma, resigned, stepped back. "*Dig,*" she commanded and handed him the shovel. We set Jakob down on a neighboring tomb, and the medic began digging right below the inscription on which Jakob's year of death was missing. I leaned on the stone slab across the way, beside Alma, with whom I watched while the young man, with effort, tossed out the dirt. I touched Alma's hand. She didn't respond. She was far away. It was her grief. She couldn't have known that I might share it in some way. She gazed, motionless, at her parents' tomb, the right side of which was being emptied to receive Jakob's body. I told the medic to step back and give me the shovel. I stepped into the hole, now about two feet deep, and started digging with vigor. I thought my body would give out right there, my muscles quivered, the calluses on my hands from gripping the iron rods of the stretcher started bleeding, my knees wobbled, but I didn't give up. I sank into the dark grave with no regard for my own body, the dampness of the dirt, and a part of me wished I'd never come back out of it.

I stopped when the shovel reached Aida Šnajder's partly disintegrated coffin. Alma sat by Jakob's body. She opened the body bag to reveal his face and gazed at the stone-like visage. She was bidding her father good-bye. After a few moments she summoned the medic. They closed the bag. I waited in the grave to receive the body. Then I lowered it gently to the floor of the grave. I had to extend the length of the dirt hole to stretch out his legs, to settle him well into his resting place, to ready him for the journey on which Charon would take him once we covered him with the earth. Several of my tears fell on the bag, not loud enough to be heard outside the grave where I was burying the secret I shared with Jakob. The medic urged me to hurry; it was dangerous. Alma called for me to come out. My tears mixed with my sweat. I don't know whether it was the tears, the sweat, or the dirt from the grave that she wiped from my face when I clambered up and out onto the ground. She passed over my cheeks with both hands at once, as if preparing me for the last part of this wretched ceremony, for our final farewell to Jakob Šnajder. Then she tossed a clod of dirt onto the plastic body bag.

V

Leaving

The sky brightening in the east was my signal to go. I'd waited all night for that moment, eyes wide open, Alma's head on my chest, soothing her with my touch every time she grew restless in the throes of another nightmare, covering her with a sheet so that the cool of morning wouldn't wake her. I saw the dawn approaching. I was out of time and I couldn't allow myself to linger. I was thinking of the blue notebook waiting for me on the grass in front of Jakob's building.

We spent our last night in Jakob's apartment. Alma wanted it that way. I couldn't dissuade her. She wouldn't consider going to her own apartment or to Ivor's. She said only that tonight she wanted to sleep in her home, in the home of her father and mother. We walked with our arms around each other through the empty streets, deaf to any danger. We were outside the war, each in our own way. In a way that we couldn't share. So we walked in silence. We didn't break the silence even when I thought, again, that I'd spotted somebody behind us. I thought I must be losing my mind on those deserted streets in the besieged city. Totally. Irretrievably.

After everything I didn't have the will or strength to tell Alma the truth. I didn't want her to know. That would only make her more miserable, far more than my leaving. And my leaving was inevitable. I didn't want to afflict the rest of her life, perhaps even make it unbearable. But maybe there was something else here that I'm only now able fully to understand. Perhaps I didn't want to lose her forever, irreparably. I know that sounds ridiculous because, after all, I walked out of her life that morning, in the end I left her.

Be that as it may, I told myself that she must never find out. There was only one more place, besides my overwrought brain, where the secret could be exposed. Mother's blue notebook. That I didn't know where the notebook was filled me with panic. If only the shell blast had destroyed forever the letter to Jakob from distant 1941, if only the blow that killed the man had also destroyed the evidence. When Alma insisted on staying at Jakob's apartment, I was appalled by the thought that the blue notebook might still be lying where I'd last seen it and we were headed right for it. The very thought that we'd walk together into the apartment and the notebook would be waiting for us on the table as the key to what had happened today—lying open like a door leading one straight into those tragic facts—cast me into despair. Nevertheless I walked calmly by her side, betraying none of my inner turmoil, my feverish search for a solution, holding her ever more tightly as if I'd made my peace with the catastrophe awaiting us at the end of the walk.

The degree to which my panic was justified I'd understand only when we entered Jakob's apartment, when I lit a candle in the living room and illuminated the same place where we'd sat that morning, face-to-face, my father and I, with our cards on the table. It was only the layout of rooms that allowed me to reach the blue notebook first and not Alma, or both of us at once. When we entered, Alma went into the bathroom without a word and lit a candle there while I walked into the apartment, groping in the dark along the same hallway through which I'd entered and exited Jakob's home earlier today. I found the matches in the kitchen, drew the curtains and the dense length of cloth with which Jakob blacked out his windows, and lit two candles. Then I spotted the blue notebook on the table. When Jakob ran off looking for Alma to tell her what he'd learned this morning, he'd left it there, as evidence for Alma, for what he intended to tell her.

The earlier intimations of panic were nothing compared to what swept over me when I heard Alma leaving the bathroom. I snatched the notebook and tried to stuff it into my pants or slip it under my filthy shirt. The notebook edges protruded. Alma was on the threshold from the bathroom, and it would take her no more than a few steps through the hallway to join me and discover me clutching the notebook. I had only one solution. Or at least so it seemed to me at the moment. I pushed the dark blackout cloth and the curtains aside and went out to the balcony. Alma called to me several times from the living room. When she went to check and see if I was already in the bedroom, I took out the notebook, thinking to rip out the pages. I opened it—*Jakob Dearest*—but didn't have the strength to tear those pages out and rip them to shreds. *"Richard? Are you here?"* When I realized Alma's voice was coming from the other side of the blackout cloth, only inches away, I flung the notebook off the balcony. I saw it flutter as it fell to the grass in front of the building. Alma pushed aside the cloth and curtain. I stepped back into the apartment.

She heated a big pot of water over a bottled-gas burner. We went into the bathroom where several candles burned. All that time we'd exchanged only a word or two. She asked me to undress. My clothing had almost completely changed color since morning, covered with dirt, caked with blood and sweat. I tossed my shirt, pants, shoes, then socks and underwear into the corner of the bathroom. I smelled the stink of my own body. She told me to sit in the bathtub. Then she came over, kneeled by the tub, and began dipping a towel into the heated water. She bathed my body. As if she were sponging away the traces of a battle from the shoulders of a deserving hero. I shut my eyes. I felt the towel stripping the grime from my face, hands, legs, belly, groin; I felt her soapy hand move tenderly over my body, then the water that my body greeted with relief, selfishly, as a prize for all its effort that day. Then she, too, undressed. In the flickering of the candle flame, her pain and fatigue made her, if not more beautiful, certainly more dignified, awe-inspiring, womanly in some mysterious way. I felt I didn't deserve to feel her next to me, hold her in my arms, press my lips to her. We sat in the bathtub facing one another. My turn. With slow movements I covered greater and greater stretches of her body, cleansing her as if I were the most obliging and trusted of servants. Alma wept aloud as if only there in the bathtub—as I rinsed her hair and kissed her eyes and cheeks, trying to collect the tears spilling from her eyes as if overflowing a dam that could no longer hold back a choppy lake—she had finally grasped what happened today and only then begun to face her loss.

I scooped her up in my arms and lifted her out of the tub. Two naked people in candlelight. I carried her, like that first night, but this time it was through our father's apartment. She pointed me to the bedroom. I laid her down on the spacious double bed. I was hoping just to settle her here and sit by her till she slept. Alma drew me to her and I couldn't resist, nor did I want to. This was the bed of her parents, Jakob's bed, the bed in which he'd spent his last night, from which he rose this morning before I appeared at the door with the blue notebook that now lay in the grass under the balcony. As if she felt me hesitating, Alma drew me, firmly, to herself. "*Let me feel something different from what I'm feeling right now . . . ,*" she whispered in my ear as a request, a command, a plea, a demand that could not be refused.

I shifted her head from my lap to the pillow, caressed her hair one last time, and pressed my lips to her forehead. She didn't wake. I wasn't sure whether I'd have been able to leave her if she'd said even one word, if she'd looked at me even once more. Her hand slipped out from under the covers. A foot appeared from under the sheet. I crept out of the room and went into the bathroom for my clothes. I dressed and for the third time I walked down the hallway, opened the door, and shut it noiselessly behind me, looking back once more—this time, truly, for the last time—at the plaque with the name "ŠNAJDER" on it.

The sun still hadn't risen on that last morning, but from the light that was spreading across the eastern horizon, it clearly would not be long. The morning was quiet and I had to hurry. Filthy as my clothes were, with dried smudges of blood all over them, I was sure I'd terrify any random passersby who might encounter me on one of the still-dark streets. There was, luckily, nobody around. Still, at an intersection I was stopped by weary armed civilians who were on sentry duty in their neighborhoods. They studied my pass carefully, comparing the picture on it with what I looked like that morning. They found my edginess suspicious, and had trouble communicating in English, and besides, I was impatient and rude. If they hadn't taken fifteen minutes of my time, I might have been at Ivor's before the first rays of sunlight. That plan would certainly have succeeded had I not spent at least ten minutes searching in a panic through the grass in front of Jakob's balcony for the blue notebook. There was no trace of it, and I couldn't imagine how it might have vanished from the grass onto which it had fluttered only a few hours earlier. I wondered who could have possibly found it there, since I was certain I was the first person to have left the building that morning. It couldn't have been the wind because there hadn't been a breath of a breeze all night. The disappearance of the blue notebook drove me to distraction, and I spun around like a cat trying to catch its own tail at the spot where, I was certain, it must have fallen, but I could no longer afford even a single lost minute. *Devil take it,* I thought, and off I dashed.

At home I found the same disarray I'd left behind. Apparently Ivor hadn't been by; I'd have been surprised if he'd risked leaving the television studio for the center of town. The upended suitcase was still there by the wall. I hastily removed Alma's things and laid them on the bed, folding them neatly one by one. I knew she'd come looking for me here soon enough. At one moment I considered a letter, a few words, but as soon as I found a pencil, grabbed a piece of paper, and wrote the first few lines, I gave up. The words that were taking shape before me were alien and cold in their generality. Loaned out for such occasions. They were so far from what I wanted to tell her that I realized I wouldn't find fitting language this morning in my groggy, underslept mind and it would be better to depart like this, with a kiss pressed to the slumbering brow, with no word of farewell. Then I reached for another sheet of paper and tried to write Ivor a letter. I got no further than *Dear friend, forgive me. I hope I'll be able to explain everything one day . . . Your R.* I took the missive to the kitchen table.

The first shaft of sunlight reached the apartment. I changed clothes quickly. I took everything superfluous out of the suitcase, and without picking and choosing I pushed photographs, money, and documents into my pockets, and once the suitcase zipper finally relented, I was ready to go. I was wrong, however, when I imagined that the path for my getaway was now completely clear.

Even before I'd reached the door, I heard quiet sobs on the other side. I flung it open and heard Emina, barefoot, in her mother's T-shirt, which obviously served as a nightgown, climb up the stairs. She peered at me through the half-open door.

"Are you leaving, captain?" she said, barely able to check her sobs. I lifted her up and carried her down the stairs.

"No, I'm just off on another one of my missions."

I brought her into her apartment. At the door I stopped, surprised, when I saw a soldier's jacket hanging in the front hall. "Mama's friend, one of those *UN* guys," she explained.

"Is he to be trusted?"

"I don't know. I still have to check him out."

"Keep an eye on him and take good care of your mama, lieutenant," I said as I laid her in bed. Her brother was babbling happily in his crib. Emina kissed me.

"Promise you'll be back."

"Promise."

"Promise for real."

"Promise for real. I'll be back soon." My voice quavered. I thought my heart would break at last right there in that child's room. "Will you do me a favor, lieutenant?"

"Anything, captain," said Emina, sitting up eagerly in her bed.

"There's a message for you to learn by heart. When Alma comes, tell her it was all true . . . all of it, from beginning to end."

I couldn't say more. I didn't know what to add while Emina worked on memorizing the message, repeating it over and over to herself.

"Just that?" she asked when she'd finished.

"I know it's not much."

"You can count on me," she said, winking, and then she shut her eyes.

I trudged slowly down the stairs with my suitcase, leaning on the wall and letting my body slide downward, as if even my legs were protesting my leaving. I was on the verge of a breakdown. I wiped away the tears and barely choked back my sobs. I stopped by the front door and tried to pull myself together. For a few moments I stood there, motionless, my hand on the handle to the outside door. Then I heard sounds from the cellar, as if somebody were down there in the pitch dark.

"Who's there?" I asked. "Come out, I can hear you."

It sounded odd, my voice in English, as if it weren't mine. The cellar was in total darkness and I couldn't see farther than a few steps. "Who's there?" I asked, but the only answer was my echo in the empty stairwell. *Yet another sign that I'm losing my mind, that I won't succeed.* I spun around and went running down the street.

From the moment when I reached the hotel where the Austrian television team was staying to boarding the UN transporter that would take me to the airport, less than two hours passed. The members of the team were noticeably dismayed when I showed up among them and demanded that they connect me to our editor in Vienna, whom I asked to evacuate me urgently from Sarajevo that same day. He promised he'd do what he could. He said he'd need to call in political favors for this. I told him to do what it took to get me out of there. Clearly, my demand came across as extremely serious, requiring urgent resolution; within half an hour I'd received the go-ahead. The transport on patrol was told to pick me up in front of the hotel and bring me out to the airport. "With a little luck," he declared as if it were the most splendid news ever, "you'll be leaving Sarajevo today." I did not respond. I wasn't grateful. I hung up and waited.

After the phone call I stopped speaking. The other journalists eyed me warily, clearly trying to guess at the reasons behind such an abrupt decision. And besides, I figured they'd seen my arrival in Sarajevo and then my disappearance into the city as the eccentricities of an over-the-hill writer. I had no wish to undermine their belief that leaving like this was just another capricious whim.

I sat on a chair, staring out the window. I was sure I hadn't dropped off to sleep, that I'd simply fallen into a thought-free state, the torpor of a person who deliberately chose that his end be elsewhere and not here where there was no possible atonement.

When I heard the rumble of the transporter, I stood, picked up my suitcase, and, without a good-bye, stepped out as if onto a train-station platform. I thought I'd simply board the white transport whose door a sergeant in a blue helmet and bulletproof vest was holding open. He looked around as if gauging the safety of the position. As I said, I intended to just board the transporter and submit, for better or worse, to the machinations of UN bureaucracy. But when I exited the building, out of the corner of my eye, I saw one of the soldiers speaking sternly with somebody.

"Simon!" I shouted, catching sight of my Sarajevo friend. They let him approach me despite the urging of the sergeant, still holding the door open, that we must leave at once.

"You're leaving, Richard?" Simon launched right in, glancing upward over the rooftops at the surrounding hills. "You're right. It's best to leave as soon as possible. I came, see, to wish you a bon voyage."

It was clear to me immediately how, in fact, he'd found me.

"You've been following me, Simon?"

"I'd rather say," began Simon again, "that our paths have crossed often in the last few days."

"Was that you yesterday? At the cemetery? On the street? And today, in the cellar? You scared me."

"Let's say that I was concerned for you, or should I say for your friend."

"Thank you, Simon," I said. "But as you already know, he died and was born again."

Simon didn't answer this time but instead dipped his hand into his long black coat and fished out the blue notebook.

"I thought it wasn't the best idea to be discarding something like this," he said, offering it to me. I clasped his elderly hand. Simon answered with a squeeze and gentle smile. The sergeant announced again that we had to leave immediately. I knew Simon would turn his back on me the next instant and vanish around the corner.

"Simon, don't you owe me something more?" I asked, and Simon's left eyebrow shot up in surprise. "You now know my friend's whole story, but I still don't know what happened in the end to Daniel and Jelena."

Over the rumbling of the transporter motor and the repeated complaints of the nervous sergeant, Simon finished his story. Jelena's life ended in Sarajevo remand. Two days after the murder at Daniel's house, she hanged herself in her cell. Franjo Kraus died a few years later, following his wife. On his deathbed, alone in his house, he called for Daniel, who refused him a last visit. They were all buried in the family tomb at the old Koševo cemetery. Despite the cross on their grave, neither Jelena nor Franjo Kraus was buried by a priest. For suicides and those who revert to their original faith, there are no last rites.

"And Daniel?" I asked. "What happened to Daniel?"

"He . . . ," concluded Simon. "He never judged again."

The clasp of our hands eased, the soldiers intervened, and the next instant I was on board the transporter. From then to boarding the plane everything progressed speedily. I let them lead me all the way to the seat on the aircraft. Then they pulled up the ramp, the plane rolled out onto the runway. I didn't have the strength to look up and out of the aircraft window at the city that spread itself out in its entirety, nestled in the valley between enemy mountains, while the plane rose into the sky, winging away from the siege.

I went to another land, another sea, to a city which, as Cavafy says in the poem that joined us, is far more beautiful than this one will ever be or could aspire to be. I knew there would be no new land, no new sea. There would be no return, because the city came with me. I wander its streets again endlessly. This city that is a cage. With no ship to take me away from myself.

EPILOGUE

Richard Richter's manuscript came into my hands in Vienna in early March 1996. Although during the war—despite numerous opportunities to do so—I did not wish to leave Sarajevo, I decided to leave the city once the siege had lifted. I knew my destination, as well as the station where I'd make a brief stop along the way. I was on my way to Paris, the only city, aside from Sarajevo, inseparably linked to my memories of Alma Filipović and Richard Richter.

◆ ◆ ◆

I traveled via Vienna. At the Südbahnhof I was met by a Mr. Z., Richard's attorney. In the fall of 1992 his letters reached Sarajevo. Mr. Z. informed me that Richard Richter had left a package for me at his office and I should come to retrieve it, *as soon, of course, as circumstances permit.*

Three and a half years passed from when Richard left the package at Mr. Z.'s office to the afternoon when one of the paralegals removed it from the huge safe before my eyes. I signed the papers and the sealed package was delivered to its addressee. On it in Richard's handwriting was my name.

Mr. Z. then said that Mrs. Ingrid Müller, Richard's aunt, "although we might, actually say his *mother,*" would like to meet you. The lady would be waiting for me at such and such a café at such and such an address if, of course, I agreed. I nodded, and that same paralegal put a call through to Mrs. Müller to confirm our appointment for the next day at nine o'clock in the morning. Mr. Z. said his office had reserved a room for me at a hotel on the Ring. I thanked them. "The taxi is waiting for you downstairs." He shook my hand and added that it had been a shock for everybody.

◆　◆　◆

It was as if I saw nothing of the beautiful city as I sat, that cold late afternoon, in the backseat of the taxi with Richard's package on my knees, seeking answers, again, to all the questions stemming from his mysterious departure from Sarajevo. I firmly believed that the content of the package, which had waited so patiently for me all these years, would help me divine his reasons. And I wasn't wrong. Still, I had no idea that Richard left me not only an explanation for his sudden exit from our lives but also with the troubled riddle of his own history and, of course, its end. After that night in Vienna I was the only person in the world who knew everything about *who* Richard Richter had been.

I opened the package as soon as I entered the hotel room. On the top I found a very old notebook with blue covers. Its importance I would understand only later that evening while reading the almost three-hundred-page-long manuscript that lay beneath. I also found several photographs taken in my Sarajevo apartment in the summer of 1992 in which Richard, Alma, and I posed, and a letter on whose envelope the author had written the unambiguous command: *Open after reading the manuscript!*

◆　◆　◆

I read the final pages as the first morning trams squealed along the Ring. Despite my exhaustion I hadn't been able to tear myself from the narration of his downfall, only briefly interrupting the reading when I cast about to recall the events he wrote about or when their painful sequence forced me to stop and muster the strength to continue. I found it hard to bear that I'd had no idea what Richard was going through in Sarajevo, and that I, myself, had been an inseparable part of his suffering. On the other hand, everything I'd not been able to figure out in our friendship, in his very arrival in Sarajevo, and finally in his almost unforgivable departure now was utterly clear. The man who had left a deep mark on me with his arrival in the city in the spring of wartime 1992 now lay exposed in these pages under the yellow glow of the hotel lamp as if he were lying on an autopsy table on which he'd autopsied himself and then shoved the results into my hands.

With the manuscript he included the blue notebook as proof of the credibility of his last statement and was adamant that I only read his letter after he'd acquainted me with all the particulars of *his* story. In his arrangements for his own end, Richard Richter had assigned me a role or two.

◆ ◆ ◆

Dear Ivor,

Knowing you—and I dare say I know you well despite the brief duration of our friendship—I don't doubt that you'll do just as I asked and that you'll open this letter only after you've read the manuscript to the last page.

We didn't part ways the way real friends should. Despite some of my comments which might have hurt your feelings, believe me you were my last friend, last but not least, as I said in all sincerity before. If you're reading this letter, you received the package which I intended for you and now you know everything. The manuscript you've read is the only copy. You're probably wondering why I left my last text to you. I'm not sure I have clear reasons for why, just as I'm not sure why I wrote it at all and what fate I hope for it.

Perhaps I owe you an apology, an apology such as a friend owes a friend for a betrayal he couldn't prevent. You now know what caused it. Maybe the riddle lies somewhere in the devastating balance of my life and the fact that at these moments you, dear Ivor, seem closer to me than all the other people I have known and loved over these fifty years. Or maybe it's just that I haven't the strength to give this truth to the world that knew me under a different guise, just as I haven't the strength to hide it, hush up everything I now know, things I wish I'd never learned as I wish that what happened in Sarajevo had never happened. I don't know. Perhaps it's that during our first encounter you said—remember?—I should send you the manuscript of my next book for you to translate, which I lied that I was writing. Now I am fulfilling your request. Don't be angry, dear friend, at my pointless bitter irony, altogether out of place in this tragic situation, but I find it difficult to resist. The answer is maybe in those conversations of ours when I could see your sharp mind, your literary talent which has all but spilled out onto paper—I sincerely envy those who will bear witness to it!—which is what, I assume, makes my trust in you, young friend, so firm. And besides, am I not, by giving you the manuscript, making good on the promise in my farewell message, that one day I'd explain everything?

I'll not ask you to burn this manuscript, because I fear that then you'd preserve it and publish it, just as I'm equally reluctant to ask you to take it to publishers as I'm afraid you'll destroy it to keep it from destroying Richard Richter, the man and writer.

You've read my last text—I'm reluctant to call it anything else—and now you know everything about me, and not just about me. Maybe I said all this because I still find it difficult to utter her name. You, I believe, may forgive me, but I don't dare expect such a thing from her. Perhaps I wrote this whole story for her so she'd one day learn the truth that could have destroyed her as it destroyed me, and maybe, I say maybe, I'm asking you now as my most trusted courier to deliver it to her. I don't know . . .

In leaving you this manuscript, dear friend, I leave you all these options. Each is equally appropriate. I hug you every bit as warmly as I'd have hugged you if I'd been able to say good-bye to you that morning in Sarajevo. If you're reading this letter, you know that you and I will never have that opportunity again.

Your R.

PS As I was finishing the letter, I heard that the National Library housed in the old City Hall has been gutted by fire. The ashes of its books are wafting around the city . . . these images come to me as manifestations of my deepest fears. I wish you all the luck, my Ivor . . .

The letter was not dated, but it would seem to have been written on August 26, 1992. In the days to follow, Richard Richter wrote a will in which he left his Paris apartment to his wife, Marianne Berger, the rights to the German editions of his books to Aunt Ingrid Müller, and the rights to the international editions to Sarajevo actress Alma Filipović. He divided among them the money in his bank accounts. Several days after the visit to Mr. Z.'s law office, Richard Richter committed suicide, shooting himself in the temple in the same hotel room where, using the name Richard Schneider, he'd spent the last months of his life, writing the manuscript he'd leave to me after his death. He was buried in Paris at the Montparnasse cemetery at his behest.

◆　◆　◆

I'd returned to the apartment just a few hours after Richard left Sarajevo. I needed help with the movie. As soon as I opened the door to his room, it was obvious that he'd left in a great rush. Most of his things were missing, and there were books and items of clothing strewn about the floor. On the bed I found several of our group photographs. On the kitchen table lay his note. His few lines in which he mentioned his hope that we'd meet again sometime in the future, when he'd *explain everything,* led me to believe he really had left the city. My assessment was confirmed later that day when I heard that Richard Richter had left Sarajevo on the morning UN flight.

My initial confusion would quickly mix with a feeling of betrayal, even deceit, and then scorn. Over the next two months, until the news of his suicide found its way to us, my thoughts about Richard and our friendship gave way to disappointment at his cowardly flight. The only explanation that made any sense put Richard with those who for months had been feeding like parasites on our tragedy and who were flocking here and then ditching us when they'd found all they needed, for which they'd be richly rewarded somewhere far away from the siege—a group to which I'd believed Richard Richter would never belong. After the news of his suicide challenged the image I wanted to sustain of him, in hopes of erasing his brief presence from my life, I went back to my work on our documentary. I soon finished it and then gave a showing and literary soirée (held, of course, in the early afternoon) dedicated to the late great writer.

The hall was packed. People still remembered Richard Richter as somebody who had boldly championed our cause and dispatched uncompromising reports about our suffering. The movie served as further proof. Some speakers even tied his suicide to his stay in Sarajevo, pathetically espousing the notion that the act was the response of a true Western intellectual to that same West which sat by observing our agony with indifference. This interpretation seemed a bit much to me, although I myself asked whether—and in what way?—the two months spent in Sarajevo had shaped his decision to take his life. Much later, reading books, studies, as well as several biographical sketches dedicated to Richard, I'd discover that this was not an isolated interpretation. Most of the authors did tie his death to Sarajevo, mostly repeating parrot-like that Richter's excursion to wartime Bosnia only additionally rocked his already-eroded *emotional equilibrium*, and the better informed among them did not forget to mention that his father had ended his life the same way.

At the commemoration I did what I could to present Richard Richter as a writer and intellectual, expressing admiration for his literary opus and unwavering engagement, and in closing I read some passages from my own translation of the novel *Closing Time*. After the audience dispersed, Alma Filipović came over.

I'd hoped she'd be there, what with the intimacy that she and Richard made no effort to conceal during our last afternoon together. Still, I hadn't known the precise nature of their relationship and therefore had no way of telling whether it had had an impact on Richard's departure or how his departure might have affected her. After we'd exchanged a few words about Richard, I realized she was every bit as baffled as I was. To my surprise she said I was the only person she could talk to about this. She wanted us to go somewhere where we could speak in private. She suggested my apartment. I agreed.

The return to my parents' place moved her deeply. She sat on the bed and struggled to hold back the tears. Over the next few hours she talked about the five days she spent with him and the death of her father. Together they buried him that night, and afterward Richard inexplicably stole out of her bed and disappeared forever. She talked about feeling abandoned, desperate, lonely, bewildered, the way she'd been enslaved to a trajectory along which, as she said, she lost first her husband, then her father, and, finally, her lover. His suicide only multiplied the questions to which she'd never find an answer and, as she added, would forever prevent her from learning "his side of the story." She said that now, after his death, there was no longer any point in hating him, but she'd never had much success with that, anyway, even with all the pain. And then there was the message conveyed to her by the little girl from our building. Emina.

The morning when she realized Richard had disappeared from her father's apartment, she panicked. She came looking for him here at my apartment. The door was unlocked. On the bed she found her folded clothing and a few photographs. Then she realized Richard had left her. She took the clothing and photos and ran out, wanting to get away from my parents' place as soon as possible. On the stairway she met Emina, who told her that Richard had had to go and that he'd left a message for her that "it was all true, from beginning to end." The little girl repeated this twice as if she'd learned it by heart and said Richard promised to come back. That was the only message he'd left her, after everything; Alma said bitterly, "A few words through a child."

I showed her the piece of paper with Richard's message. Just as I'd been mystified by his leaving so was she, and all the more so by his suicide. I comforted her, suggesting there was surely an explanation that

Richard hadn't had the strength to offer us. I added that it was such a shame we had so little of him left now. Nearly nothing. To my surprise, Alma whispered that I wasn't entirely right, and then she added, louder, that more had been left of him than I could know.

She was pregnant. A little over two months.

◆ ◆ ◆

After that day I saw Alma Filipović regularly. We often visited each other. Our memories of Richard were a firm foundation on which we chose to build a friendship. The first wartime autumn began, and we ceased hoping for a speedy end to the siege. We dreaded winter and had prepared inadequately, of course, for it. We read Richard's books. They didn't offer us any sort of resolution. I urged her to leave Sarajevo. For the child's sake.

It was at about that time that Richard surprised us yet again. Mr. Z.'s letters arrived in Sarajevo, one for Alma, the other for me. That was how Alma learned of Richard's legacy and the money waiting for her in Vienna. The raging war, the child who'd be born early next spring, and the considerable sum that allowed her to raise the child somewhere far away, in peace, were the reasons that softened her resolve about remaining in the city. She agreed to leave Sarajevo and the first opportunity to do so soon arose. Alma left that bitterly cold autumn in a convoy that was allowed passage through the enemy encirclement. I saw her off. I'll never forget her face as we stood in the cold by the bus that would take her forever from the city. She clasped my hand and placed it on her belly. We hugged for a long time. Only then did I realize how close we'd become. I almost cried. She kissed me and said she'd be back "as soon as the war is over." Then she boarded the bus. She had no idea whether she'd stay in Vienna or go on elsewhere. She only ended up staying there a day. She visited Mr. Z.'s office, signed the papers, took her money, and boarded the train for Paris.

◆ ◆ ◆

Her first letter was brought to me by a French soldier two months later. She was disconsolate. She wrote that she couldn't relate Vienna to Richard at all and that she decided to live in Paris. But only a few days after she'd arrived, she lost the child. She spent a month in the hospital. The doctors wouldn't release her for fear she'd harm herself. She was crushed and convalesced with great difficulty, as was easy to see from her letters. She should never have listened to me, she wrote in anger. The child was her only hope, and it should have been born where it was conceived. Now she'd lost all she'd had from Richard, as if *everything was cursed from the very start, as if in this world one had no right to such a love . . . for two people to be together despite everything*. She wrote asking for my forgiveness. She missed me. Her husband, Faris Filipović, found her in the Paris hospital. He didn't ask about the pregnancy, what had happened in Sarajevo. It was clear to them both that there was no point in trying to patch things up, but she could still rely on him.

Alma's letters arrived in spurts, sometimes five or six at a time. She scribbled constantly on the margins of newspapers, on beer coasters, on invitations, on theater tickets. Then she'd drop them all into a large envelope and send it to Sarajevo when somebody turned up who could deliver it to me. This was how I received a detailed description of her everyday life. The money Richard left her gave her independence, and her bank account kept growing as the number of his foreign editions multiplied. His suicide had a certain impact on sales, and Alma wrote ironically that the dead Richard was helping her financially to fill the void left by his leaving, a void that was all the more vast for the loss of his child. She described her social life, the superficial acquaintances, the solitude to which she'd sentenced herself, *wanting nothing from anybody, yet still seeking something from life,* her nostalgia for Sarajevo, her nightlife, the men who followed one after another whose faces merged in her mind. She described the city. I read her letters with an old map of Paris at hand, which somebody had left after a trip, trying to picture for myself her life in that city and the city itself. She lived in the tenth arrondissement at the Canal Saint-Martin. She wrote about the boats that passed below her window; she wrote that she was expecting my visit.

She often went to Richard's grave. She mentioned the flowers that regularly arrived from Vienna from his aunt and those brought, occasionally, by Kitty Berger. She wrote how she'd kept track of Kitty. Kitty remarried. She seemed satisfied. Alma gave up on knocking at Kitty's door. She didn't wish to disturb anybody. She herself, as said her letters that arrived all through 1993 and early 1994, had found no peace.

In the spring of 1994 her last letter came. After that she no longer wrote. My many efforts to renew our contact were ultimately met by a brief note from Faris Filipović. Alma had been killed in a car accident on a highway between Normandy and Paris. She was on her way back from an outing. The driver, her friend, was also killed. Faris Filipović was called to Paris to take custody of her body. At Alma's apartment he found my letters. He apologized for reading them. He'd seen from them that we were close. He managed to find a grave for her at the Montparnasse cemetery on its south side.

Faris Filipović could never have known—I was amazed myself when I discovered it the day I arrived in Paris and went directly from the train station to Montparnasse—that coincidence had seen to it that her final resting place

ALMA FILIPOVIC

nee SNAJDER

1962–1994

was only one cemetery avenue away from the marble stone on which was written, in silver letters,

RICHARD RICHTER

ECRIVAIN

1942–1992

◆ ◆ ◆

When I agreed to meet with Ingrid Müller, my only desire was to gratify the old woman's wish to learn something more about Richard's stay in Sarajevo. She, too, was, I assumed, trying to understand why he'd killed himself. That morning, after reading Richard's manuscript, I was impatient for our meeting. I knew what I really wanted to hear and was determined to use this, maybe last, opportunity to glean something from her, the last living participant in the events that had shaped Richard Richter's life and could help me cast light on what even Richard hadn't been able to or, perhaps, hadn't wanted to fully illuminate.

I was waiting at the designated meeting place at nine in the morning. She appeared in the doorway to the café a few minutes late. She was carrying Richard's book—*Closing Time!*—probably to help me recognize her. I waved. She was a thin, slight elderly woman who came across as lively although she was over eighty. Her stern, wrinkled visage left no doubt as to her age, but it also showed that her acuity was intact. She seemed surprised. She said she'd been expecting somebody much older. She removed her gloves and shook my hand firmly without shifting her penetrating gaze from my face, as if attempting to read there whatever had bound me to her adopted son.

That was, indeed, her first question. She sat down without taking off her coat or hat, as if she wouldn't be staying long. She was nervous. She asked me clumsily what I'd been to Richard.

"His last friend," I answered, smiling. "At least that's what he said."

She kept her eyes on me as if she doubted my answer and waited for me to continue. I talked about our friendship, about how I'd been his translator, about how Richard lived in my apartment in Sarajevo, about our work together . . .

"What did he leave you?" she asked, troubled, even before I'd finished what was a rather bare-bones report, anyway. "Forgive me for asking, but I believe you understand me."

"Nothing special," I answered. "Nothing to speak of. Some photographs, a few personal things he thought I should have, souvenirs from Sarajevo and . . . a letter."

"You're lucky. For me there was no letter. His suicide is a mystery that rips me to pieces. I'd hoped you might know more about what drove him to it. Did he mention something in the letter that would help me understand; do you understand . . . ?" Ingrid Müller choked back the tears.

"Forgive me for my candor, but in the letter, Mrs. Müller, he didn't write about what really interests you . . . ," I said. She looked over at me in surprise, waiting warily for me to continue. "Richard told me, you know, what he'd discovered in Vienna before he came to Sarajevo, as well as the *why* and *wherefore*."

The old woman frowned. As if her darkest forebodings were true, her deepest fear had finally been confirmed. Still, as if realizing she no longer needed to beat around the bush, she blurted out what had been tormenting her all these years: "Did he find . . . ?"

"His father . . . ?" I helped her.

She was silent.

"Yes," I answered. "He found Jakob Šnajder, his father in Sarajevo. Unfortunately, Mr. Šnajder was killed not long after they met."

Ingrid moved her head to the side, covering her mouth with her hand as if turning away from a nasty, wrenching scene. This was, I believe, just exactly what she'd pictured while I talked about how Richard found Jakob quickly by leafing through the Sarajevo telephone

281

directory. I never mentioned Alma, their love, or the tragic path that had led him to their father through her . . .

Ingrid listened, still as a statue. I kept for the end the fact that Jakob had believed almost his entire life that Paula had reported him to the police. But luckily Richard had given him her letter, preserved between the covers of a blue notebook, thereby resolving this half century of misunderstanding.

It seemed that I'd succeeded in my intent because Ingrid finally turned and asked nervously, her voice quavering, "So what did he conclude . . . ?"

"Who reported him to the police? Is that what you're asking?"

She kept her hostile gaze on me, waiting for my answer.

"I think he didn't know . . ."

"And Richard?" she asked.

"Richard also didn't know. He suspected Heinrich Richter. I think he probably preferred not to think any further about it. Too many blows, weren't there?"

"Yes . . . ," she said, suddenly resigned and with a deep sigh, "too many blows . . ."

We both stopped talking. Ingrid studied the title of the book she'd brought. Then she asked, as if only thinking of it just then, "Alma Filipović? Do you know her? She was only very briefly in Vienna. Too briefly for us to meet. Richard, you know, left her a great deal of money. Who was she, anyway?"

"His last love." Ingrid nodded as if that sounded reasonable, as if she'd assumed as much. "I can find no better words to describe her," I added.

Ingrid inhaled helplessly and looked out into the street. Then she stood quickly and extended her hand.

This time I did not accept it.

"It was you, wasn't it?" I said.

"Pardon?"

"You reported him, didn't you? You turned him in to the Gestapo?"

Ingrid Müller fell back into her chair as if she'd been struck. Her face blazed, her eyes were full of surprise and rage as if I'd stomped on her foot right on a lingering injury she'd hid long and well. She looked around at the neighboring tables as if fearful somebody might hear us.

"Do you have any idea what you're saying?" Her voice rose. "How dare you?!"

"You needn't put on such a show, Mrs. Müller. They're all dead now . . ." I wanted to keep her at the table, compel her to speak. "You called the police when you found out Paula was pregnant. You'd been wanting to get rid of him for a while . . . perhaps from the moment you realized you couldn't have him for yourself. Is that it?"

"You know nothing," she hissed in a half voice, looking around. "Conjecture. Rubbish."

"Jakob was reported as a Jew, not a communist as Paula believed. He said so to Richard. How did you know he was a Jew? Tell me, how could you have known?"

"Hush, young man!"

"Who told you?" I wouldn't give up. "Paula?"

"Paula told me nothing!"

"Then how? Tell me, Ingrid. I'm not a court of law. Everybody's dead, for God's sake! How did you know?!"

She didn't answer. I waited. I, too, glanced around at the other tables. There was just one middle-aged man, deep in his *Kronen Zeitung*, sitting a little farther from us.

"I guessed . . . ," she whispered. "I simply guessed. Paula once said something that made me think I might be on the right track."

Ingrid stopped again. She looked down at the table. She asked for water. We waited for the waiter to bring her the glass. Then she went on talking, staring at the table.

"When she told me of the child, I urged her to tell Andreas, I mean Jakob . . . tell him about the pregnancy and demand that he do the right thing and marry her. She said that wouldn't be possible. We quarreled. I couldn't understand. At one point she asked me whether I wanted the child to live. I said of course I did, and what could she mean by that. She told me then, for the first time ever, to shut up, that no matter how clever I was I couldn't see beyond the end of my own nose, that I had no clue what kind of a world we were living in. She locked herself in her room. We didn't speak for several days. After that night I thought about what she'd said."

"So you turned him in?"

She didn't answer.

"Paula's vagueness confirmed your hunch, didn't it? You could just as well have been wrong. Jakob could've betrayed you. All of you. If he'd wanted to."

"No. There you're wrong. When they arrested him I never once feared he'd betray us, no matter what happened. I knew that sort of person far too well. I was one of them, you know, a long time ago, before the war."

"You wanted him out of your life," I continued. "Far from Paula. You had a hunch that she alone knew of Jakob's background, and you knew full well that if he was Jewish and they arrested him, he'd think only Paula could have turned him, he'd despise her . . . The perfect solution! Then you picked up the phone and called the police."

"You said that, I didn't. Conjecture again . . . My sister and our child needed me. They needed my protection. And I gave them everything I could. That's the whole truth."

"*Your* protection?! *Your* child?!" I shouted, losing my patience. "Don't you understand that *you* killed him?!"

"There you're wrong, young man." Ingrid stood. She looked at me calmly, even with a shade of pity, and said, "I gave him fifty years of life."

This was the end of our conversation. Ingrid Müller walked away from the table with Richard's book pressed to her chest. I watched as she pulled her gloves onto her slender, bony fingers and stepped out of the café, looking left and right, and, after a brief pause, headed down the street. *Just an ordinary old woman,* I thought, *a plain old woman on the street and nothing more.* Her dowdy brown hat was soon lost in the morning crowd.

◆　◆　◆

After my meeting with Ingrid Müller, I went to the station. The train for Paris was leaving that day a little after noon. All the way to the Gare de l'Est, I couldn't shake the feeling that this was the same line that had taken Richard Richter, going in the opposite direction, to his downfall, just as it had taken Alma. I was on my way to the place where his downward spiral began, holding in my hands its full description as my most precious possession, on my way to my own fresh start. I was going to Paris, the only other city besides Sarajevo, as I said, which is indelibly associated in my mind with Alma Filipović and Richard Richter. I was on my way to their graves, knowing more about their fates than they knew themselves. Behind them they left this story, and I am its only custodian.

In the years to come I would not part with Richard's manuscript, the blue notebook, his farewell letter, Alma's Paris letters, our photographs. I carried them reverently from one rental to another, never leaving the tenth arrondissement, rereading the manuscript and Richard's letter again and again as an inexhaustible source.

Richard was wrong on one point. The talent he'd seen in me did not *spill out onto paper*. Those he envied bearing witness to it have not had the opportunity to acquaint themselves with my literary prowess in which he, it seems, believed so completely.

Until mid-2000 I hadn't found an answer to the question of what to do with Richard's legacy, with the story he'd left me, with the truth about his life, which I was jealously hiding from the world. That year in my regular visit to the Montparnasse cemetery, I noticed that the flowers which Ingrid Müller had been sending to Richard's grave had stopped coming. I telephoned Mr. Z.'s office and learned that Ingrid Müller recently passed away and had been buried next to her sister, Paula, in their family tomb. She left the apartment at Berggasse 17 to the city of Vienna, as well as her savings and the rights to the German editions of Richard's work so that a museum could be set up for *one of the most important postwar Austrian writers.*

After I heard the news, I realized that since Ingrid Müller was gone all the key players in Richard Richter's drama were dead. This helped me make sense of my role at last, perhaps the only role left for me to play before the curtain finally came down. That same day I began translating Richard Richter's manuscript, slowly, painstakingly, taking months, weighing each word, every comma, shifting his story carefully into a different language, into *my* language . . . learning, with his help, the writer's craft.

◆ ◆ ◆

In closing I should say I was not entirely right when I said I was the only person in the world who knew the whole truth about Richard Richter. There was one more person who might know, or at least suspect, its particulars, if, of course, he was still among the living. Whenever I visited Sarajevo over the coming years, I'd inquire about Simon and was mostly met with shrugs or, at best, feeble recollection. At the municipality offices they were equally helpless. Richard never learned Simon's, or Daniel's, if you prefer, surname, and I was no longer certain whether either of these names truly belonged to the old man.

I recently decided, however, to find Simon's house by following what Richard had written. After several failed attempts I thought, one afternoon, I'd finally succeeded in locating the gate through which Richard once passed to hear the story about Daniel and Jelena. There were branches thrusting through the rotten gate boards and the plaque with the address had long since fallen off. I couldn't see the house from the street and breaking through into the yard seemed well nigh impossible. I decided to ask around among the neighbors.

Simon and Daniel were unfamiliar names. Nobody could remember the man who, according to the telling, had once lived there. At the last door I knocked on, I came upon that same response. I began to despair and was seriously considering the possibility that Simon was a fabrication of Richard's, his last unintelligible literary trick. But then I was thrown a straw that I grasped at in earnest. I say *straw*, because what the old woman said to me felt like straw. I hadn't even noticed her presence in the room while I spoke to the hosts. She said she remembered a man who'd lived behind here, but he must have been dead for years now, probably died "before the war." If he survived, she added, he certainly lost his life when the house was hit by several shells in the last years of the siege, after which it burned almost to the ground. And although the members of the household warned me of the old ninety-year-old woman's faulty memory, affirming at the same time that the house had been in ruins since the war, I decided to enter the yard that very afternoon.

After a half-hour wrestle with brambles, I managed, scratched and sweaty, to reach the ruins that had been overrun by scrambling plants. Breaking branches, kicking away bricks, and rolling over beams where the house had once stood, I found the remnants of many charred and disintegrating books. I started pulling them out of the debris and looking them over carefully. Soon with an exclamation I realized I was holding fragments of old legal codices. Remembering the heavy tomes Richard mentioned in his visit to Simon's home, I was delighted that I'd finally resolved the enigma of the old man's existence.

I went on poking about the rubble. Then with a shiver of alarm I felt somebody watching me from behind. I froze and spun around, now in a panic, toward sounds coming from the undergrowth. I met staring eyes. Several curious and wary cats were following my every move. One of them pulled away from the group, rubbed up against my motionless shin, and with a slow amble made its way over to the charred wall. At the foot of the wall I saw an old-fashioned plate. As if it regularly found food here, the cat licked its rim.

Paris–Château de Lavigny–
Zaton–Dijon–Sarajevo–Chicago,
2004–2005

ABOUT THE AUTHOR

Igor Štiks was born in Sarajevo in 1977 and has lived in Zagreb, Paris, Chicago, Edinburgh, and Belgrade. His first novel, *A Castle in Romagna*, won the Slavić prize for best first novel in Croatia and was nominated for the International IMPAC Dublin Literary Award for 2006. Earning his PhD at the Institut d'Études Politiques de Paris and Northwestern University, Štiks later published a monograph, *Nations and Citizens in Yugoslavia and the Post-Yugoslav States: One Hundred Years of Citizenship*. His novel *The Judgment of Richard Richter*, originally published as *Elijah's Chair*, won the Gjalski and Kiklop Awards for the best novel in Croatia and has been translated into fifteen languages. In addition to winning the Grand Prix of the 2011 Belgrade International Theatre Festival for his stage adaptation of *Elijah's Chair*, Štiks was honored with the prestigious *Chevalier des arts et des lettres* for his literary and intellectual achievements.

ABOUT THE TRANSLATOR

Ellen Elias-Bursac has been translating novels and nonfiction by Bosnian, Croatian, and Serbian writers for thirty years. She is the recipient of the 2006 ALTA National Translation Award, an American Association of Teachers of Slavic and East European Languages award, and the Mary Zirin Prize for her book *Translating Evidence and Interpreting Testimony at a War Crimes Tribunal: Working in a Tug-of-War*. A contributing editor to the online literary journal *Asymptote*, Elias-Bursac spent more than six years at the ex–Yugoslav War Crimes Tribunal in The Hague as a translator/reviser in the English Translation Unit. Her translation of Daša Drndić's novel *Trieste* was short-listed for the Independent Foreign Fiction Prize in 2013.